Three
SISTERS

HEATHER MORRIS

ZAFFRE

First published in the UK in 2021 by
ZAFFRE
An imprint of Bonnier Books UK
4th Floor, Victoria House, Bloomsbury Square, London WC1B 4DA
Owned by Bonnier Books
Sveavägen 56, Stockholm, Sweden

This is a work of fiction, based on the personal memories of Livia Ravek and
Magda Guttman, the Shoah testimonies of Cibi Lang, Livia and Ziggy Ravek,
and the diary of Magda Guttman. Every reasonable attempt to verify the
facts against available documentation has been made. However,
many of the incidents, names, places and events are either the
products of the author's imagination or used fictitiously.

A CIP catalogue record for this book is
available from the British Library.

Hardback ISBN: 978–1–83877–262–8
Export ISBN: 978–1–83877–550–6
Signed edition ISBN: 978–1–83877–724–1

Also available as an ebook and in audio

1 3 5 7 9 10 8 6 4 2

Typeset by IDSUK (Data Connection) Ltd
Printed and bound in Great Britain by Clays Ltd, Elcograf S.p.A.

Zaffre is an imprint of Bonnier Books UK
www.bonnierbooks.co.uk

LEABHARLANNA FHINE GALL
FINGAL LIBARIES

- -

Items should be returned on or before the given return date. Items may be renewed in branch libraries, by phone or online. You will need your PIN to renew online. Damage to, or loss of items, will be charged to the borrower.

- -

Date Due:	Date Due:	Date Due:

Born in New Zealand, Heather Morris is an international number one bestselling author, who is passionate about stories of survival, resilience and hope. In 2003, while working in a large public hospital in Melbourne, Heather was introduced to an elderly gentleman who 'might just have a story worth telling'. The day she met Lale Sokolov changed both their lives. Heather used Lale's story as the basis for *The Tattooist of Auschwitz* and her follow-up novel, *Cilka's Journey*, which have sold eight million copies worldwide. *Three Sisters* is her third novel. In 2020 she published *Stories of Hope*, her account of her journey to writing the story of Lale Sokolov's life.

Also by Heather Morris
The Tattooist of Auschwitz
Cilka's Journey
Stories of Hope

Cibi, *z"l* – Magda – Livia
*Thank you for your strength and the hope you clung to
during history's darkest hour – to create a life in a
new land with loving families, to inspire us all.*

Mischka, *z"l* – Yitzko, *z"l* – Ziggy, *z"l*
*You have your own stories of survival. You have your own
stories of courage, hope, love and loss of family.
You had the love of three amazing women
and the families you created.*

Karol (Kari), Joseph (Yossi) – Chaya, Judith (Ditti) –
Oded (Odie), Dorit
*You grew up hearing the stories of your parents. You are the
richer for their endurance, resilience, courage and commitment
to sharing their past, so none of us will ever FORGET.*

*Randy, Ronit, Pam, Yossi, Joseph,
Yeshai, Amiad, Hagit – Noa, Anat – Ayala, Amir,
Ariela – Daniel, Ruth, Boaz – Lee-Or, Nogah,
Pnina, Galil, Edan, Eli, Hagar, Dean, Manor, Alon, Yasmin,
Shira, Tamar – Carmel, Albie – Maayan – Doron, Ofir,
Maor – Raphael, Ilan – Romi
AND GENERATIONS TO COME*

Note *z"l* has been added to the names to honour and
remember those who have passed away. It denotes
Zichrono livracha – may his or her memory
be blessed.

Part I
The Promise

PROLOGUE

Vranov nad Topl'ou, Slovakia
June 1929

The three sisters, Cibi, Magda and Livi, sit in a tight circle with their father in the small backyard of their home. The oleander bush their mother has tried so hard to coax back to life droops disconsolately in one corner of the small garden.

Livi, the youngest, at three years old, leaps to her feet: sitting still is not in her nature.

'Livi, please, will you sit down?' Cibi tells her. At seven years old, she is the eldest of the siblings, and it is her responsibility to chastise them when they misbehave. 'You know Father wants to talk to us.'

'No,' three-year-old Livi pronounces, and proceeds to skip around the seated figures, giving each a pat on the head as she passes. Magda, the middle sister, and five years old, is using a dry twig from the oleander to draw imaginary figures in the dirt. It is a warm, sunny, summer afternoon. The back door is open, inviting in the heat, while sending the sweet smell of freshly baked bread into the garden. Two windows, one looking into the kitchen, the other into the small bedroom the family shares, have seen better days. Chips of paint litter the ground: winter has taken its toll on the cottage. The garden gate catches a gust of wind and slams. The catch is broken; yet another thing for Father to fix.

'Come here, kitten. Will you sit on my knee?' Father beckons to Livi.

Being told to do something from an older sister is one thing; but being asked, and so sweetly, by her father is quite another. Livi drops into his lap, a flailing arm smacking against the side of his head. She is oblivious to the pain her action has caused.

'Are you all right, Father?' Magda is concerned, catching the grimace on his face as his head jerked back. She brushes her fingers down his stubbly cheek.

'Yes, my darling. I am perfect. I have my girls with me – what more could a father ask for?'

'You said you wanted to talk to us?' Cibi, ever impatient, gets to the point of this little 'meeting'.

Menachem Meller looks into the eyes of his pretty daughters. They have not a care in the world, innocent of the harsh realities of life outside their sweet cottage. Harsh realities which Menachem has lived through and still lives with. The bullet that didn't kill him during the Great War remains lodged in his neck and now, twelve years later, it is threatening to finish the deed.

Fiery Cibi, tough Cibi . . . Menachem strokes her hair. On the day she was born she announced that the world had

4

better watch out – she had arrived and woe betide anyone who got in her way. Her green eyes have a habit of turning a fiery yellow when her temper gets the better of her.

And Magda, beautiful, gentle Magda, how did she get to be five so fast? He worries her sweet nature will make her vulnerable to being hurt and used by others. Her big blue eyes gaze at him and he feels her love, her understanding of his precarious health. He sees in her a maturity beyond her years, a compassion she has inherited from her mother and grandmother, and a fierce desire to care for others.

Livi stops squirming as Menachem plays with her soft, curly hair. Already he has described her to their mother as the wild one, the one he worries will run with the wolves, and break like a sapling if cornered. Her piercing blue eyes and petite frame remind him of a fawn, easy to startle and ready to bolt.

Tomorrow he will have the surgery to remove the errant bullet from his neck. Why couldn't it have just stayed where it was? He has prayed endlessly for more time with his girls. He needs to guide them into adulthood, attend their weddings, hold his grandchildren. The operation is a risky one, and if he doesn't survive, this may be the last day he spends with them. If that is the case, however awful it is to contemplate on this glorious sunny day, then what he needs to ask of his girls, must be said now.

'Well Father, what do you want to tell us?' Cibi prods.

'Cibi, Magda, do you know what a promise is?' he asks, slowly. He needs them to take this seriously.

Magda shakes her head: 'no'.

'I think so,' says Cibi. 'It's when two people keep a secret, isn't it?'

Menachem smiles. Cibi will always have a go, it's what he loves most about her. 'That's close, my darling, but a promise can involve more than two people. I want this promise to be shared between the three of you. Livi is not going to understand, so I need you to keep talking to her about it, until she does.'

'*I* don't understand, Father,' Magda interjects. 'You're being all confusing.'

'It's very simple, Magda.' Menachem smiles. There is nothing that gives him as much pleasure as talking to his girls. Something catches in his chest; he must remember this moment, this sunny day, the wide eyes of his three daughters. 'I want you to make a promise to me and to each other that you will always take care of your sisters. That you will always be there for one another, no matter what. That you will not allow anything to take you away from each other. Do you understand?'

Magda and Cibi nod, and Cibi asks, suddenly serious: 'I do, Father, but why would someone want to take us away from each other?'

'I'm not saying anyone will, I just want you to promise me that if anyone tries to separate you, you will remember what we spoke of here today and do everything in your power not to let that happen. The three of you are stronger together, you must never forget that.' Menachem's voice stumbles, and he clears his throat.

Cibi and Magda exchange a glance. Livi looks from sister to sister to father, knowing that something solemn has been agreed, but with little idea of what it means.

'I promise, Father,' says Magda.

'Cibi?' Menachem asks.

'I promise too, Father. I promise to look after my sisters – I won't let anyone hurt them, you know that.'

'Yes, I do know that, my darling Cibi. This promise will become a pact between the three of you and no others. Will you tell Livi of this pact when she is old enough to understand?'

Cibi grabs Livi's face in her hands, turning her head to look into her eyes. 'Livi, say "promise". Say "I promise".'

Livi studies her sister. Cibi is nodding, encouraging her to say the words.

'I pwomise,' pronounces Livi.

'Now say it to Father, say "I promise" to Father,' Cibi instructs.

Livi turns to her father, her eyes dancing, the giggle in her throat threatening to explode, the warmth of his smile melting her little heart. 'I pwomise, Father. Livi pwomises.'

Gathering his girls to his chest he looks over Cibi's head and smiles at the other girl in his life, the mother of his daughters, who stands in the doorway of the house, tears glistening on her cheeks.

He has too much to lose; he has to survive.

CHAPTER 1

Vranov nad Topl'ou
March 1942

'Please tell me she's going to be all right, I'm so worried about her,' Chaya frets, as the doctor examines her seventeen-year-old daughter.

Magda has been struggling with a fever for days.

'Yes, Mrs Meller, Magda will be fine,' Dr Kisely reassures her.

The tiny bedroom contains two beds: one in which Chaya sleeps with her youngest, Livi; and the other, which Magda shares with their older sister, Cibi, when she is home. A large cabinet takes up one wall, cluttered with the small, personal possessions of the four women of the house. Taking pride of place: the cut-glass perfume atomiser with its emerald green tie and tassel, and next to it a grainy photograph.

A handsome man sits on a simple chair, a toddler on one knee, an older girl on the other. Another girl, older yet, stands to his left. On his right is the girls' mother, her hand resting on her husband's shoulder. Mother and daughters wear white lacy dresses and together they are a picture-perfect family, or, at least, they were.

When Menachem Meller died on the operating table, the bullet finally removed but the blood loss too great to survive, Chaya was left a widow and the girls fatherless. Yitzchak, Chaya's father and the sisters' grandfather, moved into the small cottage to offer help where he could, while Chaya's brother, Ivan, lives in the house across from theirs.

Chaya is not alone, despite how she feels.

The heavy drapes are drawn in the bedroom, denying Magda, shivering, feverish, the brilliant spring sunshine which now peeks above the curtain rail.

'Can we talk in the other room?' Dr Kisely takes Chaya's arm.

Livi, cross-legged on the other bed, watches Chaya place another wet towel on Magda's forehead.

'Stay with your sister?' her mother asks, and Livi nods.

When the adults leave the room Livi crosses to her sister's bed and lies down beside her, proceeding to wipe the perspiration from Magda's face with a dry flannel.

'You're going to be OK, Magda. I won't let anything happen to you.'

Magda forces a small smile. 'That's my line. I'm your big sister, I look after *you*.'

'Then get better.'

Chaya and Dr Kisely walk the few steps from the bedroom to the main room in the small house. The front door opens directly into this cosy living area, with a small kitchen area at the back.

The girls' grandfather, Yitzchak, stands washing his hands at the sink. A trail of wood shavings has followed him from the backyard, and more lie on the faded blue felt that covers the floor. Startled, he turns, splashing water onto the floor. 'What's going on?' he asks.

'Yitzchak, I'm glad you're here, come and sit with us.'

Chaya quickly turns to the young doctor, fear in her eyes. Dr Kisely smiles and guides her to a kitchen chair, pulling another away from the small table for Yitzchak to sit.

'Is she very unwell?' Yitzchak asks.

'She's going to be fine. It's a fever, nothing a healthy young girl can't recover from in her own time.'

'So what's *this* about?' Chaya waves a hand between the doctor and herself.

Dr Kisely finds another chair and sits down. 'I don't want you to be scared by what I'm about to tell you.'

Chaya merely nods, now desperate for him to tell her what he needs to say. The years since the war broke out have changed her: her once smooth brow is lined, and she is so thin her dresses hang off her like wet laundry.

'What is it, man?' Yitzchak demands. The responsibility he bears for his daughter and grandchildren has aged him beyond his years, and he has no time for intrigue.

'I want to admit Magda into hospital—'

'What? You just said she was going to get better!' Chaya explodes. She stands up, grabbing the table for support.

Dr Kisely holds up a hand to shush her. 'It's not because she's ill. There's another reason I want to admit Magda and if you will listen, I'll explain.'

'What on earth are you talking about?' Yitzchak says. 'Just spit it out.'

'Mrs Meller, Yitzchak, I am hearing rumours, terrible rumours – talk of young Jews, girls and boys, being taken from Slovakia to work for the Germans. If Magda is in hospital she will be safe, and I promise I won't let anything happen to her.'

Chaya collapses back onto her chair, her hands covering her face. This is much worse than a fever.

Yitzchak absentmindedly pats her back, but he is focused now, intent on hearing everything the doctor has to say. 'What else?' he asks, meeting the doctor's eyes, urging him to be blunt.

'As I said, rumours and gossip, none of it good for the Jews. If they come for your children it is the beginning of the end. And *working* for the Nazis? We have no idea what that means.'

'What can we do?' Yitzchak asks. 'We have already lost everything – our right to work, to feed our families . . . What more can they take from us?'

'If what I'm hearing has any basis in fact, they want your children.'

Chaya sits up straighter. Her face is red, but she isn't crying. 'And Livi? Who will protect Livi?'

'I believe they're after sixteen-year-olds and older. Livi is fourteen, isn't she?'

'She's fifteen.'

'Still a baby.' Dr Kisely smiles. 'I think Livi will be fine.'

'And how long will Magda stay in hospital?' asks Chaya. She turns to her father. 'She won't want to go, she won't want to leave Livi. Don't you remember, Father, when Cibi left, she made Magda promise she would look after their little sister.'

Yitzchak pats Chaya's hands. 'If we are to save her, she must leave, whether she wants to or not.'

'I think a few days, maybe a week, is all we need. If the rumours are true, it will happen soon, and afterwards, I will bring her home. And Cibi? Where is she?'

'You know her, she's off with the *Hachshara*.' Chaya doesn't know what she thinks of the *Hachshara*, a training programme to teach young people, just like Cibi, the skills necessary to make a new life in Palestine, far away from Slovakia and the war raging in Europe.

'Still learning how to till the soil?' the doctor jokes, but neither Chaya or Yitzchak are smiling.

'If she's to emigrate, then that's what she will find when she gets there – lots of fertile land, waiting to be planted,' says Yitzchak.

But Chaya remains silent, lost in her thoughts. One child in hospital, another young enough to escape the clutches of the Nazis. And the third, Cibi, her eldest, now part of a Zionist youth movement inspired by a mission to create a Jewish homeland, whenever that might be.

The truth has already dawned on all of them that they need a promised land right now, and the sooner the better. But, Chaya surmises, at least all three of her children are safe, for now.

CHAPTER 2

**Forested area outside Vranov nad Topl'ou
March 1942**

Cibi ducks as a piece of bread sails past her head. She scowls at the young man who threw it, but her twinkling eyes tell a different story.

Cibi had not hesitated when the call came, responding eagerly to the desire to forge a new life in a new land. In a clearing in the middle of the woods, away from prying eyes, sleeping huts have been constructed, along with a common room and a kitchen. There, twenty teenagers at a time learn to be self-sufficient, living and working together in a small community, preparing for a new life in the promised land.

The person responsible for this chance is the uncle of one of the boys also undergoing the training. Although he had converted from Judaism to Christianity, Josef's sympathies still lay with the plight of the Jews in Slovakia, despite his change of faith. A wealthy man, he had acquired a piece of land in the forest on the outskirts of the town, a safe space for the boys and girls to gather to train. Josef has only one rule: every Friday morning everyone was to return home, before the *Shabbat*, and not return until Sunday.

In the kitchen, Josef sighs as he watches Yosi throw a crust of bread at Cibi. Travel arrangements have already been made for this group – they will be leaving in two weeks. His training camp is working: eight groups have already left for Palestine – and yet here they are, mucking around.

'If the heat of Palestine doesn't kill us, your cooking will, Cibi Meller!' Cibi's attacker yells at her. 'Maybe you should stick to *growing* food.'

Cibi strides over to the young man and wraps an arm around his neck. 'You keep throwing things at me and you won't live to make it to Palestine,' she tells him, squeezing just a little.

'All right everybody!' announces Josef. 'Finish up and get outside. Drill starts in five minutes.' He pauses. 'Cibi, do you need to spend more time in the kitchen working on your bread-making skills?'

Releasing Yosi's neck, Cibi stands to attention. 'No, sir, can't see them improving, no matter how much time I spend in the kitchen.'

As she speaks, twenty chairs scrape across the wooden floor in the makeshift dining room, as young Jewish boys and girls rush to finish their meals, eager to be outside and begin training again.

Forming untidy rows, they stand to attention as their teacher, Josef, approaches, beaming. He is proud of his brave recruits, so willing to embark on a dangerous journey, leaving behind their families, their country, as war and the Nazi occupation rages around them. Older, wiser, he had foreseen the future for Jews in Slovakia and invoked *Hachshara*, believing it was their only chance if they were to survive what was coming.

'Good morning,' says Josef.

'Good morning, sir,' the trainees chorus.

'And the Lord made a covenant with Abraham . . . ?' he prompts, seeking verse knowledge from the first book of the Bible.

'To your descendants I give this land, from the Wadi of Egypt to the great river, the Euphrates,' the group responds.

'And the Lord said to Abraham . . . ?'

'Leave your country, your people and your father's household and go to the land I will show you.' They finish the sentence.

The solemnity of the moment is broken by the grumbling of a truck struggling to make its way across the clearing. After it pulls up beside them, a local farmer clambers out.

'Yosi, Hannah, Cibi,' calls Josef, 'you're first up for driving lessons today. And, Cibi, I don't care what kind of cook you are, you must learn to drive a truck. Attack it with the same gusto you attacked Yosi's neck earlier and you'll be training others in no time. I need all of you to excel at one thing so you can help with the training here. Understood?'

'Yes, sir!'

'Now, the rest of you head over to the shed. There's a lot of farm machinery inside which you will learn to use and to maintain.'

Cibi, Hannah and Yosi gather at the driver's door of the truck.

'OK, Cibi, you go first. Try not to break it before Hannah and I can have a go,' says Yosi, playfully.

Cibi advances on Yosi and, once more, an arm goes around his neck.

'I'll be driving around the streets of Palestine before you can find the first gear,' Cibi snarls into his ear.

'OK, break it up you two. Cibi, hop up – I'll get in the other side,' the farmer says.

As Cibi climbs into the truck, Yosi gives her a push from behind. Half in, half out of the cab, Cibi contemplates what she should do. She decides she will help Yosi up the same way when it's his turn.

Yosi and Hannah roar with laughter as Cibi, behind the wheel of the truck, grinds the engine into gear and bunny-hops down the road. From the driver's window an arm extends, a middle finger raised.

CHAPTER 3

Vranov nad Topl'ou
March 1942

'Livi, stop looking out of the window,' Chaya pleads. 'Magda will be home when she is well enough to leave the hospital.' She is not sure she has done the right thing by sending Magda away. As ever, she wishes Menachem was still alive. She knows it isn't rational, but she feels that the war, the Germans, her country's capitulation to the Nazis – none of it would have happened if he were alive.

'But, Mumma, you said she wasn't that sick, so why is she still in hospital? It's been days.' Livi is whining and Chaya wishes she would find a different question for her mother. She has heard and responded to this one too many times.

'You know the answer to that, Livi. Dr Kisely thought a few days' rest, away from your smothering, would help her get better faster.' Chaya allows herself a small smile.

'I didn't smother her!' snaps Livi. Sulking now, she moves away from the window, letting the curtain drop to block out a world that is becoming ever more confusing and threatening. Her mother is increasingly reluctant to let her out of the house, even to go shopping, or allow her to see her friends, reasoning with Livi that the eyes of the Hlinka Guard are everywhere, eager to round up young Jewish girls like her.

'I feel like a prisoner in here! When is Cibi coming home?' Livi envies Cibi's freedom, her plans to leave for the promised land.

'She will be home in two days. Just stay away from the window.'

The loud knock on the front door sees Yitzchak scurrying out from the kitchen, where he was chiselling a star of David from a piece of wood. As he walks towards the door, Chaya holds up her hand. 'No, Father, let me get it.'

Two young men of the Hlinka Guard are standing outside when Chaya opens the door. She shivers. The state police and, more crucially, the foot soldiers of Adolf Hitler, stand before her in their menacing black uniforms. They will not protect her or any Jew in Slovakia.

'Why, hello, Visik, how are you? And your mother, how is Irene?' Chaya refuses to show them her fear. She knows why they are here.

'She's fine, thank you . . .'

The other guard takes a step forward. He is taller, obviously angry and far more threatening than the boy. 'We are not here to exchange pleasantries. You are Mrs Meller?'

'You know I am.' Chaya's heart is beating in her throat. 'Now, what can I do for you, boys?'

'Do not call us boys.' The older guard practically spits out his words. 'We are patriotic Hlinka Guards on official business.'

Chaya knows this is rubbish. There is nothing patriotic about them. Trained by the SS, these men have turned on their own people. 'I am sorry, I meant no disrespect. How can I help you?' Chaya remains calm, hoping that they can't see the tremble in her hands.

'You have daughters?'

'You know I do.'

'Are they here?'

'You mean right now?'

'Mrs Meller, please tell us if they are living with you, *right now.*'

'Livi, my youngest, lives here at the moment.'

'Where are the others?' The second guard takes another step.

'Magda is in hospital. She is very ill and I don't know when she will be coming home, and Cibi . . . well, Visik, you know what Cibi is doing and why she is not here.'

'Please, Mrs Meller, please stop saying my name, you do not know me,' Visik pleads, embarrassed by her overtures in front of his colleague.

'Livi, then, is to report to the synagogue at five o'clock on Friday.' The second guard is peering past Chaya into the house as he speaks. 'She can bring one bag with her. From there she will be taken to work for the Germans. She must come alone, no one is to accompany her. Do you understand the order I have given you?'

'I just told you!' Chaya is suddenly terrified, her eyes burning. 'You can't take Livi – she's only fifteen.' Chaya reaches out to Visik, imploring him. 'She is just a child.'

19

Both men step back, unsure of what Chaya is capable of. The second guard puts his hand on his gun in its holster.

Yitzchak steps forward and pulls Chaya away.

'You have our orders – your daughter's name will be on the list of girls to be transported.'

Visik leans in and hisses, 'It will be worse for her if she doesn't turn up.' He puffs up his chest, needing to regain his authority, and tips his chin, laughing triumphantly as he struts back down the path.

Chaya looks at Livi, now folded into her grandfather's arms. Yitzchak's pained face fails to hide the anger and guilt he feels for not being able to protect his youngest granddaughter.

'It's all right, Grandfather. Mumma, I can go and work for the Germans. I'm sure it won't be for long. It's only work – how hard can it be?'

The room suddenly grows darker. The sunlight that had streamed through the window earlier is now blanketed by dark clouds, just to be seen peeking through the drawn curtains, a clap of thunder shakes the house, and in a moment heavy rain begins to thud onto the roof.

Chaya looks at Livi, her little warrior, her blue eyes and bouncing curls belying her determination. Livi holds her mother's gaze, but it is Chaya who turns away, clutching the front of her dress in her hands, a sign, her sign, that she is crumbling inside, the physical pain in her chest an acknowledgement of her powerlessness.

There are no words. As Chaya walks to her room, she reaches out and touches Livi's arm, her eyes downcast. Livi and Yitzchak hear the bedroom door close.

'Should I . . . ?'

'No, Livi, let her be. She will come out when she's ready.'

CHAPTER 4

Vranov nad Topl'ou
March 1942

'What are you doing, Livi? Please take those candles away from the window.'

Wiping her floury hands on her apron, Chaya advances on Livi. Why does she insist on hovering in the window? It has been two days since the Hlinka Guard told her she must relinquish her youngest daughter. They have just tonight together under the same roof. Closing her eyes, Chaya chastises herself. Why did she have to scold her? Why has she spent the last couple of days in virtual silence, self-absorbed and brooding, when she should have spent these precious hours talking to Livi, loving Livi.

'No, Mumma, I must leave them in the window. I'm lighting the way home for Cibi.'

'But you know we're not allowed . . .'

'I don't care! What can they do, take me away? They are already doing that tomorrow! If this is to be my last night in my own home for a while, I want candles in the window.'

During this exchange, Cibi has approached the house, unseen by mother and sister. She bursts in through the front door now, calling: 'Kitten, where are you?'

Livi squeals with delight and flies into Cibi's arms. Chaya is fighting and failing to hold back her tears.

'Did I hear the gentle tread of my eldest granddaughter entering the house?' Yitzchak says, with his characteristic warmth and humour.

Chaya and Yitzchak join Cibi and Livi in a tight embrace.

'Mumma, I could smell your cooking at the end of the street. I have been eating my own food for far too long – I'm starving.'

'And yet here you are, still alive,' Yitzchak jokes.

Chaya lets Livi tell her sister about Magda's confinement in hospital, reassuring her that Dr Kisely has informed them she will be fine. When Livi has finished, Chaya nods at Yitzchak.

'Livi,' he says, 'come and help me bring in some wood from the backyard for the fire. It's going to be a cold night and we want to keep the kitchen warm.'

'Must I? Cibi has just come home and I want to hear all about her adventures,' Livi moans.

'There will be plenty of time for that. Now, come on, give an old man a hand.'

When Yitzchak and Livi have shut the kitchen door behind them, Cibi turns to her mother. 'OK, what's going on?'

'Come with me,' Chaya says, leading her into their bedroom and shutting the door behind them.

'You're scaring me, Mumma. Please.'

Chaya takes a deep breath. 'Your sister is going to work for the Germans, the Hlinka came for her.' Chaya can't look at Cibi, but she forces herself. 'She has been ordered to the synagogue tomorrow. I don't know where they will take her, but we're hoping it's not for long and that . . . that . . .' Chaya sits down heavily on the bed, but Cibi remains standing, staring into the space her mother had just occupied.

'But they can't. She's just a child – what can she do for the Germans?' Cibi says, more to herself than to her mother. 'Can't Uncle Ivan help us?'

Chaya is sobbing into her hands. 'No one can help us, Cibi. I . . . I couldn't stop them. I couldn't . . .'

Cibi sits down beside her mother and takes her hands away from her face. 'Mother, I made a promise to look after my sisters. Don't you remember?'

Around a candlelit table, the Meller family shares a meal, each one of them wondering when they will do so again. Prayers are said for Magda; for their departed father; and Yitzchak's deceased wife, their grandmother. They try to enjoy each other as they always have, but what lies ahead looms large over their table.

The plates now empty, Chaya reaches for Livi's hand. Cibi extends one hand to Yitzchak, beside her, and the other to her mother. Livi takes her grandfather's hand, all the while looking across the table at Cibi. The family circle holds tight. Cibi holds Livi's stare. Chaya does not look up as tears fall unashamedly down her face. Only when Chaya can no longer contain her sobs do the girls look at their mother. Yitzchak breaks free from the circle to embrace her.

'I'll clean up,' Livi says quietly, rising from the table.

As she picks up a plate Cibi takes it from her. 'Leave it, kitten, I'll do it. Why don't you go and get ready for bed?'

With no objections from Chaya or Yitzchak, Livi quietly leaves the kitchen.

Cibi places the plate back on the table. 'I'm going with her,' she whispers. 'She's the baby and she can't go alone.'

'What are you saying?' Yitzchak's face wrinkles in confusion.

'Tomorrow I will go with Livi. I will look after her, and then I will bring her back to you. No harm will come to her as long as there is breath in my body.'

'They only have *her* name; they may not let you go.' Chaya sobs.

'They won't be able to stop me, Mumma, you know that. What Cibi wants, Cibi gets. You look after Magda until we return.' Cibi lifts her chin. The decision has been made. The candlelight catches the red in her hair, the gleam in her large green eyes.

'We can't ask you to do that,' Yitzchak says, quietly, glancing towards the bedroom door.

'You don't have to, I'm saying I am going. Now, we will need to pack two bags.'

Chaya rises from her chair to embrace her firstborn, whispering into her thick hair, 'Thank you, thank you.'

'Did I miss something?' Livi hovers by the bedroom door, reluctant to come further into the room, the tension in the air palpable. Yitzchak walks over to her and gently urges her back to the table and onto her chair.

'Kitten, guess what, I'm coming with you tomorrow!' Cibi winks at her sister. 'You didn't think I was going to let you have all the fun, did you?'

'What do you mean? They don't have your name, only mine.' Livi looks as confused as Yitzchak did, only moments ago. Livi's bravery is leaving her: she struggles to say the words, sniffs as she fights to control her tears.

'Let me worry about that, OK? All you need to know is that we're in this together from now on. Who else is going to boss you around when you misbehave?'

Livi looks at her mother and grandfather. 'Did you tell her to come with me?'

'No, no, kitten, nobody asked me to do this – I want to. I insist on it – remember our promise to Father, that we would always stay together? Magda is ill, and we can't do anything about that, but you and me, we'll keep the promise and be back home before we know it.'

'Mumma?'

Chaya cups Livi's face in her hands. 'Your sister is going with you, Livi. Do you understand? You don't have to do this alone.'

'If only Menachem was here, he would know what to do, how to protect his daughters,' Yitzchak says, his voice thick with tears.

Chaya, Cibi and Livi look at the old man as he begins to cry. It's obvious he feels guilty, powerless to protect these girls.

The three women envelope him in a hug.

'Grandfather, you are the only father I can remember – you have protected me all my life, and I know you will watch over Cibi and me, even when we are not all together. Don't cry, please, we need you to be here to look after Mumma, and Magda,' Livi pleads.

'There is nothing Menachem could have done, if he were still with us, that you haven't done, Father,' adds Chaya.

'You have protected us and kept us safe since he died, you have to believe that.'

For once Cibi has nothing to say. She wipes the tears from Yitzchak's cheeks, her gesture saying the words she cannot find.

Livi breaks the tension, looking from one member of her family to the other, then back to the kitchen table. 'Shall I clear the table?'

Yitzchak immediately starts piling the dishes. 'I'll do it. You girls get some rest.'

Cibi walks into the bedroom, but makes no move to undress.

'Are you all right?' Chaya asks from her bed. Livi is curled into her mother's side.

'Is there room in there for me? I'd like to sleep with you tonight.'

Chaya pulls the blanket aside while Cibi gets changed, and then the three women draw close, for their last night together. Cibi looks at Magda's empty bed and can only imagine how angry Magda will be when she discovers she has been left behind. She thinks of the promise to their father, that they would stick together, but what choice do they have?

After her daughters have fallen asleep, Chaya sits up, hugging herself against the chill in the room. The heavy curtains haven't been drawn tonight and the moonlight throws shards of light onto the faces of her daughters.

Small piles of clothes: dresses, sweaters, thick tights and underwear, are heaped onto the beds. Chaya picks up one garment after another, examining it, recalling when it was made or purchased, and then placing it in one of the two small suitcases. They are careful to take only the second best

26

of everything – Chaya has insisted that their good clothes remain hanging in the closet for when they return. Nevertheless, she has been mindful of the clothes her daughters favour. Cibi only ever dresses in skirts and blouses of a single colour – her fashion choices are a source of many tantrums from Magda, forced to wear Cibi's hand-me-downs, when all she yearns for are pretty, floral dresses with matching scarves. Livi, too, prefers dresses, but more from a practical perspective: two articles of clothing take longer to put on than a single dress – what a waste of time. Three dresses are packed for Livi, with an assortment of scarves to keep her daughters' wayward hair out of their eyes.

Yitzchak walks into the room juggling small cans of sardines with a cake that is under his arm, the cake Chaya had made to celebrate *Shabbat* later that day, a *Shabbat* dinner neither Cibi nor Livi will attend. Moving clothing aside, he places the food on the bed.

'Grandfather, would you take Livi outside? I'm sure she'd love to take a walk with you. Mumma and I can do this,' Cibi says.

'Can't I help?' Livi asks.

'We've got this, kitten. You go with Grandfather.'

Livi is struggling with her mother's sadness and doesn't argue.

'Don't pack any of that cake for me – you know it's not my favourite. You and Grandfather have it,' says Livi.

Cibi is devastated to be leaving the *Hachshara* without telling them where she is going. They will be expecting her back at the camp on Sunday. She thinks of Yosi, his smiling eyes . . . how long will she be gone? Palestine will have to wait for now, but she will leave one day, with her sisters, and even her mother and grandfather.

27

'Mumma, we need only a few things – not all of this! And we need harder wearing clothes – jumpers in case it's cold at night, a coat each. Please put those dresses back.'

Chaya finds herself smiling, despite her misery. 'You are a clever one, my Cibi. I know you will find a way to protect your sister.' She sighs, then remembers something she's been meaning to say to Cibi: 'Please do as you are told when you are away – you have got away with talking back to us your whole life, but I believe that now is not the time for you to speak your mind.'

'I don't know what you mean,' Cibi replies, trying to contain a giggle.

'I think you know exactly what I am asking of you. Think before you speak, that's all I'm saying.'

'Will you be happy if I say I will try my best?'

'I will. Now, let's finish packing these suitcases. We need to squeeze in some food.'

'Surely we'll be fed!' exclaims Cibi. 'We'll need books, too; I'm going to choose a couple.' She goes into the living room to examine the books on the shelves there.

'Bring me some of the linden tree tea to pack; you'll be able to drink it cold if there's no hot water,' calls Chaya. 'If ever you or Livi are feeling unwell, it's a miracle.'

Alone in the bedroom now, Chaya again picks up individual items of clothing, burying her face in each, inhaling the all-too familiar scent of her girls. She tells herself that she must be strong: her girls are brave and they will do whatever the Germans ask of them, and then they will come home. Magda will understand why she had to be sent away. The war will end, and life will return to normal. Perhaps even by Hannukah.

CHAPTER 5

Humenné Hospital
March 1942

'I want to see Dr Kisely,' Magda, half out of bed, demands of the nurse treating an elderly woman two beds away.

The two rows of twelve metal beds in the ward are fully occupied. The noises of snoring, coughing, crying and moaning make sleep, for any reasonable length of time, impossible. Magda has worked out what it means to have one of the timber-framed, fabric-filled screens placed around your bed: something unpleasant is about to happen to a patient. On the small bedside table is a photo of Magda's family.

A small desk sits at the head of the room, where the nurse in charge is now seated, watching over her domain, issuing instructions. 'Get back into bed, Magda. Dr Kisely will be doing his rounds shortly, you'll see him then.'

'I don't want to get back into bed, I want to go home. I'm feeling fine.'

'Either do as I say or I'll tell Dr Kisely you've been misbehaving.'

With all the petulance of teenagers through the ages, Magda swings her feet back into bed and sits cross-legged on top of her blankets, sighing heavily. Bored and more than a little confused as to why she is still there – her fever broke the day before – she is longing to get home to Mumma, Grandfather and Livi. Her mother hasn't visited once, adding to her general sense of unease: something is wrong, but what? Once again, she wishes Mumma had let her join Cibi for *Hachshara*, but, as the ever-obedient middle child, Magda's help around the house has been invaluable.

She is still lost in her thoughts when Dr Kisely enters the ward and approaches his first patient. 'Dr Kisely!' Magda exclaims.

The nurse hurries over to Magda, telling her to shush and wait her turn.

Dr Kisely watches the exchange, and says a few words to his patient before walking over to Magda. 'Good morning, Magda. How are you feeling today?'

'I'm fine, Doctor. There's absolutely nothing wrong with me and I want to go home now. My mother and grandfather need me.'

Dr Kisely unwraps his stethoscope from around his neck and listens to Magda's chest. The women in the beds next to hers strain to see what he is doing, to listen to what he is saying. Everyone is so bored of being in hospital.

'I'm sorry, Magda, but you still have a little infection in your chest. You're not ready to go home.'

'But I *feel* fine,' Magda insists.

'Will you just listen to the doctor?' the nurse scolds.

Dr Kisely perches on Magda's bed and beckons her to lean in. 'Magda, I need you to listen to me,' he whispers. 'It would just be better for you and for your family if you stayed here a few more days. I didn't want to have to tell you like this, but I see I have no choice.'

Magda's blue eyes are wide with fear. To Dr Kisely she looks much younger than her seventeen years: in her thin nightie and braided hair she could be thirteen or fourteen. She nods once, for the doctor to continue; she was right, there is something very odd going on.

'I don't want to scare you, but the truth is the truth.' The doctor sighs and looks at the stethoscope in his hands, before meeting Magda's eyes once more. 'The Hlinka are rounding up young Jewish girls and taking them to work for the Germans. I want to keep you with your family if I can, and if you're in hospital, you're safe. Do you understand?'

Magda's eyes flick between the doctor and nurse. She reads concern and sincerity on their faces. She herself has heard talk of the Germans needing young people to work for them, she just never imagined these 'young people' might include her and her sisters. Her heart begins to race. Her sisters! Is Cibi still safe in the woods? And Livi?

'My sisters!' she breathes, now gripped by a fear so strong her voice is barely audible.

'It's OK, Magda. Cibi is not at home, and Livi is too young. You just need to stay put until the guards have found enough young people to send away, and after that you'll go home. I need you to be strong for just a little while longer. Let the staff here take care of you. Remember that your mother and grandfather gave their permission, so please don't disappoint them, Magda.'

The nurse takes Magda's hand and smiles at her reassuringly, but Magda is not reassured. She made a promise to her father, formed a pact with her sisters, and now each of them is in a different location, with no way of knowing how the others are faring.

Magda can only nod her consent to stay in hospital. She lies down in her narrow bed and stares up at the ceiling, tears of anger and frustration – and fear – welling up in her eyes.

CHAPTER 6

Vranov nad Topl'ou
March 1942

'Don't look back, please, Livi. I beg you, don't look back,' Cibi urges her sister.

The girls step off the front path, out onto the street. In the doorway, their mother is sobbing in their grandfather's arms. Livi *had* glanced back as she pulled shut the front gate. Her whimper of pain at witnessing her mother's distress felt like a club to Cibi's heart, but she had to be strong for Livi, for their mother.

Cibi straightens up and, transferring her small suitcase from one hand to the other, she grasps Livi around the waist, and the two sisters march on and away. 'Just keep walking, that's it, keep step with me, you're doing well, Livi. We'll be back home before you know it.'

It is a bright spring afternoon. The air is crisp and clear, the sky a deep cerulean blue. Livi's dark brown curls glint in the sun, while Cibi's waves bounce and settle, bounce and settle as she walks. They are aware of the neighbours lingering in their front gardens, watching, as the sisters, and the other Jewish girls, make their way towards the synagogue. Instinctively, maybe stubbornly, Livi and Cibi stare straight ahead.

Cibi is not sure her words of comfort are having any effect on Livi. Her sister leans into her, trembling a little. Where are they going? What will be expected of them? But the question which plagues Cibi more than any other, concerns Livi: will she be allowed to stay with her sister?

Fifteen years old and small for her age, how would Livi cope on her own?

'Magda should be here with us,' says Livi, cutting into her thoughts. 'Aren't we always meant to be together?'

'Magda is safe, that's what's important now. You and I have each other – we'll do the work, come home and then we'll be together.'

'And our pact, Cibi, to never be apart—?'

'There's nothing we can do about that now.' Cibi didn't mean her words to sound so strident: Livi is crying now.

'Promise me, Cibi,' says Livi, between sobs. 'Promise me we will come home, and that we'll be with Magda, Mumma and Grandfather again.'

'My sweet kitten, I promise you that one day soon, we'll walk back down this street and go home. I just don't know when – but I will protect you until my last breath, which will be a long time coming. Do you believe me, Livi?'

'Of course I do.' Livi's tears have abated for the moment. She squeezes Cibi's arm. 'You're Cibi. Nothing stops Cibi getting what she wants.' The sisters exchange a watery smile.

Cibi takes in the other young girls, carrying small suitcases just like theirs, walking in the same direction. She notes the weeping mothers dragged back inside their houses by distraught fathers. They are walking through a nightmare. Some of the girls are on their own, others with their sisters or cousins, but no one crosses the street to walk with their friends. For some reason, they know this journey must be made alone.

'Livi, do you know why there are no boys here?' Cibi asks.

'Maybe they've already taken the boys.'

'We would have heard if they had.'

'Why only girls, though, Cibi? What good are girls for hard work?'

Cibi forces a laugh, anything to ease the tension. 'Maybe someone has realised we can do anything boys can do.'

Their orders had been clear: to report to the synagogue at 5 p.m. on *Shabbat*. They are greeted by the sight of Hlinka guards standing either side of the doors to the education block next to the temple. The block houses a large classroom where the girls, since early childhood, have received religious instruction. Cibi, as ever, is in awe of the synagogue, the towering building where she and her family have prayed and been comforted by friends following the death of their father and grandmother. Forever a place of safety and security amongst her own people, today the building offers no such comfort. The Nazis have ruined it. The Hlinka guards have ruined it.

The girls are herded inside the classroom while the few parents who had chosen to ignore the order to stay away are screamed at, hit with batons and told to go home.

'Stay here,' Cibi says to Livi, letting go of her sister and dropping her suitcase. Hurrying outside, Cibi grabs hold of a young girl who is clinging to her mother, refusing to be parted. A guard is striking the woman on the back, over and over, but she won't let go of her daughter. A small crowd watches this brutal spectacle in horrified silence.

'I've got you, come with me.' Cibi's courage is more evident than her fear at this moment.

The girl loses her grip on her mother as Cibi pulls her away. Crying, screaming, the girl reaches out for her mother again, who is now being dragged away by the guards.

'I've got her, I'll take care of her, Mrs Goldstein,' Cibi shouts, as she chivvies the girl – Ruth – inside.

More and more girls enter the room, their fear written large on tearful faces. The room is full of grief and desperation.

'Ruthie, Ruthie! Over here,' a voice calls.

Cibi looks around to see Evie, her young neighbour, beckoning Ruthie Goldstein.

'That's your cousin, isn't it?' asks Cibi, and Ruthie nods.

'I'll be OK now,' she tells Cibi, with a watery smile. 'She's my family.'

Cibi goes back to where she left Livi. 'We should find a space by the wall if we're to be comfortable,' she tells her, leading Livi away from the centre of the room.   .

The sisters stay standing, waiting for instructions, watching as more and more girls are ushered into the room. Despite the crisp morning air the room is stuffy, and noisy, as girls call to one another, and sob. Once a room full of happy childhood memories, it is now a hostile space.

As the daylight fades, two small bulbs in the ceiling are turned on to emit a dull, yellow glow over the room.

Suddenly, and without warning, the door is slammed shut and the girls' fear intensifies.

'I'm scared, Cibi! I want to go home!' Livi cries.

'I know, me too, but we can't. Let's just sit down for a bit.' Now, with their backs against the wall, Cibi places Livi's

36

suitcase between her legs before doing the same with hers. 'You must look after your case at all costs, do you understand? Don't let it out of your sight.'

'What will happen to us?' Livi asks.

'I think we might be staying the night, so we should get comfortable.' Cibi places her arm around Livi's shoulders, drawing her head onto her chest, holding her tight. 'Are you hungry, Livi, my kitten?'

Livi is crying again, shaking her head.

'Just close your eyes and try to get some sleep.'

'I couldn't possibly sleep.'

From somewhere deep inside, Cibi recalls the words to the Czech lullaby she sung long ago to baby Livi. Softly, she begins to sing.

My Little Angel	*Hajej můj andílku*
Lie my little angel, lie and sleep,	*Hajej můj andílku hajej a spi,*
Mum is rocking her baby.	*matička kolíbá děťátko svý.*
Lie, sleep sweet, little one,	*Hajej dadej, nynej, malej,*
Mum is rocking her baby.	*Matička kolíbá děťátko svý.*
Lie my little angel, lie and sleep,	*Hajej můj andílku hajej a spi,*
Mum is rocking her baby.	*matička kolíbá děťátko svý.*
Lie, sleep sweet, little one,	*Hajej dadej, nynej, malej,*
Mum is rocking her baby.	*Matička kolíbá děťátko svý.*

Cibi hugs Livi tight. Within a few minutes she hears her breathing slow. Cibi sends all the love she feels for her little sister into the sleeping child. 'I won't let anyone hurt you,' she whispers into her sweet-smelling curls.

Leaning back against the wall, Cibi watches as other girls struggle for space to sit down, negotiating a back to lean against, a spot by the wall. Some of them open their suitcases and remove small tins, hunks of bread, cheese. They offer the food around. Cibi thinks about *Hachshara*, and wonders what everyone is up to at the camp. On Sunday they will question where she is, why she hasn't come back. She tries not to think about Mother and Grandfather, sitting down to a meagre supper at home. Will they even be able to eat? Cibi wonders whether Magda is better. She wishes she was here, but maybe she's better off in the hospital.

Comforted by this thought, Cibi closes her eyes, and remembers happier days.

'We'll look at your sleeping arrangements tomorrow, once we know how many of you are willing to stay and do the training, to become part of Hachshara. *Meanwhile, find a space and try to get some sleep. I promise you will all get beds, mattresses, blankets and pillows tomorrow.'*

'Where are all the boys?' one of the girls calls out. Cibi notes her cheeky grin, her shining eyes.

'In another part of the camp. And before you go looking, it's a long way from here.'

'I'm Cibi, what's your name?' Cibi asks the cheeky girl. They are lying side by side on the wooden floorboards, pulling their coats tight around their bodies to ward off the wind blowing through the large gaps in the walls.

'Aliza. Nice to meet you, Cibi. Where are you from?'

'Vranov. You?'

'Bardejov, but not for much longer. I can't wait to get to Palestine.'

'I know what you mean. I can't believe I'm actually here,' Cibi says, giggling nervously.

38

'Do you think we will train with the boys?' Aliza asks no one in particular.

'Is that the only reason you're here, to meet boys?' The girl lying beside them sits up.

'No, I want to go to Palestine,' Aliza tells her.

'Well, I'm only here for the boys,' a voice from the back of the room calls out.

'Hands up those who are here because they want to go to Palestine,' says Cibi, so that the whole room can hear her.

All the girls in the room sit up, and everyone raises their hands.

'Now hands up all those who are here because they want to meet boys?' Cibi asks.

The girls all exchange glances, more giggles and once again, every hand is raised.

Instead of sleeping, as instructed, the girls talk and joke, exchanging names, towns of origin, ambitions.

Cibi feels an intense sense of pride in her decision to be there amongst these strangers, united in their purpose. Her sacrifice to leave her family and follow her dream of becoming a pioneer in a new and promised land will be worth it. She will work hard to reach Palestine, and then she will send for her sisters, for Mumma and Grandfather. In this small room, devoid of bedding but replete with a sense of adventure, the camaraderie amongst the women underpins Cibi's fervent wish to begin Hachshara as soon as possible.

She is one of the girls who will have a bed tomorrow night.

Aliza stands up. 'Why do we think the boys are here?' she yells.

In unison the girls shout back: 'To go to Palestine, AND TO MEET GIRLS.'

Cibi wakes with a start.

'I want my mumma! I want my mumma!' A girl's plaintive wail echoes into the room.

Livi stirs, softly moaning in her sleep. Cibi whispers soothing words and Livi settles once more.

As the early spring sunshine sneaks through the high windows, the girls wake, stand, and stretch. Again, they ask of one another: *Where are we going? What will be asked of us?* There are no answers and soon the room falls silent, the girls sinking back to the floor to wait. Some eat from the rations in their cases. At least the room feels less bleak in sunshine, and more reminiscent of the days of old.

'Wake up, Livi. It's time to wake up.' Cibi gently nudges her sister, whose slumbering head rests in Cibi's lap.

Sitting up, Livi looks dazed, staring around the room, confusion in her eyes.

'Would you like something to eat, Livi?' Cibi prompts.

'I'm not hungry,' says Livi, her eyes taking in the girls, some of whom are crying.

'You have to eat something. We don't know how long we'll be here.'

Cibi opens her suitcase, looking for the food buried under and around her clothes. She takes the cake her mother had made for *Shabbat* dinner. Unwrapping it from the achingly familiar tea towel, Cibi inhales the aroma of Mumma's cooking. She breaks off a small piece and hands it to Livi.

'I don't want any, you know I hate this cake,' Livi complains, brushing Cibi's hand aside.

'All the same, we need to eat it. It won't last and we need to save the tins. Doesn't it mean anything to you that Mumma made it with her own hands?' Cibi grins and holds out the cake to Livi once more.

40

Begrudgingly, Livi takes it and begins to nibble, rolling her eyes at each morsel, pretend-gagging as she swallows. Cibi forces her own portion down – her mouth is dry and the cake tastes of ashes.

'I'm thirsty, I need something to get rid of the taste.' Livi is beginning to whine and Cibi suddenly feels exhausted. She would like to whine too.

'You will have to wait. I'm sure we will be given something soon.'

They don't hear the door open, but jump to their feet as a voice booms, 'Up on your feet, it's time to go!' The Hlinka guard slaps his baton into the palm of his hand.

Snapping the suitcase shut Cibi stands up fast, grabbing Livi's case as she rises. 'Hold on to your case, Livi,' she reminds her sister. 'You are not to let anyone take it from you, do you understand?'

Livi nods, her eyes on the doors at the front of the room from which more guards are entering their space. The girls are corralled into two lines and led outside. They squint in the bright sunshine of a beautiful day.

Cibi pushes Livi ahead of her, holding on to the back of her coat. They mustn't lose each other, whatever happens. One side of the street is lined with Hlinka guards, and on the other side are the girls' families, desperately calling to their daughters, granddaughters and nieces. They have broken curfew to be there: Jews can no longer wander where they will at whatever hour they choose. They are risking beatings and imprisonment, but for many, the punishment will be worth it to see their beloved children. Cibi knows that her mother and grandfather will not be amongst the crowd. They have never once left the house on *Shabbat*.

41

The Hlinka begin to march the girls down the street, away from the synagogue and the grief.

'Where are we going?' whispers Livi.

'This is the way to the station,' Cibi says, pointing ahead. 'Maybe we're to catch a train.'

As the plaintive cries of their families fade, new voices – angry, hate-filled voices – greet them as they make their passage through the town. Their former friends and neighbours are hurling rotten fruit and stale bread at their heads, yelling their joy that the Jews are finally leaving. Cibi and Livi are stunned by the taunts, the full-throated bile being dispensed from snarling mouths. What has happened to these people? These are the very individuals their grandmother had attended during childbirth; the same ones who shopped in their mother's store or sought her wise counsel.

They pass Mrs Vargova, the cobbler's wife. Cibi had taken their shoes to be repaired as and when they needed new soles or some stitching. Often Mrs Vargova would not allow her husband to charge for his work, reminding him the girls had lost their father after he had been injured fighting for their country. Now she is part of this roaring crowd, her hair out of its tidy bun, hanging loose and deranged around her shoulders, while she tells Cibi, Livi, and all the other girls that she hates them, that she wishes they would die.

Cibi pulls Livi close. She can't prevent her sister from seeing or hearing what's going on, but this is all she's got: a warm body, enveloping arms. Cibi raises her chin, unlike the girls around them who are crying and wailing. This hateful crowd won't get her tears.

'Hi, Cibi, I didn't think you were selected to leave today.' Visik, her childhood 'friend' turned Hlinka traitor, is walking towards them. It was simply the promise of a smart black uniform that turned Visik into a monster. Cibi ignores him.

'What's the matter with you?' he probes. His dull eyes look her up and down. 'Why aren't you crying like all the other weak Jews?' He walks with them, as if they're taking a pleasant stroll together in the sunshine. Cibi pulls Livi closer, and at the same time sidesteps so she's shoulder to shoulder with Visik, turning to meet his eyes

'You will never have the privilege of seeing me cry, Visik. And if I ever think about crying, I'll just remember your ugly face, and I'll laugh instead. And as for weak, I'm not the idiot who needs to hide behind the uniform of a thug,' Cibi spits.

An older guard joins Visik. 'Get them back into line,' he orders him.

'And then take this little boy back to his mumma,' Cibi hurls after him, as she and Livi move back into the throng of girls.

'Cibi. What are you doing?' Livi's eyes are wide with fear.

'Nothing at all, Livi. That felt really good.'

The train station looms into view: Cibi was right. She remembers the pleasant trip they'd made the previous year, to Humenné, to visit relatives. Now, they are hustled through the station to the platform, the guards shouting and pushing the girls onto the waiting train. They shuffle on board, place their cases overhead and find seats. No one is crying anymore; instead, they are quiet, each young woman contemplating the family she has left behind, and the unknowable future stretching out ahead of them.

Slowly the train pulls away from the station. Livi rests her head on Cibi's shoulder. They gaze out of the window at the bright spring day, the familiar fields moving slowly past. Several times the train stops with no indication of where they are: fields to the left and right, and the stunning, still snow-capped Tatra mountains in the distance, bidding their citizens goodbye.

The train conductor makes his way down the aisles, empty mugs hanging from the fingers of his left hand, while in his right he holds a jug of water. As he hands Cibi and Livi a mug each and proceeds to fill them to the halfway mark, he mouths a 'Sorry', giving them a sad smile. Cibi glares at him, but Livi says, 'Thank you', drinking down the water in single gulp and handing back her mug.

The train eventually pulls into a station, with signs telling them they have arrived in Poprad. The doors to the carriages are flung open. Hlinka guards step inside each carriage and shout, 'Out! Out!'

On the platform, new Hlinka guards are wielding long black whips, snapping them into the girls' faces as they disembark from the train.

'They won't hit us, will they, Cibi? We haven't done anything wrong, have we?' Livi whispers.

'Of course we haven't,' Cibi tells her, hoping her voice doesn't betray her own fear.

A few feet away from where they stand, waiting for the next set of instructions, a girl approaches one of the guards and opens her mouth to say something when the guard raises his whip and strikes her on the arm. Several girls react, yelling at the guard, dragging the injured girl away. Cibi grabs hold of Livi as more guards flood the platform, ordering hundreds of girls into long lines, ready to start marching once more.

They haven't been walking for very long when they are stopped in front of an enormous wire and steel fence, on the other side of which Cibi spies a number of imposing, dark buildings.

As the girls enter what is obviously a military compound, they note the army insignias on the vehicles, the barracks lining either side of the solitary road running the length of the fenced-in enclosure. Cibi and Livi join a group of girls being herded towards a two-storey barracks. Once inside, the door is slammed behind them. Slowly, the girls sink to the floor, claiming a space to sit down, lie down or curl up in despair.

'Do you think they will give us something to eat?' Livi wants to know.

'I don't think we can expect anything more than what we got last night,' Cibi answers.

'But that was nothing.'

'Yes, nothing. Let's wait a little longer before we go back into our cases.'

Sobbing and whispering, voices rumble around this room and the room above. But there's nothing to be done. Cibi and Livi lie down and using their jumpers for pillows, their coats for blankets, they eventually fall asleep, too tired to feel hunger, fear or longing.

The next morning, when there is still no word from the guards, the girls are subdued. Cibi believes being left alone in this room to imagine the worst is part of the Hlinka's plan. Terrified, hungry women will be far easier to manage.

Livi grabs her suitcase and climbs onto it to peer through the window into the courtyard beyond.

'What can you see?' Cibi asks, as others gather around.

Pushing up onto her toes, Livi squints through the murky glass. Letting go of the windowsill with one hand she attempts to wipe away the dust with her sleeve. Losing her balance, her arm smashes through the glass before she tumbles to the floor, unleashing a shower of broken glass.

Cibi quickly pulls her away from the scene as the other girls also move into the depths of the room, wanting no association with the broken window.

'Are you all right? Are you hurt?' Cibi brushes fragments of glass from Livi's hair, her coat.

'I'm fine,' Livi answers, quickly.

'Well, let me look at you.'

Cibi begins examining Livi's face for stray shards and then she takes Livi's hands. There is a long, bloody gash running down the middle of Livi's right palm. Blood drips onto the floor. Cibi lifts her skirt, grabbing the white linen petticoat underneath. Bending over, she sinks her teeth into the fabric, making a small tear and then proceeds to rip off long strips of cloth, with which she wraps Livi's wound. Almost immediately, blood begins to seep through the white cloth.

In shock, Livi watches her sister wrap her injured hand. She feels no pain.

The door is flung open, and three guards enter. Without a word, each of them grabs two girls by the arms and drags them outside.

Everyone in the room watches in horror, girls clinging to one another as the door is once more slammed shut.

An hour or more passes before once again the door is opened and the girls are ordered outside. Those who pick up their suitcases have them snatched away as they cross the threshold. Cibi hears a guard telling one girl that her suitcase will be there when she returns. They never see them again.

The girls are led into another building, a large space with a kitchen area at the back. They line up and find themselves in front of the six girls who had been taken earlier and who now hand them a small tin plate, a small pile of over-cooked cabbage and a piece of bread the size of their fists. Maybe this was once a dining room, but there are no tables and chairs, so the girls sit on the floor forcing the tasteless food into empty stomachs.

On their return to their barracks, buckets of water, mops and scrubbing brushes greet the girls. They are told they are to scrub the room until it shines. They take turns washing and rewashing the floor, each girl working until they have all scrubbed at least once, watched over by guards.

They spend the rest of the day sitting, standing, crying. Late in the afternoon they are taken back to the dining room and fed a small piece of potato and a slice of bread each.

Back in the barracks, one of the girls reminds them it is *Pesach*, Passover. But how can they take part in the rituals demanded of them in here? The girl points at a blonde-haired teenager who is sitting alone. 'Her father is our rabbi. She should know the order of prayer, the rituals.'

All eyes turn to the girl, who nods and clicks open her suitcase to remove the *Haggadah*. Soon, everyone is gathered around joining her in prayer. A heavy sadness settles on them.

The next morning, once more without breakfast, the girls are marched out of the compound, and back to the train station. Once again, whip-carrying Hlinka guards mark their journey.

The train is waiting on the platform, engine fired up and ready to go. But the girls are ordered past the rows of carriages, towards cattle wagons at the back of the train.

'Get on board!' the guards yell, over and over. But the girls don't move. Cibi feels like an animal caught in the headlights of a car. They can't mean they should climb into a vehicle meant for transporting cows, surely?

'Cibi, what's happening?' Livi cries.

'I don't know, but . . . but these wagons, they're for *animals*.'

But the Hlinka guards are serious. The whips are extended and used to shepherd the girls into the wagons, despite the fact they are so high off the ground. The cursing, yelling, and hitting continues, all attempts at decorum abandoned, and the girls scrabble to climb aboard, reaching out to then help those on the platform to clamber inside.

Cibi pushes Livi up into the arms of a girl who lifts her into the wagon. The stink of cow manure mingles with the very real smell of their fear.

The girls are packed inside, standing room only. Bolts are drawn across the heavy doors and the only light comes from shards of sunlight pouring through the wooden slats of the walls.

Practically everyone is crying now; those nearest the walls are screaming, smashing their fists against the slats, demanding their freedom.

Cibi and Livi have entered a waking nightmare. There is no respite from the close proximity of other bodies, from the wailing, the terrible thirst and gnawing hunger. The train stops many times, sometimes briefly, sometimes for lengthier periods, but the door stays closed. Cibi tears more and more strips from her petticoat to change Livi's bandages, until only the waistband remains.

48

Finally, the doors creak open. The sun has slipped below the horizon, but even this half-light makes them squint. Cibi's heart almost judders to a halt when she spies the uniforms of the Nazis. It's the SS. She has only ever seen them in Grandfather's newspaper, but the dark grey jackets, the swastika in the bright red strip on their sleeves – there is no mistaking it. They line the platform, facing the wagons, holding their rifles in one hand and the leads of large, barking dogs in the other.

The girls start to jump down and the dogs strain to snap and snarl at them. Two girls are bitten the moment they land.

'Faster, faster,' the Germans scream, striking those they deem too slow with the butts of their rifles.

Cibi and Livi move fast, leaping out of the wagon and standing to one side. They have arrived at what is obviously another compound. There are floodlights illuminating buildings, whole streets beyond the gates. They look at the sign above the wire fencing and read: *ARBEIT MACHT FREI*. Cibi knows enough German to decipher the meaning. *Work sets you free.*

But then Cibi and Livi become transfixed by the shaven-headed, hollow-cheeked men who now swarm the train. In blue-and-white striped shirts and trousers, they move like rats fleeing a sinking ship as they clamber into the wagons and begin to throw the girls' suitcases onto the platform.

Cibi and Livi watch one man pick up an empty sardine tin, Livi almost retching as he runs a finger around the inside, sucking on it before holding the tin to his lips to drain the last of the oil. He looks up and notices the sisters watching him, but he carries on licking the tin, unabashed.

The line of girls begins to move towards the gates.

49

'Listen to me, Livi,' Cibi whispers urgently. 'We will eat stones, nails, and whatever we can get our hands on, but we must survive this place. Do you understand?'

Speechless, traumatised, Livi can only nod 'yes'.

Part II

The Gates of Hell

CHAPTER 7

Auschwitz
April 1942

'Just keep walking, Livi. Stay in line,' Cibi murmurs to her sister.

Once they are through the gates, the girls are led down a tree-lined street, the first flush of spring leaves waving in the cool breeze. Heat emanates from the harsh overhead lighting and Cibi is ironically reminded of a warm summer evening. They pass a grey concrete building, meeting the blank stares of young men and women who gaze back at them, expressionless, from the windows. Cibi shivers – they could be the *Yeshiva* boys, the shaven-headed youth who study the *Torah*. But she can't allow herself to think about home, about her friends. She must stay alert. Red-brick barracks line both sides of several of the streets the girls pass through. Tall trees and pretty flowers in neat garden beds adorn the earthy plots in front of each building, giving the illusion of a welcoming home.

Finally, the girls are led into a red-brick, two-storey building, where they find themselves face to face with its other occupants. It is a vast room, with high ceilings, but as large as it is, it is still a tight fit for the hundreds of inhabitants inside. At least a thousand, thinks Cibi. The loose straw on the floor reminds her of a stable or barn, somewhere animals would sleep – not girls. The smell of manure adds to the impression that this room is for livestock.

'They've put us in with boys!' Cibi whispers, incredulous. But she can see that there are girls here, too . . . will the sisters end up like them? Wide-eyed and skinny? Blank-eyed and desperate?

The boys are in uniform – Cibi thinks it is Russian soldiers' uniform: worn khaki trousers and button-down shirts, a yellow-bordered red star with the hammer and sickle. Cibi thinks they are looking at the girls with pity, probably because they know only too well what awaits them. Or maybe they just don't want to share this confined space with them.

'I think they're girls, Cibi.' Livi is unable to tear her eyes away from the emaciated figures who are still staring at them, in silence.

'Welcome to Auschwitz.' A boy steps forward. 'You're in Poland now, in case they haven't told you. This is where we live.' He waves a hand around the room, at sacks of straw scattered on the ground. Surely they can't be expected to bed down on these things? Cibi thinks.

'What happens now?' a scared voice calls out.

'You sleep with the fleas,' another answers.

'But we haven't eaten,' the first cries, scared, tired.

'You're too late. You'll eat tomorrow. I warn you, you will also have your heads shaved like us – they shave *all* of your hair – and you will be put in a uniform like this. And then to work. Never resist. If you do you will be punished, but so might we.'

The figure lowers his voice to a whisper. Cibi notes his eyes: pretty eyes in a thin boy's face. Livi is right, these boys are girls. 'The SS are everywhere,' she says, conspiratorially, 'but it's the *kapos* who look after us we have to be wary of. Sometimes they're worse than SS. They're prisoners, just like us, but you must never trust them – they have chosen their side.'

Prisoners. The word startles Cibi. They are in a prison, and they will remain there until the Germans decide they can leave. Attempting to hide her fear, Cibi springs into action, claiming a lumpy mattress in the middle of the dark room.

'Come on.' She takes Livi's hand and gently pulls her onto the 'bed'. They lie down fully clothed, and in their coats, the straw crackling beneath their bodies, poking through rough hessian to scratch at their hands and heads. Cibi wishes they'd been allowed to keep their suitcases – perhaps they'll be reunited with them tomorrow.

One by one, the girls find beds and settle down, but there are not nearly enough, and two, three, four girls have to squeeze together, like sardines.

Livi is crying, softly at first, but then she is sobbing. Cibi folds her arms around her sister and wipes away her tears with her sleeve. 'It's all right, Livi. You're hungry; we're both hungry. Tomorrow we'll eat, and it will be daylight and we'll feel better. Please stop crying, I'm right here with you.'

But Livi's tears are contagious, and soon the room is full of sniffing and gasping sobs.

Girls stumble to their feet, tripping over each other as they head for the door. Voices call out to them to stop, come back. 'You'll get us all into trouble!' a voice yells – very obviously now, a girl's.

'Go back to bed. It's worse out there than it is in here!' shouts another.

Livi's sobs slowly subside, and the room falls silent, until a cry of, 'Something bit me!' and the reply: 'It's just fleas. You'll get used to it.'

It is still dark when the girls are woken at 4 a.m. by the *kapos* shouting at them to get moving.

It is bitterly cold. Cibi and Livi slept fitfully, and now they are chilled, hungry and thirsty. Rubbing sleep from their eyes, they follow the inmates who have learned the rhythm of the morning ritual, lining up to use the makeshift bathroom of long troughs with dripping taps and open toilets.

Cibi and Livi hold on to each other as they begin to file out of the room, but then Cibi lets out a cry and stumbles, falling to her knees.

'Cibi, Cibi, what's wrong?' Livi says.

Cibi rips off her shoes and socks to reveal feet alive with jumping fleas. Cibi holds the socks she had just removed in one hand and stares, paralysed, at her feet. Around them the girls climb over the straw sacks to get outside.

'Cibi, you're scaring me. We need to keep moving!' Livi cries, shaking her sister's arm.

Cibi looks at the socks and flings them away.

'It's OK, it's OK. We just need to wash your feet. I'll help. Come on.'

But Cibi pulls away from Livi. This is her problem, and she must be strong for her sister.

A young, shaven-headed girl pushes her way back through the crowd and grabs Cibi's discarded socks. 'She'll need them,' she tells Livi. 'I shook out all the fleas.' Livi is stunned by the girl's tone: robotic, utterly devoid of emotion. But it is an act of kindness all the same.

Livi takes the socks with a nod and shows them to Cibi. 'The fleas are gone. Please put them back on.'

Cibi says nothing but doesn't resist as Livi pulls the socks onto her feet, and then buckles her shoes.

Cibi and Livi join the others trudging out of the building. Outside they are separated from the old-timers and marched to another building. In daylight, the streets and buildings don't look nearly as inviting. SS officers now line the pavements, rifles strung across their backs, handguns holstered on their hips. Prisoners spill out from buildings like the one Cibi and Livi have just spent the night in. They pass a group of men shuffling along beside them – a glance here and there, but no one makes eye contact.

Eventually, the girls are ordered into a windowless room, where they are instructed to undress. Cibi is grateful, for the moment, that they haven't been warned of what's to come, grateful that Livi has been spared, even for a few hours, the reality behind the blank stares of the hairless inmates.

When some resist, their male and female guards think nothing of slapping them. Cibi and Livi and every other girl try to hide their nudity with hands and arms. The sound of men's laughter fills their ears as they shout obscenities at the naked girls.

'Your jewellery – don't forget those pretty diamonds you have in your ears, girls. We want it all,' their *kapo* calls out, laughing. She is a tall woman with short, curly black hair, and a single missing incisor.

Cibi reaches a hand to one ear and then the other. The small gold earrings with their tiny red stones had been fixed to her lobes on the day she was born by her grandmother, who had just delivered her. This would be the first time they had ever been removed. Cibi struggles to find the clasp holding them in place. She watches with growing horror as the *kapo* rips earrings at random from girls' ears. Blood pours from split lobes as hysterical crying fills the room. She hopes Livi, wherever she is in this hellish room, has managed to remove hers. As she pulls them free she finds the *kapo* is standing in front of her, hand outstretched to take the precious tokens of a grandmother's love. She thinks briefly of Magda, and thanks God her sister is many miles away.

One by one the girls are called into the centre of the room, to be inspected by the *Schutzstaffel*, SS guards, who continue to leer at the young female bodies paraded before them. Cibi remembers her grandfather telling her again and again, *Humour will save you. Laugh, and if you can't laugh, put a smile on your face.*

Raising her head to her examiners, she puts a brave smile on her lips. She feels the flutter of a hundred butterflies in her stomach. When she is called, she slowly makes her way forward to stand in front of a man dressed in striped trousers and shirt. He is the barber. He snips off lengths of her chestnut hair and she watches the waves fall onto the growing mound at his feet. He flicks on a crude shaving machine and runs it over her head, reducing her once proud head of hair to stubble. Not finished, and to her shame, he drops to a knee. Spreading her legs, he directs the machine to her crotch, where he removes her pubic hair. She tries not to think of little Livi enduring the same humiliation. Without meeting her eyes, he nods for her to move on.

They are then herded into another room.

'Into the sauna with you all,' another *kapo* shouts.

This room features large iron tanks filled with dirty water. Puddles of loose hair float on the surfaces of them all. Cibi climbs into the nearest one. This is not like any sauna she has heard of. Cibi's mind begins to drift away from this place, back to her home, to Magda and Grandfather and everything she holds dear. If she can hold them in her mind maybe it won't be so bad here.

'The water is dirtier than we are,' says a girl, clambering out of the bath. 'And colder.'

The freezing water snaps Cibi out of her trance. Her body has grown numb from the cold, as numb as her head and heart.

Having climbed out, and dripping with water, Cibi takes the clothes thrust at her. Dressed in the same Russian prisoner-of-war uniform as the older inmates, Cibi finds the harsh fabric of the khaki shirt irritating to her tender skin. The matching breeches threaten to fall down with every step.

The rough clothes cling to her damp body, providing no warmth. The *kapo* thrusts a piece of paper into her hands. She reads the digits scrawled onto it: 4560.

Back in line once more with the other washed and shaved inmates, Cibi doesn't resist when she's called forward.

Another man in blue-and-white stripes sits at a desk at the front of the room in which her hair was just shorn. He holds out his hand for the scrap of paper and tells her to sit down.

The numbers which stand in bold black letters against the grubby white are etched into the skin of her arm.

The pain is intense, shocking, but Cibi shows no reaction. She won't give this man her agony.

Outside once more, Cibi joins hundreds of girls, who, like her, are desperately searching for a familiar face. But no one looks familiar any more. In identical clothes and shorn heads, there is nothing left to distinguish them.

And then Cibi hears her name. She doesn't move as Livi runs to her, embracing her before pulling away and staring at her oldest sister. She runs her hand over Cibi's naked head. 'What have they done to you? Cibi, you've got no hair.'

Looking at her sister's own naked head, Cibi doesn't reply. Livi is clutching her arm and wincing, tears of pain streaking pink cheeks. The pain of Cibi's tattoo is equally intense – she can feel the blood running into the creases of her elbow, and wonders about infection. Putting her arm around Livi's shoulders, she steers her sister back to the building with the flea-infested mattresses. It is not until the sisters sit cuddled together that they look at their arms.

'Your number is only one ahead of mine,' Livi says. She wipes away the dried blood so Cibi can see the butchered number: 4559.

When all the girls from Vranov have returned to their room their *kapo* enters, accompanied by four emaciated men struggling to carry two cauldrons, a crate of small metal mugs and another containing bread.

'Form two lines and come and get your food. You haven't done anything today so you will only have half a cup of soup and one piece of bread. Anyone who pushes or complains will get nothing,' the *kapo* roars.

Taking their mugs and bread back to their mattress, the girls compare the contents of their 'soup'.

'I have a piece of potato,' Cibi says. 'Do you?'

Livi stirs the weak, brown liquid, shaking her head. Cibi pulls the potato out of her mug, and takes a small bite. She plops the rest into Livi's mug. They spend the remaining time before lights out picking the fleas from each other's necks and ears. The old-timers return after dark. On their way to bed they smile at the new girls, and shake their heads in sympathy.

Another 4 a.m. wake-up call. *'Raus! Raus!'* is screamed into the room, accompanied by the hammering of a baton on the walls. After a visit to the bathroom to wash away as many fleas and bedbugs as they can, Cibi and Livi receive their first breakfast in Auschwitz: a ration of bread the size of their palms, and a drink of lukewarm liquid they were told was coffee, but which bears no resemblance to any coffee they have tasted before.

'Soup and bread for dinner, coffee and bread for breakfast,' Livi mutters, forcing the coffee down her throat.

'Remember what I said when we arrived – we will eat stones and nails, whatever we are given,' Cibi replies.

'We should have kept the linden tea,' Livi tells Cibi, as if they had had a choice in the matter; as if they should have asked the guards to wait a moment until they had removed the precious leaves from their suitcases before leaving them behind in the cattle wagon.

Outside, a flurry of snow attempts to carpet the road on which the girls now stand in rows of five. Livi and Cibi shiver, their teeth chattering.

Cibi reaches for Livi's hand in an attempt to comfort her. She feels the soft touch of fabric and carefully pries apart Livi's fingers. 'How have you got this, Livi?' she whispers.

'Got what?' Livi is holding a small pouch containing a sacred coin their mother had sewn into both girls' vests on the night of their departure.

'Where did this come from?' Livi asks, oblivious to the fact it is in her hand.

'You tell me. How have you held on to it?'

'I-I don't know.' Livi doesn't take her eyes off the coin. 'I didn't know I had it.'

'Listen to me.' Cibi's voice is harsh, and Livi startles. 'When we start moving, you have to drop it. Just let it go. We can't be caught with it.'

'But it's from Mother; she gave it to us to keep us safe. The rabbi blessed it.'

'This coin will not keep us safe, it will only get us into trouble. Will you do as I say?' Cibi insists. Livi hangs her head and nods. 'Now, hold my hand and when I let go, that's when you drop it.'

For two hours the girls stand in line as their numbers are called out. Cibi realises that the numbers are the ones etched into their swollen arms. She pulls up her sleeve to memorise hers and instructs Livi to do the same. This is their identity now.

Finally, their numbers are called. Once they have been assigned to their work details, Cibi and Livi march out of the gates, past the station, towards the town of Oswiecim.

Outside the camp, empty fields surround them; in the distance, smoke billows from small farmhouses, and unseen horses neigh their presence. The SS stride up and down the rows, those with dogs encourage them to bark and snap at the girls.

Cibi slows down until the girls behind catch them up. Glancing around to make sure none of the guards are nearby, Cibi gently lets go of Livi's hand. She hears the soft thud of the pouch as it hits the muddy slurry on the ground. She takes hold of Livi's hand once more, squeezing gently, to communicate the message that they have done the right thing.

They enter a street of houses without roofs, some without walls. Mounds of rubble line the empty road. The old-timers move towards the brick ruins; others clamber up onto the rooftops and begin to throw down bricks and tiles. Those on the ground weave and duck to avoid the falling missiles, not always succeeding.

'You two!'

Cibi looks around to see their *kapo* staring at her and her sister.

'Come here!' she instructs, and the girls hasten towards her.

'See that?' She is pointing to a four-wheel cart a hundred metres away. There are a couple of girls strapped to the front of the wagon in a harness, dragging it along. As though they are horses, Livi thinks. 'They will show you what to do.'

The girls hurry away to once again come face to face with the blank eyes of prisoners who have been here far longer than they have.

'You're on the back,' one girl says.

Livi and Cibi move to the back of the cart and await further instruction.

The girls at the front begin pulling the cart towards a newly demolished house, where bricks are piled in long rows near its foundations. Several girls stand by, waiting. Livi and Cibi start pushing.

When they reach the rubble, the girls start to load the bricks into the cart.

'Don't just stand there, help them!'

Nudging Livi into action, Cibi starts heaving the bricks into the cart, just as the *kapo* walks up to them.

Livi throws in a brick, where it strikes another, chipping off a corner.

'Break one more and there will be consequences,' the *kapo* snaps.

Cibi thinks of Magda and feels a wave of relief riding the length of her spine. She has been spared this torture. She wishes Livi weren't here – she looks and seems so much younger than all the other girls. She is brave, but she is still so little. How will she even handle this work?

CHAPTER 8

Vranov nad Topl'ou
April 1942

Chaya is seated by the window, in the very same position Livi occupied only days earlier.

'We will hear her when she gets home, Chaya. Please, come away from the window.' Yitzchak lays a gentle hand on his daughter's shoulder and feels the rigid muscles tense beneath her skin.

Chaya doesn't drop the curtain; she will not miss Magda's arrival. 'Father,' she says, her eyes trained on the street. 'I don't know how we'll tell her about the girls.'

Yitzchak sighs. He has been worrying about the very same thing. 'I will make some linden tea,' he says in response, and Chaya nods.

Chaya presses her face to the window, and her tears slide down the glass as she mumbles prayers, clinging to her faith, needing to believe these powerful words will reach Cibi and Livi, no matter how far away they are; that, somehow, they will hear them and know she is yearning for their safe return.

Turning to receive the steaming china cup from Yitzchak, Chaya misses the moment Dr Kisely pulls up outside the house. Magda is out of the car before he even comes to a full stop, racing up the path.

When Magda bursts through the door, Yitzchak quickly takes Chaya's mug before she drops it. He steps aside to allow mother and daughter to collide in an embrace.

Dr Kisely appears in the doorway, placing the small bag containing Magda's belongings on the floor. Yitzchak and the doctor grasp hands. There is nothing to say as Dr Kisely glances around the room, sensing that Cibi and Livi are no longer there.

'And Magda?' Yitzchak finally says. 'She is recovered?'

'She is healthy and well.' The doctor's mouth twitches in a half-smile, but it doesn't reach his eyes.

'Chaya,' says Yitzchak, turning towards his daughter and granddaughter, still locked together. 'It's time to tell Magda.'

Magda pulls out of her mother's embrace. 'Tell me what? And where are Cibi and Livi?'

'Come and sit down, my darling,' Chaya says, her voice full of tears.

'I don't want to sit down.' Magda looks at her grandfather. 'Do you know where they are?'

When Yitzchak doesn't reply, Dr Kisely clears his throat. 'I must leave now, but if you feel unwell or your fever returns, I'll come back immediately.'

Yitzchak takes Dr Kisely's hand once more and thanks him. He watches the doctor walk to his car before shutting the front door and turning to meet the fearful eyes of both Chaya and Magda.

'Please sit down, Magda. It will be easier.'

The women take the sofa and Yitzchak positions himself on the only other comfortable chair in the room. Magda squeezes Chaya's hand tight, and Chaya welcomes the pain.

'Your sisters have gone to work for the Germans, Magda. We don't know where they are, but they weren't alone; many of our girls were taken that day.'

'Taken to work for the Germans?' Magda is aghast. Didn't Dr Kisely tell her that her sisters were safe? Didn't he promise her that Livi was too young and that Cibi was away? 'It can't be,' she says.

'I wish it wasn't true,' says her grandfather.

'But when?'

'Two days ago. They all left two days ago.'

'On *Shabbat*?' Magda is slowly processing the fact that her sisters are not in the house, that Cibi is not at the *Hachshara* and that Livi isn't in the garden.

Yitzchak nods.

'Why would they do that? Why would they go off to work for the Germans?'

'They had no choice, my precious child. The Hlinka guards had Livi's name on a list, and Cibi went with her to look after her.'

'For how long?'

'We don't know,' says Yitzchak, sighing. 'Hopefully not for too long. There is talk they are going to work on German farms. They may be there all summer.'

Magda turns to her mother. 'Mumma, why did you let them go?'

Chaya begins weeping then, burying her face in her hands. Magda puts an arm around her shoulders, drawing her closer.

'Your mother couldn't stop them taking the girls, Magda. No one could stop them.' Yitzchak's voice breaks and he retrieves his large handkerchief from a pocket to swipe away his tears.

Suddenly, Magda releases her mother and gets to her feet. 'We need to find out where they are so I can join them,' Magda pronounces.

Chaya gasps. 'We promised your sisters we would keep you safe. Here, at home.'

Magda looks at her mother, defiance lighting up her eyes, a snarl on her lips. 'We made our promise too, don't you remember, Mumma?' She turns to Yitzchak. 'Have you both forgotten our pact to stay together?'

'Stay where?' says Yitzchak. 'We have no idea where they are.'

'Uncle Ivan could help us. He's still here in Vranov, isn't he?' Magda is flushed, in shock, but determined.

Chaya nods slowly. 'Of course he is.'

'I want to see my uncle *now*,' insists Magda. 'He knows people. He has contacts. He can help us.' Perhaps he has heard something useful, she reasons.

She is staring at the back door, which leads to the house on the other side of the lane, where her uncle and aunt live with their three small children.

'We've spoken to Ivan and he has promised he will do all he can to keep us safe and in our home – that is all he can do.' Yitzchak says firmly. He runs the handkerchief over his face once more.

Slowly, reluctantly, dazed by the terrible news, Magda collapses back onto the sofa and Chaya wraps her in her arms, trying to be the parent every desperate child needs.

CHAPTER 9

Auschwitz
Spring 1942

The *kapo* picks up the broken brick and waves it in Livi's face before shoving it into her hands and instructing her to place it carefully back into the cart. Cibi is looking at the blood from Livi's wound, smearing the brick as she lays it down. When the *kapo* walks away, Livi tries to wrap her bleeding hand in her shirt.

The gash in Livi's palm has not healed and Cibi attempts to tear a strip from the thick fabric of her uniform shirt but it is too tough.

'Use your left hand. I'll cover you.' Cibi shields Livi from their supervisor's eyeline as they work.

When the cart is full of neat stacks of bricks, the *kapo* gives a nod to the two girls in charge of the sisters.

'Get to the back, you two,' they're told again. 'Push.'

They can hear the girls at the front straining in their harnesses. Cibi and Livi push against the back of the cart, but it doesn't budge.

'Push, you lazy bitches. Harder!'

Cibi puts her shoulder against the cart and indicates for Livi to do the same. Eventually, the cart begins to ease forward.

They make slow progress as the ground is littered with broken bricks and tiles, pieces of timber, the shattered remains of what were once people's homes.

The girls are soon sweating from their exertion, despite the cold air and strong wind. Cibi can't remember ever having worked so hard, not even at the *Hachshara*. She casts a sideways glance at Livi: with only one good hand at her disposal, her sister is struggling. The cart moves down a pitted road, passing fields, some of which have the new growth of potatoes pushing up through the frozen soil. They come to an empty field, where several men are awaiting their load. Piles of bricks have already been delivered and stacked. One man tells the girls where to position the cart. He and another help them unload and together they add the bricks to the existing piles.

With the cart empty, the return trip is faster. They repeat the whole exercise once more before being told by their *kapo* to take a break. Sitting down, their backs against the cart, Cibi examines Livi's hand.

'Someone should take a look at this, Livi. When we get back, I'll ask if there's a clinic, or a nurse,' Cibi whispers.

'I'll need a clean shirt, too,' says Livi, a tremble in her voice. 'This one is covered in blood.'

'We can wash your shirt. Come on, let's get back to work.'

'But we haven't been told to. Can't we rest a little longer?'

'We could, but I want to impress the *kapo*, keep her off our backs. Come on, you can do it.'

By the end of the day the girls have made four trips with their cart. Cibi shivers as she recalls the scenes from earlier in the day, when several girls in their group were struck by bricks and tiles, haphazardly launched from the ruins. They are also wary of the random slaps and punches their *kapo* distributes freely to any who, in her opinion, is shirking. Exhausted, they drag themselves back to their block and the meagre rations that await them.

After they have swallowed their bread and gulped down the soup, Cibi approaches their *kapo*, dragging Livi behind her. She holds up Livi's injured hand.

'*Kapo*, is there somewhere we can get some first aid for my sister? She cut her hand on the journey here and it's still bleeding. It needs to be bandaged if she is to keep working.'

The tall woman glances at the hand being held out to her. 'The hospital is in the next block along. Maybe they will look after you, maybe not,' she tells Livi, smirking, as she points down the street towards the gates of the compound.

As Cibi and Livi take the first couple of steps, the *kapo* calls out: 'Go alone. You don't need your big sister to hold your hand.' She sniggers at her own joke. 'And don't call me "*kapo*" – my name is Ingrid.' She smiles to reveal her missing tooth, and Cibi suddenly feels sick.

She gives Livi a gentle push. 'You'll be fine. I'll save us a space to sleep.'

The compound is now floodlit again. The sun has set and the girls have completed their first full day of work at Auschwitz.

Cibi settles down against a wall to wait for her sister. Later, as she is trying to smooth the lumpy mattress, Livi bursts through the door calling her name.

There are at least a thousand girls in the room, some sleeping, some still awake, or talking quietly in small groups. Cibi stands up and waves until Livi spots her and begins to weave in and out of the mattresses towards her.

Cibi notes the tear-tracks on Livi's face – pink flesh revealed amidst the brick dust that covers her fine, delicate features.

'What's wrong? Are you all right?' asks Cibi, as Livi collapses into her arms. She lowers her sister onto their mattress and grasps her bandaged hand. It seems to have been treated, at least.'What's wrong?'

Livi continues to sob until finally she can get a sentence out: 'Why didn't you tell me?' she cries.

'Tell you what? What's happened?'

'I went to the hospital.'

'Did something happen?'

'I saw.' Livi has stopped sobbing. Her eyes are wide with fear.

'Saw what?' Cibi asks, suddenly feeling very cold.

'There was a mirror in the room. Why didn't you tell me what they've done to me?'

Cibi takes Livi's face in her hands and brings it close to her own. For the first time in days she smiles. 'Is that all? You saw your own reflection in a mirror?'

'My hair . . .' Livi says, running her fingers over her scalp, pulling them away in disgust. 'They cut off my curls.' Livi is looking past Cibi, into the room, at the hundreds of other shorn heads. Her eyes are glassy, unfocused. For a moment, Cibi wonders if she should slap her sister, snap her out of her shock. Finally, Livi turns her wide blue eyes on her sister. 'They were cutting off my hair?' she whispers. Her hands go once more to her head. Tears fill her eyes.

'But, Livi, what did you think they were doing with that machine?'

'I . . . I didn't want to think about it. While it was going on, I imagined it was Mumma fiddling with my hair. You know how she likes to pin up my curls.' Livi lapses into silence as the truth dawns on her. She shivers.

Cibi understands now: some things are just too awful to accept. Maybe it's a good thing – who knows what they may yet have to endure? Maybe it's a skill she too will have to learn to cultivate.

'I am your mirror, Livi.' Cibi waves a hand around the room. 'We all are your mirror from now on.'

Livi nods and closes her eyes.

'Let's just lie down, OK?' Cibi doesn't have anything else to offer her sister but the oblivion of sleep.

'But the fleas . . .' Livi's eyes snap open.

'Like us, they're hungry too. We just have to learn to ignore them.'

'But yesterday, you . . .'

'Yesterday was a lifetime ago.'

Back at the demolition site the next day, and before they begin work, Ingrid asks if any of the girls know how to read and write. When no one answers – it's obvious to Cibi by now that invisibility is one way of escaping her cruel attention – their *kapo* becomes enraged. She repeats the question, louder and louder. She isn't giving up. Aware of the SS guards hovering close by, Cibi recalls her decision to try and impress these people in the hope that she and Livi might, in some small way perhaps, accrue some favours. If she puts herself forward, maybe the sisters won't have to work on the demolition site.

'I can read and write,' Cibi says.

'Who said that?' Ingrid demands.

Cibi boldly takes a step out of line, her eyes staring straight ahead. Ingrid is not a Pole like the other *kapos*; she is German. Cibi wonders if she was a criminal or political prisoner – the few reasons why a German national would find themselves in Poland, in Auschwitz. Cibi is grateful that she and Livi can understand and even speak a little German.

Ingrid thrusts a clipboard and pencil at Cibi.

'Write down everyone's name and number and make it quick.'

Taking the clipboard, Cibi approaches the girls in the front row and begins to write down names. The girls raise their sleeves to reveal the tattooed numbers on their arms and Cibi also copies these onto the sheet of paper. She hurries up and down the rows of girls and, when she's finished, she hands the clipboard back to Ingrid.

'These are all correct?' Ingrid asks.

'Yes, Ingrid.'

'We shall see.'

The *kapo* turns over a page. Running a finger down the list she calls out: 'Prisoner 1742, what is your name?'

The girl whose arm bore the number 1742 calls out her name. It is correct. Ingrid recites more numbers, receives more responses.

With Cibi still standing beside her, Ingrid waves at one of the SS guards. He saunters over to them, his swagger stick bumping his leg as he walks. Ingrid presents him with the list.

'How did you learn to write so beautifully?' he asks Cibi.

With a bravado suited more to life in the *Hachshara*, she meets the guard's eyes. 'I didn't grow up in the woods; I went to school,' she replies.

Glancing at Ingrid, she sees the *kapo* turn away to hide the smile that might get her into as much trouble as Cibi.

The guard harrumphs. 'Give her the job keeping your records,' he says to the *kapo*, before stalking off.

'Well, well,' Ingrid says, laying a hand on Cibi's shoulder. 'You are neat *and* accurate. But your mouth will get you into trouble if you're not careful. You are more useful to me alive than dead, so no more cheeking the guards. Do you understand?'

Cibi nods. She doesn't like being touched by Ingrid, but then again, isn't this what she wanted? To curry favour with those who might hurt them?

'Each day you will record new prisoners and cross out those who are absent. Is that clear?'

'Yes, Ingrid. I can do that. I'd be happy to do it,' says Cibi.

'Now, off to work, all of you!' Ingrid barks. And as Cibi turns away to join Livi and the others in her detail, she adds, 'You keep your job on the cart.'

Livi approaches her big sister, shivering in the cold, terrified of what Cibi's interaction with the *kapo* and the SS guard might mean for them.

'Who is this?' Ingrid asks. It is clear she does not recognise Livi from the night before.

'My little sister.' Cibi takes Livi's bandaged hand.

'You look cold,' Ingrid says to Livi.

Livi nods, her teeth chattering. There is no denying that Livi looks younger than every other girl on the demolition site. She barely reaches Cibi's shoulder and while she's not yet as emaciated as the other girls, her prison uniform hangs off her slight frame. Cibi can't help but catch a glimpse of something soften in Ingrid's eyes.

The next day, when Cibi and Livi line up in the courtyard before they leave for the building site, Ingrid drops a heavy coat across Livi's shoulders. 'You're about my sister's size,' she tells her. 'What are you, eleven, twelve?'

'Fifteen,' whispers Livi, too terrified to meet Ingrid's eyes.

Ingrid turns away abruptly and begins to lead the girls out of Auschwitz.

The other girls are jealous of Livi's coat, muttering under their breath, and Cibi worries that Ingrid's attention has marked them out. Could there be repercussions for this favouritism from a German *kapo*?

When they reach the demolition site, Cibi checks off the names of the girls, and hands the clipboard to Ingrid before she begins to once more load the card with bricks. And once again they push the laden wagon to the field, where they gratefully acknowledge the Russian prisoners of war who help them unload. Nothing is said about Livi's coat. It is clear, in any case, thinks Cibi, that Livi works as hard as the rest of them, despite her injury.

As spring blossoms, the forest beyond the field grows lush with green leaves. Crops have been planted at the edge of the woods by the prisoners, hoping a good yield will provide them with more sustenance.

The road, despite the change in the weather, remains an obstacle course, with deep muddy potholes one day and the next, a trail of stones and rocks where the mud has dried out. It is on a very wet day when the front wheels of the cart dip into a crater and hold fast. The girls pile stones beneath the wheels to ease its passage out of the hole. Livi is at the back pushing, while Cibi and the other girls pull from the front. As the wheels slowly start to turn, Livi notices something poking out of the thick mud. It is a small knife. With its wooden handle, it nestles perfectly in the palm of her hand. Grateful for the pockets in her Russian army breeches, she hides the knife and carries on pushing.

Later, in the dark, in bed, she takes it out to show Cibi. 'It's worth millions to us here,' she tells her sister, eagerly. 'We can cut up our food, ration it.'

'You know what they'll do if they find this on you?' Cibi hisses.

'I don't care,' Livi snaps back. '*I* found it, so it's mine. You wouldn't let me keep the coin, but I'm holding on to the knife.' Livi tucks it back into her pocket. It *will* be useful, Cibi will eat her words one day.

One morning, a week later, Livi doesn't wake up when the SS guard runs his baton along the walls of their room. Cibi prods her, feels her sister's forehead.

Livi is hot, flushed and sweating.

'Livi, please, you have to get up,' Cibi pleads.

'I can't,' Livi croaks, without opening her eyes. 'My head hurts. My legs. Everywhere hurts.'

The girl in the bed next to theirs leans over and also touches a hand to Livi's head, and then she pushes a hand under her shirt.

'She's hot all over. I think she has typhus,' she says quietly to Cibi.

'What? How?' Panic washes through Cibi.

'Flea bite probably, maybe a rat. Hard to know which.'

'But what can I do?'

'See if they will let you take her to the hospital. It's the only place she will survive. Look at her – there's nothing of her, and she's ill. She can't work like this.'

'Will you stay with her while I find Ingrid and ask if I can take her to the hospital?'

The girl nods.

Ingrid frowns and even seems a little concerned. She nods her consent and Cibi races back to Livi, heaving her onto her feet and supporting her as they cross the room. She remembers, just in time, to slip Livi's knife into her own pocket before exiting the block.

The girls are lining up outside and Cibi pushes her way through, stumbling as she half carries her semi-conscious sister. She thinks of their father then and wonders what he would make of Cibi's role of responsible older sister at that moment. Is it her fault Livi has typhus?

Cibi hands her sister over to a stern nurse who instructs her to leave immediately, despite her protestations. She has no choice. When Cibi rejoins her detail, Ingrid tells her that she will be joining the girls on the rooftops: her job will now involve hurling bricks and tiles down to the workers on the ground.

For three days Cibi goes to work with no news of Livi. But at least she's in hospital, not sweating and suffering on a bed made of straw, all alone. Cibi loses herself in her new job and looks forward to the regular breaks this heavy work entails. Their only meal is lunch, when the cart will turn up with five cauldrons of soup and five servers. Cibi has heard the crazy stories of what goes into these 'soups', and then sees it with her own eyes: a toothbrush, a wooden bangle, rubber bands, floating amidst the onions and sardines. The detail shares a rare laugh the day a girl pulls a comb from her bowl of soup and loudly announces: 'I have a comb, if only I had some hair.'

On the third day of Livi's confinement, Cibi climbs down from the roof and studies the mass of girls waiting to be called forward for their soup. She has noticed something strange about this lunchtime routine: most of the girls are looking in the direction of the plump server with the two long brown braids. Her hair alone is odd as, to Cibi, she looks like she's at least seventy years old. Cibi makes her way off the roof and joins the girls waiting for their food. Now she too looks at this braided cook. When Cibi catches her eye, she smiles. The cook does not return the smile – God knows no one has once smiled since they arrived here – but she does beckon Cibi forward. The ladle is dipped deep into the pot, spooning not only thin, tasteless liquid into Cibi's bowl, but a big chunk of meat too. The woman gives Cibi a nod and casts her eyes back over the hungry girls to see who next she will favour with her largess.

Cibi sits alone and gulps down her soup, until the chunk of meat is revealed at the bottom of her bowl. Looking around to make sure no one is watching, she picks it up with her fingers, licking it dry before stuffing it into her pocket, beside Livi's small knife. She will find a way to go to the hospital on her return and share it with her sister.

But when Cibi enters the block later that evening, she finds Livi waiting for her inside. Livi is almost better and some of the colour has returned to her cheeks. Cibi puts a finger to her lips and reaches into her pocket. She opens her hand to reveal the piece of meat. Livi's eyes go wide. With the knife she cuts the meat into thin slivers. It is a feast of unknown origins, but the girls don't care.

Over the next three months the number of prisoners increases dramatically. They arrive by train in their hundreds, filling all the buildings in Auschwitz, and replacing those who have died, either from illness or at the hands of the SS. Cibi and Livi hear rumours of a killing room, a bunker below ground a few streets away where men, women and children enter alive, and are carried out dead. The girls have seen male prisoners pulling carts loaded with bodies. It's too awful for Cibi to process, so she decides instead to believe they died from disease.

Livi's hand heals as the sisters grow weaker. Like everyone, they now take each day as it comes, feeling a glimmer of satisfaction when they close their eyes at night: they have survived another day of demolition detail. More than once they have seen what happens if an SS guard is feeling particularly vindictive; a chipped brick, a toppled pile – and a bullet fired. They have had to help carry dead girls back to Auschwitz, at the end of a long hard, harrowing day.

But the knife continues to puncture their misery with moments of joy. Cibi uses it to cut their bread into small portions: some to be consumed immediately, the rest to be saved, giving the ability to ration their food. It's not much, but it gives the sisters a secret and with it a tiny amount of control over their chaotic lives. Livi keeps it with her at all times: concealed in her breeches by day, under her mattress at night.

Boys from Slovakia started arriving a few weeks after Cibi and Livi, but they didn't stay in Auschwitz. The sisters knew where they were, however. The bricks the girls continue to drop off at the field are being used to construct new housing blocks, and across the road from this site vast wooden rooms have been erected. It is within these structures that the Slovakian men are now housed; it is obvious to all that a new camp is being built.

Cibi can communicate with the Russian prisoners of war because she is familiar with Rusyn, the Ukrainian dialect spoken in eastern Slovakia. But the whispered conversations she shares with the men reveal nothing new about their situation. Livi, still the shy, innocent teenager, never joins in these exchanges. Cibi is glad: this place hasn't taken everything away from her little sister.

And then one day, the men have some answers for Cibi. These new brick buildings are to be women's housing. A women-only camp.

Birkenau.

CHAPTER 10

Auschwitz-Birkenau
Summer 1942

By June, the sisters are navigating their days in silence. The grinding exhaustion of manual labour and scarcity of food has worn them down. Cibi notes the arrival of summer with a weary acceptance that they might remain in this place, this terrible place, for years – or until they die, as so many others have. Every night she wonders how they have survived another day. Even the idea of her family begins to feel like a half-remembered dream she had a long time ago. Cibi tries to imagine what Magda is doing, whether she is safe, whether the Hlinka guards are still looking for her. She keeps a watchful eye on Livi, who is getting thinner by the day, often mute, often moving from place to place in a dazed trance. But Livi also works hard; she is brave, well-liked by the other prisoners, and Cibi is proud of her.

There is no let-up in their treatment: despite the raging heat, the daily abuse of their bodies and minds continues, but as August approaches, the promise of cooler days beckons. Cibi and Livi have endured illness, injury, starvation and 'selection'.

Once harmless, this word has come to symbolise their greatest fear. Paraded before the SS, the girls must appear fit and healthy, show no sign of weakness, no tremor in their hands or faces. Those who fail this examination are 'selected' – and never seen again.

The heat has been so oppressive illness is everywhere, and what little food they have often spoils. But, today, a little breeze scatters dry leaves on the ground around them as they line up outside their block, gazing dumbly down the street at all the other blocks and the thousands of other women and girls. The silence is palpable as they await roll call. But, Cibi notes, catching sight of trucks positioned at the end of the road, something is different today.

A female German SS officer patrols the street, pausing to talk to the guards of each block. 'Some of you are moving to another location today.' The officer stands beside Ingrid, shouting instructions into their faces. 'Get into your work details and follow your *kapo*. Those of you who can't walk may use the trucks.'

Cibi quickly moves towards Ingrid once the officer has moved on to the next block. By now she and the *kapo* share an odd kind of friendship. It has grown slowly, but surely. There is something about Livi which has thawed a corner of this woman's heart. Cibi never probes – it is enough to receive her small mercies.

'What does she mean, "another location"?' Cibi is suddenly breathless: fear has crashed through her fatigue and dull-headedness. Life is bad, but they understand the rules here, at Auschwitz. Will they have to start all over again, with different guards, different routines, new tortures?

'You are to going to live in Birkenau. Just do as you are told, and *don't* get in the truck, whatever happens. You must walk – understand? Rita will be your new *kapo*.' Ingrid glances around, noting the position of the SS guards. She lowers her voice. 'I have asked her to look out for you and . . . and Livi.' Ingrid turns her back on Cibi and walks away. Cibi knows she will get no more out of her *kapo*, the risk is too great for them both.

Cibi watches Livi look longingly at the trucks, but she tugs hard on her sister's arm, and they walk out of the gates together, heads held high. Cibi glances up at the words she has read on exiting and entering the compound every day for the last five months: *ARBEIT MACHT FREI*. What rubbish, none of them are free. They are prisoners, treated like animals, their lives worth nothing. This 'freedom' means only death.

Once again they walk the road to the building site.

'I think we're about to be reacquainted with our bricks,' Cibi tells Livi, slipping an arm around her sister's shoulders.

'The buildings the Russians were putting up? But they aren't finished.'

'Some are. Do you think they care if they're half-built? For the likes of us?' Cibi bites her tongue; it would be so easy to lash out at their captors, to reveal that she has given up hope, but she must remain strong, for Livi. 'Maybe it will be better where we're going, kitten.' Cibi plants a kiss on her sister's cheek, but Livi just carries on stumbling along the road.

The sun beats down on the girls; the dry dusty track throws dirt into their faces. Ahead, a girl faints. An SS officer marches over, takes his pistol from its holster and shoots her in the head.

Cibi and Livi don't break their stride as they manoeuvre around the girl's body. They have learned to appear indifferent; never to register shock or fear, anger or horror. To survive one must remain invisible. Drawing attention to yourself, however insignificant the detail, is often all that's needed for an instant death.

'She should have taken the truck,' Livi whispers.

'It wouldn't have made any difference, whether she was on the truck or on the road,' says Cibi. Livi looks puzzled. 'Have you seen any trucks go past? Look around, we're almost there and not one has driven by. Those girls are not coming to Birkenau.'

Livi doesn't answer. Now she understands.

They walk on in silence. Ahead, the girls are turning off the road into the new camp where completed brick blocks sit side by side with those still under construction. There are three 'streets', each containing a row of five blocks. A wire fence surrounds the compound, and wooden watchtowers have been erected to keep an eye on the new residents. Armed SS guards watch from above, rifles trained on the girls. More nonsense, thinks Cibi wearily. What can even a thousand half-starved wretches do to these men?

They await instructions in a wide clearing.

'Before you go into your new homes you need to get your numbers inked again. Too many of them have faded,' a female SS guard yells at them.

Livi looks at the number on her arm. Cibi does the same. All around them girls are looking at their left arms.

'I can still see my number,' Livi says.

'I can see most of mine,' Cibi replies.

'Get in line,' the guard yells.

The girls shuffle into something resembling a line.

'Livi, is that Gita? Ahead of us?' Cibi points a finger. 'Gita, Gita,' she calls out.

A girl turns round, smiling when she sees Cibi and Livi. It is their school friend.

'I didn't know you were here,' Gita whispers. 'How long?'

'Months,' Cibi replies. 'You?'

'Same. I wish we'd met on the train from Vranov – I feel like I've been here my whole life,' sighs Gita. 'I'm working in the laundry.'

'Well, we've been delivering bricks.' Cibi points to the new blocks.

'You can thank us for the new luxury accommodation,' says Livi, a twinkle in her eye.

'Really?' Gita seems shocked. 'That sounds so hard.'

'I'm sorry you're here, Gita.' Livi is staring at her feet, the twinkle gone. 'Sorry that we're all here.'

'No talking!' a guard screams.

Gita turns round to face the front and they continue to shuffle forward.

Livi and Cibi watch as Gita steps up to the desk and the tattooist, who will eventually refresh the numbers on every arm of every girl in line. Gita looks frightened, reluctant to hold out her arm. Cibi's breath catches in her throat. *Please, Gita,* she wills her friend. *Just let him do it.* They watch the tattooist gently take Gita's hand; he says something to her and Gita seems to relax a little.

When it's Cibi's turn, the tattooist is still watching Gita walk away.

He is a gentle man and when he's done, he whispers, 'I'm sorry.'

The sisters, their arms once again dripping blood, enter Block 21. Gone are the wooden floorboards and straw-filled mattresses of their first 'home'. The ground here is solid grey concrete. The large, airless room is lined with tiers of wooden-slatted bunks. There are no blankets, and no mattresses at all, just loose straw the girls will have to gather and line their bunks with if they are to get any sleep at all.

Cibi thinks about winter, just a couple of months away, and shivers. Two rooms stand empty either side of the front doors.

'But where are the bathrooms?' Livi asks.

'They must be outside, Livi. We must have missed them, but let's not worry now.'

As more girls are ordered into the room, Cibi and Livi find a bunk and soon two more girls join them. These bunks are for at least four people. They have just begun to make their introductions when they're startled by the sound of a baton slamming against the door, over and over.

The girls fall silent as a slim figure walks into the room. Her clothes bear the emblem of a black triangle, denoting her as a criminal prisoner. The number 620 is stitched onto her shirt. She has fair, shoulder-length hair and a button nose. Cibi thinks she's almost pretty.

But her features twist with sadistic pleasure as she spreads her arms to encompass the bunks, the concrete floor, the brick walls. 'Welcome to your new home, ladies. I am Rita, your new *kapo*. If you are wondering about the bathrooms' – she pauses for effect – 'forget it.' She is laughing now, peering into the girls' faces, none of whom is brave enough to make eye contact. 'If you need to relieve yourselves you will have to walk to the end of the camp, and do your business by the fence, under the eyes of the SS in the watchtowers.' Her horrible smile grows wider. 'If you're out after dark, you will be shot.'

Rita walks the length of the room slowly, sneering at the girls huddled together. Cibi is startled by Rita's obvious delight in their fear, their weakness.

'Tomorrow you will be assigned your new work details. I suggest you spend today getting to know your new home.' She turns on her heel and sweeps out of the room.

Cibi is amazed this new *kapo* is a friend of Ingrid's and she doesn't hold out much hope that she will look out for them. She is about to tell Livi what she's thinking when Gita comes into the room and approaches their bunk.

'Isn't Magda here?' she asks, glancing around the room.

'No, Gita. Hopefully, she's safe at home with Mumma. She was in hospital when we left,' Cibi says.

'Is she all right?'

'It was just a fever, she's fine. And your sisters, are they here?' asks Livi.

'No, they only wanted one of us. Franny has her two small children and thankfully Rachel and Goldie were too young.'

The three girls hug before Gita returns to her own bunk. Livi stares after her; while she's glad Gita's sisters aren't here in the camp, she also feels sorry that Gita is on her own. She reaches for Cibi's hand. 'Does it make me a bad person to be glad you're here with me, Cibi?'

Cibi too is staring at Gita. 'I know exactly how you're feeling, Livi,' she says, squeezing her sister's fingers.

At rollcall the next morning, Rita puts the girls into their groups. Some are lucky enough to be sent to the laundry, sewing room, sorting room or mail rooms, but, as the location of these jobs is still at Auschwitz, they will be required to make a twice-daily two-mile trek to and from the main camp.

Rita walks up and down the rows of remaining prisoners, now and then grabbing an arm to read a number. She approaches Cibi, who holds out her arm before Rita can touch her. Rita's eyes move from the number to Cibi's face and then to Livi's, who is standing beside her. 'She your sister?' she asks Cibi.

'Yes, Rita.'

She leans in close, to whisper in Cibi's ear. 'Ingrid asked me to look out for you two. There's not much I can do, but she's a friend and there aren't many of those around. You're to work in the sorting room, the *Kanada* they call it. A *kapo* is expecting you.' Rita has blue eyes, just like Magda's, thinks Cibi. Maybe it's a sign that she isn't as evil as she first appeared to be. Rita squeezes Cibi's wrist hard and Cibi doesn't even flinch. 'Don't make me regret doing this favour for a friend,' she hisses. 'Now, get in line. You're going back to Auschwitz.'

Cibi takes Livi's hand and quickly they join their detail to begin the walk back to their old camp.

Arriving back in Auschwitz Cibi and Livi head for the *Kanada*, the building they know to be the sorting room, where, with white kerchiefs tied around their heads, they will rummage through the belongings of newcomers, just as once their own suitcases had been mined for whatever the Nazis deemed valuable.

CHAPTER 11

Auschwitz-Birkenau
Autumn 1942

E ach morning and evening, as the sisters walk to
Auschwitz and then back to Birkenau, Cibi's fear of the
approaching winter months escalates. The sisters gaze
forlornly at the forest beyond Birkenau, noting the change
of season: green leaves turn red, then yellow, and begin to
fall. They reminisce about the wonderful times they spent
with their grandfather in Vranov. Following the death of
Menachem, Yitzchak had taken it upon himself to educate
the sisters on the joys of the forest. They knew how to identify
the bracken, and the ferns which snuggled at the base of the
trees, which species of fungi was safe to eat, and how to
avoid the more attractive but deadly mushrooms that littered
the forest floor each autumn.

'I bet we'd find mushrooms in there,' Livi says regularly, wistfully. 'Don't you remember, Cibi? You, me and Magda, with our baskets full of berries and apples?'

Cibi rarely responds because it is a fantasy, and fantasies are dangerous in this place. But, more than that, she doesn't want to bring thoughts of Magda into the camp. The image of her sister at home with their mother is the only picture that brings her any real solace.

When the snow begins to fall, the sisters smuggle back a blanket and a couple of coats from the sorting rooms, but they are still cold.

The *Kanada* is a land of plenty. The sisters' job is to scrutinise the confiscated items of the new prisoners for secret caches of food, money, jewels – anything of worth. Watched over by the SS, the girls feel along the seams of trousers, the hems of skirts, the collars of coats. When something is discovered, they unpick stitches and retrieve secrets. Cibi has uncovered a ruby, Livi a diamond. Temptation is a reality for all the girls in the sorting rooms, but Cibi won't risk their lives for a gem, no matter what such a treasure might buy them. But some of the girls do, especially now in winter, as the desperation for food, extra clothing, some kindness, sets in.

After this, they group together similar items of clothing: shirts, coats, trousers and underwear. The rooms are warm, and the work less exhausting than the building site, for which the sisters are grateful.

Returning to Birkenau in the evenings, Cibi occasionally catches sight of a girl burying her stolen wares in the hard earth beneath the snow. The girl will then wait for an opportunity to smuggle the gems, or whatever she has buried, to the rumoured *privileged* male prisoners who, in turn, will barter with willing SS officers, for food.

Occasionally, Cibi nudges Livi into slipping on an extra pair of socks, or winding a scarf around her neck: small, negligible items that carry little risk, but make all the difference to the unrelenting conditions of their lives. Sometimes, when she can, Cibi takes extra items back to the block for one of the other girls.

Some of the girls exchange undergarments for a bread ration, but neither Cibi nor Livi can bring themselves to 'sell' what they smuggle. Occasionally, they find food amongst the belongings – a stale end of bread, a half-rotten cake – and even these they have handed over willingly, apart from a couple of times, when, close to starvation, their hunger had overwhelmed their fear of capture and they stuffed rock-hard, weeks-old dough into their mouths.

'Livi, Livi, look at this,' Cibi whispers to her sister who is pairing socks together one day, adding them to the pile in front of her.

Beneath the pile of coats she is sorting through, Cibi's palm is open.

'What is it?'

'It's a franc, a French franc. Isn't it the most beautiful thing you've ever seen?'

Livi looks once more at the coin and into Cibi's glowing eyes. Her sister hasn't looked so hopeful in a long time.

'It's beautiful, Cibi, truly, but what can you do with it?'

Cibi seems to snap awake, closing her fingers around the coin. She marches across the room, towards Rita, and hands it over. Cibi then returns to her post and carries on rifling through the coats. For a few moments, she was walking the streets of Paris, watching the river Seine sparkling in the moonlight, admiring the couples walking arm in arm, who smiled at her as they ambled on their way.

That evening, Livi lags behind the others as they trudge back to Birkenau. Cibi hasn't spoken a word to her or to anyone else since she let go of the coin. The snow is falling as the light fades, and the lights in the watchtowers are still a mile away. Rachel, another of their detail, catches up with Cibi, drawing her attention to Livi, who is dropping further and further behind the group. Cibi smiles at Rachel, grateful that she and many of the others have taken on big sisterly duties for the youngest of their group, for Livi.

Initially a little cross that Livi has not tried to keep up, Cibi chides her to hurry up: 'What's wrong? Why are you being so slow?' asks Cibi, when eventually Livi has caught up.

Tears slide down Livi's face as she points to her feet. 'My feet are frozen. I don't think I can walk any more,' she sobs.

'Everyone's feet are frozen. Just try and keep pace with me.'

Livi places a hand on Cibi's shoulder and lifts her left foot to show Cibi that the sole of her shoe is missing. Her tender skin is raw and gritty and bloody.

'When did you lose it?' Cibi, now concerned, peers at Livi's foot.

'After we walked out of the gates at Auschwitz.'

'Put your arm around me and hop, OK?'

Sheltered by the rest of the group, the sisters make it back to the Birkenau gates. As they are about to step over the threshold, they spy the regular line of SS guards, on the lookout for those they deem too weak to work.

Cibi removes Livi's arm from around her waist. 'You must walk through the gates on your own now, Livi,' Cibi tells her. 'Hold your head up, ignore the cold, just keep moving. Act like you want to be here.'

Just ahead of the sisters are a couple of girls whose shoulders droop. They might as well be sleep-walking they move so slowly. Livi tries not to stare as the guards pull them aside. Livi knows instinctively that there will be two vacancies in the *Kanada* tomorrow, two vacancies which will be fought over. She does not intend to create a third.

Back inside the block, Cibi helps Livi up onto their bunk. She gently wipes away the blood and the grit and massages her sister's foot back to life. Cibi blows warm air onto her toes and very slowly they turn pink.

'Before we are locked in for the night, we must show Rita your shoe. She might help us,' Cibi tells Livi.

The sisters head for the front of the block where their *kapo* stands watching the girls as they return from their various work details. 'Hurry up or you'll find yourself visiting the gas chamber in the morning!' Rita yells.

'What is she talking about'? Livi whispers. 'What's a gas chamber?'

'Livi, I don't think we should talk about it now,' says Cibi.

'Why not? What is it?'

'Livi, please. Let's just sort your shoes out, OK?'

But Livi won't take another step. 'Cibi, please don't treat me like a child! Tell me what it is.'

Cibi sighs, but her sister is right. How can anyone be a genuine child in this place? She meets Livi's wide eyes.

'Where do you think they take those who fail the selections? Tell me, what do you think happens to them?'

'They die?'

'Yes, they die. In the gas chamber. But that's not for you to worry about. I won't let anything happen to us, not as long as I have a single breath in my body.'

'Is that what the smoke and the smell is about? They burn them afterwards?'

'I'm sorry, Livi.'

'And somehow, *somehow,* Cibi, you are going to stop them gassing us, burning us?' Livi asks, her voice rising. 'Tell me how exactly you're going to do this.'

'I don't know, kitten. But I've kept us alive until now, haven't I? So come on, let's get you some new shoes.'

Livi trails after her sister, a new dread in her heart now. She wonders if asphyxiating on poisonous fumes is painful.

'Livi's shoe is missing an entire sole, Rita,' Cibi tells the *kapo*, showing her the shoe. 'Please, can she go and get a new pair?'

Rita looks at the shoe and at Livi standing before her, eyes averted.

'Do you know where to go?' she asks.

'To the storeroom at the front of the camp?' Cibi says.

'Hurry, then, I'll be locking up soon. You don't want to get caught outside.'

Cibi and Livi race to the small building where an odd assortment of extra shoes and clothes are housed. Inside, they meet a *kapo* they have never seen before, and Cibi hands her Livi's soleless shoe.

'I'm size 39,' Livi pipes up.

The woman points to a bench where just three pairs of shoes languish.

Livi walks over to inspect them. 'But I can't wear these,' she says. 'They're all too small!' Livi is exhausted, her foot is throbbing and for a moment she forgets where she is. 'I'm size 39,' she repeats, petulantly.

Neither girl is expecting the response that follows. The *kapo* strides towards the girls, her eyes on Livi, and slaps her hard, twice across the face. Livi stumbles into the wall.

'I am so sorry we can't provide you with your correct shoe size, madam. Perhaps you would care to come back another day,' the *kapo* sneers.

Cibi grabs a pair of shoes with one hand, and Livi's arm with the other, and drags her out of the building. Once outside, she stops and holds up the shoes.

'Lift up your leg, Livi,' she whispers.

Livi's cheeks are red. She doesn't respond.

'Please, Livi, let's just try and get these on.'

Livi is staring at Cibi's mouth.

'What's wrong with you?' Cibi urges.

'I can't hear you! I can't hear you!' Livi cries, shaking her head, trying to clear the ringing in her ears.

Cibi gets to her knees, attempting to push Livi's feet into the shoes, but they are at least two sizes too small. She is grateful Livi can't hear her as she quietly pleads with her mother for guidance. The shoes don't fit and Livi will surely die if she has to walk to and from Auschwitz in bare feet. Above the wind, above the barking of the dogs and snarling SS, Cibi hears her mother's reply. *Put the shoes on your sister's feet.*

So she tries again. Livi, feet numb from cold, can't sense her toes as they're crushed into the too-small shoes.

But the uppers *are* made from canvas, which, after a couple of journeys to and from Auschwitz, gives, at least enough to make the shoes slightly more comfortable. They have ribbed wooden soles, which become packed with snow on the long treks. The girls joke that Livi is getting taller. Livi responds that she is now the big sister. She knocks off the snow from her soles, and returns to her usual size. This twice-daily ritual provides a small oasis of amusement for the sisters.

Despite Cibi's initial reservations, she and Livi grow bolder in the sorting rooms, smuggling extra clothes back to their block, holding on to just enough to provide a little extra warmth in these cold months and giving away the rest. Cibi hides jewels and money in her pockets, makes trips to the toilet pit where she drops them: she would rather they disappeared for good than the Nazis get their hands on them. They are only searched at the end of the day when they leave the *Kanada*.

The weather is ruthless, however, providing enough of a motivation to cancel out whatever loyalty exists between the women, and often Cibi and Livi return to their bunks to find their own clothing missing. There are no confrontations: everyone is desperate.

New arrivals continue to create tension: fights break out and old allegiances dismantle. The new girls need clothes if they're to survive and the old-timers won't share. The SS step up the selections during rollcall, singling out the weak and the sick for extermination. To Cibi and Livi, it feels as though they're taking place every day, as more and more girls disappear.

Christmas heralds a new outbreak of typhus, hitting their block hard, and Cibi is struck down. Within days she is delirious with fever, but every girl knows that if she remains in the block when the workers leave for work in the morning, she won't be there when they return.

For the next two weeks, Cibi is half carried to and from Auschwitz. At night, Rita turns a blind eye to Cibi shivering and sweating beneath a pile of donated clothes, as fever wracks her emaciated body. Livi holds her sister's hand all night, while Cibi thrashes around their bunk. Cibi's thirst is barely quenched by the sips of water the girls smuggle in. Sometimes she sees Magda's face, hovering above her own, willing her to get better. At other times it is Magda who feeds her crumbs from the broken biscuits the girls have 'liberated' from the sorting rooms.

With an enormous effort, she gathers her strength each time they pass through the gates of Auschwitz or Birkenau, and Livi urges her, just as Cibi had done, to walk unaided past the watchful eyes of the SS. The bad weather often plays in their favour too, as the SS guards have no desire to hang around in the snow.

Cibi's recovery is slow, but steady. She holds the delirious mirage of Magda in her mind, and that helps, but she makes no mention of her dreams to Livi. If Magda is in her head, her heart, that's enough.

On Christmas Day the girls are given the day off, but a Christian Christmas means nothing to them. They have missed Hanukkah, have had to work long hours when they should have been lighting the *menorah* candles in the windows of their homes, reciting the prayers with their families. But for the German guards, the SS and the *kapos*, Christmas is a day for feasting and drinking, not exterminating.

Christian festival or not, the girls are glad to receive a Christmas present of hot soup with noodles, vegetables and meat. It is an absolute feast, and for Cibi, it is also the first meal she has been able to eat unassisted. She hopes the food will give her the strength to get up the next morning and return to work unaided.

That night, as the sisters curl up with their two other bunkmates, Cibi whispers, 'Goodnight,' to Livi.

'Is that all you're going to say?' a perplexed Livi asks.

'What else is there to say?' Cibi closes her eyes.

'Our prayers, Cibi. Our nightly prayers. Even when you were delirious you still prayed before you went to sleep.'

'There will be no more praying, little sister. No one is listening to us.'

Livi hugs Cibi close and shuts her eyes. But, as exhausted as she is, sleep will not come. She thinks of their mother and what she would say if she knew Cibi had abandoned their faith. They hadn't missed a single night of giving thanks for their family, their friends, the food they ate, and the homes that sheltered them. She thought of Magda. Cibi was so sure Magda was safely at home, but what if she was wrong? What if Magda was in another camp, just like this, but without the comfort of a sister?

The following day, Cibi and Livi, along with the rest of the white kerchief detail, are feeling re-energised as they march towards Auschwitz. It is incredible what extra food and a good night's sleep does for their morale.

'Do you know what Rita just asked me?' says Livi. The girls are in the sorting rooms; Cibi has just returned from a bathroom visit.

'I can't imagine. What did Rita ask you?' Cibi begins to sift through the jumpers and skirts and trousers.

'She asked if I could machine type.'

'And what did you say?' Cibi lays down the clothes and meets Livi's eyes.

'Well, I said "no", of course.'

'Go and find her now, Livi. Tell her that I can type.' There is a new urgency in Cibi's voice.

'I can't, Cibi. You know I only speak to her when she asks me something.'

'Oh, Livi, really! Stay here.'

Cibi strides across the room towards Rita who is circling the office, stopping now and then to talk to the girls, presumably asking them the same question.

'Rita, Livi said you asked her if she knew how to type and she said no.'

'That's right, I'm now asking . . .'

'I know how to type,' Cibi blurts. 'I learned at school. I can use all ten fingers and . . . and I'm good at arithmetic, too.' She is trembling, unsure of what she has just offered herself up for.

'Come with me,' snaps Rita, and leads Cibi towards the office at the front of the sorting room.

An SS officer sits behind the larger of the two desks that fill the small room. On the smaller desk sits a typewriter, a pile of blank paper, a tray and some pencils. Rita introduces Cibi to the officer, telling him she is the new clerk and will be typing up the daily log of clothes the girls had sorted.

The officer, Armbruster, acknowledges Cibi with a nod. He is a slim man in his fifties at least; his grey hair and the wrinkles around his eyes give him an air of wisdom. He could be her grandfather. Rita sits down at the smaller desk and holds up a typed list. She hands Cibi several handwritten pieces of paper that contain the details of the clothing compiled, and ready for transport. She explains how Cibi is to create a daily log itemising the men's, women's and children's clothing. She is to send one copy with the daily transports, keep one copy and create a monthly log. Errors will not be tolerated.

When Rita leaves the room, Cibi places a piece of paper in the typewriter, and winds it on. With a confidence she is yet to feel, Cibi begins to type, 'Men's clothing', using only two fingers.

'Is that how you type?' Armbruster asks.

Cibi looks at the German officer. 'No. I learned how to type with all ten fingers, but I can do it quicker with two,' she replies.

'Give me the page when you're done, I'll check it before it goes out.' He turns away.

Cibi slowly compiles a list of clothing using the new figures from the scraps of paper. When she has finished, she dramatically pulls the sheet from the machine and takes it to Armbruster.

Back at her desk, she starts the women's clothing list. She is still working her way through when the officer appears at her side.

'You made some mistakes, and I have corrected your spelling, and you will have to do it again,' he says, without the all-too familiar note of threat in his voice. 'And take your time to get it right. It isn't a race.'

1943 is a new year, it is no different to 1942. Livi works in the *Kanada*, and Cibi is SS officer Armbruster's clerk, so at least they are still together in the white kerchief detail. Cibi is still not praying, but each night she whispers, 'Mumma, Magda, Grandfather,' and pictures them at home, safe in the little house in Vranov. Each night she pulls Livi close. And these are the ways in which they keep going.

CHAPTER 12

Vranov nad Topl'ou
March 1943

'It's time, Magda. Get your coat and go.' Chaya is whispering, careful not to wake Yitzchak from his nap in the armchair.

Magda remains curled up on the sofa, where she has been shifting her focus between the unlit fireplace and her sleeping grandfather.

'Magda, get up! You have to leave! They will be here soon,' Chaya repeats, but with more urgency.

'Why, Mumma? What is the point? They will get me sooner or later, and maybe this way, I can join Cibi and Livi,' Magda replies, not budging from the sofa.

Chaya retrieves Magda's coat from its peg by the door and drops it onto her lap. 'Magda Meller, put this on and head over to Mrs Trac's. I spoke to her a short while ago and she is expecting you.'

Standing but not moving to put on the coat, Magda looks once more at her grandfather. She can tell he is awake, aware of their exchange. She wonders if he will get involved. Whose side will he be on? But he doesn't stir.

'It's been nearly a year, Mumma. We can't keep on living like this. Look around you, we have so little left to sell, at what point do we give up? When there are no chairs to sit on? No beds to sleep in? All of it gone for a loaf of bread!'

'They have taken two of my daughters and I will not let them have you. I still have some jewellery to sell but, right now, I need you out of the house. It is just for one night.'

'I'll go this time,' says Magda, finally, pulling on her coat. 'But can you please ask Uncle Ivan if he has any more news?'

'I will. Now, off with you.'

Magda kisses her mother on the cheek, before kissing her grandfather lightly on the head. 'I know you're awake,' she whispers.

Opening his eyes, he smiles, his eyes locking onto Magda's. It breaks her heart.

'Good girl, you must always do as your mother asks. Now, run along.'

Standing and stretching, Yitzchak joins Chaya at the window as Magda opens the door, checking left and right for Hlinka guards before she trips down the path, steps onto the street and then runs to the house directly opposite.

As the neighbour's door closes behind Magda, Chaya drops the curtain.

'I will get us something to eat,' she says.

'I'm not hungry, you eat,' says Yitzchak. 'I'll have some linden tea, if we have any left.'

Mrs Trac has been looking out for Magda. She knows the Hlinka Guard will soon come looking for any remaining Jewish girls and boys. They come on *Shabbat*, when they know all the Jewish families will be at home. Her own children, now adults and living in Bratislava, are protected by their Roman Catholic faith. How they chastised their mother when they heard she had been hiding Magda in the house; her faith will not protect her if she is caught hiding a Jew.

'Hurry, my dear, they could knock on my door at any moment. I have put a little bread and cheese up there for you.'

'Thank you, Mrs Trac, you didn't have to do that, but thank you. I don't know how we can ever repay you for taking such risks for my family.'

'You can repay me by staying alive and punishing those who would hunt you down. Now, it's time to hide.'

Pausing just long enough to give her neighbour a warm hug, Magda hurries to the chair in the narrow hallway, above which is a small trapdoor. She pulls it open and climbs into the small space beyond. After that, she pulls herself up into the ceiling cavity.

The light from the hallway illuminates a plate of bread and cheese. Magda knows from experience that as soon as the trapdoor is back in place, she will be in pitch-black darkness. She quickly notes the blankets and pillow nearby, where she will lie in wait until she hears the familiar tap from below to tell her to come down, the next morning. She hears the sound of the chair scraping along the wooden floor as Mrs Trac drags it back to the kitchen. She hopes it hasn't left any telltale marks leading straight to her hiding place.

A short while later, Magda hears a loud banging at the front door and a voice telling Mrs Trac to 'open up'.

The squeaking of the front door tells Magda that Mrs Trac is now face to face with some Hlinka guard.

'Is there anyone else in the house with you, Mrs Trac?' a guard asks.

'Laszlo, you know my son and daughter now live in Bratislava with their families. Why would they be here?'

'We have to ask, you know that. Do you mind if we come in and have a look around?'

'And if I did mind, would that stop you?' a defiant Mrs Trac fires back.

'Step aside so we can come in,' another guard demands, clearly impatient with the back and forth.

'Shut the door behind you. You're letting in the cold,' says Mrs Trac.

Magda listens as footsteps move away from the front door and head towards the kitchen. She holds her breath as she now hears pacing directly beneath the ceiling space in which she is hiding. Might they spot any skid marks from the chair?

'I hope you don't expect me to make you tea,' says Mrs Trac.

'We're fine, we don't need anything,' Laszlo replies.

'Have you seen anything of the Meller girl from across the road?' the other guard asks.

'I have children of my own to worry about, never mind anyone else's,' Mrs Trac replies sharply.

'We are just asking if you have seen her recently. She has been spotted in town from time to time, but she's never at home when we call round. What can you tell us about her?'

'Well, she is a very beautiful girl. Are you interested in asking her to go out with you?'

'Please, Mrs Trac.' Laszlo's voice again. 'Do not impede our investigation. You must let us know if you see her. We have urgent questions for her.'

'Why? What can that girl possibly know that you don't?'

'Come to us if you see her. That's all we're asking.'

'I'm looking around right now, and I don't see her. Do you?'

'Thank you for your time. We will see ourselves out.'

Magda hears the footsteps head away, and then the front door click shut. She picks up the bread and lies down on one blanket, covering herself with the other. She is glad Mrs Trac can still afford fuel for her wood burner – she feels the warmth of it through the ceiling. The smell of woodsmoke is comforting too.

The scraping of the chair along the wooden floorboards below wakes Magda the next morning. She hears the *tap, tap, tap* of the broom handle on the trapdoor.

Magda is stiff from her night in the confined space, and she descends slowly. Pulling shut the trap she heads for the bathroom, and then joins Mrs Trac in the kitchen, who is drinking a cup of tea.

'Thank you for the bread and cheese. I ate the bread, but do you mind if I take the cheese home for Grandfather? He misses it.'

'You must. I can give you some more if you would like?'

'No, no! This is more than enough'. Magda nods at the cup Mrs Trac is raising to her lips. 'Linden tree tea?'

'Would you like a cup, my dear? I have plenty, thanks to your mother.'

'No, thank you. We still have some and I had better head home. Mumma and Grandfather will be worrying.' Magda touches the woman's shoulder. 'Thank you, Mrs Trac. I don't know how . . .' Her words catch in her throat.

'Don't thank me, girl. Just give my love to your mother and grandfather and I will see you next Friday. All right?'

'I will. But let's see how the weather holds up. I might be able to go into the forest now that it's getting warmer.' Magda leans over and kisses Mrs Trac on the cheek.

'Any news of your sisters?'

Magda shakes her head. She has no words to express her desperate concern for her sisters.

Preoccupied now with fresh concern about her missing sisters, Magda doesn't immediately respond to her mother's questions about the night she spent across the road, and the guards' visit.

'Magda, please come back down to earth,' pleads her mother.

'Grandfather!' says Magda, emerging from her trance. 'Where's Grandfather? I have something for him.'

'I'm here, Magda. What is it?' Yitzchak walks into the sitting room from the backyard and holds out his hand for the gift Magda is offering him.

'It's from Mrs Trac,' she announces.

Yitzchak stares at the small, yellow block of cheese.

'She shouldn't have,' Yitzchak says, in a muffled voice.

'Well, I can't take it back.'

Yitzchak meets the eyes of his granddaughter and daughter. Pain is etched into every line, every wrinkle, on his face. There should be five people in this room with whom to share this unexpected treat.

Chaya reaches out and strokes his arm.

'Come and sit down. We'll share the cheese,' he says. 'Chaya, will you make us some tea? I think there is a little *Shabbat* bread left over from yesterday. We will have a feast; we will give thanks for our good fortune.'

Yitzchak leads the way. Chaya loops an arm through Magda's, needing to feel the solid reality of her daughter.

'Is Uncle Ivan coming over?' Magda whispers.

'Yes, he will be here soon enough, but I don't know what you think he's going to tell us.'

The cheese and bread are gone and the last of the tea is being poured when they are startled by a light tapping coming from the back door.

'It's just Uncle,' says Magda, jumping up to open the door. He immediately sweeps her up into his arms.

'You are safe, you have survived another Friday,' he whispers into her ear.

Joining Chaya and Yitzchak at the table, all eyes turn to Magda: it was she, after all, who has been pestering him for news.

Feeling the weight of their gaze, Magda looks away.

'I don't have any news of your sisters, Magda,' Ivan says. 'Just rumours.'

An expectant silence fills the small room. Ivan clears his throat. 'It's hard to find out very much. But I did hear one thing about your sisters' transport – I think Cibi and Livi have been taken to Poland.'

'Poland?' Chaya explodes. 'The Germans took them to *Poland*? What on earth for?'

'You forget, sister. The Germans have occupied Poland.'

There is a new light in Magda's eyes. Yitzchak reaches across the table and takes her hand, shaking his head as she opens her mouth. 'Do you know where in Poland, Uncle?'

'No, Magda. And your place is here, with your mother. We will all stay here as long as we can.'

'And Clive, your friend at the council office – he has always been a great friend to our family, my son. Have you seen him?' Yitzchak asks.

'Occasionally, Father. He has done all he can to protect us. Every week he puts our name at the bottom of the list of Jews who live in Vranov, but now . . .' Ivan sighs. 'Now, there are only a few names ahead of ours. It is only a matter of time.'

'There's more, Ivan, I can hear it in your voice,' insists Yitzchak. 'Tell us everything.' The old man lays his hands flat on the table, sits up straighter.

Ivan takes his time to respond, looking from Chaya, to Magda, and finally back to Yitzchak. 'I have heard they are starting to round up the very young children now, as well as their parents, grandparents, aunts, uncles . . . everyone.'

Chaya lets out a low moan. 'What do they want from us?' she asks.

'I don't know, I just don't know.' Ivan stands up and starts to pace the small room. 'There may come a time when all three of you will need to hide on *Shabbat*. Either at Mrs Trac's or in the forest.'

Chaya catches Ivan's hand as he begins another circuit of the room. 'Is that what you're planning to do, with Helena and the children? Go into the forest every Friday night?' Chaya's despair grows with every word that leaves Ivan's mouth.

'Sister, I will do whatever it takes to protect my family and that includes the three of you.' Ivan smiles at Chaya, but it is a hollow expression. His eyes are as full of fear as her own. 'How are you for food? Do you need money?'

'I still have some of our mother's jewellery, but I don't want to sell it.' Chaya's eyes fill with tears. 'It's all I have left of her.'

Now it is Ivan's turn to lose patience. 'Don't be silly, Chaya! Do you think she would want you to hang on to trinkets while your family starves? Promise me you will sell it if you need to.'

Chaya hangs her head.

'She will do it,' Yitzchak says.

'Magda, are you still going into town to do the bartering?' Ivan asks, moving towards the back door.

'Yes, Uncle, but only once a week.'

'I will give you the names of some people who will pay you a fairer price for the jewellery. They're not Jews, but they are sympathetic to our situation.'

Ivan pulls open the door, and Magda, Chaya and Yitzchak rise from the table. 'Come for dinner tonight,' he says, before he leaves. 'The boys keep asking after you, and Helena would love some female gossip.' He offers Chaya a conciliatory smile, which she returns.

'We will, thank you, Ivan. Please tell Helena we would love to share a meal with you all,' Yitzchak says.

CHAPTER 13

Auschwitz-Birkenau
Spring 1943

'Wake up, Cibi. Wake up.' Livi nudges her sister.

It is dark in the room and everyone else is asleep.

'What is it? Leave me alone,' Cibi murmurs.

'You were singing in your sleep,' whispers Livi.

'Was I?' Cibi sighs and opens her eyes. Slivers of light stream through the cracks in the mortar, and Cibi can just make out the contours of Livi's face, and the fear and concern in her sister's eyes. 'It was just a dream,' says Cibi, pulling Livi close. 'Grandfather Emile was here. He took our hands and led us through of the camp.'

'Here? In Birkenau?' Livi is aghast. She can't make sense of the image. It is too strange.

'He took us to the sauna. Grandfather Yitzchak was waiting for us, playing "Hatikvah" on Mumma's baking pan.

It was so odd, Livi. The pan had strings attached to it, like a violin.'

'Are you sure you're not going mad?' Cibi can hear the smile in Livi's voice, but also the concern. They have seen girls lose their minds completely, guaranteeing their death.

'Shut up, Livi. I haven't finished. You remember how we would always join in with him when he sang "Hatikvah"? Well, we did it in the dream too. Our grandfathers told us they would look after us.'

'Do you believe they can look after us, Cibi?' Livi asks.

'I believe anything is possible. Look at us, Livi. We've been here almost a year and we're still alive.'

'It's only thanks to you; I wouldn't have survived on my own.'

'You are stronger than you think, little sister. Now, go back to sleep.'

The next day, after they return from the long, cold, walk from Auschwitz, Rita follows them to their bunk. In her arms she carries a bundle of clothing. She hands Cibi two blue dresses – typical attire of the German housewife – along with a couple of dark blue aprons and new white head kerchiefs.

'On Sunday morning wear these dresses,' Rita tells them.

'Why?' asks Cibi.

'Just do it. And put them under your mattress to keep them safe from thieving hands.'

As Rita walks away, Cibi and Livi study the clothes. Without a word Cibi looks around to see if anyone is watching. Several girls have witnessed the exchange with Rita. Cibi carefully pushes the clothing beneath their mattress.

On Sunday morning, after rollcall and breakfast, Rita appears beside their bunk.

'Come on, you need to change. Now,' she orders. And Cibi retrieves the clothes.

Cibi and Livi quickly pull off their tattered, dirty dresses and replace them with the fresh garments.

As Cibi begins to slide the apron over her head, Rita steps in. 'Let me help you. It has to be perfect.'

The *kapo* carefully smoothes the apron flat before wrapping the ribbons around Cibi's waist, folding the pleats just so. When she is satisfied, she does the same for Livi. Rita stands back to admire her work. 'It's important you look pretty. Now tie the kerchiefs on.'

The other girls in the room watch this pantomime in silence.

Rita returns to the front of the block before calling for everyone to line up outside.

The girls in Block 21 join all the other girls from the women's camp in the assembly yard. The snow has stopped falling and the sun now shines on a picture-postcard winter's day. A large, black, shiny car drives up to the block and several SS officers, uniforms crisp and gleaming with medals, step out of the vehicle. The senior German female officer, who is rarely seen out and about in the camp, now comes forward to greet them, saluting.

Thousands of women stand in neat rows watching this scene unfold.

The officers speak in low voices with the female officer, and then, with the camp *kapos* on their heels, they begin to walk up and down the rows of women. As they come to stand before each prisoner, one or other officer points left or right. The *kapos* immediately indicate for each prisoner to move to the left or right of a large area at the far end of the yard.

'It's a selection!' Cibi whispers. 'Remember, Livi, stand tall and pinch your cheeks to give them a bit of colour.'

It feels like the sisters have been standing to attention for hours when finally the Nazis arrive at Block 21. It is impossible to tell which instruction – left or right – means certain death, as they see strong, relatively healthy, girls being sent in both directions.

Cibi watches as the men draw closer. They will reach her before Livi. Without saying anything, Cibi swaps places with her sister.

Along the line, their friend, Lenke, is holding out her hands for the officer to inspect. They are red and swollen from the cold.

'They sent Lenke to the left,' whispers Livi. 'Is that good? Perhaps we should hold out our hands too.'

Cibi glances at her hands. A dirty bandage covers a wound on her index finger. She rips it off, dropping it onto the snow and then standing on it.

'Leave your hands by your side. Stand tall. Look strong and healthy,' Cibi hisses.

As the men come closer, Cibi feels faint. She struggles to control her breathing. In and out. In and out. Was this it? Was this the moment their fates were to be decided?

The officers pause in front of Livi, and Cibi can't fault her for the way her sister throws back her shoulders and lifts her head. The men offer her a cursory glance before sending her off to the right.

Now Cibi waits. I will live, she thinks. I must live. Magda's face flashes before her eyes, and then her father's. The sisters will be reunited one day, she vows, and they will keep their pledge not only to survive, but to thrive. An officer pauses in front of Cibi. She swallows hard. He is taking his time to look her up and down. As he steps away, already turning to take in the next girl in the row, he flicks a hand to the right.

As Cibi and Livi gather with the other girls in the far right-hand corner of the assembly yard, they are still clueless as to which fate awaits them. Are they to be spared or are they headed for the gas chamber?

'Why did you swap places with me?' Livi asks.

Cibi stares at her feet in silence.

'Cibi! Tell me why you wanted me to be inspected first?' Livi insists.

'I had to make a decision. That's all,' Cibi replies. 'Please don't ask me to explain.'

'You have to tell me.' Livi gestures at the courtyard, at the camp beyond, at the world. 'We're in this together. You have to tell me what you were thinking.'

After a long pause, Cibi meets Livi's eyes. 'If you were sent to the left then I would have followed you. That's all. No matter where they sent me, I would follow you.' Cibi's eyes glisten with tears.

'Even to your death? Is that what you're saying?' Livi gasps, eyes wide and wild.

'Yes.' Cibi nods, and the tears spill out of her eyes. 'But I believe we're safe. I believe we've been saved.'

'And what if you were sent to the left, what was I supposed to do? Tell me, Cibi, what was I supposed to do?'

'I would have made sure you were out of sight before I went to the left, that you wouldn't see me and couldn't follow.'

'How could you? You made that decision for yourself! What about me, how do you think I could have gone on living if you were dead?' Livi's face is vivid with her anger.

'I'm sorry, Livi. Please. I keep telling you, you are stronger than you think. If I die you must go on living. Someone has to be around for Magda. For Mumma and Grandfather.'

Several of the girls in their group listen to the conversation between the sisters. Many are weeping. Livi moves away from Cibi, unable to accept her sister would sacrifice her own life just so Livi wouldn't have to die alone.

One of the girls puts an arm around Livi's shoulder, hugging her tight. 'I don't have a sister to look after me, to make such a decision for me. She believes she is doing the best for you. And she is.'

Livi looks at Cibi, who is staring straight ahead.

The wind has picked up and snow is falling heavily once more. There are several blocks yet to be inspected, but the Nazi officers have had enough. They speak to the German officer before climbing into their car and driving off.

The girls continue to stand in the snow, watching as thousands of women to the left of the courtyard are marched to the gates of the women's camp, where they are ordered to remove their shoes. The shoes form a mountain. The women are led, barefoot, down the path that leads towards the gas chamber.

Cibi was right, but it gives her no satisfaction. They had been saved. By Rita.

Finally, the German officer approaches Cibi and Livi's group. She tells them they are to head to the sauna, and to take the path through the men's camp on the other side of the road, which bisected Birkenau camp.

The girls march through the snow as the male prisoners stare at them. They don't seem to even register them as women.

Arriving at the baths the girls are told to strip naked. Once again, they endure the humiliation of having their heads, armpits and crotches shorn of hair by male prisoners. Cibi stares at Livi; she is a skeleton wrapped in transparent skin. She runs her hands over her own ribcage, counting every single bone. If she is Livi's mirror, then surely Livi is hers.

Cibi's first thought on entering the sauna is that they are about to be gassed. But instead of gas, jets of steam pour from the vents in the ceiling. Initially the heat is delicious – it has been a long time since either of the sisters had felt any real warmth, but soon it becomes stifling, unbearable. Girls are fainting around them. Cibi and Livi hold each other up, coughing, struggling to breathe. I was wrong, Cibi thinks. This is just another way to kill us.

Finally the vents are turned off. The steam evaporates when the doors are opened; around them lie dozens of unconscious girls on the wet concrete floor. Those still standing are ordered to drag them out of the room. Cibi and Livi each take a hand of one girl and, as gently as they can, they pull her across the floor and out of the room. Outside, the cold air immediately revives them; those still inside the room are helped by freezing jets of water which now gush out of the vents.

They are led into yet another room and Cibi gives thanks when she spies the mounds of clothes laid out on a table.

Initially delighted by the sight of underwear, shoes and socks, Cibi cannot fathom the sense behind the dresses that are now being handed out. They appear to be cocktail dresses, garments fit for nothing but parties.

'Are you serious?' Cibi asks the *kapo* in charge. 'How can I wear this?' She is holding up a dress made from a sheer, thin fabric, with a low cleavage and three-quarter length sleeves.

'This is what's been sent over. Your choice. These dresses or nothing.'

Cibi turns to Livi, who is laughing at her. She holds up the dress. 'Anyone coming to the ball with me? Where is my prince?' she jokes, stepping into it. Cibi bows to the other girls. Their relief at holding on to their lives for just one more day has released something, the impulse to be a silly teenager, a desire to laugh.

Livi's dress is made from a similar material in green, but the sleeves are short, so she has also been given a cardigan.

'May I have a cardigan too?' Cibi asks the *kapo*. 'I don't think this dress is going to keep me very warm.'

The woman tugs on Cibi's sleeves. 'You already have sleeves. And anyway, you wouldn't want to cover up such an elegant gown.'

After a sleepless night on the damp floors of the sauna, the girls are led back to the women's camp, where a delegation of senior SS officers is waiting for them.

'I am Commandant Rudolf Hoess. Tell me right now, if there is anyone here who doesn't want to work or doesn't know how to work, step forward and you will be put to death immediately. I can say this freely now – you all know what happens here if you don't work or you get sick.' Hoess pauses for effect, a tight smile on his thin lips. 'You heard me right. There are no more secrets between us. It is your choice.'

This delegation, like the last, departs in a shiny black car. A new female SS officer steps forward.

'I am SS Officer Grese. I am now in charge of you and this entire camp. You have made it through selection. There will be many more prisoners joining us in the coming weeks. I have ordered that girls with four-digit numbers be passed over during selections. If you work hard and stay healthy you will continue to live.'

With a start, Cibi takes in her meaning. As the camp has grown so have the numbers, and now many girls carry five digits on their arms. The girls who arrived at the same time as she and Livi have only four-digit numbers on their arms. They are almost all Slovakian and number in the hundreds; they have been there the longest of any prisoners. Cibi wonders why they should be spared, rationalising that maybe it's because they have been in Auschwitz almost as long as the officers, *kapos* and guards, and therefore they are well-trained and familiar with the rules of the camp.

Livi and Cibi are exempt from the selections: a chink of hope. Now they just have to survive the rest.

The girls are ordered to squeeze into just three blocks; the remaining twenty-one will be allocated to the new arrivals. They don't need to be told that the last block in the camp, Block 25, or the 'Death Barracks', has a special purpose: those who are too ill to work are housed there, and every morning its inhabitants are sent to the gas chamber.

Walking to their new block Cibi and Livi see Cilka, the young Slovakian girl who has her own room in Block 25, where she oversees the women who are bound for death.

'You know why she's in there, don't you, Livi?' says Cibi.

Livi shakes her head. She can't imagine how or why Cilka is there, living amongst women who are bound for imminent death.

'They say the commandant visits her for sex,' whispers Cibi.

'For sex?' says Livi. 'She has sex with *him*?' The young girl is aghast: she would rather die than sleep with a Nazi. 'How can she do it, Cibi? Why?'

'Like us she has chosen to survive, so don't ever judge her, Livi. Do you think she wants to be in Block 25? Or that she flirted with the commandant? We all choose to stay alive any way we can.' Cibi is passionate about this idea and she needs Livi to understand. 'If she refused him, she'd be dead,' she adds.

'But I couldn't do it, Cibi. I just couldn't.' Livi hangs her head.

'Then be thankful you're not in her position. It must take a certain type of courage to wake up every morning and just carry on.'

In their new block, the sisters are delighted to find clean, warm blankets.

The next morning, as if the night before had never happened, they go back to work at Auschwitz in the *Kanada* sorting rooms. Their very first task is to select suitable clothing, relieved at last to discard the curious cocktail dresses for the rough woollen garments of a prisoner.

But, once again, the sisters are thwarted by the footwear. There are no boots available and frostbite continues to ravage the girls' feet. As winter rages around them, it is Cibi's turn to suffer. On some of the colder days, she needs the help of her friends to make it to and from Auschwitz.

Finally, when she can barely put one foot in front of the other, there is nothing to do but ask her boss, SS officer Armbruster, for help. She gathers her courage and makes her plea, and the officer receives her words with a nod of his grey head.

Cibi has already sensed that he is not like the other officers, preferring the quiet of the office to the peacock strutting of so many of his peers. If he doesn't like what she's saying, he is more likely to tell her to stop whining and get on with her work than order her death.

But, Armbruster tells her to sit down and take off her shoes. As she gently pulls off her socks, the flesh on the soles of her feet come away, sticking to the socks. There is also a powerful decaying smell which fills the room and makes Cibi recoil. This is what death smells like, she thinks. It's just waiting for the rest of me to catch up.

Armbruster looks at her feet but says nothing. He leaves the room and returns with a basin of warm water. While Cibi soaks her painful feet in the water, Armbruster once again leaves the room, this time returning with ointment, clean socks, sturdy shoes and a box containing several small canisters. They are filled with tea leaves, some with added herbs and spices, some with tiny, dried flowers. He fills the small kettle and places it on the wood burning stove.

Armbruster asks Cibi to select the tea she would like to drink.

'Have you any linden flowers?' she says quickly, her heart suddenly racing.

'I don't think so. I don't know that tea. These are from my wife, who knows I like a cup of tea before I got to bed.'

Cibi unscrews the lids of several of the canisters, inhaling deeply the scent of the leaves. She chooses the most pungent and hands it back to Armbruster.

Without a word he makes Cibi a mug of hot, strong, spicy tea.

For the next few days basins of warm water are delivered to Cibi by Armbruster. She sips on a different tea each day, while her feet soak.

But while the wounds of one sister heal, the other begins to suffer. Livi starts to complain of stomach cramps. She is even paler than usual and Cibi worries she has typhus again.

Cibi begins to rush through her office work, so she can help Livi with the sorting. The train tracks have been extended, linking the camps, and now transports of prisoners arrive at Birkenau too, in their hundreds, day and night. The girls have their work cut out for them in the sorting rooms. Cibi hears the rumours about the ghettos in Poland being cleared, the elderly and very young executed, and the young men and women transported to Auschwitz. She overhears Armbruster discussing with a colleague the large numbers of residents being moved out of the town of Lodz. She doesn't know where Lodz is, and tells herself it doesn't matter – what matters is sorting through as quickly as possible the precious possessions they bring with them.

They keep their minds and their thoughts on their jobs.

In the sorting room, Cibi is emptying a suitcase onto the table. She picks through the clothing, separates the underwear from the skirts. A stale waft hits her full in the face. She continues to rummage until she finds the source of the bitter stench. Wrapped up in a piece of cotton is an onion, its juices permeating the garments that surround it.

'Livi, come over here,' she calls to her sister.

Livi glances at her from where she is hunched over a table sorting socks. Cibi can see her stomach is hurting again. Livi shakes her head, wary of the *kapo*. But the woman is busy delivering more suitcases into the room.

Slowly, Cibi makes her way over to Livi, the onion held firmly behind her back. 'I have something for you. I want you to eat. It will make you feel better,' she says, holding the onion out to Livi.

Livi's eyes go wide, her nose wrinkles. 'I'm not eating raw onion,' she announces.

'Livi, please. Don't you remember what Grandfather used to say? *An onion is the best medicine in the world.*' Cibi pulls the little knife from Livi's breeches and starts to cut the onion into quarters in her hand.

'Please don't make me!' Livi moans, pinching her nose between her fingers.

'Yes, that's good. Hold your nose. Now, open your mouth.'

'No!'

'Do it!' Cibi insists.

Livi opens her mouth and Cibi pushes the quarters of raw onion between her teeth until Livi swallows, one by one. Tears run down her cheeks as she chews and, eventually, swallows.

'I want you to eat it all.' Cibi is smiling with what she hopes looks like encouragement, and Livi, laughing and crying, eats the whole onion, bite by tiny bite.

The next morning, Livi wakes up feeling much better. The sun is shining, and winter is giving way to spring. The trees in the forest are flush with new growth.

Later, Cibi places a piece of paper in the typewriter and types the date. *29th March 1943.* Suddenly, her hands start to shake. Her head dips to her chest as it dawns on her that it has been almost exactly one year since she and Livi left their home. A year since she has seen her mother, grandfather and Magda. For a moment, she pictures the three sisters on that afternoon, so long ago now, when they made a promise to never be apart.

Magda's features are crystal clear to Cibi. She closes her eyes, desperate to hang on to the image of her beloved sister, lays her head on the desk, and remembers . . .

CHAPTER 14

Vranov nad Topl'ou
1939

'*H*urry up, Magda! Cibi and Livi are ready to go!' *Yitzchak calls.*

'*I'm coming. I just want to put a cardigan on; it's so cold outside,' Magda yells back.*

'*It's not cold. You* are *cold! Even when it's hot outside. Come on, if we don't hurry someone else will get the flowers,' shouts Cibi.*

Magda is doing up the buttons on her thick cardigan when she leaves the house. Cibi and Livi wear tunic dresses with a short-sleeved blouse. Yitzchak has on the jacket, shirt and tie he only ever wore outside. He holds a folded cotton sheet in his arms.

'*Are we all ready?' he asks.*

Since the girls have been forced to abandon their education months earlier, twelve-year-old Livi is no longer able to take part in games and sports with her school friends. She is getting restless at home, all day, every day. Livi loves having someone to take her out and about, someone who shares in her passion for wandering the forest, learning the names of the flora and fauna, collecting mushrooms. Cibi also shares her sister's love of the outdoors, but Magda is different, preferring to stay at home with Chaya to help her prepare meals and manage the household chores. When he can, Yitzchak drags Magda along: it is important to him that all the girls have an understanding and respect for their environment.

'Let's go, girls!' Yitzchak leads the way down the front path of their home.

Today's expedition is just to the end of the street, to the Catholic church – a large mosaic above the wide wooden doors shows an image of Christ, a hand raised to bless all who pass through – and priest's residence. As they draw closer, the church bells ring out. The girls have grown up to their chiming rhythm. It is a comforting, reassuring sound because it calls forth the devout to celebrate baptisms and weddings, and to mourn the loss of loved ones.

The girls would run to the end of the road when the bells rang to admire the brides dressed in white, and dream of the time when it would be their turn to become wives.

Today, the bells tell them it's midday. They gather at the foot of the steps and stare up at the doors; the priest will appear as soon as the final bell chimes.

'Come on, hurry it up!' Livi mutters, jumping up and down on the spot; she has important work to do.

With a flourish both doors creak open and the priest steps out. Dressed in black trousers, a black shirt and with his clerical collar, he raises a hand in welcome to Yitzchak and the girls. His face breaks into a wide smile and he walks down the steps to greet them.

'Shalom, *Yitzchak,'* the priest says, gripping the old man's hand. 'How are you, my friend? Your dear wife Rachel is still very much in my prayers.'

'I am well, Father, even now, during these troubling times,' *Yitzchak replies.*

'Can we go now, Grandfather? It's my turn to climb the tree and shake the branches,' *Livi pleads.*

'Patience, Livi. Remember your manners. Say hello to the Father first,' *Yitzchak chastises.*

'I'm sorry, Father. How are you?'

'I am very well, young Livi. And you?'

'I'm fine. It's my turn to climb the tree, you know.'

'I do. And we will leave very soon.' *The priest turns to Magda, who is shivering.* 'Are you sick?' *he asks her.*

'She's fine, Father,' *Cibi says.* 'She just feels the cold. We're all well.'

'Well, then, let's go and find that tree you seek. Which one is it again, Livi? The large oak out the back?' *he teases.*

'No, Father! It's the linden tree. We're to fetch flowers from the linden tree,' *an exasperated Livi fires back.*

'Of course. To the linden then. Follow me.'

But the girls run ahead and the priest and Yitzchak walk slowly behind, knowing that their young charges will wait by the gates to the priest's home. He will open it and release the girls into the yard, in the centre of which stands the great linden tree.

He pretends to fumble with the keys, prolonging the girls' excitement, but finally the gate is open and they stream through.

The old man and the holy man watch the sisters shriek and chase each other onto the manicured lawn. They are twelve, fourteen and sixteen years of age, but they might as well be toddlers.

The magical tree dominates the garden. It is shelter on a summer's day, a peaceful place any time of year, its soothing presence guaranteed to ease the worst of moods. The eldest of Vranov's parishioners don't remember a time when the tree wasn't there, making it easily over one hundred years old. The tree, straight and very tall, looms above the town, the highest point for miles.

The girls dance around the tree, kicking up the early fall of flowers. They are there to shake the remaining flowers off its branches.

'It's been a good summer,' Yitzchak observes, taking in the prolific flower growth: delicate pale yellow petals snuggled amongst the emerald green leaves.

'It has indeed,' says the priest. 'There should be enough to keep the neighbourhood in tea for many months.'

'Come on, Grandfather,' yells Livi. 'Spread the sheet. I want to start climbing.'

Yitzchak and the priest unfold the sheet and spread it on the ground.

Cibi reaches up and grabs a branch, shaking it gently. A veil of flowers tumble down.

'No, Cibi! Let me get up there. You know it's my turn to shake the branches first,' Livi yells at her sister.

Cibi giggles. 'Sorry, I couldn't help myself.'

'Give me a hand, then. Help me up.' Livi lifts her arms to grab the lowest branch and her sisters hoist her up. She climbs and climbs.

Then: 'Here I go,' she yells. Slowly, rhythmically, she starts bouncing on a thick limb, holding on to others above for balance. Cibi and Magda below twirl around as thousands of the delicate flowers float down, landing on the white sheet.

Livi moves around the tree, shaking and bouncing. She has flowers in her hair, covering her clothes. She squeals with delight. 'I'm going to climb up higher,' she calls.

'Livia Meller!' commands her grandfather. 'You are not to climb any higher.'

'But, Grandfather, I can do it. Don't worry! And there are so many flowers up here.'

'It's time to come down, my dear. Look at the sheet. We have more than enough for our needs. You must learn to always leave plenty for others.'

With one last strong bounce, Livi reluctantly begins to climb down until she is back on the ground. The sheet is indeed densely laden with the fresh flowers which, once dried, will provide the tea – the elixir, as her mother calls it – to not only warm their bodies, but also to ward off and even cure any ailments that may befall them in the coming winter months.

The girls each take hold of a corner of the sheet. Yitzchak reaches for the fourth corner, his arthritic joints making bending difficult, but he manages.

'One, two, three!' Livi shouts, and the four of them take a few steps towards the centre of the sheet, pulling up the sides. The flowers gather in a large pile in the middle. Livi hands her corner to Cibi while Magda hands hers to her grandfather. The sheet is then pulled closed and with goodbyes and thank yous to the priest, they walk out of the gate, onto the footpath and towards home.

On the way they pass Lotte Trac with a white sheet tucked under her arm and her older brother, Josef.

'Hope you left some for us,' Lotte says, with a warm smile.

'There's millions this year.' Livi laughs. 'Absolutely millions.'

CHAPTER 15

Auschwitz-Birkenau
June 1943

The sisters enter their second year of captivity and Livi is clearly depressed. Most mornings Cibi has to drag her out of bed for rollcall. She refuses to eat, so Cibi has to push the food into her mouth, or save it for later. Cibi chides her often, and it only makes Livi withdraw further.

But this morning, it is Cibi who is unresponsive.

'Livi! Wake up.' The sisters share their bunk with two other girls, one of whom has a hand pressed to Cibi's forehead.

'Leave me alone,' Livi replies, rolling away.

'It's Cibi. She's burning up. Can't you hear her moaning?'

Livi is defiant. 'She's fine. Just leave me alone.'

'I think she has typhus,' whispers the girl and Livi, finally, sits up and stares at Cibi, who is shivering beneath their single blanket. Cibi spasms, flinging an arm into Livi's chest.

'Ow! Cibi, stop it,' wails Livi.

'Can't you see she's sick!' their bunkmate says.

Livi climbs out of the bunk and feels Cibi's forehead. Her hand comes away wet. She turns to the girl, who is staring at her, expectantly.

'I don't know what to do. Cibi looks after *me*.'

'Well, now it's your turn to look after her. Go and talk to Rita. You're lucky, she seems to like you.' There is no malice in the girl's voice: in this place, you take your luck where you can find it, and no one will judge you.

Livi turns away to pull on her clothes. She heads for Rita's room, calling over her shoulder, 'Will you watch her? I'll be right back.'

'Who is it?' Rita sounds groggy, and Livi hopes she hasn't woken her.

'It's Livi. Cibi is sick.'

The *kapo* is wrapping her hair into a scarf when she opens the door. 'What's wrong with her?'

'It might be typhus. She's very hot. And she's not talking.'

Rita pushes past Livi and heads for the girls' bunk. The girls stand back as she approaches, wary of the slaps she freely distributes should you get in her way.

Cibi's teeth are chattering now, and sweat pours down her face and neck.

Rita reaches up to the bunk above and snatches down a blanket. She wraps it around the semi-conscious Cibi. 'Outside. All of you,' Rita orders the girls. But Livi doesn't move. 'I will mark her present on rollcall,' she tells Livi. 'She'll stay here and if anyone asks about her, just tell them I needed her in Birkenau today.'

'Do you think we should take her to the hospital?'

132

'It's not a good time, they're clearing it out at the moment.' Rita pauses for this to sink in and Livi understands. Periodically, the hospital is subject to the selections. 'Now, go and have your breakfast and get to work. Behave as if it's just another normal day.' Livi's heart is simultaneously hammering and sinking. Nothing about this day or any of the others is 'normal'.

In the sorting rooms, she folds and packs men's shirts in a trance. When anyone asks where Cibi is, Livi rolls out Rita's answer. She is joined on her break by another white kerchief girl, who asks after her sister.

'I think she has typhus,' Livi says. The girl holds out her hand, the fingers uncurling to reveal a large bulb of garlic. 'I found this in a case. Will you give it to her later? It's garlic, much better than an onion for a fever.'

'Our grandfather said onions were the best,' Livi says, staring at the bulb.

'Just take it. It's as good as an antibiotic, I've heard.'

Livi pockets the garlic and thanks the girl.

As soon as Livi returns to Birkenau, she races to their block, to their bunk, where Cibi is no longer sweating or shivering, but sleeping.

Rita appears at her side. 'I got some water in her, but she hasn't opened her eyes all day.'

Livi pulls the garlic from her pocket and shows it to Rita.

'Someone gave this to me.' Livi bites her lip, then decides she doesn't care if it gets her into trouble. 'They said it would help.' Rita nods and Livi raises the entire bulb to Cibi's mouth and tries to force it between her lips.

'Not like that!' snaps Rita, grabbing it from her. She cracks the bulb open against the side of the wooden bunk. The

133

cloves fall to the floor and Livi bends to pick them up. She watches Rita peel the skin off a single clove, which she hands it to Livi. 'Like this.'

Livi takes the clove and pushes it into Cibi's mouth. Cibi stirs and tries to spit out the garlic, but Livi clamps a hand over her mouth, shutting off her airway. Suddenly, Cibi's eyes fly open.

'Are you trying to kill her?' Rita slaps Livi's hand away.

Cibi's eyes slowly focus on the two women looming over her.

'Don't you dare spit it out, Cibi,' warns Livi. Cibi begins to chew. 'Do you remember the onion you gave me when I was ill?' Livi takes Cibi's hot hand and holds it to her chest. 'Well, this your onion.'

After Rita has left them alone, Livi retrieves the small knife from her pocket and slices the cloves into two, which she feeds to Cibi until the whole bulb is gone.

Cibi stays in the block for the rest of the week, only joining Livi outside on Sunday, their day of rest, to sit in the sun. As they walk to their favourite spot in the camp, a place where they know they will meet other girls from Vranov, they pass a lone figure sitting in the dirt.

'Isn't that Hannah Braunstein?' asks Cibi.

The sisters sit down beside Hannah. She is picking at the sores that cover her arms and legs.

'Hello, Hannah. Do you remember us? Cibi and Livi, from Vranov?' Cibi asks, gently.

Hannah looks up, and a small smile of recognition flits across her sallow features.

'We used to come to your mother's bath house on Sundays,' Livi adds.

'I remember. You were always nice to me.' Hannah looks past the sisters. 'Where is the other one? Aren't there three of you?'

Cibi and Livi exchange a pained look. 'She's still in Vranov with our mother and grandfather,' Cibi replies.

'Are you all right?' Livi presses.

'I'm OK.' Hannah goes back to picking her sores.

Cibi wraps her arms around the girl, drawing her close. She strokes her back, her arms, and whispers words of comfort. Cibi tells her she will get better.

Livi moves behind Cibi and begins to part her hair, searching for lice. Cibi's chestnut waves are growing back, but who knows for how long? With delicate fingers, Livi begins to draw out the lice and squash them between her fingernails.

'Hannah, would you like me to murder your lice when I'm finished with Cibi's?' she asks.

'No. Thank you, Livi. I'll let my lice die with me.'

'You're not going to die, Hannah. We won't let you,' insists Cibi. 'You're not well. You'll get better. I've just been ill, and look at me now.'

Hannah doesn't respond.

'Promise me you'll ask your *kapo* for some medicine for your sores?'

Hannah sighs and meets Cibi's eyes. 'I promise. I'll ask her. But for now, will you just sit with me in the sun?'

'Of course we will,' Cibi says. 'And we'll meet next Sunday, too. You can show us how much better you are.'

The following Sunday Cibi and Livi hurry to the same spot, but Hannah isn't there. They ask the girls from her block if they have seen her, one of whom tells them that

Hannah was taken to the hospital and never returned. Livi remembers Rita telling her how they were clearing out the hospital and wonders if it has happened again. In silence, the sisters walk away to find a space where they can sit in the sun and murder each other's lice, alone.

Cibi worries this episode will plunge Livi back into despair, but the warmer weather, along with a cache of food they recently found in the sorting room, are working to keep her sister's demons at bay.

Over the summer months, new arrivals stream into the camps, and more and more selections take place. Cibi surmises this is mainly due to a lack of space, in Auschwitz or Birkenau, to house them all. Time and time again, Cibi and Livi stand together with their block while the officers examine the girls' naked bodies for injuries, wounds or sores, the sight of which would immediately consign them to the gas chambers. But the SS officer, Grese, kept her promise: those with the four-digit numbers are always returned to the block.

As the seasons change, autumn giving way to an early winter, Livi is struck down with typhus. Cibi desperately scours the contents of the incoming suitcases for onions, garlic or anything she can give to her little sister for strength. She finds a bundle of cloth hiding what looks like tiny green plums. She brings them back to the block, but before she feeds them to Livi, she takes a bite, and spits it out in disgust.

'Where did you get that?' A young girl is hovering by Cibi's shoulder, a Jewish girl from Greece. Cibi quickly folds the fruit into their cloth wrapping.

'What?'

'Those olives, where did you get them?'

'Olives?'

'Haven't you seen olives before?' the girl asks, smirking.

'No, never. And they taste horrible!'

'Can I have them, then? If you don't want them? I'll swap you for my bread.'

Cibi notes the shine in the girl's eyes and dumps the cloth bundle in the girl's hands. 'Take them. And you should never give your food away, but because my sister is ill, I'm grateful. Thank you.'

But Livi's fever hasn't abated and each night she thrashes around the bunk, making it impossible for anyone else to sleep. They are worried it will be noted if she misses many more rollcalls.

Finally, Rita tells Cibi it's safe for Livi to go to the hospital now: the selections are over for a while. She should be safe and she needs antibiotics or she won't survive. Together the women carry Livi's tiny frame between them.

After leaving her at the hospital, Cibi walks away with a heavy heart. Has she just broken her promise to stay with her sister, to protect her? Will this be the last time she sees her? She hears their father's voice telling them to always stick together; she imagines Magda beseeching her to never leave Livi's side.

Cibi turns round and races back to the hospital. Breathlessly, she tells the Polish nurse that it's fine, that Livi is looking better, that she doesn't need to stay after all. Cibi will take care of her.

The nurse holds up a syringe with one hand and lays the other on Cibi's shoulder, and looks steadily at Cibi. 'Your sister is how old? Eleven? Twelve?'

'She's fifteen,' says Cibi.

The nurse frowns. 'Well, she's tiny in any case. I'm about to give her some medicine that will help. And you can trust me. I promise I'll take care of her. Sisters, eh? You're lucky to have each other.'

Once again Cibi walks away from Livi, but now her heart is a little lighter.

'She'll be fine with that nurse,' Rita tells her later. 'She's a Polish prisoner not a German volunteer. Be grateful, because they're as bad as the doctors.'

The next day Livi is semi-conscious and able to make sense of her surroundings. She is told she will spend a few days on the ward before being sent back to her block.

The twelve beds in the ward are full. Some of the girls are sleeping, some are quietly moaning. By the afternoon, Livi feels a little better. She smiles at the girl in the bed next to hers, whose face and neck are a strange shade of yellow. Does she have a sister looking out for her, as Livi does? Probably not, she thinks and reaches a hand across the divide.

The girl does the same.

'I'm Livi,' Livi whispers, squeezing her fingers.

'Matilda,' says the girl, with a weak smile.

At that moment, the Polish nurse sweeps into the room, with Mala on her heels. Mala is a prisoner, just like them, but she's also the 'translator' for the Germans. Polish by birth, they say she can speak French, Dutch, Russian and German. The two women enter the tiny room where the nurse stores the medicine and close the door.

Livi looks at Matilda, who has fallen asleep, still holding her hand. Livi feels her own eyes closing.

It is getting dark when the nurse shakes Livi awake. 'Livi, you must get up. Right now!'

Livi opens her eyes. Where is she? The lights aren't on and in the dim light she can see the outlines of the girls bodies beneath their blankets.

'Livi, come on.' The nurse pulls aside Livi's blankets and takes both her arms, hauling her upright. 'We need to move. Now.'

'I can't,' says Livi. 'I don't feel strong enough.'

The nurse pulls Livi's legs over the side of the bed and lifts her onto the floor. 'Please, Livi. We must go now.'

Under protest, Livi is hurried out of the ward and out of the building.

'But where are we going?' Livi doesn't have shoes on and within minutes she is hobbling over the gritted path towards the latrine block. 'Can't I go to the toilet in the hospital?' Livi asks, perplexed.

'Just keep walking.'

Once inside the block, the nurse pushes Livi into an empty cubicle. 'Stay here until I return. Do you understand? Do not step outside.'

Livi slumps into the corner. It smells foul and the floor is soaked in urine, but she can't stand up any longer.

It is early evening when the nurse returns. Livi has fallen asleep despite the stench. The nurse's voice hisses at her to wake up. Without a word she is led, limping, back to hospital.

Now, Livi gazes around the empty ward. 'Where have they gone?'

'Block 25,' the nurse replies, through pursed lips.

'Block 25?' The truth is slowly dawning on the young girl. She meets the nurse's teary eyes. 'You saved *me*?' Block 25, where you spend your last night on earth before you are taken to the gas chamber, emptied every afternoon and filled every morning. Livi knew it was Death's waiting room. And she has escaped its clutches.

'I promised your sister I would take care of you, didn't I? When Mala told me a selection was taking place, I saved who I could, and that was you.'

It was clear now, that that was what they had been talking about earlier; Mala, enjoying certain advantages as a translator, was privy to the knowledge of forthcoming selections.

A tear splashes down the nurse's cheek. She gazes around the empty room. 'I would have saved more if I could.'

Livi reaches for the nurse's hand, but she is already turning away, heading back to her tiny room full of medicine.

When it's dark, Livi gets out of bed and, wrapping herself in a blanket, slowly shuffles out of the hospital and back to her block. She has escaped with her life, today she is lucky; how many more times will luck decide if she lives or dies?

Livi's strength returns and on Sunday she decides she needs some fresh air. She and Cibi find their preferred spot on the grass and, sharing a blanket, they raise their faces to the winter sun.

'Rita's coming,' whispers Livi suddenly, as the *kapo* approaches the sisters. The girls get to their feet.

'I have a new job for you, Livi,' Rita says, without preamble. 'And you start tomorrow.'

'A new job?' Cibi says. This is the worst news. They cannot be apart.

'I've put your name down to be one of the couriers delivering messages for the SS. Don't look so worried – it isn't a hard job.'

'What will I have to do?' asks Livi. She looks at Cibi for the answer, but Cibi is staring at Rita.

'Tomorrow morning, after everyone has left, I'll take you to the front gates where you will wait to be given messages. You will then deliver these to the officers all over the camp. It couldn't be simpler.'

When Livi doesn't respond, Rita raises her voice. 'Do you understand?'

'Will she be safe?' asks Cibi. 'I mean, the SS . . .' She trails off.

Rita raises an eyebrow, but smiles. 'No one working as a messenger has ever been hurt. They are lazy bastards, these men. If they can get away with sitting around on their arses all day, then that's what they'll do.'

'It's OK, Cibi, I can do it,' says Livi.

'Mostly, you'll just be standing around and waiting. It's boring work. But it's safe.' With that, Rita turns on her heel, leaving Livi to wonder if this woman has any understanding of the word *safe*.

Rita is right: Livi's new role as a messenger is easy work. Together with a couple of girls, she stands at the entrance to Birkenau, beside the small office where the Nazis are on duty, monitoring the comings and goings of all who enter. The girls grow bold, risking a chat now and then, as they wait to be sent hither and thither with messages around the camp.

When Livi returns to the gates one afternoon after distributing the mail, she finds herself alone, the other girls still busy with their own deliveries. It is almost the end of the day and the men working outside the camp are returning.

Some of them are hefting between them the bodies of prisoners who died that day. With bullet wounds, cracked skulls and broken limbs, these men didn't drop dead of exhaustion. Livi watches them numbly. When did she become so immune to brutality on this scale?

Two SS officers are standing either side of the gates watching the men stagger into the compound. A male *kapo* is pacing up and down, screaming at the men to keep moving, to hurry up.

'Give me your stick,' the *kapo* says to an SS officer. 'This is the only way to get them inside.'

The officers exchange a smile before one pulls a baton from his belt and hands it to him. Livi knows she should leave – nothing good is about to happen here and she doesn't need to see anymore – but she finds she can't move.

The *kapo* raises the baton and launches himself at the incoming prisoners, beating them about the head, the torso, laughing all the while, cursing the men for being so stupid, so lazy, so weak. Those who collapse under his blows are quickly pulled to their feet and dragged away. Two prisoners, however, are not fast enough to catch the proffered hands, and they remain on the ground, struggling to get to their feet, failing.

Livi looks away as the *kapo* bears down on them. She hears the repeated thuds of his baton cracking bone and skull. When she looks back the prisoners are obviously dead, a bloodied heap of rags and blood. But the *kapo* appears to have lost his mind – he continues to strike out with the baton, breaking fragile bones and pounding his hatred into Jewish flesh.

'That's enough!' orders one officer, holding out his hand for the baton. The *kapo* doesn't hear him, lost in his work.

'I said, *that's enough!*' the officer screams. The *kapo* gives the pile one last kick and then wipes the bloody stick on his trousers before handing it back.

And then he sees Livi.

'Want some too, do you, girlie?' he sneers, revealing two rows of broken, yellow teeth. He is a squat man with wild eyes, his unkempt black hair hanging in damp ribbons around his sweating, filthy face. 'Give me back the stick,' he yells to the SS officer. 'I'd like to have a go at her.'

Livi feels herself float away. She is staring at this animal, but she is also hovering over this scene, looking down at him, at the bodies of the dead men, at the officers, one of whom is now planting himself in front of the *kapo*.

'Leave her alone. She works for us, not you.'

'I could kill her with my bare hands,' spits the man. 'And enjoy it.'

'Girl, get out of here,' the other SS officer says, over his shoulder. 'Go back to your block.'

'I'll remember you, girlie. Isaac never forgets a face.'

Livi snaps back into her body and runs.

Every day they witness the trains entering Birkenau and disgorging the thousands of men, women and children abducted from their homes. They watch as the SS, with a flick of their wrists, consign the inmates to the right – the camp, or to the left – the gas chamber. Livi, in her new role as a camp messenger, can't avoid the distress of these families as they await their fates and, once again, she begins to withdraw.

Tomorrow will be 16 November, my birthday. I will turn seventeen, she tells herself. Will I see eighteen? She wonders what Mumma would make for her birthday tea, if Mumma were there – no, if she was back home with Mumma. Cibi would remind her that she is still the youngest, Magda would search the backyard for a flower from the oleander bush.

Livi decides to say nothing to Cibi, or anyone else. Tomorrow will be a day like every other day there. All she has to do is wake up and keep moving.

The next morning the sisters woke up to heavy snow showers, which haven't abated. Now, in her position at the gates of Birkenau, waiting for the messages she will deliver around the camp, Livi watches another train pull in; men and women clamber down from the carriages into three feet of snow, where they huddle together, frozen and terrified on the platform.

Livi can't seem to avert her gaze. Occasionally she catches the eye of one or other prisoner, but she quickly glances away.

It is still snowing when the selection detail arrives. In a heavy coat, one officer considers the crowd, before flicking his hand to the left, to the gas chambers. Today, it is not their age or their health or gender which has sealed their fate, but the weather.

That night, when the sisters climb into their bunk, they discover that their blanket has been stolen. Cibi and Livi cuddle together for warmth. They are wearing every single item of clothing they own, including their shoes. The freezing wind howls around the block, forcing its way through the cracks in the mortar, the gap beneath the door. Snot from their noses forms icicles.

Instead of sleeping, Livi whimpers, quietly, to herself. 'Cibi, are you awake?' she says, finally.

'Yes. What is it? Can't you sleep?'

144

'I don't think I can keep doing this. And now, without our blanket, we'll freeze to death. Cibi, if we're to die tonight, I don't want it to be in here.' Livi starts to cry.

Cibi reaches out with gloved hands and holds Livi's face. She blows warm air onto her sister's icy cheeks. She swallows once, twice. She feels something like a punch in her stomach. Livi is right. They will die in this block and, in the morning, their frozen corpses will be loaded onto a truck with hundreds of others and taken away to be set on fire.

'Let's go,' is all she says, and Livi nods.

The girls quietly climb out of the bunk and tiptoe across the concrete floor. Cibi pushes open the door and the girls take a step. They are almost blasted back into the room by a flurry of snow and wind, but they keep going. They hug the walls as they round the block, behind which lies the forest. Together, hand in hand, they head towards the electrified fence.

'When I say run,' Cibi whispers into the falling snow, 'run!'

Cibi and Livi take a last look at the camp; at the floodlights illuminating the brooding buildings; at the gates, which will never set them free; at the empty watchtower.

The faces of Mumma, Magda, Grandfather and their father are never far away. In a strange way, these images give the sisters strength.

Together they take several steps. Cibi pauses for a moment and Livi knows the next word, the last word she ever will hear from her sister, will be 'run'.

'Don't do it!'

The girls jump and turn round.

'Don't do it,' the voice repeats. A silhouette of a slim figure hovers in the shadows of the block.

'You can't stop us!' says Livi, squeezing Cibi's fingers tightly, as if to urge her forward.

'I know I can't. But just tell me why. Why tonight? What is so different about this night from any of the others?' It is a girl's voice, plaintive, faltering.

She steps out of the shadows and Cibi recognises her as one of the new girls.

'Someone has taken our blanket,' says Livi. 'And we don't want to die in there, in that stinking bunk in that stinking room. There, is that enough of an explanation? Will you leave us alone now?'

'Come inside. I promise I will find you a blanket,' the girl says.

Cibi looks into her sister's eyes and senses hesitation. They could run now for the fence, hold on for an instant and this would all be over.

'If there's a small chance we can live long enough to see Magda and Mumma one more time, then we should take it,' whispers Cibi. 'Shall we go back? Or shall we go forward?'

Livi doesn't move for a long time. She stares at her boots and then, almost painfully, she puts one foot in front of the other and leads Cibi back towards the block.

Inside, Cibi and Livi watch the girl who has tempted them back inside move around the room, tugging at the blankets of the sleeping occupants. When she meets resistance, she lets go. She does this again and again, until, finally, she lightly pulls two heavy blankets free.

She hands these to the sisters without a word and goes back to bed.

The next morning as the sisters prepare to leave for rollcall, Cibi looks across to the bunk from which their blankets were liberated. Two girls lie bonded together; their eyes are open, staring sightlessly at the ceiling. Cibi turns away, her mind a necessary blank.

146

CHAPTER 16

**Vranov nad Topl'ou
December 1943**

A flurry of snow follows Magda into the house. She pulls off her coat and shakes it, scattering soft flakes onto the threadbare rug. 'I don't believe it, Grandfather,' she says, hanging her wet coat on the peg. 'I just don't believe it.' She holds out a small cloth bag to her grandfather.

'What is it?' he asks, his face suddenly pale. 'What happened?'

'It's not bad enough that I got given stale bread even though I could smell the new loaves coming out of the oven, but that Mrs Molnar went out the back and found an especially dry loaf – just for me! I wanted to throw it at her.'

'Is that all?' Chaya comes into the room, drying her hands on her apron. 'Let's just be thankful we have bread.' She forces a smile.

'No, that's not all, Mumma. Far from it.'

Chaya's smile fades. 'So tell us,' she says.

'As I was leaving the store Mrs Szabo snatched the loaf out of my hands and threw it on the floor. They were all laughing. I hate their faces!' Magda's cheeks are pinched pink from the cold weather, but she isn't chilled; if anything, she is too warm, her fury as powerful as a roaring fire. 'I wanted to leave it there and walk away, but how could I?'

Her blue eyes are bright, defiant. Yitzchak is pleased his granddaughter is angry. Anger is better than dejection, but all the same he is distraught she has been humiliated in public, and worse, that he can do nothing about it.

'They might be horrible to your face, Magda,' says Chaya, 'but they haven't reported you to the Hlinka yet. For that we can be grateful.' And it's true: none of the smug 'patriots' in town have given her up, yet. But maybe it's just a matter of time.

'Well, you're home now,' adds Chaya. 'Come and have some soup. You must be frozen.'

Now Magda rests her head on the table. 'Do you know what else I saw?' she says, almost to herself.

'Go on,' Yitzchak says, holding his breath.

'Do you know what the date is?' Magda raises her head.

'We celebrated the beginning of Hanukkah two days ago, so today must be the 24th of December.'

'It's Christmas Eve,' Magda says. When no one responds, she adds, 'And there is a war going on, correct?'

Yitzchak slowly nods.

'And yet,' Magda is suddenly angry again, 'you should see the houses and stores, all lit up in celebration. I mean, how can they, Mumma? Grandfather? When people are being killed? When we have no idea where Cibi and Livi are or when they'll come home? But these people, these "friends and neighbours", all they care about is filling their stomachs and buying presents.' Magda deflates and Chaya puts her arms around her daughter. There is nothing else she can do or say. The women weep.

Yitzchak quietly places a bowl of steaming soup on the table. 'Magda, eat now.'

'If it's Christmas Eve, maybe they won't come knocking on our door,' Chaya says, hopefully.

'It's *Shabbat*, Chaya.' Yitzchak shakes his head. 'They always come on *Shabbat*.'

'But maybe Mumma's right, though,' Magda says. 'They might take the night off.'

Chaya and Yitzchak exchange a look.

'We can't risk it,' he says, looking away.

'Are you sure, Father? It's snowing, and Mrs Trac is still away.'

'I'm sorry, Magda.' Yitzchak is trying to sound firm, but his voice trembles. 'We can't take a chance, it just isn't worth it.'

'Perhaps for a few hours only, then,' suggests Chaya. 'They won't visit more than once on Christmas Eve.' She would take Magda's place if she could, in a heartbeat.

'It's OK, Mumma, honestly. I'll be fine, I know where to hide out of the wind.' Now it's Magda's turn to force a smile. 'I have a secret place.'

'That's good!' announces Yitzchak. 'But don't tell us.' He picks up Magda's thick braid and gives it a small tug. 'If we don't know, we can't be forced to reveal it.'

'Oh, I think you know where it is – I'll give you a small clue but that's all. Don't try and guess.' Magda's eyes are twinkling now.

'Oh, we're playing games, are we? All right then, give me a clue.'

'Hope and strength,' she announces.

Yitzchak smiles, nodding.

'And what does that mean?' Chaya says, perplexed.

'You don't need to know, daughter.' Yitzchak winks at Magda.

'Oh, so now we're keeping secrets?' But Chaya is smiling. 'I think I like it that the two of you have a secret. You should keep it.'

'And now I must go to my secret,' Magda says. She picks up her bowl of soup and downs it one long gulp.

Following a long-established routine, Yitzchak proceeds to wrap up some bread and cheese for Magda's night in the woods. He adds an oatmeal cookie which Ivan's wife, Helena, gave them yesterday. Chaya forces layer upon layer of clothing on Magda until she is fat with vests and jumpers. She wears three pairs of socks and squeezes her feet into her mother's boots, thankfully a size larger than her own. From a cupboard Chaya produces the only article of clothing she has kept of Menachem's: a long, heavy army coat. It comes down to Magda's feet. The heavy blanket from the bed Magda once shared with Cibi is folded and placed in a drawstring bag.

The sun is minutes away from setting when Yitzchak snuffs out the candles, opens the front door and ushers Magda into the night. The snow is still falling and flimsy flakes glide through the dull yellow light of the streetlamps.

She doesn't see a single soul as she hurries towards the forest. Above her, the clouds part to reveal a galaxy of stars, lighting her way. The moon, just a thin sliver tonight, offers her nothing.

Naked branches sway and creak in the wind in the forest. Magda is no longer scared of the long shadows they throw in her path; instead, they feel like wide-open arms, welcoming her back into their sanctuary.

Sliding down a small bank, Magda finds her way to the small cave of earth that has been a second home to her these long months. She brushes away a thin covering of snow on the ground before settling down, her knees curled up under her chin, out of the wind and snow. She is hugged by the thick blanket, by her father's warm coat. Pulling the collar to her nose she believes she can still smell the masculine, familiar scent of her father. She feels his presence and falls asleep knowing he is watching over her.

In the morning, Magda opens her eyes to the dazzling glare of the sunlight bouncing off the pure white snow beyond her cave. She listens, hears nothing and slowly crawls outside. Her bones creak and complain as she stretches and jumps up and down to get the blood flowing.

Making her way back through the forest she is on edge, alert for signs of other people. It would take nothing for someone to report a strange girl wandering the woods early in the morning. Echoing into the streets, as she walks home, are the excited cries of children unwrapping their Christmas gifts.

Yitzchak opens the door before her hand is even on the latch. There is an urgency in his eyes as he grabs her arm and draws her inside. He shuts and bolts the door before making his way to the window to peer outside. The coast is clear: no one has seen her arrive.

'They came twice, Magda,' he says, his eyes still on the street. 'The last time was only an hour or so ago.' He turns to her. 'I think you'll need to stay away longer in future.'

'I have hot tea for you. Come and have something to eat,' Chaya calls from the kitchen.

From the folded blanket Magda produces the parcel of food Yitzchak had so carefully prepared for her last night. She has not touched it.

'I gave you the food to eat, Magda. How do you expect to stay warm if you have nothing inside you?' Yitzchak chides.

'I wasn't hungry, Grandfather – I was too busy sleeping. And now you can share it with me.'

Chaya takes the heavy coat from Magda's shoulders, stroking it lovingly before she returns it to the cupboard in the bedroom.

CHAPTER 17

Auschwitz-Birkenau
December 1943

There was to be no special meal and no day off this Christmas. There was, however, a gift from Cibi for Livi. That night, as they climb into their bunk, Cibi, with a great flourish, pulls a small, knitted, white woollen hat from her pocket. It even has ribbons.

'What is this?' Livi squeals.

'A hat, silly! It will keep your head warm. Let me put it on for you.'

'I'm not a baby, Cibi, I can do it myself. But isn't it a bit small?' Livi is tugging it hard over her ears. It's a snug fit but Cibi is delighted. She ties the ribbons into a neat bow under Livi's chin.

'I can feel my head getting warmer.' Livi is equally thrilled.

'Now, lie down,' Cibi instructs.

Livi does as she's told and Cibi tucks a blanket around her body.

'Come and see my baby,' she calls to the girls in the room, laughing. They gather around, smiling at the girl in the white bonnet. She is seventeen now, but so thin she looks like a child.

'Where did you get it?'

'I found it in a case of baby's clothes,' Cibi says, proudly, refusing to relive the pang of sadness that had gone through her when she had first opened the case.

'Can you get me one?' another girl asks.

'And me? I'd like to be a baby too,' one quips.

'I'll see what I can find. I never thought to look at the children's clothes.' Cibi pauses and gestures to the emaciated figures standing around them. 'Look at us, we're no bigger than children, anyway.'

Livi sleeps well that night, the best she has all winter. Each morning, she carefully tucks the bonnet under her mattress.

'You still here? I thought you went to God a long time ago.'

Cibi is at her desk in the *Kanada* office. An SS officer stands before her. She remembers him from the demolition site. 'You'll go to God before me,' Cibi hisses, under her breath.

'I barely recognise you,' he says. He looks her up and down. Her hair is even longer now, the waves sitting on her shoulders. She wears mostly clean clothes and she thinks she could pass for a secretary in any office.

'Would you like to move to the *Kanada* at Birkenau? I can arrange it,' he says. Despite her hostility and bravado, he is eyeing her almost kindly. 'You survived when I didn't think you or any of the early arrivals would – I'm just offering you a new job so you don't have to walk to and from Birkenau every day,' he says, and then adds, 'We're not all monsters.'

'Aren't you?' says Cibi. 'And, no, thank you. I've done my share of sorting dirty, stinking clothes.'

'What about the post office? I could have you moved there, if you'd prefer.'

Cibi looks up from the typewriter. Is he playing with her, she wonders.

'I would like that,' she says, slowly. 'Are you being serious?' A job at Birkenau would suit her very well. The walk is lonely without her sister, especially during these bitter winter months.

'Leave it with me,' the officer says, turning away.

The snow is falling hard as Livi sets off to deliver a message to the medical block. She is halted in her tracks when a truck pulls out in front of her. Two SS guards climb out of the canvas-covered van. The canvas flaps swing back into place, but not before Livi catches a glimpse of the naked women huddled inside.

She takes a step back when a young woman jumps out, landing in front of the SS guards. She raises her hands in the air. She doesn't seem to feel the cold or the snow. 'Shoot me now, because I will not walk into your gas chamber!' she yells.

Livi takes a step back, and then another, wary of becoming the victim of a stray bullet.

The guards point their rifles at the naked woman. One takes aim, but another guard slaps his arm down. Livi notes

155

the cruel smile on his face as he tells the girl she is not to be granted the easy death of a bullet. Instead, she is to die like all her kind – slowly, painfully, gasping for air as the gas robs her of her life. He moves towards her, swinging the butt of his rifle into her stomach. She collapses, but struggles to her feet and starts to run, to Livi's horror, towards *her*.

But the rifle swings once more through the air and connects with her skull. She goes down. Her blood colours the snow pink. When she makes no attempt to stand up, a guard grabs her arm and drags her back to the truck. The women haul her inside.

As the vehicle moves off, Livi drops to her knees, dry retching. When will this madness end? Her eyes find the blood and she waits for the snow to obliterate this new horror before she moves off. Her fingers close around the little knife in her pocket, her talisman now. She imagines plunging it into the heart of the SS officer who wielded his rifle against a naked woman in the snow.

Later, Livi doesn't tell Cibi what she witnessed earlier that day. She hasn't told her about Isaac either, the crazed *kapo*. It's easier somehow, to not speak of these things. And there are newcomers, in any case, to distract them.

The sisters watch these fresh inmates repeat the questions which consumed them on arrival: *Why are we here? What will they do to us?*

One of the girls introduces herself as Vanoushka and asks if any of them have read Oscar Wilde's story of Dorian Gray. Several laugh at her, incredulous she is talking about a *book* and *reading* while they wait at the very gates of hell. Undeterred by their mockery, she says, 'Let me tell you about *The Picture of Dorian Gray.*' She holds her audience rapt as she recounts the story. Gasping and giggling, the girls learn of the sensual and sinful twists and turns of Dorian's life and his longing for Sibyl. Like every good storyteller, she ends her tale on a cliff-hanger, the girls begging for more. Vanoushka promises further adventures the following day.

The next evening Vanoushka waits until the lights go out. Everyone gathers by her bunk while she delights them with the story of the infatuated artist, Basil, the painter of Dorian's portrait.

These sessions become a lifeboat for the girls to cling on to, but especially so for Livi. Slowly, the memory of the bloody woman in the snow begins to recede. She and Cibi both dream about finding their Prince Charming, and sitting for portraits while a famous painter fixes their images in thick oils onto canvas.

When, finally, Vanoushka has exhausted Oscar Wilde's masterpiece, she offers the girls other stories from other books, but they only want more of Dorian Gray. She must go back and repeat his adventures again and again. Livi finds these tales as comforting as the feel of her knife in her palm. Somehow, they remind her of home: Mumma used to read to her in bed as a child, and Livi finds herself desperate to share these memoires with her mother now. She just prays she and Cibi will live long enough to see her again.

The SS officer had been true to his word and now Cibi works at Birkenau. Sorting mail at the post office is easy enough, and she no longer has to make the trek to Auschwitz; but, most importantly, she no longer has to be parted from Livi.

A few months earlier, the Theresienstadt family camp had been established within Birkenau, housing German, Austrian,

Czech and Dutch Jews from a north-western ghetto in Czechoslovakia. Letters and parcels, often containing food, arrive regularly for these prisoners and Cibi's role is to note the names and addresses of the prisoners receiving this mail. She types up the information and sends it to an address in Switzerland.

Initially, Cibi doesn't know *who* in Switzerland receives this information, but the answer comes to her a short while later when food parcels start arriving for these families from the Red Cross. There are numerous rumours about the ghetto, with many saying it was a propaganda machine for the Germans to show the outside world it cared about its Jews, treating them well, feeding them, displaying their largess to the Red Cross, before sending them to extermination camps across Nazi-occupied Europe.

'This family is no longer here,' Cibi tells her supervisor one morning, while handing him a small, unopened box.

'Doesn't look like there can be much in there. Open it.'

She lifts the lid to find a tiny box of chocolates and two tins of sardines. Her supervisor takes the chocolates, but hands her the sardines without a word.

Cibi gives one tin to her co-worker and takes the other to a dark corner of the mail room. She cannot risk being caught trying to smuggle the tin back into the camp, so she must eat it now. Peeling back the lid, Cibi gulps down the tiny, salty fish and pours the oil into mouth. With her finger she wipes the inside of the tin clean. Almost immediately, her gorge rises as she remembers the day she arrived at Auschwitz, more than two years ago, and she thinks of the man she and Livi saw: thin, shaven-headed, dressed in baggy, striped prison clothes; he had clambered into their cattle wagon and picked up an empty tin, and, just as she had done, he wiped a skeletal finger around its oily insides, before sticking it into his mouth.

Cibi feels faint. There is no difference now between her and that man, apart from the clothes she stands in. It is while she is lost in this dark memory that the door to the mail room opens and an SS guard enters. His lips are moving, but Cibi has missed his first sentence entirely. She stares at him stupidly.

'I said, come with me!' he barks. Letting the sardine tin drop, Cibi follows him outside to where a truck is waiting. 'Get in!'

Cibi runs to the passenger side and climbs into the truck, fully present now. She is in an SS truck with an SS guard. There is only way this is going to end. She thinks of Livi, who may never find out what has happened to her. She thinks of Magda, of her mother and Grandfather.

The SS guard glances at her, noticing the trembling fingers that cover her mouth. 'I'm not going to hurt *you*,' he tells her. There is a matter-of-factness in his voice. Cibi releases the breath she has been holding, and tentatively meets his eyes. 'I need you to pick up some parcels at the front gate and take them back to the post room where they should have been delivered in the first place. When I find out who was too lazy to walk them round I will have them shot.'

Cibi is still trying to steady her breathing. It is cold outside, but she needs the fresh air. 'Do you mind if I wind the window down?' she asks, and the soldier gives a curt nod.

Cibi leans into the wind, gasps in the cold air and feels calmer.

A large open truck is driving towards them. As it sails past she is blasted by the voices of men roaring in song. She turns in her seat to catch sight of naked male prisoners in the back. They stand tall and chant the song she herself has sung so many times at synagogue.

Her heart may have slowed down, but the shock Cibi received when the SS guard ordered her into the truck has weakened her grip on herself. An icy fear flushes through her now, and she clutches her chest as she feels she is starting to fall apart. What little hope she has of surviving this place flies out of the open window, chasing the men destined for imminent death.

How soon before the SS come for her, strip her naked and drive her to the gas chamber?

Livi can't understand why Cibi is avoiding her. These days, her sister stays later and later at the post office, often sneaking back into the block once the lights have gone out. As they lie in bed at night, she seldom responds to Livi's whispered questions. Livi resolves to talk to Cibi on Sunday, their day off, but when Sunday rolls around, Cibi mutters she has work to do at the post office, and slips away.

Livi wanders around the camp, stopping now and then to talk to the other girls, but she doesn't hang around for very long. She's worried about Cibi. Maybe, she wonders, Cibi has witnessed one or two unsettling episodes herself, and been struck mute by them. But Cibi is her rock, Livi reasons, she can't just *disappear*.

Livi heads for the gates which divide the two women's camps. They're open today, as they are every Sunday, allowing family and friends to reunite for short periods.

Livi's blood runs cold when senior SS officer Mandel appears on her magnificent black horse, and rides over when she sees Livi. Mandel is universally feared: cold-eyed and vicious, she wears her long red hair in a high ponytail, even though she's too old for such a girlish hairstyle. Never one to use her words when a baton will do, Mandel is famous for lashing out during rollcall. She is known as 'The Beast'. It is rumoured that if you look her directly in the eye, she will have you shot or sent to the gas chamber. No one is in a hurry to find out if it's true.

'Do you know why these gates are open?' Mandel demands of Livi.

Struggling to stay calm and to avoid the woman's eyes, Livi explains that Sundays are visiting days, and that the women are allowed to mingle with friends who live in the opposite camp.

The officer tosses a large key at Livi and tells her to lock both sets of gates: everyone is to remain where they are and if they're not where they should be when the gates are shut, they will be punished. Striking her heels into the horse's flanks, Mandel rides off.

Livi begins to warn the women they must return to their camps, that they must pass on the message, and hurry. She starts to make a great show of pulling the gates closed as women streak past her to their rightful blocks. They are screaming at Livi not to lock them in as Mandel gallops up once more.

'Hurry,' shouts Livi to the stragglers. 'Hurry!'

Livi is locking the gate as Mandel jumps down from her horse and strides up to her. 'I told you to lock the gates immediately,' she screams into Livi's face.

From the corner of her eye, Livi sees Rita approach, but she can't save her from the fist swinging into Livi's face. Knocked off her feet, Livi lies stunned on the ground. Her bladder releases and she feels hot urine puddle beneath her.

Mandel, her work done for the moment, climbs back onto her horse, and issues her final blow: 'Send her to the hole!' she screeches at Rita, before riding off.

Rita offers Livi a hand and hauls her to her feet. 'I can't get you out of this.' she says, but the young girl can't speak: she knows that she is lucky to be alive.

Livi follows Rita to the back of the women's camp. There, a girl is standing, up to her shoulders, in a hole in the ground. There is no way Livi can drop down into it, it's too narrow. Instead, she must climb through a short dirt tunnel and come up into the hole. It is only once she is fully upright that Livi understands the torture of this punishment. Back to back, their arms trapped by their sides, neither girl can move – they can barely breath – and they must stay like this all night.

When Cibi returns to the block that evening for dinner, Rita explains that Livi has been sent to the hole.

'I need to see her,' Cibi pleads. 'Please, Rita. She can't do it alone.'

'She has to. You go anywhere near her and you'll end up in there too, or worse.'

'But she's my little sister, I have to look out for her.'

'She's a lot stronger than you think. She'll be back at work in the morning, you can see her then. But tomorrow night, she will return to the hole.'

Livi isn't cold, she is numb. She can no longer sense her hands and fingers and it feels like her chest is caving in with each breath she takes. She and the girl she is pressed up against exchanged names after Rita left, but then there was nothing else to say, and it hurt to talk. She senses Agatha feels the same, because the girl remains silent. During the night, Livi nods off but then starts awake. This happens a hundred times, maybe two hundred.

In the morning, Rita hoists the girls out of the hole.

When Cibi sees her, she is afraid for a moment. Livi's blouse is torn and filthy, the curls which have started to grow back are caked in mud. Livi holds her shirt closed, having lost all the buttons in the tunnel.

'Aren't you happy to see me?' Livi asks, forcing a grin, and Cibi runs to her, crushing her against her chest, brushing the dirt out of her hair, repeating over and over, 'Are you all right? Are you OK?'

Vanoushka finds Livi a new blouse.

As she puts it on, she notices the number stitched onto the lapel. 'I have a new number. Look, Cibi – now I have two,' Livi tries to joke.

'That means I can sleep in and you can answer for me at rollcall.' Vanoushka laughs.

That evening, Livi reports to the hole for another sleepless night on her feet. A very tall female SS officer in a spotless uniform is watching Agatha climb out. She turns to Livi. 'Your sister told me it was The Beast who sent you here,' she says.

'It was,' says Livi, wondering if this is a trap. Agatha scurries away into the dark.

'You see this?' The officer points to the insignia on her uniform. 'I outrank the bitch. She can't throw her weight around here like she used to, and I'm enjoying undoing every single order she gives. Go back to your block, little girl.'

Without having to be told twice, Livi races back to the arms of her sister.

CHAPTER 18

Vranov nad Topl'ou
April 1944

'Magda? Magda Meller? Is that you?'

Magda pulls her scarf around her face. She dips her head to her chest and picks up speed.

'Magda Meller! Stop where you are!'

Magda stops, berating herself. Why did she believe she was invincible when everything around her had gone to hell? She turns round to see the familiar smirk on Visik's face. Her old school 'friend'.

'Visik, what do you want?' Magda is trying to hide the tremble in her voice.

'You. We've been trying to speak to you for months, and don't pretend you don't know.'

'And who is "we"?'

'Me and my colleagues in the Hlinka Guards, that's who.'

'My colleagues and I,' Magda corrects him. She hates his smug face, his stupid uniform. He is a little boy pretending to be a man, and he won't get the better of her.

'Don't get smart with me. We've come to your house every Friday – tell me where you've been hiding.'

'Hiding? Why should I hide? I've probably just been out with my friends. Oh, but that's right, isn't it, Visik – you wouldn't know what a friend is.' Despite herself, a tiny bit of Magda is enjoying this exchange. It may be her only chance to show him her contempt.

'You can't talk to me like that anymore, Magda. I could have you shot, and maybe if I shot you myself I'd even get a medal.'

Magda has had enough. 'What do you want, Visik? I have shopping to do.'

'We'll be at your house on Friday, as usual, and you had better be there. It's time for you to join your sisters, don't you know?' he teases, an infuriating grin on his mouth.

Magda is alert now, the sniping forgotten. She takes a step towards this man-boy. 'Do you know where they are?'

'Of course I do, I . . . I know everything.' But Magda hears the hesitation in his voice.

'You know nothing,' she hisses. 'Because you are nothing but a little boy playing with a big gun. Why don't you go home, Visik, to your mummy?'

Magda turns her back on him and strides off, but she is less sure of herself now. Why hadn't she done as her mother had asked and gone straight home after the shopping? Why had she had to stop by the little boutique on the main street to admire the dresses? She doesn't have any money for a new dress, even if she had somewhere to wear it. Now Visik knows she is still in Vranov, and that is bad.

While she is slamming the few tins of fish she managed to find in the grocery store onto the kitchen counter, Chaya comes into the room, and watches her for a moment. 'What's wrong with you?'

Magda ignores her. She doesn't need her mother berating her too, all for the sake of a dress she will never own.

'Maybe seeing your cousins tonight will put you in a better mood,' Chaya offers.

'My cousins?'

'Your uncle and aunt have invited us to have dinner with them.'

'Is that because they know we've nothing to eat?' Magda snaps, staring at the three solitary tins of fish.

'We have food, and haven't you just been shopping?'

'Look at it, Mumma. It's nothing!' Magda says. 'It would have been better for everyone if I had left with Cibi and Livi.' The words are out of her mouth, and it's too late to take them back. Her mother's eyes fill with tears.

'Ladies, ladies, what's going on? I can hear you from the garden.' Yitzchak enters the room through the back door.

'Nothing, Grandfather, it's nothing,' Magda says, quickly. She doesn't need an interrogation right now.

'Magda thinks we would be better off without her,' Chaya mumbles. 'She wants to be with her sisters.'

'Magda, is this true?'

'Yes. No! I don't know. But we have so little to eat. And . . . and you would have more.' Her grandfather is half the size he was two years ago, and he was a slight man even then.

'Stop it, Magda. Don't you think we've all had the same idea? How is it helpful?'

'I'm sorry, Mumma.' Magda reaches for her mother's hand. 'I didn't mean it, but, it's just so hard. How much longer can we live like this? How much longer can *I* live like this? Hiding, scared of my own shadow? Worrying about my sisters?'

Chaya pulls Magda to her chest, stroking her hair. 'Some linden tea, that's what we all need,' she whispers. And Magda nods.

'Maybe Ivan will have some news for us tonight,' Yitzchak says, hopefully, as he fills the kettle. Setting it on the stove, he stokes the embers beneath to life. There is no wood left, so they will have to settle for lukewarm tea. 'Magda, I'll need to collect some more wood tomorrow. Will you help me?'

'Of course I will.' Magda smiles.

Later, as they cross the back garden to Ivan's house, Chaya pauses to look at the new buds on the oleander bush. She has tended this bush since she was a child, bringing it back to life time and again. Her family joked that as long as the oleander bush thrived, so would they. It is flourishing now, giving them all a little hope that Cibi and Livi are also flourishing.

After dinner, when her young cousins are in bed, and the adults are sipping tea around the fire, Magda breaks the comfortable silence.

'Uncle, something's wrong, isn't it?'

Her uncle has been avoiding her eyes all evening. He gives a heavy sigh and nods.

'This is the reason I invited you to dinner tonight: we need to talk.' Ivan places his cup on the small coffee table and lays his hands on his knees. Helena, his wife, is staring at her shoes.

'Ivan, Helena! You're frightening me. Please tell me what's going on.' Chaya's hand rests over her heart.

'It is no longer the young they are after, Chaya. They are coming for all of us.'

A hush falls over the room as this sinks in. Yitzchak slowly gets to his feet and crosses the room to sit beside Chaya.

'And where will they take us?' asks Yitzchak, finally, breaking the silence.

'I don't know,' replies Ivan. 'No one does. But it's obvious they now want to clear every Jew out of Vranov. Maybe the whole of Slovakia.' He looks at Magda, who is staring at her mother and grandfather, her mouth hanging open. Helena touches Ivan's shoulder and he turns to her, pulling her into his arms. 'I can't even protect my own family,' he says.

Magda is shocked to see her uncle's distress. He had always been the strong one, never thinking twice about entering government buildings to demand to speak to whoever was best placed to give him information.

'Brother, as long as we stay together, we can survive anything,' Chaya says, softly. 'It's time for you to stop feeling so responsible for us. None of this is your doing.' Chaya's voice breaks and she covers her face with her hands.

'When will this happen, son?' Yitzchak asks. Magda hears authority in his voice: he is now the strong one.

'It could start at any time.' Ivan has adopted the posture of defeat and, like his sister, elbows on his knees, he buries his face in his hands.

Helena strokes his back. 'We should be packed and ready in any case,' she adds, bleakly.

Ivan raises his head to look into the faces of Magda, Yitzchak and Chaya. There is guilt and shame in his eyes, and Magda's heart breaks for him.

168

After that, there is nothing left to say, and the Meller family makes their way home. The moment they step through the back door, Magda races to the sideboard in the living room and begins to rummage around in the drawers. 'Mumma? Where are all the photos?' she yells.

'Photos? Now? We just need to get some sleep. Please, Magda.'

'Just tell me where they are,' Magda insists.

Chaya reluctantly lights a lantern and, with Yitzchak, heads to her bedroom. 'I'll fetch them.'

'Mumma?' Magda yells once more. 'Can you bring a pillowcase?'

'What's wrong with her?' Magda hears her mother ask her grandfather.

'How should I know?' he says, and she can hear a tiny smile in his voice. 'She's your daughter.'

When Chaya and Yitzchak return with the photos, Magda is brandishing the silver candlesticks – a wedding present that Chaya has vowed never to sell.

'What are you doing with those?' Chaya demands.

'Give me the pillowcase and the photos, Mumma. Please.'

Chaya and Yitzchak watch as Magda folds the items into the pillowcase.

'Can you get a chair from the kitchen, Grandfather, and place it beneath the trap door?' Magda asks.

'What are you doing?' Chaya is becoming exasperated. She is tense with worry about what tomorrow holds, exhausted by the thought of what will happen to them all.

'Isn't it obvious? I'm hiding our things.'

'Can't we just take them with us?' says Chaya.

'Do you think they'll let us keep our candlesticks, Mumma?' Magda's eyes are bright, determined.

169

Of course, Magda is right, thinks Chaya. Their houses abandoned, who will stop anyone entering and stealing their things? Not the Hlinka, not the Nazis and not her neighbours.

'Let her do this, Chaya,' says Yitzchak, dragging the chair to the trapdoor, just as Mrs Trac had done for Magda so many times before. 'They'll be safe up there.'

Yitzchak moves to climb onto the chair, but Magda draws him away. 'It's all right, Grandfather, let me do it. I've had the practise.'

Pulling herself up, Magda disappears into the tight cavity. Her head appears a moment later and she holds out a hand for the lantern and the pillowcase.

'Mind you're not startled by the mice,' Yitzchak tells her. 'Or you'll drop the lantern and set us all on fire.'

Magda smiles when she hears a giggle escape her mother's lips. Now, lying flat on her stomach, Magda crawls to the furthest corner of the dark space. Tucking the possessions under old clothes and crumbling newspapers, she crawls away, then eases herself back through the hole. 'Now we can go to bed!' she announces.

The next morning, mother and daughter find Yitzchak dressed and ready to go out.

'Why are you dressed like that?' Chaya asks. 'Aren't we supposed to be packing?'

'Before we do all that, Magda and I are going to find some firewood. I need a cup of tea and so do you.'

Magda is ready in seconds. Yitzchak waits for her outside with a small cart built for the single purpose of gathering kindling.

Ever since Yitzchak moved in with Chaya, this has become a regular routine for grandfather and granddaughter, and

170

the moment they step into the dense bushes, with the sun filtering through the leaves, Magda enters her happy place. She remembers the years Yitzchak has spent patiently teaching her the names of every bush and tree, every mushroom and flower.

As Magda skips ahead, marvelling at the summer growth around her, Yitzchak scans the forest floor for stray, dry branches. He doesn't mind that Magda has run off into the depths of the woodland; he is just happy that today she is happy.

'Grandfather! Come and look at this.'

Yitzchak leaves the cart and follows Magda's voice, to find her sitting by a large oak tree. 'I've found a flowering sword lily,' she tells him. Magda is cupping the delicate, funnel-shaped flowers in her hands, the glorious purple-pink blooms nod in the breeze. 'It's here all on its own, just for us,' Magda says, smiling up at her grandfather.

Magda's simple delight touches Yitzchak deeply, but now his mind turns to his other granddaughters: how they would love to be here, he thinks. Cibi, inquisitive as ever, would be scanning the forest for other flowers, refusing to believe the lily was alone. And Livi? He would be begging her not to pick it!

'Now I know where you hide when you come to the forest at night, my Magda! And what can you tell me about the sword lily?' Yitzchak tests her.

'They are a genus of the gladiolus family.'

'And what is the meaning of the word "gladiolus"?'

'It means strength of character, Grandfather. It means never giving up. *And*, it is part of the iris family, which signifies hope.' Magda, initially pleased she is able to roll the answers off her tongue, now looks away from Yitzchak, into the trees beyond. She is thinking about the word 'hope'.

'Strength and hope,' repeats her grandfather. 'Our special, secret words. These are the finest qualities a person can have. Qualities I see in you, Magda, and in your sisters.'

Magda meets his eyes. He is her protector and her teacher. She is crying now, her tears falling onto the petals of the sword lily.

Later, in silence, they pull the kindling-laden cart home, moving slowly, each wondering whether this might have been their last excursion into the forest.

'I was about to come looking for you,' Chaya says, as they heave the cart to the kitchen door.

'Magda found a sword lily in bloom,' Yitzchak tells her, with a grin.

Chaya looks at Magda, who turns away from her mother, still lost to her thoughts. The small living room is strewn with their belongings: suitcases, clothes, books and non-perishable foods lie in piles on the floor and sofa and armchairs.

'Strength and hope,' she says to Magda. 'Now I understand the secret of where you have been hiding in the forest.'

'Yes, Mumma.'

'We will need both these qualities in the days ahead.'

'Yes, Mumma.'

'I'll get the stove going,' Yitzchak says. 'While you finish packing.'

While they are sipping from mugs of fragrant linden tea and staring at the mess around them, the Hlinka arrive.

They are to report to the train station tomorrow morning. The time has come.

CHAPTER 19

Auschwitz-Birkenau
March–September 1944

Cibi and the other girls working in the post office receive new orders. Handed dozens of postcards, they are instructed to write to the relatives of the family camp's residents informing them that the prisoners are alive and well, and ask that they send food.

Cibi knows these prisoners are almost certainly dead.

'Why are we doing this?' Cibi asks the post office supervisor, a severe woman with little interest in answering questions.

'You know better than to query your orders. Just get on with it.'

That night, Cibi tells Livi of the strange task she has been assigned. She fears that the numbers being sent to the gas chambers are increasing, and wants to know if Livi has heard rumours, or read any of the messages she delivers. Livi considers Cibi's agitation. By now she knows that Cibi's work is very different to her own. While Livi just delivers messages around the camp, her sister is confronted on a daily basis by the reality of the death all around them. Hundreds, thousands of letters and parcels, are being delivered for the ghosts of the dead.

Livi explains that she is careful never to so much as glance at the messages she delivers, not even those without envelopes. It is far safer to remain ignorant, however often she might be tempted to look.

'Keep your eyes open, little sister. I have a bad feeling,' Cibi tells her.

The next day Livi watches the transfer of prisoners, with their possessions, from the family camp to the recently cleared quarantine camp which sits next door.

Livi tells Cibi this dark news. And there's more. She also saw a doctor enter the camp and leave with several small children.

'A doctor?' A nondescript man in a white coat who is often seen around the camp, trailing groups of very young children, springs to Cibi's mind. Surely not him.

'I think it was him, Cibi,' Livi whispers. Neither of them wants to think about Josef Mengele or the terrible rumours that follow him all over Auschwitz-Birkenau.

Twenty-four hours later, all of the family camp prisoners are dead. The sisters do not speak of it again. They cannot. They hold each other close at night, and each day pray that they will be together again that evening.

Spring eases into the summer and the sisters' routine doesn't falter. They work, eat what they can and sleep. It is as though they have lived there for ever. But while the warmer weather makes their lives easier, it does nothing to diminish their awareness of the crematoria chimneys spewing their ash every morning, as they line up for rollcall. There is much about the camp they take for granted: the meagre food rations, the stealing, the random beatings – but they will never get used to the smell of the smoke. Part of their routine, an unspoken part, is to ask themselves, every day, *Is today our last day on this earth?* The answer comes at bedtime, as they cuddle together for comfort. *We survived another day.*

The trains continue to arrive several times a day, hauling their human cargo into Birkenau. Livi, from her position at the gates, witnesses families from Hungary disembark, only to be marched straight to the gas chambers and crematoria. The trucks trundle their possessions to the *Kanada*.

Cibi's new supervisor at the post office, SS officer Elisabeth Volkenrath, treats the girls well, often allowing them to share amongst themselves the food parcels destined for the dead. Volkenrath is young and very pretty: her long, strawberry-blonde hair hangs in a single thick plait down her back, and she has blue eyes and full red lips. Cibi notices the other officers staring at her, but she only has eyes for her husband, SS officer Heinz Volkenrath.

One morning, Cibi catches him entering her office and, shortly afterwards, she hears Volkenrath giggling. When Heinz opens the door to leave, he is adjusting his clothes.

'We are just married,' Elisabeth Volkenrath whispers to Cibi, after he has left.

Cibi is wary of her apparent openness. This officer has as much blood on her hands as any in Birkenau or Auschwitz. But now she winks at Cibi whenever Heinz visits. He isn't so keen on Cibi, however, glaring at her whenever he comes calling. And Cibi despises him back. One day, she chucks the newspaper he had casually dropped on her desk before entering Volkenrath's office into the small stove in the corner of the room.

'Has anyone seen my paper?' he asks, pulling on his jacket after another 'session' with his wife. Volkenrath hovers, smiling stupidly at his shoulder. 'I put it down here.' He points at Cibi's desk.

'Did you want that?' Cibi asks, smoothly. 'I thought it was rubbish.' Cibi indicates the stove. 'So I threw it in the fire.'

Suddenly, Heinz is towering over her. 'You did what?' he says, slowly.

'I put it in the fire,' Cibi repeats, faltering a little now.

Without missing a beat, Heinz has pulled out his pistol and aimed it at her head. Cibi shrinks back, her senses suddenly screaming. Gone is her bravado. Gone is her small victory. Now, she thinks only of Livi. She has been stupid, cavalier with her life. For nothing.

Volkenrath gently pushes his arm aside. 'She didn't mean anything by it,' she says, briskly. 'She's a tidy one, that's all.'

Very slowly, Heinz holsters his gun and strides out of the post office, slamming the door behind him. Cibi lets out her breath.

'Don't ever cross Heinz!' Volkenrath snaps. 'And next time I won't stop him, so be warned.'

A few days later, the post office girls are tending to a delivery of boxes that have been dumped outside the building. Cibi is helping her workmates sort their contents. She enjoys the rhythm of this work and she likes Rosie from Bratislava, a new recruit to the small team.

Rosie is on her knees, gazing into the box of books she has just opened. She picks them up, one by one, reading the titles. Cibi joins her, noting that many are prayer books. The girls turn them over in their hands.

'What are those?' A kapo has appeared from nowhere. He grabs a book, inspects the title, turns the pages. In seconds, he is hurling the books to the ground and stomping on them until their spines are broken and their pages torn. He is showing off to the SS officers who are lurking close by, that much is obvious. But then Rosie is suddenly on her feet, tall and defiant, cursing the kapo, firing words of abuse into his face.

Cibi is convinced one or other of the officers will execute her on the spot but she is powerless to help. But the kapo merely kicks the detritus of the books aside and laughs.

An SS officer wanders over to them. 'What are you so upset about?' he asks Rosie. 'They're just books!'

Cibi, on her feet now, takes Rosie's arm, trying to pull her away, trying to stop her from digging her own grave, but Rosie shrugs her off. And then Cibi has an idea.

'Let me tell you a story,' she says, stepping in front of Rosie and towards the SS officer. 'One day, the gold asked the iron, Why do you shout when you are beaten? I get hit too, but I keep quiet. The iron replied, I cry because the hammer is made from iron – it is my brother and that hurts me. You are hit by a stranger.'

The officer turns away without a word.

The next day, the officer turns up at the post office with a grey box, which he hands to Cibi.

She opens it to reveal a prayer book covered in pale grey leather.

'This is my gift to you. A good luck omen so we won't lose the war.' He smirks.

'We also pray for our enemies,' Cibi replies.

The officer is staring at her now, his head on one side. 'Don't you remember me, Cibi?' he says. 'I'm Eric. From the *Kanada*?'

Cibi wonders why this SS officer would care whether she remembered him or not, but she has given up being surprised by anything that happens in this place. She looks him up and down. 'You look thin,' is all she says.

'So do you.'

'I am a prisoner. You're not.' Cibi is feeling bold.

'These days I live off vodka. Food has lost its appeal.'

Cibi marvels at the fact they're having a conversation. 'Are you sick?'

'Only in the head.' Eric sighs and runs a hand through his hair. He points a thumb over his shoulder. 'Usually, I'm stationed by the gates, where the transports come in.' He looks at his boots. 'Where they make the selections.'

Cibi's curiosity turns to cold, hard, unsentimental fury. Is he expecting sympathy from her?

Understanding, even?

'Eric, why don't you go and pack your suitcase and go back to your mumma?' Cibi says, turning her back on the young man.

She is thinking of this exchange, trying to understand why Eric was so keen for Cibi to know he has a conscience, when she sees a little girl standing by the door to the post office. The mail room is next to the hospital block where Mengele houses his 'children'. Too many times Cibi has witnessed his shiny black car pull up outside and disgorge the unremarkable man along with the little girls and boys. She has watched him herd the children through the doors

178

of the hospital, joking with them as he hands out sweets. Cibi has no idea what happens to those children exactly, but it can't be good.

'Hello,' the little girl says.

Cibi takes a step towards her, aware of the SS officers lingering close by.

'Hello,' Cibi says, hesitantly. 'My name is Cibi. Do you have a name?'

'Irinka.'

'That's a beautiful name, and you're a beautiful little girl.'

Irinka smiles shyly and opens her mouth to say more, when a nurse approaches. 'There you are. Come along now, Irinka. You know you're not meant to be outside.' The woman's tone is sickly sweet.

'Bye, Cibi,' the little girl says, taking the nurse's hand.

Cibi's stomach turns as she watches the little girl disappear through the hospital doors. The fresh air feels cloying suddenly, the sun a furnace. Cibi hurries back inside the post office, where Volkenrath is patrolling the room. Cibi can see she is in a good mood.

'What's going on with the children in the hospital?' Cibi asks, nonchalantly, as she pulls a stack of letters towards her. She begins to open them methodically, noting down the names and addresses of the would-be recipients.

'If they're in the hospital, then they must be sick,' Volkenrath replies.

'They don't look sick, or act sick,' says Cibi, lightly.

'Well, they are. I've been on the wards and they are all in bed – some of them are definitely receiving treatment.'

Cibi nods, acknowledging she won't get anything more out of Volkenrath. Maybe it's better not to know. Maybe it's better they're in the hospital: most of the children arriving in Birkenau these days are sent to the gas chamber immediately.

'Can I tell you something?' Volkenrath moves closer and Cibi's skin crawls.

'Heinz and I want to have a baby,' begins Volkenrath, in a low voice. 'That's why he's always here. I cuddled some of the younger ones next door, and there was this one little girl – she can't have been Jewish, she had beautiful blonde hair – do you know what she asked me?'

Cibi shakes her head slowly.

'She asked me if I had an egg. She wanted to eat an egg. That's strange, isn't it?' Volkenrath's voice is wistful and Cibi finds this intimacy disturbing.

A few days later Cibi unpacks a box of food and finds a hardboiled egg. She thinks of the girl who wanted an egg and takes it into Volkenrath's office. 'Look what I found,' she says.

Volkenrath doesn't look up. 'What?'

'It's a hardboiled egg. You said there was a little girl . . .'

Volkenrath is out of her chair in seconds, holding out her hand for the egg. 'Thank you, I'll take it to her straight away.'

A short while later, Volkenrath storms back into the post office and heads straight for her room, slamming the door behind her.

The girls glance nervously at one another. Cibi takes a deep breath and decides to find out what has happened. She opens the office door very slowly and peers inside. Volkenrath is sobbing, her head on the desk.

Cibi enters the room and pulls the door closed behind her. 'Are you OK?' she asks hesitantly.

The officer sniffs loudly and looks at Cibi. Her blue eyes are red and her cheeks bright pink. Strands of blonde hair have escaped their braid and stick to her face in damp clumps.

'No,' she says. 'I'm not OK.'

'Was she not there?' Cibi asks with genuine compassion.

'She was there. I found her and handed her the egg.'

'So that's good. Isn't it?'

'She started screaming and wouldn't take the egg. Then she ran away and hid behind one of the nurses. She wouldn't even look at me.' Volkenrath begins to cry again.

'Oh . . .' Cibi feels somehow responsible and suddenly very anxious. 'I'm really sorry. I shouldn't have given it to you.'

'It's not your fault. Now leave me alone.' The officer turns away from Cibi, wiping her eyes with her fingers.

Cibi shuts the door behind her and turns to face her watchful co-workers, all of them waiting for an explanation. 'You know she wants a baby. I think she gets upset when she sees the little ones,' Cibi offers.

She waits all morning for her punishment, but none comes. Volkenrath appears a little later, her usual grim smile back on her face.

'Have you heard?' Rosie whispers, later that same day. The girls in the post office mostly work in silence, opening boxes, sorting contents, setting aside items of value. Cibi can lose herself in these tasks; she can almost forget where she is at times.

'Heard what?' Cibi says, distracted.

'About Mala, the interpreter.'

'What about her?' another girl asks.

181

'She's escaped!' Rosie is gleeful. She has Cibi's full attention now. 'She and her boyfriend Edek have escaped together – they've been gone for days. How exciting is that?'

'You're sure?' Cibi is trying to make sense of the word 'escape'. To flee this place, to live without fences, without beatings, without the guards. She doesn't often let herself think of her life before Birkenau. The camp has expanded to stifle her memories of a different time, and she rarely imagines life after the camp.

'The Nazis are going crazy,' Rosie informs them. 'One of the girls who works in the administration block told me they're all blaming each other to save themselves.'

'I hope she makes it,' Cibi says, quietly. 'I hope she makes it and can tell the world what's going on in here.' She dares to allow a small flicker of hope to ignite.

The girls are animated that night. Cibi and Livi, their hunger and fatigue forgotten for a moment, engage in the joyful speculation about Mala's escape. Mala, the talented translator from Belgium who had been assigned 'protected prisoner' status by the Nazis. The girls guess she must have used her freedom from the constraints the rest of them have to endure to somehow get away. She is a hero to every prisoner, and stories of her bravery escalate as the weeks pass. They hang on to the fantasy that they will be saved once Mala has revealed the truth of their situation.

But the weeks become months and there is no Allied rescue. The transports from Hungary arrive each day, the gas chambers and the crematoria function morning and night. No one mentions Mala's name anymore.

One September evening, after everyone has returned from their various work details, they are instructed by the

SS officers to gather in the assembly yard. Organised into long, semicircular rows, they form a horseshoe shape around a central clearing in which something, obviously, is about to happen.

Livi, standing beside her sister at the end of a row, hopes an announcement is to be made. She prays that they are not about to be punished, or forced to watch a punishment. But it is still a shock to the sisters when Mala – naked, filthy, thinner than ever – is marched into the clearing by SS officers, and shoved to the ground. Bloodied and bruised, the young girl staggers to her feet, standing as straight as she can manage, a defiant tilt to her head. Livi finds the tiny knife in her pocket and closes her fingers around it.

'Oh, Mala,' she says, under her breath. 'What have they done to you?'

And then SS Mandel steps into the compound. Her high ponytail catches the setting sun and glows red. Livi thinks she could be anywhere between forty and sixty years old. Livid patches of rouge on her cheeks make her look like a clown. She is not on her horse today, but she is no less intimidating as she begins to strut up and down the rows, berating the girls furiously, telling them to forget about escaping, that they are wasting their time even thinking about it. Look at Mala, they had found her, hadn't they, and they would find any girl who was stupid enough to test them. There was no corner of the earth that the Germans could not cover. Mala wasn't so clever after all, was she? She and her 'boyfriend' – Mandel spat this word from her mouth – had been recaptured so easily. He was being hanged right at this very minute, but Mala wouldn't be so lucky – hanging was too good for Mala. She would be burned alive.

While Mandel is raging in their faces, she doesn't see what is going on behind her – what every other prisoner is now witnessing. From the matted remains of her dark hair, Mala withdraws a small blade, which she drags along the length of her arms, from wrist to inner elbow. Into the eerie silence between Mandel's outbursts, she lets out a low moan and collapses. Mandel spins to find her 'prize' lying on the ground, blood gushing from her arms.

'She is not to die like this!' she rages. 'She is to die by fire!'

An officer runs into the clearing with a wheelbarrow. Mandel points at Livi and another girl. 'Load her in and take her to the crematorium. Now!' she screams.

'Let me go!' says Cibi, grabbing her sister's wrist, but it's too late: Livi is moving past the girls into the clearing.

With the other prisoner, Livi heaves the emaciated, bloody body of Mala into the wheelbarrow. The girls each take a handle and began the journey to the crematoria.

Mala is barely conscious, moaning softly. Two officers walk a short distance behind them.

Once outside the women's camp, on the road heading towards the crematoria, the girls slow their pace. The SS do the same. Without exchanging a single word, the girls have acknowledged they will let Mala die in the wheelbarrow. She is quiet now – it shouldn't take long. They walk slowly, staring straight ahead, aware that Mandel might appear at any moment.

As they draw closer to the crematoria Livi looks at Mala. The girl's face is relaxed, her eyes are open, staring blankly up at the sky.

'She's dead,' Livi whispers.

'Good.'

Two male prisoners are standing at the entrance to the crematoria when they arrive. They stare at the girl in the wheelbarrow, before wheeling her away without a word.

The girls walk in silence back to the camp.

CHAPTER 20

Vranov nad Topl'ou
September 1944

Yitzchak is dressed in his finest suit, a white shirt and tie. Clothing totally unsuitable for a hot, late summer's day, but he would not be seen in public in anything less. Chaya wears her simple, functional black dress. With tiny buttons from collar to her midriff, the dress skims her calves and a black belt cinches her slim waist. Her hair is in a red and gold scarf; after all, she is a proud Slovakian woman and these are the colours of the traditional folk costume. Chaya tucks her black-stockinged feet into her sturdy shoes and throws a coat over her arm.

There was much discussion between mother and daughter as to what Magda should wear. They are going on a train journey and they don't want to be uncomfortable. All that sitting around required some preparation. In the end, Magda wore a plain blue skirt and a collarless blouse covered in blue and yellow flowers. She decided against stockings, but insisted on wearing her best shoes: slingbacks with a silver buckle. She also packed some 'sensible' shoes. Magda refused the scarf Chaya pressed on her. She wanted her hair to be loose and wild, *All the better for holding my head up high*, she told her mother.

A small suitcase carried by each of them, they leave the house.

Magda turns to lock the door, but Chaya calls out. 'Don't!'

'Don't what, Mumma?'

'Don't lock it. It's a lovely door and I would hate for it to be broken.'

Of course! Mother is right, thinks Magda. And didn't she hide the candlesticks, their photos? They are hated by this town. These *neighbours* would think nothing of breaking down the door to steal their things.

'Don't underestimate them, Magda. They mocked your sisters on the day they were taken from me. They will race each other to our door once we've gone.' Chaya's eyes alight on a figure further up the road: Mrs Cerny, leaning on her gate, watching the Mellers. 'She is one of *them*,' hisses Chaya.

Yitzchak has been watching this exchange in silence. Now, he picks up Magda's suitcase and hands it to her. 'Magda, put the key in your pocket. Maybe the neighbours will steal from us, maybe they won't. A locked door will not stop them.' He puts his arm around her shoulders and draws her close to him for a moment. She can hear his heart beating, slow and steady. Magda takes in a deep breath and, finally, with a last look at the only home she has ever known, she joins her family as they begin their reluctant march up the street.

Mrs Cerny looks away as they pass. Chaya keeps her eyes on the road ahead, but Magda cannot hold her tongue. 'If you step foot inside our house I'll find out. And then I will come back and curse you and your entire family!'

'Magda! Please!' says Chaya, taking Magda's arm, urging her on.

'Leave her be, Chaya,' snaps Yitzchak. 'She is only saying what we're *all* thinking.' He doesn't look at Mrs Cerny, but spits on the ground as he moves past her gate.

Mrs Cerny's eyes narrow, but she holds her tongue. Magda is glad her mother is gripping her arm so firmly, otherwise she would be tempted to slap the smug look off the woman's face.

The rest of their journey is in silence, each lost to their thoughts. Will they ever see these landmarks again? The church? The linden tree?

The station is heaving with friends and families they have not seen for many months. They share stories of hiding, of bribing government officials, of selling everything they own but the clothes they stand in. Many are overjoyed to see each other, believing their friends had long since been abducted by the Nazis.

The guards are checking off the names of everyone on the platform; many receive no response. Magda shivers each time this happens, and prays they are safely in hiding.

'The Kovacs haven't answered,' she whispers to her mother. 'But I saw Mrs Kovac in town last week, so I know they're still here. Maybe we should have tried harder to hide.'

'Hide where?' asks Chaya. 'Sooner or later, they will find the Kovacs, Magda. And what do you think these monsters will do when that happens?'

When the rollcall is over, they are ordered to board the train. 'But where are we going?' a voice shouts.

'You will find out when you get there,' comes the terse reply.

Yitzchak, Chaya and Magda squeeze together on a double seat in a crowded carriage.

'It's better to be squashed against someone you know,' Yitzchak tells them with a smile.

Magda, by the window, watches the river Topl'a speed by as the train picks up pace. In the past, the river was the natural border between the town and its invaders. She has crossed it only a few times, most recently when she went to hospital in Humenné – the time she was saved and her sisters weren't. She doesn't look back as the river disappears from view. She doesn't need to: she will return.

Magda sees the rolling hills of the countryside, green pastures, forests, and then the stunningly beautiful Tatra Mountains, more rivers, a lake. She whispers to herself the names of the towns they pass through: Poprad, Ruzomberok, Zilina. The train changes track and an hour later they stop at Nováky.

The guards scream at the passengers to disembark. While some of the elderly need help, Yitzchak doesn't. He strides down the aisle and offers a hand to Chaya and Magda as they climb down, as any gentleman would do. They are relieved to be outside, in the fresh summer air. Magda yawns and stretches.

The prisoners are marched down the length of the platform and onto the street, where the locals of Nováky have gathered to gawp.

'For shame,' Yitzchak mutters.

Magda begins to understand the true nature of what lies ahead of them when some of the prisoners refuse to go any further, insisting on knowing where they are being taken. The Hlinka guards draw their batons and lash out, regardless of age or gender, violently herding the crowd forward. The subdued crowd falls into a heavy silence, a silence composed from despair, thinks Magda. The Mellers hold hands; they can't lose each other, they have already lost too much.

They move towards what is obviously a school at the end of a street: play areas and chalked concrete denote children's games, but there are no children in the building. They are led into the main hall – all glossy floorboards and climbing frames – and from there divided into smaller groups and allocated classrooms. Magda gazes around at the tiny chairs, forgotten pencils, dusty desks. At the front of the room, mathematical equations are scrawled on the blackboard.

Their guard informs them that this is where they will be spending the night, so 'get comfortable'. Yitzchak immediately finds them a space along the wall. Everyone does the same, as the guard watches, a glint of amusement in his eyes. With their backs to the wall, they sit down and stretch out their legs, staking their claim to whatever floor space is available.

'There are toilets and washing facilities outside. Someone will take you when it's your turn,' the guard says.

'What about food?' Yitzchak asks.

'I'm sure you all have food in your cases, old man. Why don't you eat that?' the guard snarls, before turning his back on the room and shutting the door.

190

Yitzchak and the other men in the room get to their feet and head to a corner of the classroom to talk in hushed voices.

'What was that about?' Chaya asks, when Yitzchak returns.

'Typical,' he sighs. 'Everyone has a different plan and no one can agree on which to implement.'

Magda's eye blaze. 'We must do something, though, surely?' She can't seem to rid herself of her hatred of the Hlinka guards, some of whom Cibi was at school with. These old 'friends' of hers, striking the old men and women with batons . . .

'Some want us to stay put and see what happens, others want us to break down the door, beat the guards and run away, and a few want to barter their way out of here.'

'And you? What do you want to do?' Magda persists.

'What can I do? I have no money to buy our freedom and I am too old to fight.' He meets Magda's eyes. 'I can't risk doing anything that might hurt you or your mother.'

'So we wait? Is that what you're saying?' Magda knows her anger isn't very useful, but she can't help it. She wants to spit and kick and punch. 'I want to fight!' she says, vehemently.

'Don't even think about it!' Chaya snaps. Magda abruptly stands up and walks away; she doesn't trust herself to say another word on the subject.

Magda weaves her way in and out of legs and bodies, towards her friend, Zuzana, who she has just spied on the other side of the room.

Zuzana gets to her feet as soon as she spots Magda approaching and the girls find a couple of chairs, out of the earshot of the adults. They talk animatedly about the miracle of their survival, how they escaped the *Shabbat* abductions, how their families managed to endure the ever-diminishing rations of food.

'To begin with, they sent me away,' Zuzana tells Magda. 'To our non-Jewish relatives on the Ukrainian border.'

'Why on earth did you come back?' Magda asks, incredulous.

'They weren't very kind to me. They had a farm and it felt like I was the only one doing any work. I felt like a slave, Magda. But that isn't the reason I left. They'd heard that anyone caught sheltering Jews would be deported, so they sent me home.' Zuzana had been back in Vranov only a couple of weeks.

That first night in the classroom is hot and uncomfortable. Before they settle down, the conversation is focused on food, how much they should eat and how much they should save. Yitzchak produces a pocket-knife and rations their bread, cheese, dry biscuits. One by one, everyone else does the same for their families.

Magda is relieved to be allowed outside the next morning, but her mind is on more than the fresh air. In the small playground, she finds that two other 'classrooms' have also been released. Magda and Zuzana join a group of teenagers.

'I say we attack them,' one boy says, squaring his shoulders.

'And when we're free in the streets of Nováky, what do we do then?' Zuzana asks. No one has an answer for that.

'It's funny,' muses another boy. 'School always did feel like a prison.'

Nothing has been resolved between the teenagers by the time they are shepherded back into the classrooms.

Another day and night passes in a fug of ignorance as to what lies in wait for the prisoners, and Magda's 'class' becomes despondent.

In the afternoon of the third day, a Hlinka guard hands around rations of bread and coffee. From her suitcase, Chaya takes out a jar of pickled vegetables to mask the taste of the stale loaf. She shares it with the other families until the jar is empty.

They endure two long weeks of confinement, with little change to their routine. They are fed twice a day, allowed to exercise for an hour, and the rest of the time they are locked into their classrooms. All talk of rebellion abates after a couple of men who demand an audience with those in charge never return to their families.

By the end of the second week, Magda has lost track of the days. This is how they break our spirits, Magda thinks. But then, one morning, before breakfast, a guard enters the room. When everyone is silent, he glances at his clipboard and calls out, 'Magda Meller. Identify yourself.'

Magda, Chaya and Yitzchak stand up.

'Wait! You're not *all* Magda Meller,' he snaps.

'I'm Magda. This is my mother and grandfather.'

'Then tell your mother and grandfather to sit down.'

'What do you want with her?' says Yitzchak, standing in front of his granddaughter.

'That's none of your business, old man. Now move.'

'We go where she goes!' Chaya insists. 'She's my daughter.'

The guard gives a nod of his head to some guards in the hallway, signalling for them to come inside.

'It's all right, Mumma,' Magda says, as they approach. 'I'm sure I'll be back soon. And save some of that delicious bread for me.' She winks at her mother, but Chaya grabs hold of Magda's sleeve, pulling her away from the Hlinka guards. Magda pats her mother's hand and gently removes it. She can almost hear the bristling tension in the limbs of these boys, and doesn't want to test them. 'Mumma, please. I won't be long.'

'Chaya, please come away. Now!' Yitzchak's eyes are fixed on the guards: they are seconds away from striking her, he knows it. He leads Chaya back to their chairs.

'Don't forget to save me some bread,' Magda calls, with a grin. Her heart is hammering so hard she's amazed she got the words out. She waits for the classroom door to close behind her before she rounds on the guard with the clipboard. 'What do you want with me?'

'You'll see,' is all he says, leading her along the hall towards the back of the school and into the administration block. She enters a large foyer where several other teenagers, mostly girls, are also waiting. The guards abandon them to their fear for two hours. The room falls into silence, insurrection forgotten.

Eventually the guards return, five of them, and the teenagers get to their feet.

Whatever is about to happen to her, she will find out right now.

'You will go with my men,' says one, presumably their leader. 'And you're to leave immediately.'

'Go where?' a boy asks.

The guard fires back the usual answer. "You'll find out when you get there.'

'What about our families?' Magda has finally found her voice. She thinks of her mother and grandfather pacing the small classroom, waiting for her to return.

'They will join you later. Enough questions. In the school-yard I want you to line up and wait for my instructions.'

'You can't do this!' explodes Zuzana. 'You can't separate us from our families!'

'Make some trouble, I dare you,' the guard says. 'And your family will pay for it.' When the room falls silent once more, the guard nods, once. 'Good. Go.'

The schoolyard is empty but, glancing up, Magda catches sight of faces pressed against the classroom windows. She doesn't see her mother. Parents call out to their children as they're led out of the school grounds and away.

Magda recognises the route they're taking: they're heading back to the train station. I was right, she thinks glumly, as they are led onto the platform, where a train idles on the tracks. She has never felt more alone. Is this what Cibi and Livi went through? Did they feel abandoned and terrified? Of course they did. Cold sweat seeps through her thin blouse as she boards the train to watch the town of Nováky disappear.

Magda jolts awake as the train grinds to a halt. How long has she been asleep? The memory of being separated from her mother and grandfather rushes in and the hollow pit in her stomach growls.

They have arrived in the city of Banská Bystrica in central Slovakia.

Once again they're on the march. The midday sun beats down on them. Once more they find themselves in a school, in small classrooms.

'Do you think they will feed us?' a girl asks when the guards have locked them inside. 'I'm starving.'

'I'm sure they will,' placates Magda. The last thing they need is to become hysterical.

'I don't have any other clothes with me,' another girl says.

'None of us do,' says Magda. 'We're all in the same boat, so let's just sit down and get comfortable.'

It is dark when the guards return to take them to the toilets, after which they are fed stale bread and coffee.

Magda hopes to sleep now she has something in her stomach, but the bread feels like a rock in her tummy, and the coffee has left a sour taste in her mouth. The despair she sensed in the crowd, as they marched towards the first school, now washes over her. She stifles her sobs, but around her, no one is making the same effort. Eventually, exhaustion overwhelms her and Magda falls asleep to the sound of girls crying.

Two toilet breaks, an hour of exercise and two meals a day: the same drill as Nováky, but its familiar routine brings Magda no comfort.

One night, Magda dreams of streets filled with Hlinka guards fighting with the townspeople of Vranov. Jews and non-Jews alike battle the men for the sake of the town, for the end of Nazi tyranny.

'You need to get out,' a voice tells her and then says it again louder.

But Magda wants to fight the guards. She's not going anywhere. Her eyes flick open, she isn't dreaming. A figure hovers in the doorway, saying the same words over and over: 'You need to get out.' Magda sits up; everyone is on their feet now, disoriented, alarmed. What is going on?

The stranger is a big man, with dark curly hair that hangs in damp coils around his face. He has a cut on one cheek, bloodied knuckles. He is sweating profusely, breathing hard.

196

'All of you. Come on. You need to run!' he yells, waving at the girls to start moving.

Magda is instantly alert. This is what they've been waiting for, she realises – to be rescued! The girls shove and push each other out of the way as they scramble for the door.

Magda enters the schoolyard just as the first faint rays of sun announce a new day. She stops for a moment to take in the chaos unfolding around her. Young men with Hlinka rifles and batons charge through the crowd of teenagers, urging them off the school grounds, into the town beyond. Magda reaches for the arm of a man. 'Where do we go?' she asks.

'Anywhere. You're free now. Don't you realise what's going on? We're taking back our town, this country!'

'Who *are* you?' shouts Magda as the noise of girls crying, men shouting and guns firing intensifies.

'Resistance fighters!' he yells back. 'Word came through last night to begin our attack. This is happening all over Slovakia right now.' With that, he disappears back into the crowd.

Magda looks around for Zuzana, for any familiar face, but it is chaos. On the street, she runs in the same direction as everyone else. Shop windows are smashed, cars overturned, a bullet screams by her ear. Magda stumbles into a small alleyway to avoid the gunfire. It is a dead end, with a large, foul-smelling dumpster parked outside some double doors at the end of the alley. She tries a handle, but the doors are locked. The noise from the street is getting louder. Men are shouting; are they Hlinka or Resistance fighters? She has no way of knowing. Magda hides behind the dumpster.

Curled up on the ground, hidden from view, she stays there until night falls. Whenever she creeps up the alleyway to peek out, the same scenes of chaos play over and over: people running in all directions, men and guards fighting with fists, with guns and knives, women still crying, screaming for help. Some have suitcases, some have pushchairs loaded with either babies or possessions. Don't they know where to go? Magda wonders as she crawls back to the dumpster and allows sleep to overwhelm her senses.

The next morning it is quiet. Magda watches the street for long minutes, but no one passes and, finally, with a deep breath, she decides to leave the alleyway. There is their prison school at the end of the road and abruptly she turns to walk in the opposite direction. Rounding a corner, Magda finds herself on a large main road, and she is no longer alone. A German tank powers towards her, followed by armed soldiers marching alongside a large canvas-covered truck.

'You there! Hold your ground.' The soldiers raise their guns and Magda stumbles as her head begins to swim. She holds on to a wall for support and an image of the dumpster flashes through her mind. If only she had stayed put. Was it all for nothing in the end?

The guards fire questions at her, barely waiting for her answers.

'Magda Meller,' she replies. 'I'm . . . I'm from Vranov. Yes, I'm a Jew.'

And then she finds herself being led away, a captive once more, to the truck. Pulling aside the canvas flaps, a guard nudges her in the ribs with his rifle. 'Get in.'

The truck follows the tank, stopping every so often to take in new prisoners. Soon, it is full. Magda's companions are men and women and children. All of them have the same terrified, exhausted expressions. Magda realises her own face is a mask of theirs. The truck speeds up now that its hold is full of cargo. When she pulls back the flaps she sees two German military vehicles sailing along behind them. There will be no escaping this time.

They reach their destination in the late afternoon.

This is no empty school – she hears the whine of iron gates creaking open before the truck pulls up and everyone is ordered out. The sun is still shining but it's losing some of its heat. Magda is grateful for the cool breeze.

Razor wire runs along the perimeter of the high concrete walls of the compound. Large four-storey concrete buildings surround a central clearing. Everything is grey.

'It's a prison,' a woman gasps.

A prison guard approaches, and to Magda's horror, he is pointing at her. 'Step forward, miss!' he commands. 'Welcome to Ilava prison.' The officer smiles from ear to ear. 'Your little insurrection has failed – the German Army will not be defeated by a rabble of untrained freedom fighters. You will now be our guests until we decide what to do with you.' He turns away from Magda, to another guard. 'Take them to their cells. But her' – he points at Magda – 'she is to have a cell of her own.'

The second guard grabs Magda's elbow to lead her away, but she shrugs him off. He is taking her towards one of the grey blocks. Inside, the cavernous, echoing space is a hive of cells, metal walkways and fetid air. Magda is placed in a tiny room on the ground floor. As the door clangs shut behind her, she inspects her cell. A wire bed with a thin mattress is pushed up against one wall, a steel toilet without a seat is in the far corner, and there is a small table and a chair at the head of the room. She can almost touch both walls with her fingertips when she spreads her arms. Instead of processing where she is and what will happen to her, Magda lies down on the lumpy bed and loses herself to sleep.

Hours later, the sound of a heavy key turning in the lock startles her awake. Magda is not ready for this, whatever 'this' is. But it's just a guard with her dinner, which he hands over without a word and leaves. She stares at the stew with its indistinguishable brown lumps, and the half loaf of soft bread. For a moment the sight of the food banishes all other thoughts. She eats fast, not tasting the stew or the bread and it is over all too soon. This is the most substantial meal she has eaten in days, in months.

The sun has set, and the lights in her room suddenly go out. For a moment she is in complete darkness. It is then, as her eyes begin to adjust, she turns to the narrow window above the desk, to see the moon. Magda feels her way back to bed.

The next morning, after another good meal of sweet porridge and more bread, she places the chair on the table and ascends the rickety structure to look out of the window. From this position Magda finds herself staring directly into the exercise yard below. She hears whispered conversations, but can't make out any actual sentences. One of the inmates catches her eye. He looks familiar. Very familiar.

'Excuse me,' she calls, thumping the window.

The man stops, looks around.

'Up here. I'm at the window.'

'Hello up there,' he says, with a smile.

'Are you Mr Klein from Vranov?' she asks.

He looks surprised and his smile grows wider. 'I am. And who are you?'

'Magda Meller. You were my maths teacher – you also taught my sister, Cibi. Don't you remember me?'

'Magda! Of course I remember you. But what are you doing here? Is Cibi here too?'

'No. I'm alone. And . . . and I don't really know why I'm here.' Magda spies a guard advancing on Mr Klein and she ducks.

'Move along. Or do you want me to help you?' threatens the guard.

'Look after yourself, Magda. I'll be here tomorrow,' Mr Klein throws over his shoulder.

Now Magda has something to look forward to. For the next three mornings, she has a brief exchange with Mr Klein. He makes her laugh with stories about Cibi's behaviour in class. She knows he wants to cheer her up, because she has told him about what has happened to her family.

He can shed no light on what will become of either of them.

On the fourth day, Magda finds herself being marched out of the block, with no breakfast and no warning. In the prison courtyard, now thronging with hundreds of other inmates, Magda waits her turn to climb into one of the trucks. Those who show the slightest sign of hesitation are encouraged with the swipe of a baton or the butt of a rifle.

It isn't far to the train station, maybe half an hour, and when they reach their destination, instead of carriages with seats, Magda and the others are ordered into cattle wagons.

Inside, it is stiflingly hot and it stinks. She has no water or food – no one does. For the entire journey, Magda alternates between shutting her eyes, praying for sleep and looking for Mr Klein. In neither case is she successful. The journey takes the whole day and the sun is setting when the prisoners are ordered out of the wagons.

Magda leaps down before she is pushed, and lands not on the platform of a station, but onto train tracks. Powerful lights overhead illuminate the scene. Hundreds of people surround her; some have suitcases and bags, as if they're visiting family. Dogs bark as they strain on their leashes, hungry for something. Maybe our blood, thinks Magda, dazed by the lights and faint with thirst.

And then she spies the emaciated figures in the blue-and-white striped uniforms, darting in and out of the crowd, snatching the belongings of the prisoners.

'*Schnell! Schnell!*' new soldiers scream. And Magda knows this German word. *Faster!*

'Where are we?' Magda asks, catching the eye of one of the thin men.

'Welcome to hell,' he says, his eyes darting back and forth between the prisoners.

'Where is hell?'

'Poland. You are in Birkenau.' And then he is gone.

CHAPTER 21

Auschwitz-Birkenau
October 1944

September has rolled into October, bringing with it a change in Cibi's mood. She is snappy and short-tempered with everyone, even Livi. Her concentration is suffering, and when her mistakes are pointed out to her in the post office, she answers back, knowing this is risky behaviour, but at a loss to stop it.

When Cibi leaves the post office each day, it is often to the sound of a train pulling into the camp, and she finds herself walking towards the gates. She has no strong desire to be a spectator of the selections, but she does it anyway, whenever she gets the chance. She feels she owes something to these prisoners, a moment of solidarity perhaps, a few seconds of empathy. She is equally hopeful, yet terrified, of seeing her family step off the trains.

Day after day, she sees the new prisoners being shoved out of the carriages, many falling flat on their faces or backs, only to be trampled by the next in line. It's the same ritual every time: the train arrives and chaos ensues. There is no orderly exit; everything is designed to keep the prisoners in a perpetual state of fear.

'I will be moving to Auschwitz,' Volkenrath tells her one morning. 'To run the post office. Would you like to come too?'

'Why not?' replies Cibi, with a sarcastic smile. 'You know what they say about a change being as good as a rest.'

'Very good. I will sort it out.'

That night, Cibi tells Livi she has put both their names on a list to return to Auschwitz, where they will work in the post office.

The next morning, Cibi is more alert than Livi has seen her in weeks. 'We're not going to Auschwitz,' Cibi announces.

'Why not?' Livi asks, sleepily.

'Last night Mumma came to me in my dreams. She told me to stay in Birkenau.'

'It was just a dream, Cibi! I want to go to Auschwitz! I want to work in the post office. I hate being a messenger. Don't you know what it's like to see the trains every day? Watch them send everyone to the crematoria? Please, Cibi, please can we go to Auschwitz?' Livi pleads.

'No.' Cibi is firm. 'I have to find a way to take our name off the list.'

'Because you had a dream about Mumma?'

'Yes.'

'But what about me, Cibi?' Livi is furious. 'I'm not a dream, I'm real!'

'You have to trust me; we must stay here. I don't know why but we must.'

The fire has gone out of Livi's eyes and now she just looks miserable. 'I am only here because you have kept me alive, Cibi. I wouldn't have survived without you.' She looks at her boots. 'If you say we should stay, then I guess we should.'

Cibi clutches Livi's face in her hands. 'How many times do I have to tell you, you're stronger than you think. It's your strength that keeps me going.'

'How did Mumma look when you saw her in your dream?' Livi suddenly seems very young to Cibi.

'She looked happy, kitten. I could smell her perfume. She was playing with her wedding ring. You know how she was always twisting it on her finger? She said it made her feel like Father was still with us.'

'We'll stay here then, Cibi, don't worry. Mumma is always right.'

Three days later, it is Livi's turn to wake Cibi. Cibi has been more like herself in the days since she dreamed of Mumma, and Livi is relieved.

'Happy Birthday, Cibi,' she whispers.

'How do you know it's my birthday?' Cibi says, sitting up.

'Two days ago, I saw a calendar on one of the Nazi's desks, so I asked him what the date was, and then I worked out that today is your birthday.'

'Thanks, Livi.' Cibi gives her a tired smile. 'I guess we can celebrate the fact that I've survived to see another birthday.'

'Do you want to make a wish?'

'Not really.' Cibi grins at her sister. 'Every single wish I've made over the last couple of years has bitten me.' She waves a hand around the room. 'We still wake up every morning in this place.'

Livi nods her head slowly. 'Well, maybe you can tell Volkenrath it's your birthday and she'll let you have some food from one of the parcels.'

'I don't think she'll care too much that it's my birthday.'

'OK, then. All you're going to get is a "happy birthday" from me. Happy birthday, Cibi.'

Cibi hugs her little sister for a long time. 'Am I really twenty-one?' she whispers into Livi's ear.

'My big sister is twenty-one.'

'Wow.'

As Cibi heads towards the post office, Leah hurries up to her. Leah is from a different block, but Cibi knows her from Vranov. She was transported to Auschwitz a few months after Cibi and Livi arrived. Cibi knows Leah works in the crematoria, although they have never discussed exactly what she does there.

'Cibi, wait. I've been looking for you. I've got something to tell you.' Leah is breathless, excited, bursting with her news.

'Tell me.' Cibi's heart constricts.

'It's Magda! I saw Magda!' she says, grinning.

Cibi freezes.

'I'm telling you, it was Magda. I'm sure of it.'

Cibi swallows hard, heat fills her face and for a moment, her vision swims. She grabs Leah by the arms and shakes her. 'Why didn't you tell me sooner?' Cibi yells at her. 'Tell me where you saw her!'

'Let go of me, Cibi.' Leah shakes herself free and rubs her arms. 'I told you, I've been looking for you. I saw her three days ago.'

'Do you know it's my birthday today, Leah?' Cibi is now suspicious. How could Magda be here and she didn't know it, didn't feel her sister's presence? 'You wouldn't be so cruel to say such a thing just because it's my birthday?'

'No! That's a horrible idea. I'm not a Nazi, Cibi.'

'I'm sorry, Leah.' Cibi is ashamed, and then alarmed when she remembers where Leah works. 'You didn't see her at the crematoria, did you?'

'Yes. No! Not exactly, I *was* at the crematoria but I could see the selection taking place at the station. That's where I saw her.'

'And Mumma, my grandfather?'

'I didn't see them, but that doesn't mean they weren't there, I just didn't see them.'

'Do you know where she is now?' Cibi feels a sudden urgency. She looks around the camp, as if Magda might be standing in the shadows waiting to leap out and announce her presence.

'All I know is that she's with the survivors, and they were heading towards the family camp, but I don't know if that's where they ended up. She is in here somewhere, Cibi. I promise you.'

Cibi pulls the girl to her chest and hugs her tight. 'This is the best birthday present I have ever had, Leah,' she tells her friend.

As desperate as Cibi is to tell Livi about Magda, she decides not to say anything until she knows for sure Magda is here and that their sister is alive.

Once again, she struggles to concentrate on her work, her mind racing, but this time it isn't due to despondency, but to a growing desperation to find out where Magda is. And then she seizes her opportunity. Unwrapping a large parcel containing not only food but women's clothing, Cibi checks to see whether the addressee is alive or dead. She knows everyone from the Theresienstadt family camp is dead, but she checks anyway. A red line has been drawn through the name. Cibi also knows that, according to Leah, the new selection has probably just been taken to the family camp. If Magda is anywhere, she is there.

Cibi takes the parcel to Volkenrath's office. 'I have a parcel that needs to be delivered to the family camp. Is it OK if I take it over?'

'Just do your job,' comes the short reply. Cibi breathes a silent sigh of relief.

To walk or to run? Cibi does both. The longer she takes to get there, the longer she can cling to the possibility that she is about to be reunited with her sister. As she approaches the camp she slows to a dawdle, preparing herself for whatever she might find. She decides to tell Livi nothing if Magda is not there. Right now, her biggest fear is running into her little sister, as the family camp is only metres away from where Livi stands each day at the front gates.

At the gates of the camp, the block leader insists she hands over the parcel. She reads the name and tells Cibi that the person this parcel is addressed to could not possibly be here, that there is no one there from Greece. Cibi tells her that Elisabeth Volkenrath asked her to deliver the parcel personally. The *kapo* holds her gaze for a moment, but then reluctantly waves her through.

Cibi steps inside every block in every row, calling out Magda's name, before moving on to the next. The girls and women are dressed in civilian clothes and they still have their hair. Not for long, though, thinks Cibi grimly. Most of them wear head scarves, making it difficult for Cibi to identify Magda's thick brown hair. Twice, Cibi thinks she sees her, only to be bitterly disappointed.

With only two blocks left to check, Cibi notices a group of young women sitting in the sun, plucking at blades of grass while they talk. Such a normal scene, Cibi feels dizzy at the sight of it. One of the girls stares into the October sun, leaning back on her elbows. Cibi can't see her face, but she recognises the posture.

She shouts, 'Magda!' Cibi's voice is trapped in her throat and all that comes out is a stifled squeak. But one girl in the group is looking at Cibi, bemused by this flushed figure standing perfectly erect, clutching a box and struggling to shout a name. Now the whole group is nudging one another, pointing at Cibi, and finally the girl staring at the sun turns too. For a moment, Cibi can't move, can't speak, she hears a buzzing in her head. Is this a dream, will she wake up?

Or is that really Magda standing up, calling her name, running towards her?

The sisters collide, shrieking. They say each other's names over and over. Now they are crying, asking questions, giving no answers. Right here, right now, the only thing that matters is that they are together.

The girls in Magda's group, painfully moved by this reunion, hug one another too, echoing the sisters' embrace.

'Livi? Where's Livi?' Magda is desperate know.

'She's here, Magda. She's as well any of us can hope to be,' Cibi tells her.

'Can you take me to her? Now?'

More and more girls gather around. There is little enough good news in this place, and just a glimmer of it is contagious. Everyone wants to hear their story, but Cibi is suddenly aware of the potential danger of being discovered in an area where she should not be.

'Which one is your block?' Cibi asks her sister urgently, taking her hand.

But Magda doesn't move for a moment. She is staring at Cibi as if she's finally seeing her.

She looks her up and down slowly, touches her short hair, her shoulders, arms. 'What have they done to you, Cibi?' Magda is crying again, but Cibi can't do this right now. She knows what she looks like, she knows her face is gaunt and her body fleshless. They need to keep moving.

'We can talk later, Magda. Come on.'

Magda's block is the same as any other, featuring desperate girls sitting on their bunks staring into space. Cibi opens the parcel and pulls out the clothes, instructing Magda to change. While she is undressing Cibi hands the box to one of the numb-faced girls.

'There's food in here, you can share it.'

The girl looks inside the box, her eyes go wide. She nods at Cibi, and smiles a 'thank you'.

Once the sisters are outside again, Cibi finds Magda's friends. 'I need your help,' Cibi tells them. 'You won't get into any trouble, don't worry. OK?'

When the girls nod eagerly, Cibi thinks they must like Magda very much to take any sort of risk after what they have been through.

'The block leader saw me come in alone, but I want to leave with Magda. I need you to distract her while we slip out. Can you do that?'

The girls, grinning now, nod again and move towards the front gate. Cibi and Magda press against the walls of the block closest to the gates.

The girls start chattering loudly, arguing as they head towards the gate. Once they have the attention of the *kapo* they escalate their fight, pushing and shoving, now moving past the gate towards the opposite side of the camp. The *kapo* begins to follow them, telling them to stop talking, to walk in orderly lines, to return to their block.

And Cibi grabs Magda's hand and the sisters slip through the gate and speed-walk towards the women's camp. Cibi takes her into Block 21, which is empty. There is still an hour to go before everyone returns. Now they sit on Cibi and Livi's bunk, arms wrapped around each other, in silence.

Finally, Cibi takes a deep breath. There is one question that can't wait for Livi's return.

'Mumma? Grandfather?' is all she needs to say.

Magda looks at her lap, her shoulders begin to heave. 'I don't know where they are,' she sobs.

'It's OK, Magda. It's OK. Were they on your train?'

'I don't think so. I didn't see them, anyway. We got separated a while back.'

'That's good news. Maybe they won't come here at all.' Cibi is gentle with her sister, keen to spare her the painful

211

questioning, but at the same time she needs to know what has happened to their mother.

'We were at home until July,' Magda tells her.

'Really?' Cibi is delighted to hear this. 'Just a few months ago?'

'Yes. But, Cibi, there's so much to tell you – too much. And I want to know so much too. When did you and Livi come here?' Magda looks around the block, at the bunks, the grey concrete, and shivers.

'We can talk about that later, with Livi. Can you tell me a little about Mumma and Grandfather and what happened?'

Magda nods. She wants to talk about them, but at the same time she doesn't want to make their absence real.

'They started clearing Vranov of all the Jews in July and that's when they caught up with us. We were together for a while and then the Hlinka took me away.' Magda is suddenly lost in her memories and falls silent.

'Took you where?' Cibi nudges.

'They took me to Banská Bystrica, to a school, but then the Resistance arrived and freed us.' Magda's eyes shine for a moment as she remembers her night behind the dumpster. 'I was actually free, Cibi, can you believe it? But then the Germans caught me and took me to a prison.'

'A prison?'

'Ilava prison. Do you remember Mr Klein? He was there.'

Cibi looks puzzled. 'Our maths teacher? He was in the prison too?'

'He was. He remembered you. We talked a lot, but then . . .' Magda falters, remembering the cattle wagons.

'What?'

'Then I was brought here, Cibi.'

Just then, girls begin to pour through the doors; it's the end of the day, which means Livi will be back any minute.

'Listen, Magda, I don't want you to be frightened by what you see and hear in this camp – you're safe now, you're with your sisters. I'm going to go outside to prepare Livi. Will you wait here?'

Girls continue to arrive, several glancing Magda's way before collapsing onto their bunks.

Outside Cibi paces. Where is Livi? Why does she have to be late, today of all days? Finally, Cibi sees her and runs to meet Livi, who listens, incredulous, while she learns that Magda is there, in the block, waiting to meet her again. But before she runs inside, Livi's eyes ask another question, and Cibi shakes her head. No, Mumma and Grandfather are not here.

Magda meets Livi in the middle of the vast room, and once more girls gather around to cheer this happy reunion.

That night, for the first time in almost three years, the Meller sisters are together.

The next day Cibi takes Magda to the post office and puts her to work. Luckily, Volkenrath left for Auschwitz the day before and their new supervisor has no idea who should be working there and who shouldn't. Cibi knows none of the other girls will give them away after hearing their story.

'What's her number?' Rosie asks Cibi. Cibi reaches for Magda's left arm, pushing up her sleeve, and is shocked to see bare flesh. Without a number her sister doesn't exist.

'You don't have a number?' Rosie breathes.

Cibi is still staring at Magda's arm. 'She's just arrived, Rosie, of course she doesn't have a number. What will we do?' Cibi is panicking and Magda wants to comfort her, to tell her it doesn't matter, that they will sort it out somehow, but Cibi knows this place, and it is clear that this missing number is a very bad thing.

'I saw the tattooist working outside a few minutes ago,' Rosie says. 'Maybe he's still there, he could do it.'

'What number?' bursts out Magda. 'What are you talking about?'

Cibi pulls up her sleeve, revealing the tattoo on her left arm. Rosie does the same.

'Stay here,' Cibi says, heading for the door.

'Where is she going?' Magda asks.

'To see Lale,' Rosie tells her. 'He'll give you a number, and then you'll be as safe as the rest of us.' Rosie grins, and Magda begins to understand the grim sarcasm of the Birkenau girls.

Outside, Cibi finds Lale sitting at his small desk, patiently inking numbers into the arms of men. Two SS guards hover close by, their backs to the queue, and Cibi takes her chance and approaches the desk.

'Lale.'

'Hello,' he says, looking up from the arm he is about to tattoo.

'I need your help,' Cibi says, urgently.

'Go on.' Lale traces the numbers written on the man's arm with his tools. The man tenses, but doesn't otherwise react.

'My sister is here; I've smuggled her into my block but she doesn't have a number.'

Lale pauses and looks at Cibi. 'Where is she?'

'In the post office. We work in the post office.'

'Then go back to work, and when I'm finished here, I'll find you,' offers Lale, before bending once more to his task.

An hour later, true to his word, Lale pokes his head round the door of the post office, and beckons for the sisters to come outside.

His bag of tools waits for them in the shadows of an adjacent building.

'I'm Lale,' he tells Magda. 'And I hear you need a number.'

Magda is scared. She has seen Cibi's arm, the arms of all the girls in the post office, and by now she knows it will hurt to have this indelible mark stabbed into her flesh.

'I can't give her a four-digit number, Cibi. It will have to be a more recent one.' He pushes up Magda's sleeve and punches A-25592 into her skin. Magda does not flinch.

Cibi exhales a long sigh of relief as the number appears on her sister's arm. Later this evening, she will beg Rita to add her to morning rollcall and, finally, Magda will officially exist in Birkenau.

'Go back to work, girls,' he says to the sisters, packing away his tools. 'Tomorrow will be a good day.'

Over the next few days, as Magda begins to understand the true nature of her sisters' lives in the camp and what they have witnessed, rumours of the Russian military advancing on the Germans offer small slivers of hope.

On a cool morning at the end of October, Livi is delivering a message to the administration block when the first train of the day arrives at Birkenau. Livi pauses to watch the men, women and children on the platform. They are terrified; they probably don't even know where they are.

Children run in and out of the crowd, needing to burn off excess energy after days of being cramped inside a cattle wagon. A little girl is chasing an older boy, the boy bumps into an old man and the girl stops to apologise. He leans over to pat her shoulder and then straightens up to look around.

Something strange is happening inside Livi's chest: it's as though her heart wants to get out. She scrunches her eyes, rubs them hard, but she's not mistaken, she would recognise this man anywhere. She feels hot and then very cold when she sees the woman beside him.

Mumma!

Shifting from foot to foot to get a better look, Livi doesn't know what to do. She can't leave, she can't stop looking at her mother, but she has to move, she has to find her sisters.

Cibi and Magda are sorting through mail when Livi bursts through the door of the post office. From the look on Livi's face, from her glittering eyes and blood red cheeks, Cibi knows something has happened. She needs to take Livi outside before she gets them all in trouble.

'Stay here,' Cibi tells Magda, and pulls Livi through the doors. 'Tell me.'

'It's Mumma, Cibi! She here, and Grandfather.' Livi pauses to catch her breath; she points to the front gates of the camp. 'The train, they just arrived on the train.' Livi places her hands on Cibi's shoulders and shakes her. Her sister's eyes have glazed over; she too is struggling to breathe, but they don't have time for that. She shakes Cibi again. 'We have to help them!'

'But Magda . . . We need Magda, too,' Cibi pants.

216

'Two of us running out is bad enough, Cibi.' Livi is tugging on Cibi's sleeve to *move*. 'Magda is new here – she gets caught, she dies.'

The girls cross the short distance between the post office and the train. Standing side by side, they watch the hundreds of new arrivals dragging their feet along the platform as the prisoners in their familiar striped uniforms dart in and out of the cattle wagons grabbing their possessions.

'I can't see them,' says Cibi, her eyes desperately searching the faces.

'Over there!' Livi points. 'I just saw them over there.'

Cibi freezes as her eyes come to rest on the SS officers who will be handling the selection. 'Kramer, Livi. I have to talk to him,' she says.

'No, Cibi! You can't. Please!' Livi grabs hold of Cibi's arm, but Cibi isn't listening to her. She shakes free and strides towards the officers. As she approaches, the men turn and look at her. Cibi feels very small, a weak animal in the midst of powerful hunters, but she gathers her courage.

'Commander Kramer. I have just seen my mother and grandfather on the platform. I beg you to spare them.' Cibi doesn't cry – she's too scared to cry, but her hands are shaking. She digs her nails deep into the palms of her hands, and the pain makes her brave. 'They are all I have left in this world.'

Kramer looks her up and down and gives a sharp shake of his head. 'I have decided their fates – not you, little girl. Your mother and grandfather will be with their god soon enough.'

'I am begging . . .' Cibi doesn't see the hand that strikes her. It happened so fast, knocking her off her feet. From the ground, she stares up into the sneering, hateful face of the German officer. She feels the urine slip out of her body. Suddenly, there is a commotion on the platform and, for a moment, Kramer turns away, distracted. Cibi feels herself being dragged to her feet as someone whips the scarf from her head. She is surrounded by other girls, all of whom have removed their headscarves. Kramer turns around again, looking for Cibi, but the girls, identical in their emaciation, stare back. Unable to identify Cibi amongst them, he turns away.

'Come on, run!' Livi says urgently as she grabs Cibi's hand and pulls her away towards the fence that divides them from the new arrivals.

The trauma of having been assaulted by Kramer flashes away as she and Livi once again turn their focus on the hundreds of men, women and children slowly walking towards the building, where she knows they will be told to strip naked before being taken to their deaths.

'There! There they are!' Cibi suddenly screams. Her hands grab the fence, shaking it as if to bring it down. Livi is frozen, her mouth open and soundless. Cibi tries to call out but her voice too, has suddenly deserted her. Another girl joins them. She doesn't need to be told the sisters are looking for their mother. It's obvious.

'Mrs Mellerova!' the girl shouts. Once, twice, three times.

Chaya hears her name and turns around.

'Mumma,' Cibi cries, banging her fists on the wire. 'Mumma! Mumma!'

The snaking line of prisoners draws closer, there are only a few feet between them now.

'It's me, Mumma! Cibi!'

Chaya is looking around, her eyes failing to find her daughter. Yitzchak's head is cocked, catching Cibi's words in the air. And then Chaya sees her, and stumbles. Yitzchak catches her. 'Cibi? My Cibi?' her mother cries.

Mother and grandfather hang on to each other, diminished.

'Yes, Mumma, it's me!' Cibi is struggling to speak – she can barely stand to look at them; her proud, once erect mother is gaunt, hunched, hanging on to an old man.

'And Livi?' her mother cries. 'My baby?'

Cibi has forgotten Livi is standing mute beside her. She realises her mother and grandfather have not recognised her. She puts her arm around Livi's shoulders, drawing her close.

'She's here Mumma. Here's Livi.'

'Mumma,' Livi croaks. 'I need you.'

'My baby!' Chaya wails, as Yitzchak catches her once more, her legs threatening to give way. But they can't stop, the line is moving.

Cibi and Livi walk alongside them, their eyes locked onto their mother.

Chaya is trying to say something, but her words are strangled, unintelligible.

'Magda!' shouts Yitzchak. 'Is Magda with you?'

'Yes! She's here. She's fine,' Cibi calls back.

Cibi watches Yitzchak lift Chaya's hand to his mouth and kiss her fingers. He is saying something to Chaya: his lips are moving but the sisters can't hear him. The old man is smiling. Smiling and nodding.

'You are all together, my child,' he says. The line of prisoners is turning away now, her mother is disappearing into the nameless crowd.

219

'Mumma, Grandfather,' pleads Cibi. 'I'm sorry. I'm sorry. I'm sorry.'

'Look after your sisters, my darling.' Her mother's final words.

'Mumma,' Livi whimpers.

For the first time since leaving her home almost three years ago Cibi collapses. She sits on the ground, sobbing. In a few minutes it will all be over: her mother will be a corpse, she will never see Grandfather again. She hangs on to the fence, shaking it, shaking it, willing them to turn round and come back.

Livi kneels beside her, peeling her fingers from the fence.

'They're gone, Livi,' she says, rubbing her face.

'I know, I know,' Livi whispers, kneeling and hugging her sister. The girls are crying hard now, beyond the comfort of each other's arms.

'Girls, you can't stay here, it's not safe.' A male prisoner hovers over them, looking around anxiously. 'Come on. You need to get up and go back to your block or wherever you should be.'

Their arms around one another, the sisters head back to the post office in silence.

'You need to go back to work, Livi,' says Cibi, at the door. 'Don't give them any reason to come looking for you. I'll tell Magda about . . .' The words catch in her throat, but Livi understands. She kisses her sister hard on both cheeks and turns to leave.

Magda is unaware of the horrors of the killing chambers, has not yet witnessed the piles of bodies wheeled through the streets towards the crematoria; all she knows is that her mother and grandfather are dead, and that she will never see them again. She buries her face in her hands and sits down to cry.

Before the day is over, a friend who works in the *Kanada* next to the crematoria, enters the post office and asks Cibi to step outside.

'I think this belongs to you,' she says, handing over a plain brown handbag. Cibi takes it, immediately recognising it as her mother's. She smells it, holds it to her chest and closes her eyes. 'How did you know?' she whispers.

'There's a photo inside of your sister. And . . . and a wedding ring.'

Cibi flicks the clasp and opens the bag. The photo shows Livi at thirteen years old, smiling happy. And then she finds the ring. Slipping it onto her finger she wonders why her mother ever took it off. She'll never know. She places the items back in the handbag and snaps the clasp shut.

* * *

Cibi is back at the fence the next day, watching the new arrivals endure the selection. She feels empty inside, depleted. As the officers attempt to corral the prisoners into lines, Cibi has the sudden urge to hammer on the fence and scream at them to *run*, that they are headed for the gas chamber to die. Turn on your captors! she wants to yell. Do something!

But she is not brave enough, and she has to stay alive herself, for her sisters.

But the prisoners are not being killed today; instead, they are being marched towards the Hungarian camp. Why?

But Cibi has seen enough. She doesn't understand what's going on, why a selection hasn't taken place and it's a waste of her time trying to figure it out. Turning away, she hears a man's voice from the crowd calling her name. For a moment she feels disorientated, as though her grandfather has somehow survived and is now amongst this new group of arrivals.

She peers into the sea of figures until she alights on a group of very familiar faces. No, it can't be, but it is.

Uncle Ivan and Aunt Helena and their children.

Cibi's heart is racing, her emotions churning. She is over-joyed to see them, heartbroken they are here. Will she have to watch them too, being driven towards the gas chamber one day?

Her aunt and uncle have moved on but, for now, they are safe.

Cibi returns to the platform the next day and the next, observing that all the new arrivals are now being housed in the Hungarian camp, that no one is being exterminated. Are the gas chambers broken? she wonders. But what crushes Cibi and her sisters is the idea that their mother was murdered the day before these killing machines fell silent.

Every night now, Cibi lies awake, mulling over this cruel idea. Nothing Magda or Livi say brings her any comfort.

On Sunday, the three sisters make their way to the Hungarian camp, where they wait for Uncle Ivan to appear. When he does, the girls call and wave until he sees them. Cibi is glad he is on his own – this will be hard enough even without the presence of the children and her aunt.

'My girls,' he says in tears. 'I hoped never to see you in here.'

'We hoped the same, Uncle,' says Magda. She finds she can't look at her him, can't begin to tell him the news he is waiting to hear. She glances at Cibi. *You do it*, her eyes tell her, and Cibi understands.

'Mumma and Grandfather, Uncle . . .' Cibi begins. Livi is already crying, her face buried in Magda's shoulder. Ivan seems to visibly deflate before their eyes. He leans against the fencing, his fingers gripping hold of the wire.

'Tell me,' he says, his voice thick.

But Cibi doesn't know how to say the words. Should she tell him of Grandfather's smile? Of Mumma's parting entreaty, of the look on her mother's beautiful face, stoic and prepared to meet her terrible fate? In the end, she needs only two words. 'They're gone.'

Their fingers push through the holes, entwine, and the family weeps.

CHAPTER 22

Auschwitz-Birkenau
Winter 1944

It is winter when the rumours start circulating. The girls from the administration block are privy to the talk amongst the officers, and they share everything they hear. They are adamant the Germans are losing the war, the Russians are on their doorstep. And why shouldn't they believe these rumours, when the sound of shelling, night after night, keeps the girls awake? Aerial battles are fought overhead. The SS is now destroying the records of all the Jews, all the other prisoners, gypsies and Russian POWs they have killed.

This is why the murders have stopped.

In a frenzy of activity, the prisoners, men and women, find themselves allocated to new work details. Both Livi and Cibi are informed that they are being moved back to Auschwitz to work and to live, but Magda is to remain in Birkenau. Rita, despite their pleas, cannot help them – no one can. Once again the sisters will be separated.

'It won't be for long,' Cibi reassures Magda. 'We'll find a way to get back to you.'

But Magda is despondent. She doesn't understand this place and without Cibi and Livi to guide her she worries she will put a foot wrong and end up dead. On the morning her sisters depart for Auschwitz she refuses to wave them goodbye and instead remains in the block. She is angry with them; she can't help feeling abandoned, and soon she falls into the all-too familiar despair for her mother – if they had only been allowed to stay together, she could have entered the gas chamber by her side. Maybe this would have been better, she doesn't know anymore.

On the day of their departure from Birkenau, Cibi and Livi dress in every item of clothing they own, and after rollcall hundreds of girls begin the march back to Auschwitz, back to the place where this nightmare began.

Now, just like the other girls in the block, Magda doesn't have a job to go to. The days unravel, and she spends more and more time curled up in the bunk she once shared with her sisters. There is no comfort in having all this space.

Only a few officers are out in the snow, ordering the girls through the gates, telling them to move faster, calling them lazy, work-shy, filthy Jews. But it's not the soldiers that Livi is afraid of: she has seen Isaac. He is wrapped up warm against the cold, sharing a joke with the officers when he sees Livi. He raises a hand in greeting, Livi stares at her boots. She is afraid she is going to wet herself.

'I see you, girlie,' is all he says, as she joins the long line of girls walking away from Birkenau.

She doesn't speak a single word the entire length of the journey, but then neither does Cibi. Each girl is wrapped up in her thoughts, but they are broadly similar thoughts. Will they die before they reach Auschwitz? Despite their layers, it is freezing. Why can't Magda join them? Will she be safe at Birkenau? And finally, if they are to die, why can't they do it together? Livi is shaken by her encounter with Isaac, but takes some comfort in the fact that she no longer has to worry about seeing him around the camp.

Now they pass through the gates Cibi had hoped to never lay eyes on again. Livi had almost stopped believing Auschwitz had ever existed, but here they are, cut off from Magda, only two miles up the road, but a universe away.

Livi and Cibi are put to work in the Auschwitz post office together, sorting letters and parcels as they arrive, in much the same way Cibi did in Birkenau. They are sent from families throughout Europe and beyond. No effort is made to locate the addressees, no journal consulted to see where the prisoner might be, whether they're dead or alive. Cibi continues to open the parcels and separate the contents into edible and inedible, and burn the letters. The girls work to the sound of planes flying overhead, bombs dropping. Everyone wants to stay inside these days, fearful of attack, but not Cibi. She wants to be outside to see their saviours before they arrive, and welcome them.

One morning, on her break and lost in her thoughts, Cibi finds herself under the *Arbeit Macht Frei* sign. She looks up and wishes a bomb would drop on it right now, even though she stands directly beneath the evil signage. She doesn't really register the black car which has just driven through the gates until it pulls up beside her.

The window rolls down to reveal a pretty officer with strawberry-blonde hair. 'What are you doing here?' Volkenrath asks. She seems genuinely pleased to see Cibi.

'They moved us back here,' Cibi says, and then adds, desperately, 'We've been separated from Magda.'

'And who is Magda?'

'My sister. There are three of us, but she only just arrived a few weeks ago. She is still in Birkenau. Can you help me?'

Cibi's pleas seem to fall on deaf ears, because Volkenrath doesn't respond. Instead, she rolls up her window and the car moves off.

Neither Livi nor Cibi sleep that night, worrying that Cibi has put Magda in danger. The officers, however friendly they might appear, are not at the beck and call of the prisoners. They are by turns indifferent, or deliberately cruel.

Cibi can't settle down to work the next morning, and once again finds herself back at the main gates. She watches cars and trucks pull in and out of the camp. No one pays her any attention. And why would they? A half-starved wretch who can't even keep the promise she made to her father. Magda was here and she lost her. She wonders what would have happened if they had simply refused to leave Birkenau. Cibi shivers.

Once more, Cibi fails to register the same large black car roll up and stop next to her. Volkenrath is winding down her window and Cibi gulps, convinced she is about to be castigated for dawdling.

'Hey, Cibi,' say Volkenrath, her painted lips parting in a smile. 'I have something for you. Here is your jewel.' She rolls up her window and Cibi wonders what kind of cruel trick is about to played on her.

The passenger door opens and a figure steps out and shuts the door behind them. The car speeds off, leaving Magda in its wake. She stands in the snow, wearing all her clothes.

'That officer is a good friend to you, Cibi,' is all Magda says, before she bursts into tears.

'They're hanging on to whatever scrap of humanity they have left,' Cibi says, bitterly, as she pulls Magda into her arms. 'I'm not grateful to them for anything. But we're together again, as we should be, and that's all that matters.'

As the girls head back to Cibi's block, they notice the ladders propped against the naked trees lining the streets of Auschwitz. Men are attaching colourful lights to the bare branches.

'I guess it's nearly Christmas,' Magda says.

'Christmas in a death camp.' Cibi sighs. 'Nothing makes any sense anymore.' She looks at her sister properly for the first time in days. 'So, what happened?'

As the sisters walk, Magda tells Cibi the whole story. She was working in the post office when Volkenrath walked in and called out her name. Before whisking her out of Birkenau, for ever, she instructed Magda to return to her block and grab her meagre bundle of clothes.

'Then we got in her car and she didn't say another word. I was too scared to ask her where we were going.'

'Maybe she's pregnant at last,' says Cibi, grinning. 'Finally found a bit of compassion in her dried-up heart.' Cibi looks wistful for a moment and then takes Magda's hand. 'Come on. Let's go and find Livi. I don't know how many times the poor thing can handle being separated from you.' But

Cibi tugs at Magda's sleeve before they enter the post office. 'Did you see Uncle Ivan before you left?' she asks.

Magda just shakes her head.

Livi looks up from the parcel she is unwrapping when her sisters walk through the door. Her face breaks into a huge smile.

'I knew you would come,' is all she can manage as she buries her face in Magda's shoulder.

'Hmm,' says Magda. 'Even so, I'm going to miss having our old bunk all to myself.'

That evening, the sisters join the other prisoners, along with the officers and guards, to walk the streets of Auschwitz and marvel at the bright lights that cover every tree. It is a crisp, clear evening, and the buildings and trees are covered with a thick layer of snow. Flakes dance in the glow of the perimeter tower lights, throwing a kaleidoscope of colour around the camp. For a short time, the sisters forget themselves as they wander this colourful landscape. It is almost beautiful enough to instil a tiny drop of hope in their hearts.

The prisoners are given Christmas day off, and extra rations. The revelries of the SS can be heard throughout the camp, but the girls ignore them. Instead, they gather to talk about past Hanukkah celebrations, reliving their favourite memories, when Cibi pipes up that Christmas Day, 1942, is her favourite. Livi stares at her sister in disbelief. That year she had been weak with typhus and, for a while, she had wondered if she was going to survive. But it was their 'feast' of soup with noodles and meat that had restored her energy, just enough to get to work the next day.

Hearing this story for the first time, Magda weeps. 'Remember our promise?' she says, finally.

'I'll never forget it,' Cibi replies.

'Me, neither. Even though I don't remember making it,' Livi chimes in.

'You said "I promise" in your little voice when Father asked you to honour our pact,' Magda says, with a giggle.

'No, Magda! She said "I pwomise"!'

'Shall we say a prayer for Father and Mumma and Grandfather?' Magda is suddenly solemn.

'I stopped praying a long time ago. Can we just talk about them, instead?' says Cibi.

Magda decides not to probe, this evening is about Mumma.

'I miss Mumma's cooking, especially her bread,' says Livi, sighing.

'I miss going to the bakery with her every Monday morning with the dough for the loaves. And I also miss going back to collect them later,' Magda recalls. 'I really loved those walks with her. Just the two of us.'

The girls spend the rest of the day in a reverie of nostalgia. They talk about their lives back in Slovakia, about their parents and the rows and squabbles they shared, but it's only Cibi who has any solid recall of their father. Somehow, Magda's presence has helped Cibi to look back, to be less afraid that once she lets herself remember happier times, she will no longer be able to carry on.

The next day, it's back to work and all three sisters head for the post office to open what they now call 'the death packages' – their recipients deceased.

'Hey! Look what I've got here!' Magda's cry jolts everyone out of their silent thoughts.

The girls stare at the large fruit cake which Magda has unwrapped. The smell of dried fruit and cake permeates the air.

'Let's eat it. Fast,' a voice says.

'It shall be our Christmas cake,' Livi agrees.

Cibi picks up the note it came with and her face falls. 'Stop! Stop!' she says. 'Don't touch it.'

The girls turn their puzzled frowns on Cibi. 'Listen,' she says, holding up the note. '"If you eat the contents of this package, you will die," it says. Put it back in its box,' Cibi instructs Magda. 'And no more food is to be eaten from packages.'

The mood in the camp is tense as the new year approaches. The girls are ordered to remain inside after the Christmas celebrations. The bombing they hear throughout the day and night is getting closer. Planes fly over the camps, and missiles are dropped. On occasion, the girls huddle together, their hands over their ears as the shelling outside grows louder. And once, even the officers joined them, charging into the block and slamming shut the door, hunkering down in an opposite corner with the same terrified expressions on their faces as the girls.

On 3rd January, the girls venture outside for the first time that year. The sun is shining and the sisters turn their faces to the sky, when a loud banging suddenly breaks out nearby. They follow the sounds to a courtyard, the same courtyard where Cibi and Livi were lined up when they first arrived at Auschwitz. A figure is staring up at the structure being erected. It is Volkenrath.

'We're making our last stand,' she cheerfully tells the sisters.

'What is it?' asks Cibi.

'Don't you recognise them? They're gallows.'

Cibi steps back, and then Magda and Livi do the same. The banging gets louder as planks of wood are added to the construction.

'You're going to hang us?' she gasps.

'They're not for you. They're for the four girls who smuggled in explosives to blow up Crematoria Two. Tomorrow they will pay for their crimes. And you will get to watch.'

Cibi and her sisters look at the gallows, but specifically at the four hooks from which the nooses will be strung.

That evening, the girls are warned that they are not to look away when the 'criminals' are hanged. They are to watch every second of it, or they too will die.

Sleep does not come easily that night, and equally, breakfast is hard to swallow the next morning.

The blocks stand together in long rows in front of the now completed gallows. They don't have to wait long before the girls, their faces scarred and bruised, are marched up the wooden steps.

For several minutes an SS officer berates those watching. He repeats the threat that any girl who looks away will be the next to be hanged. Cibi notes the strong presence of SS officers, their eyes trained not on the gallows but on the girls.

Cibi stands between Magda and Livi, holding their hands. They have been told that the four girls smuggled the powder explosives in under their fingernails, and in the hems of their dresses, from the ammunition factory where they worked. The explosives had been received by those in the men's camp who planned to carry out the detonation, with the aim of the destruction of one of the Nazis' killing factories. Cibi wonders what happened to the men, but only for a moment, because now they have to focus on these young women, whose courage and acts of resistance have cost them their lives.

'Think of Mumma,' whispers Magda, as the four girls are instructed to climb onto the chairs beneath the hovering nooses. 'Do you both remember when we took the linden tree leaves home in the sheet? How thrilled she was?'

Both Cibi and Livi nod slowly, their eyes trained on the ropes being secured around the girls' necks.

'Fill your minds with her face. Her beautiful face.' Magda's voice catches.

'She made us tea with the fresh flowers, didn't she?' says Cibi. The chairs are kicked away and Cibi gasps but she doesn't look away.

'It was bitter,' says Livi. 'The flowers should be dried first. But I remember the cake.'

'It was a fruit cake . . .' Magda begins, as the girls begin to twitch.

It is only after the girls have stopped twisting in the frigid air, and the senior SS officers have left, that the girls are allowed to return to their blocks. No one speaks. There is nothing to say.

For the next four days, the bodies of the dead girls swing from the gallows.

Cibi notes the new year: 1945. She wonders where they will be in January 1946 – surely not in this place. Maybe they will be dead. But, a couple of weeks later, the sisters and everyone else in their block are told they will be leaving.

'Where?' a voice calls, speaking out loud the question on everyone's mind.

'Just a walk,' Volkenrath tells them. Cibi can read nothing in her expression.

'How far?' Cibi asks, confident Volkenrath will answer her.

'If I knew I would tell you,' comes the reply.

'Are we free? Are you letting us go?' Cibi persists.

Volkenrath smirks. 'That is not what's going on. You will be escorted to another camp.' She claps her hands once, twice. 'And you should thank us – we're taking you away from all this bombing.'

'Do we have a choice? I would rather stay here where we have a roof over our heads and take my chances with the bombs,' another voice cries.

Volkenrath snaps to attention. 'You do not have a choice. I didn't have to come here and tell you anything.' With that she storms out.

Once again, the girls dress in every single item of clothing they own, and then they drape their blankets around their shoulders. Once they are gathered outside, under a new shower of snow, they are told to start marching.

They pass through the gates Cibi and Livi first entered three years earlier. Now, they march out together, the three of them. The sisters turn their heads to read the letters emblazoned above, *ARBEIT MACHT FREI.*

'Does this mean we are free?' Livi asks.

'Not yet . . . Not yet,' Cibi answers.

Magda looks at her sisters. They are so thin, weakened by the years of struggle. How will they possibly survive this weather?

CHAPTER 23

Death March
January 1945

Cibi, Magda and Livi stumble, trip and catch themselves time and again as they plough the deep snow, arm in arm. They can no longer feel their fingers, their faces. The bombing draws closer. Surrounded by thousands of girls and women, all departing Auschwitz, the sisters head into the unknown.

'Stay on your feet,' hisses Cibi. Gunshots echo in the air as those who can no longer keep pace, those who have collapsed into the snow as though it were a bed, are dispatched with a bullet. 'If one of us goes down, we all go. Remember that,' she adds. They won't let go of each other, and they won't fall, they each decide.

Livi turns round to survey the multitudes of women joining the throng.

'Look, Cibi, it's the women from Birkenau,' says Livi. Hundreds of women have been added to the queues streaming away from Auschwitz.

Cibi feels like lying down and dying right there on the ground, despite her advice to her sisters. They are mere specks in this vast landscape of women marching towards yet another hellish unknown. Is God watching us, she wonders? Of course he isn't. Cibi eyes the guards who keep pace alongside the women, shouting '*Schnell!*' and lashing out with the butts of their rifles, their icy fists.

'Remember the promise!' urges Magda, rousing Cibi from her despair. Her sister has not endured the beatings, the starvation, the degradation she and Livi have endured. Magda is still hopeful, so Cibi inhales a stream of icy air and releases a fog of breath.

'We stay together no matter what,' she responds.

'We are strongest when we are together,' adds Livi. The young girl's cheeks are hollow, but they are pink. Cibi is glad, she looks *alive*.

They walk on. There are no breaks. No food or water, but when the officers move away to hammer at some poor girl who lacks the strength to carry on, they scoop up hand-fuls of snow to melt on their tongues.

'Remember how we used to make chocolate snow?' Magda asks, after a long period of silence.

For Cibi, the image of her mother stirring a steaming pan at the stove, amid the companionship of her family, feels like a scene from a story she read a long time ago. But she drags herself into the conversation, for the sake of her sisters.

'It would be too hot, and we'd go outside . . .' begins Cibi.

'. . . and add snow to it!' Livi is staring into the sky. Icy flakes land on her face. Her hand closes around the little knife, deep in her pocket.

'Frozen chocolate, you used to call it,' Magda says. 'If only we had some cocoa and a bit of sugar, we could make some now.'

'The sugar won't dissolve without boiling water, though,' notes Livi, wisely. 'We need more than hot water and sugar and chocolate.' She turns her face away from the skies and stares at her boots. 'We need Mumma.'

Cibi draws Livi close. This is why she has to keep going. She can't let them give up now. 'She's with us, Livi,' Cibi says. 'And Grandfather. They're walking with us right now. We just can't see them.'

'I can feel them,' Magda whispers. 'Mumma is next to you, Livi, and Grandfather is beside Cibi.'

'Well, I can't feel them.' Livi's voice breaks. 'And I'm not a baby, to be fed fairy tales.'

'Would it help if I told you a story?' Magda asks. 'Not a fairy tale,' she adds, hastily.

Livi is still staring at her boots. 'Is it a happy story?' she asks, quietly.

'It is. It's about the last time Grandfather and I went into the forest for kindling.'

'Tell us the story. Please, Magda,' Cibi says, desperately. Anything to keep their minds off this endless torture through the snow.

'It was a glorious summer day,' begins Magda. 'Everything was alive in the forest, even the ferns waved to us when we entered. Grandfather was pulling that funny old cart of his, you know the one? The heat, it's hard to imagine it now, but it was a blanket around my shoulders.' Magda pauses, lost in her own memories.

'Keep going,' urges Livi.

'Well, we were quite a way in, the bees and insects were going crazy, when I came across a sunny clearing.' Magda turns to her sisters, a question in her eyes. 'You remember the big oak, don't you?'

Cibi and Livi nod. The girls are still walking, taking care where to place their feet, wary of rocks beneath the snow which might upend them any moment. Their toes are numb, every part of them feels dead, but Magda's story of sunshine is beginning to thaw their hearts at least.

'I noticed a flash of colour, just by the trunk of the oak, so I ran over to it.'

'What was it?' Livi asks, fully engrossed. 'And don't you dare say an elf or fairy.'

'Don't be silly, Livi. This is a true story.' Magda wants to get it all out now. She wants her sisters to feel the heat on their skin, to be dazzled by the blinding glare of the sunshine when she looked up into the canopy of leaves. To feel their ears twitch with the buzzing of insects.

'It was the most magnificent sword lily I have ever seen. Just one. Those beautiful pink flowers didn't look real. Grandfather and I stared at it for ages, and then he asked me if I knew the meaning of the word "gladiolus".'

'Do you?' Livi says, her forehead scrunching, as if she's trying to recall the meaning herself.

'I do. Don't you?'

'I do,' Cibi says.

'I don't,' Livi says. 'Magda, please keep going with the memory. What did you say?'

Cibi marvels at their younger sister. They are surely headed for their deaths, yet she is lost in Magda's story, caught up in the summer's day, in the appearance of a magical flower.

'The gladiolus symbolises strength, Livi,' Cibi tells her.

'And do either of you know what family of plant the gladiolus belongs to?' Magda asks. She is stamping her feet as she walks, trying to get a little blood flowing into her toes.

'Don't tell me! Don't tell me, I know this. Just give me a minute,' says Livi.

Cibi and Magda give her a few moments.

'Iris! It belongs to the iris family,' Livi blurts out, with pride.

'Well done, Livi. And now a harder question. Do you know what the iris symbolises?' asks Cibi.

Livi thinks for a moment and slowly shakes her head. 'I don't think I ever knew that,' she says, quietly.

'Hope, little sister,' says Magda. 'It means hope. Seeing that sword lily before we were taken away gave me strength and hope. And that's why I'm telling you both this story now. We Meller girls must stay strong and carry hope in our hearts.'

After a long silence, Livi says, 'I can feel Mumma and Grandfather with us now.'

The girls are still marching as night falls. The sound of bombing still stutters in the distance, but the noises are definitely moving away. Someone whispers that the Russians are winning, driving the Germans back, and that they are marching away from the Russian fighters. The sisters struggle to free their feet from the snow with each step. It is now

past their knees, but they keep going because the only altern-
ative is a bullet.

They walk through the night and into the dawn, into
the day. The snow has eased up and the sun shines on the
thousands of walkers. Cibi, Livi and Magda step over the
thin corpses of those who could not take one more step.
They watch as other girls pause to remove the shoes of
the dead.

'How can they do that?' gasps Magda.

'We've seen worse,' says Cibi. 'And if we needed extra
clothing, I'd do the same.'

While the sun shines and the road ahead looms long
and white, Cibi begins to wonder which of the sisters will
collapse first. She hopes it's her. She is struggling to breathe
now; it takes effort to fill her lungs and even to expel
the air.

'Halt!' The SS guards are suddenly animated, screaming
at the girls to stop walking. The sisters freeze in place. They
each have the same thought: they will die now, out here in
the anonymous Polish landscape. Their bodies will be buried
by the falling snow only to be discovered, perfectly preserved,
in the spring.

But their guns are holstered. Instead, the officers direct
the hundreds of women off the road towards a large barn
into which they slowly file. Dozens at a time collapse onto
the straw covering the ground.

'My feet are dead,' groans Livi, reaching for her shoes.

'Don't take them off,' Cibi warns her. 'Your feet will swell
and then you'll never get them on again.' Cibi gathers hand-
fuls of straw and packs them around her sister's feet. 'This
will warm them up.' She does the same for Magda and then
for herself.

The sisters hunker down, keeping on their coats, laying the blankets they've been wearing across them. Despite their hunger and the bitter cold, they fall fast asleep.

The officers tell them it's time to go and the sisters jump to their feet. Magda urges those around them to stand up, not to give up now. Some women never wake up, and their shoes and coats and cardigans are carefully and gratefully removed by those who need them. Those who refuse, begging the officers for a little longer in the shelter of the barn, are executed on the spot.

They are on the road again. The sun is shining, but its warmth is an illusion; within minutes, the girls are chilled to the bone. The snow is packed hard and the women slide over the ground.

'A town!' gasps Livi. Ahead, the outline of dark buildings against the blue sky. They make slow progress, but the fact they have a destination drives the women forward.

'Oh, dear,' says Cibi, as they enter the town. She points towards the train station at the top of the main street. 'This isn't good.'

The 'train' is a line of open-air coal wagons.

'At least we can stop walking for a bit,' encourages Magda.

'*Schnell, schnell!*' the officers command, and the women climb into the filthy compartments. Black coal dust sticks to their damp clothes; it finds its way into their noses, eyes and mouths. The women cough and splutter as they stand, once again, packed tight, unable to move an inch.

As the train pulls away it starts to snow.

The wagons rumble along the tracks. No one has said a word for hours. It's still very cold, but the fact that they are so close together provides a little insulation.

'Can you hear the fighting?' says Cibi. And then the wagons jerk as the ground beyond explodes, scattering shrapnel over their heads. It can't be avoided, there's no room to duck. The women swerve, stumble, slip on the wet floor.

One woman and then another and another pass out. They're dead already, thinks Cibi, and soon enough, their features become rigid, their eyes glaze and mouths gape. Cibi turns away from these fresh corpses and catches a conversation between a few of the women. Should they throw the bodies over the side? They'd have more room if they did. But no one moves.

In the early hours of the next morning, the coal wagons arrive at another camp. Cibi hears the name 'Ravensbrück' uttered by the SS guards.

As the sisters pass through the gates, Cibi notices a very young girl sitting on the icy ground, weeping. Cibi nudges her sisters and moves to kneel beside the girl, whose teeth are chattering. She is blue. She can't be more than ten or eleven years old.

'Have you got separated from someone? Your mumma?'

The girl shakes her head and Cibi reaches for her hand. 'Would you like to come with us?' The girl's watery eyes meet Cibi's. She nods.

Cibi helps her to her feet.

'These are my sisters, Magda and Livi. Can you tell us your name?'

'Eva,' comes a whisper.

'Eva, you can stay with us until we find someone you know,' Cibi says.

'I don't know anyone anymore,' Eva tells them in her quiet voice. 'They're all dead. It's just me.'

Livi puts her arm around Eva, hugging her as they walk.

There is no one to tell them where to go or what to do. Hundreds of women mill about the camp, seeking shelter – it's the most they can hope for right then. Their SS guards have abandoned them.

Eva and the sisters are finally accepted into a block. The bunks are all full, they will have to make do with the floor, but Cibi is simply grateful they are no longer outside. There is warm water flowing from the taps in the bathrooms and Cibi soaks her scarf to wipe away the coal dust from their faces.

'Strength and hope,' Magda mutters, as Cibi wipes.

'I don't need strength and hope,' says Livi. 'I need food.'

The sisters have not eaten a morsel for two days, and it becomes clear there is not enough food in this camp to feed its inmates and the new arrivals.

'They are looking for volunteers to go to another camp,' Eva tells them. 'We might get some food there.'

The four girls, rested and washed, head for the administration block and, an hour later, they are on their way to Retzow, a sub-camp of Ravensbrück, in the back of a truck.

'Stay strong, sisters,' mumbles Cibi. But her thoughts are scattered. Why is she asking them to stay strong when she feels so weak, so utterly drained of energy and hope? They will die in this truck, or at the next camp, or on another death march. Her father's face flashes in front of her eyes. Now I'm hallucinating, she thinks.

'You are stronger together.' She hears his words as clearly as if he were sitting there beside her. Cibi's eyes shoot open. She was dreaming, but that doesn't matter. He was right, *is* right. She can't give in to her fear. Her sisters will sense it and they will give up too.

Once through the gates of Retzow, the women are lined up for registration. When it's Cibi's turn, she tells the officer she is from New York, in America. She winks at Livi and Magda.

'It was just a joke,' she tells them afterwards.

'How is that funny?' asks Magda.

The truth is that Cibi doesn't know why she did it, but maybe it's because there is no war going on *in* America right now, and that's exactly where she would like to be – as far away from Europe as she can imagine.

The sisters have just learned they are in Germany.

The sisters and Eva enter their new block with a rosy flush in their cheeks. They have just eaten and now they have beds to sleep in. Magda claims a top bunk and is helping Eva up when their new *kapo* steps into the room. All chatter stops immediately.

'I need girls to work at the airfield,' she says, staring around the room. The short, rotund woman with spiky black hair speaks slowly in German, so that everyone will understand her. 'It is a bombsite. Our enemies want to destroy us, but they will not win. If you help to clear the runway of debris and fill the craters, you will receive extra food.'

Cibi exchanges a look with Magda – extra food because it's so dangerous, their eyes say. But they don't need to think twice. They decide to take Eva with them. While she's too small for this work, she is still better off in their company.

The next day finds the sisters at the airfield, along with dozens of other volunteers, loading shrapnel and unexploded bombs into wheelbarrows and taking them away. The day after they fill the cleared craters with gravel.

Slowly and methodically, the women clear small areas, and enjoy the bread, milk, potatoes and even pudding they are offered on their breaks. The sisters eat slowly, devouring every morsel, only returning to work when they have the energy and enthusiasm.

One afternoon, Cibi is startled by the sound of an approaching aircraft. Air raid sirens scream across the airfield and the sisters watch the SS guards flee to the bunkers.

'Run!' a voice yells.

'To the kitchens!' shouts another voice. And then Cibi, Livi, Magda and Eva, and all the other workers, are pounding the tarmac to the corrugated iron shack that functions as a kitchen.

Outside, bombs are exploding as they crash into the airfield.

'Better to be killed by the Allies than the German pigs,' the cook announces to the room. 'And if we must die here, at least our stomachs will be full. Come on. Eat!' she commands.

The sisters stuff food into their mouths and their pockets.

When the all-clear sounds, the women return to the airstrip to find their careful work undone by fresh blasts.

The work the next day is back-breaking, but somehow they fall into the rhythm of their labour.

'This is easy work for us,' jokes Cibi to Magda. 'We had to clear an entire demolition site when we first got to Auschwitz.'

'The bricks had to be placed "just so",' says Livi, delicately placing a piece of shrapnel into the wheelbarrow. 'If it chipped or cracked, you would be cracked.'

It is easy, but it is also thankless work: for every crater they fill, another bomb decimates it until, one day, Cibi

245

announces to Magda and Livi they won't be going back to the airfield. There is no point, it's too dangerous, and no one seems to be monitoring them anyway at Retzow. Cibi waits for their *kapo*'s admonition, but none comes and the sisters confine themselves to the camp, accompanied always by little Eva.

Spring arrives and a strange malaise settles over the camp. The guards are distracted. The inmates are fed, and counted at rollcall, but few do any work. They are all waiting for something to happen.

'Cibi Meller, show yourself.' A female guard is standing in the doorway of the block, reading her name from a sheet of paper.

It is raining and the sisters are lying in their bunk, listening to Eva tell the story of her mother – a kind woman who loved the little girl, but who was taken away one morning, along with a dozen other women, never to return.

Cibi squeezes the girl's hand and climbs down off the bunk, Magda and Livi on her heels.

'I'm Cibi Meller,' she announces.

'Come with me. It's your lucky day.'

'Why?' asks Cibi, following the guard into the camp.

'You're being sent to Sweden.' She eyes Magda and Livi. 'Not all of you. Just Cibi Meller,' she snaps.

'We go where our sister goes!' Magda insists.

'Sister? But your names aren't on the list.'

'What list?'

'The Red Cross is taking all American prisoners to Sweden and then back to the United States,' the guard informs them.

Magda and Livi exchange a look and burst into laughter, but Cibi isn't laughing. Her joke has backfired, and now the

Germans will separate them. 'I'm sorry,' says Cibi, in a small voice. 'It was a stupid joke. I'm from Slovakia, not New York.'

'Do you think I care about your jokes? Your name's on the list and you're coming with me.'

Before she follows her, Cibi turns to her sisters. 'Go back to the block. I'll sort this out. Don't worry. Please, don't worry.'

Magda and Livi stare after her, their laughter a bitter ring in their ears.

And, sure enough, Cibi returns eventually and climbs into the bunk where her sisters wait for her. 'I had to work hard to persuade the clerk,' she explains. 'He took pity on me in the end, I guess.' But, Magda observes, Cibi doesn't look relieved. Her brow is furrowed, as if she's trying to work out a problem.

'What else?' she asks.

Cibi takes her sisters' hands. 'He told me they're emptying the camp,' Cibi says, slowly. 'We might be taken on another march.'

A few days later, the inmates of Retzow are lined up and led out of the camp. Once again, the SS monitor the walkers, but this time, fallen inmates are not struck or shot, they are just ignored. The road they are walking on has been bombed, and the girls have to step carefully to avoid twisting an ankle in a crater. They pass bombed-out German vehicles, the limbs of dead soldiers scattered over the ground. The forests and fields of the German countryside are lush with plants and flowers as the heat of the midday sun pounds down – just as the snow had done months earlier. They walk slowly, Cibi and Livi each holding one of Eva's hands.

247

'Have you noticed the guards are disappearing?' says Magda. 'I just saw one wander off into that bit of woodland and he didn't even look back.'

Cibi and Livi glance around. Cibi steps out of the line and looks back at the hundreds of women behind them. She lets out a long slow breath. 'You're right. Where have they all gone?'

'They're abandoning us,' another prisoner says. And then another echoes the same line.

Soon Cibi and her sisters are surrounded by a group of women.

'It's time to leave,' one says.

'We can take our chances,' adds another.

'I'd rather be shot in the back than spend another day, another hour, imprisoned by the Nazis,' says a third.

'Let's do it!' says Cibi. 'Let's move to the side of the road.' Her heart is in her mouth as she meets her sisters' eyes, but Magda and Livi nod. They too are hopeful, feeling a sudden strength in their limbs. They can't face another march, another camp, another cruel order from a heartless man.

Magda wonders for a moment whether they should leave Eva, but one look at her, clutching Livi's hand, convinces Magda the little girl must stay with them for now.

A group of ten women begins to walk away from the line, into the field by the side of the road. But they don't make it very far before they hear footsteps running up behind them.

'Halt! Halt or I'll shoot,' comes the bark of an SS officer.

Cibi turns round slowly to face the young soldier. He stops running and raises his rifle. Cibi places herself in his line of fire, shielding the women behind her.

'You are so young,' she says. If she is to lose her life now, she doesn't want to do it on her knees, begging. She wants to look her killer in the eye. 'You could just turn and walk away.' Cibi takes another step.

'If you take one more step I will shoot,' he says.

Cibi takes another step.

'No, you won't,' she whispers. 'Shoot me and the rest of us will swarm all over you like angry bees. How many of us can you shoot before we tear your eyes out? I'm showing you some mercy, so run away.' Her heart is hammering; maybe he can even hear it. No one is more surprised than Cibi when the soldier turns his back on the women and flees.

When she turns round, some of the women have covered their eyes, and Livi's face is buried in Magda's shoulder, Eva pressed against her belly.

'Well, that was easy,' says Cibi, letting out a breath. Her sisters run into her arms, both of them crying. 'Hey, hey,' she says, holding them away. 'Come on, it's OK. Let's keep moving. It's time to go home.'

CHAPTER 24

Germany
May 1945

In the late afternoon sun, the women watch the long column of prisoners shuffle away. No one else joins them, and they turn towards the field where the tall grass shifts in the afternoon breeze. It is a perfect summer's day, thinks Cibi, despite the distant sound of bombing. The women exchange names and camps: two are from Auschwitz, Eliana and Aria are Slovakians like them; of the four Polish girls three are from Ravensbrück and one from Retzow – Marta and Amelia are cousins who found each other on the march. They are all in their teens.

At the far edges of this vast landscape of green, Cibi spies a spire in the distance: a village perhaps? But villages mean people, Cibi thinks, German people.

'They'll hand us over,' Livi says. 'The moment they see us they'll fetch the SS.'

'But we need to eat. If I don't get something soon, I may as well go back and join the march and wait for a bullet to the head,' Eliana from Slovakia says.

'Let's take a vote,' says Cibi. She knows they can't go on for much longer. But she can't make this decision for them; her confrontation with the guard has shaken her, despite her bravado. 'Hands up if you want to head to the village for food.'

Eight hands shoot up. It's decided.

Cutting across the fields, the group joins a road which will take them directly to the village. They quicken their pace, and then they slow down. Sauntering towards them are two SS officers, rifles slung casually over their shoulders. Cibi tenses; will her wits save her life again, or will she get everyone killed this time? She hastens to the front of the group and leads the way, her head held high. As the men draw closer, she averts her eyes. The whole group is staring at the ground, but they keep on moving, keep walking. And then the men draw level and they too keep going, sparing them barely a glance as they stroll on.

No one says a word.

The village appears to be deserted. The streets are empty and every shop is shut and house boarded up. They make their way down a long street, towards a large building with its doors hanging open.

'Maybe it's a warehouse,' observes Aria, the other Slovakian. To each other, they speak in German, each of them knowing just enough to be understood by the others.

Entering the cavernous space on tiptoe, the girls are fearful, peering left and right, under tables and up to the rafters, but there's no one in there either. And then they are spreading out, entering rooms off the main hall, finding cleaning equipment, bags of cement, anonymous machinery.

'Food!' yells Magda. She has found the kitchen and is flinging open cupboards, pulling out drawers. She finds hard lumps of bread, some wizened scraps of cheese, soggy tomatoes and tins of sardines. Livi uses her knife to open the tins and they eat without speaking.

Within minutes the girls have devoured the lot.

'I'm going to see if I can find out what's going on,' Cibi says. 'We need help if we're to get home. Everyone stay here until I come back.' Cibi has washed her face and hands, dusted off her clothes, but she knows there's no disguising her identity. She is a Jewish prisoner, an escaped Jewish prisoner. She looks like a skeleton and she is going to have to be very careful.

'I'm coming with you,' says Magda, taking her arm. They insist that Livi stay behind with Eva and the other women, and for once Livi doesn't argue.

The sisters wander across the street towards a cobbled courtyard bordered by a row of small houses. They peer inside the windows, but again, there's no one around. A large cowshed stands next to the house at the end of the row and Cibi beckons Magda forward.

Piles of hay litter the milking stalls, but there are no cows, and no milk. As they turn to head back to the warehouse, they hear a low moan coming from the stall at the far end of the shed.

'Let's go, Cibi.' Magda is scared of losing their tentative freedom, and Cibi has risked too much for her already. But Cibi isn't moving.

'I'm going to take a look. Go and stand by the door and get ready to run.'

Cibi tiptoes over to the stall. From beneath a mound of hay a bare foot protrudes. She brushes aside the straw to reveal a leg, then a torso – a man. He is dressed in the rags of a Jewish prisoner. Cibi gets down on her knees and examines his body for an injury but finds none.

His eyes flutter open.

'What's your name?' she asks, softly. He starts to speak, but his words make no sense to Cibi.

'Magda, go and fetch the others,' she calls over her shoulder.

Soon the whole group is standing around the sick man. Eliana pushes through with a wooden mug of cold water, which she holds to his dry lips. After a few sips, he closes his eyes and falls asleep.

For the rest of the night, the girls take turns to sit by his bed in the straw and talk to him, reassure him that the worst of their nightmare is over, that help is coming and he, just like them, will return home to his family. One by one the girls fall asleep and when the dawn breaks, flooding the cowshed with light, they wake to find he is dead.

'We have to bury him,' says Magda. 'We're not in the camps anymore. He deserves this final dignity.'

Livi and Eva find shovels, and in the courtyard, with the four Polish girls, they begin to dig deep into the grassy patch beside the cobbled clearing. Magda and Cibi search the one house whose door isn't locked for food, but there is none there, either.

'What are those for?' Cibi asks. Magda is holding a bottle, a pen and a piece of paper.

'You'll see,' she says, and the girls head back to the court-yard. As they're shutting the door behind them, the front door of the house next door creaks open.

Magda and Cibi flinch, step away. But it's just an old woman.

'What are you doing? Who are you?' she asks.

Cibi clears her throat. 'Isn't it obvious? We've escaped from the camps and we're going home, but need to bury someone first.'

The old woman looks into the courtyard, where six girls are busy digging a hole in the dirt.

She sighs and shakes her head. 'There's a graveyard just down the road, you should bury him in there.'

'You're right,' says Magda. 'Of course. We should have looked for the cemetery.'

'I would wait until after dark if I were you, someone might see you. You still have enemies in this village. Stay in the cowshed for now, and I will bring you what little food I have.'

When the woman has shuffled back inside, Cibi explains the new plan to the group. The old woman, true to her word, returns at dusk with hunks of black bread and potato soup in a small tureen. Barely a full meal for one person, the ten girls sip from the pan and pass it on, sip and pass until it's all gone.

And then they wait for nightfall, huddled together in the dark, in the straw, their slow breathing the only sound in this strange, deserted village, which may or may not house their enemies.

Later, they take their shovels to the graveyard and dig another grave. Four girls drag the dead man to his final resting place and lower him into the hole. Magda scribbles the number on his shirt onto the piece of paper, slips it into the bottle and corks it. She throws it into the hole, and then all ten girls heap soil over the body.

The moon is full, lighting up their solemn faces. Cibi, Livi and Magda stand together, their arms around one another.

'Someone should say the *Kaddish*,' says Aria.

The girls bow their heads, and Magda begins to recite the words she knows from the funeral services in their synagogue. This is the first time she has spoken them aloud; they are not meant for the lips of women, but Magda had memorised them all the same. Soon all the girls are reciting the ancient Aramaic prayer.

'If they find his number,' says Magda, before they turn to leave, 'they will be able to trace his family.'

'We'll sleep here one more night,' announces Cibi, back in the cowshed. 'We leave at first light.'

For two days the sisters, Eva and the six women wander the German countryside. They find berries to eat, the roots of weeds; they gorge themselves on windfalls and drink cold water from bubbling streams. But they are tired of walking, tired of this aimless meandering, despite their freedom.

'I can't take another step,' Livi wails, stopping in her tracks.

'Come on, Livi, one step in front of another – you can do it, you must do it,' Magda encourages.

'I need to rest. Please, Cibi, can we just rest for a while'? Livi begs.

The Polish cousins look like ghosts; everyone has stopped walking.

Cibi sees a small lake at the edge of the field they are crossing, bordered by tall trees. 'Let's go and sit by the water for a while,' she suggests.

They walk slowly through the grass and drop to the ground, finding patches of shade in which to lie down and fall asleep.

When Livi wakes up it is to the sight of hundreds of butterflies tripping through the air. One dares to perch on her nose; she goes cross-eyed trying to focus on its delicate beauty.

'Look at Livi,' she hears Aria say. 'Don't move.'

The girls watch the butterflies land on Livi's face, in her hair, on her arms.

'It's the most beautiful thing I've ever seen,' says Magda, choking back her sobs.

And then it's time to go. They leave the butterflies to their fun and head for the road.

The hours on the road, the nights sleeping in fields, or stables, wherever they can find shelter, give Cibi and Livi too much time to think, and they hate it. Neither sister can banish the memories of life at Auschwitz and Birkenau, and they realise now that these episodes of brutality will be lodged in their minds for ever.

At night, Livi wakes up screaming, Cibi breathless and sweating. Magda tortures herself with the question, *Would Mumma still be alive if we had stayed together?* Maybe they should have all hidden in the forest, day after day, out of the clutches of the Hlinka. She says none of this to her sisters – she feels an overwhelming guilt for what they had to endure in her absence.

Eva is a comfort to them all, listening avidly to the tales of their childhood, when so much of this little girl's was spent in the camps.

'I can't find any happy memories,' Livi cries one morning, sleep deprived and rattled.

'Then let me help you,' Magda tells her. 'Do you remember the doll Father gave us?'

Livi nods.

'Cibi?'

'I do. It was the most beautiful thing we ever owned,' Cibi replied.

The women are walking once more across another field. The sun is high in the sky. There is no sign of life but their own.

'And do you remember how, after he died, whenever we held the doll, Mumma would tell us stories about him?'

'I don't remember him at all,' Livi says.

'That's OK, kitten, that's what older sisters are for,' Cibi says.

'Kitten?' muses Livi. 'I haven't heard that in while.'

Cibi realises she hasn't called Livi 'kitten' in a long time and wonders if this is a good sign. A sign that they are becoming the girls they were before.

'Well, you're a kitten to me. A tiny thing I need to look after. You were such a small baby too, I think that's where it comes from.'

'I remember her crying a lot when she was a baby,' Magda adds.

'I did not!' But Livi is smiling. 'Tell us some more memories, Magda. Ones when we were all together.'

The girls walk and talk and, very gradually, Cibi and Livi feel their minds latch on to happier times and hold on.

'Look, cows! Lots of cows,' Livi yells. It is late afternoon. The sky is awash with pink streaks. The colour has returned to the women's cheeks. The girls gaze at the black-and-white shapes in the distance, at the edge of some woodland.

'There might be a farmhouse nearby,' Aria says.

'Or we could just kill a cow and cook it over a fire,' Eliana adds. Everyone starts to laugh, tickled by the image of ten frail women chasing a cow around a field, with nothing to kill it with but their hands.

The group draws closer to the woods, to the wide path leading through the trees. They leave the open skies and head into the cool shade of oak, spruce and pine.

The path veers off to the right and the girls keep moving until they reach a paved courtyard on the outskirts of the forest, and set eyes on the large house which looms in its midst. A path skirts around the courtyard, joining a road beyond the woodland.

'It's a castle!'

'It's the biggest house I have ever seen!'

Livi hammers at the heavy wooden doors. But no one answers.

'I don't think there's anyone home. Some of you go round the back and see what you find.'

Magda, Livi, Marta and Amelia run towards the back of the house. They return a minute later.

'The house is open round the back,' Magda tells them. 'But, there's another dead man in the yard.'

The group now gathers around this new dead body.

'He must have lived here. Look at his clothes, they're so fancy,' Livi says.

'Can we look for some food first?' Eva cries, plaintively. 'I'm starving.'

'No,' says Cibi, firmly. 'We're not animals, to fill our stomachs beside dead bodies. We have to bury him now.'

The girls hunt the outbuildings for shovels, spades, anything that will help them dig the hole as fast as possible. Cibi points to the immaculately manicured lawn beyond, in which a small fig tree blooms with new fruit. 'That's the perfect place for him,' she says.

The girls take turns to dig. Magda finds a wheelbarrow and, together with Livi and two others, they load the body into it. But Livi won't pull the barrow, the memory of moving Mala to the crematorium still painfully fresh in her mind.

Magda, once again, opens her mouth to recite the *Kaddish*.

'But what if he's not Jewish?' Marta says.

'I don't think it matters anymore what your religion is, not when you're dead,' she replies. 'These are words of comfort, whether you believe in a God or not.'

With heads bowed, the *Kaddish* is spoken over the grave of an unknown man, by everyone but Cibi.

The group gathers at the back door of the house, Cibi holding them there for a moment, while she gathers her resolve.

'There could be a hundred people hiding in there.' Marta cannot shake off her fear, and she and Amelia huddle together, visibly shaking.

'Two hundred,' says Amelia. She found her cousin on the march and she isn't about to lose her now.

'We need food,' says Livi.

'We'll go inside and look around,' Cibi decides. 'But I'm pretty sure if there were two hundred people in there they would have heard us by now.' She can feel its isolation, its neglect.

She leads the way into a kitchen the size of her house in Vranov. She was right – people have left in a hurry: there are still dishes in the sink, bread only recently gone stale on the long table in the centre of the room. The girls perform their routine of opening cupboards, rifling through drawers. Magda finds a small cache of preserved fruit and vegetables, a few cans of fish and processed meat. And then Marta and Amelia find the prize: a large walk-in pantry, with jars upon jars of food on the shelves. They cry in relief.

The girls gather at the kitchen door which will lead them into the rest of the house.

'We stay together,' says Cibi.

They walk, open-mouthed, through the luxurious rooms. Living rooms and libraries, studies and boot rooms. Livi opens one door to find a lift, but no one is prepared to try it, instead they ascend the staircase by foot. There are just too many bedrooms, thinks Cibi. How many people live in this house? The beds are draped with opulent silks, while thick wool rugs cover the polished parquet boards. Gold taps adorn the elegant bathrooms and the girls leave muddy boot prints all over the pale marble floors. They enter walk-in wardrobes, the walls lined with shelves housing soft jumpers, shirts. Shimmering dresses dangle from tasselled hangers. In the chests of drawers they find underwear, which the girls model against their own bodies, giggling, before carefully replacing them.

And then they find the mirror. Standing in front of the ornate frame above the fireplace in the master bedroom, the ten girls pause to absorb what has become of them. Livi and Cibi barely recognise themselves. The Polish cousins begin to weep, and Eva buries her face in Magda's arms.

'Let's get out of here,' whispers Cibi, and in silence the girls go back downstairs.

They make for the dining room, pausing to run their hands along the surface of the long table, around which are arranged twenty elaborately upholstered chairs. The sideboards reveal an impossible array of glassware, whose drawers contain fine silver cutlery. At the far end of the room the French windows open out onto a small courtyard with a beautiful lawn extending into the formal gardens.

'I haven't sat in a room at a table for so long,' Eliana says, quietly. Nine heads nod up and down. No one makes a move to pull out a chair.

'I don't want to sit in here,' says Cibi. 'It feels all wrong. But I don't think the owners of this wonderful home would mind if we borrowed their table and chairs.'

'Where are the owners?' asks Magda.

'Gone,' replies Cibi. 'However gorgeous this house is, there's a lot of dust.' Now the girls peer at the sideboards, the surface of the table, the parquet floors. Cibi is right, whoever lived here has been away for a while.

Cibi moves to the French windows. 'Let's take it all outside.'

The girls pull away the chairs and position themselves at either end of the table and heave it through the doors and onto the grass. They return for the chairs and then for the food. Livi and the two Slovakian girls disappear into the vegetable garden beyond the lawn and return with carrots, lettuces. Livi wipes the blade of her little knife before she pockets it.

Just as they are laying their produce on the table, a figure rounds the corner of the house and stands before them on the lawn. He is dressed in rough cotton trousers, a thick shirt. 'Who are you?' he barks.

At once the group gathers around Cibi, instantly on their guard.

Livi closes her hand around her knife; he isn't so big and there are ten of them.

Cibi once more finds herself stepping forward, clearing her throat. 'We were prisoners of Auschwitz,' she tells him, firmly. 'And now we've escaped.'

The man doesn't speak for a long time. He looks at the girls, who are suddenly self-conscious in the rags hanging from their emaciated bodies.

His voice breaks as he utters the words: 'Help me round up my cows and it would be my honour to give you some warm milk and fresh cheese.'

'Do you know where the owners are?' Cibi points to the grand house.

'I have no idea,' he says.

Five of the girls go off with the farmer, and the others all return to the vegetable patch. Within an hour they are laying the table with milk, cheese and bread from the farmer, tomatoes and fresh vegetables from the garden, and pickles and tins of fish from the pantry. Eliana has discovered the wine cellar and she has uncorked two bottles of fine red wine, which are waiting to be poured into crystal glasses. Candles adorn the length of the table and the silver cutlery gleams in their flickering light.

As the sun sets, the girls take their seats.

'We've survived the camps,' says Cibi. 'We survived the marches. We're not home yet, but today, tonight, I think it's time to celebrate our freedom. Our freedom march!' She raises her glass.

'Our freedom march!' the girls echo. They clink glasses and, smiling, begin to reach for the food. They eat slowly, savouring every mouthful.

The moon is full, throwing a spotlight on her sisters, and Cibi is finally confident that whatever lies ahead for them, they will face it together.

CHAPTER 25

Germany
May 1945

The whole group is unanimous in their desire to rest and gather their strength before they decide what to do next. That first night, the sisters agree they cannot sleep in any of the bedrooms, and, to their surprise, the other women feel the same. They gather blankets, pillows and throws and hunker down in the dining room.

Magda, with Livi's help, draws up a roster of work for the girls. Some of them will help the farmer with his cows, others are allocated chores around the house. For two weeks, the group works, eats well and slowly, and each of the women finds her strength returning. Their hair grows thick and glossy, and pale cheeks fill with colour. The sisters' dreams are as disturbing as ever, and at least three of the women wake up screaming every night, but that's what this moment of respite is for: some time to heal more than their bodies.

Cibi steps out of the house, preparing to head over to the farm; it is her turn to help the farmer round up his cows. All the air in her lungs escapes in one long gasp when she sees the open-bed trucks parked in the courtyard.

Soldiers.

She takes a step back, one hand on the door, the other at her throat. The fear is sudden and painful, she feels faint and stumbles into Magda, who is standing behind her.

'It's OK, Cibi,' whispers Magda. 'They're Russians. Look at their uniforms.' The men are indeed wearing Russian uniform. Cibi scrambles to recall her Rusyn dialect.

The officer in charge identifies himself and asks, 'Are you the owner of this house?'

Cibi wants to laugh, but she just waves at her rags, at the equally ragged figures who now crowd around her. 'No, sir. We are escaped prisoners from Auschwitz.' She pulls up her sleeve and holds out her arm to show him the tattooed numbers.

The officer shakes his head slowly and speaks in a low voice to the other officers in his truck.

'How did you escape?' he asks.

'The march, we ran away from the march.'

'Do you know why you were marching? Where you were going?'

Cibi didn't know – so much made little or no sense: the violence, the torture, the killing machines. She had learned never to question orders. She shakes her head.

'They were going to use you to bargain for their freedom,' he tells her, adding, 'and other reasons too: to carry on working for them, but also to stop you telling your stories to the Allies. Thank God you escaped.'

The girls shuffle awkwardly from foot to foot; none of them wants to imagine more camps, more work, more brutality.

Cibi tilts up her chin and stands straighter. 'It's behind us now,' she says. 'We want to look forward.'

The Russian officer smiles and nods. 'I agree. Will you show me around the house?' he asks.

Cibi nods and steps aside to let him into the room, where the girls' crumpled bedding covers the floor. After a tour of the house, the officer returns to the living room. 'You are all Jews?' he asks. The girls fidget and grumble, reluctant to answer: how has being Jewish ever helped them?

'We're all Jewish,' Cibi says firmly, with a defiant nod of her chin.

'I promise you will come to no harm,' the officer says. 'Not from me or my men. You have my word. I am also a Jew.'

Cibi informs the officer of their routine: the cleaning and collecting of vegetables, and the rounding up of cows in exchange for milk, bread and cheese.

'I need to talk to this farmer,' he tells Cibi. 'We Russians need meat!'

Cibi witnesses the transformation of one of the outbuildings into a slaughterhouse for pigs, and introduces a new chore into their roster. They will now help to prepare food for the soldiers.

'I know it's pork,' Cibi tells the group. 'But we don't have to eat it.'

'I'd eat it,' says Livi, giggling. 'If there was nothing else, but it does stink.'

All this work has taken a toll on their clothes, and now the pungent aroma of pork fat is embedded in their tatters.

'Help me sew these into dresses?' Cibi corners Magda on her way to the farm. She is holding up old curtains she found in a cupboard, and has also uncovered an ancient sewing machine.

Now, every night, Cibi and Magda cut cloth to the measurements of the girls and soon they have functional dresses made of blue and red cotton. Eva dances in her new clothes, delighted. Livi thinks she is turning back into the little girl she was before the camps, despite the haunted expression in her eyes.

Another couple of weeks pass in the happy company of the soldiers, after which Cibi decides it's time to move on. They are stronger now and they have new clothes and food. They pack bread, cheese and salami into the capacious pockets of their new dresses and head to the farmer's house to say goodbye.

'The Allies have taken over Brandenburg,' he informs them, scrawling out directions on a scrap of paper. He hands it to Cibi. 'That's where you should go.'

The sun is shining on the girls as they head away from the house, waving a warm goodbye to the Russian soldiers.

As the afternoon grows hotter and then cooler, Cibi is on the lookout for a place to sleep. They find a barn. The next night they sleep in a cowshed. Cibi is grateful to the locals who donate food as they march on.

As they near Brandenburg, the group is joined by hundreds of others heading in the same direction, towards safety.

'We are all survivors,' Cibi tells her sisters. 'We have all been beaten, starved and tortured, but look at us, we're still moving, still alive.'

Brandenburg city has been reduced to rubble and the girls navigate the destruction as they make for the huge army base set up to assist and repatriate the dispossessed. It is here the sisters say goodbye to the six girls who joined them on their freedom march. The Polish girls will stay together as they try to find their way back to Krakov, and Eliana and Aria are now firm friends, so no one is on their own. Eva, of course, will remain with the sisters. It isn't a tearful farewell in the end; together these girls regained their humanity, and that can only be celebrated.

*   *   *

Cibi gazes up at the blond soldier talking to her in English, a language she has no knowledge of, but she understands he is there to help her. Around her, broken girls fall to their knees, kissing the hands of American soldiers.

'Where are you from?' Another soldier asks her in German, and Cibi reels off the details of their identity and their escape from the camps.

'But you're not *from* Auschwitz,' he says. 'That's not your home. Where did you live before?'

'Slovakia,' whispers Magda, because Cibi has lost her voice.

'Hungary,' calls another voice.

'Poland.'

'Yugoslavia.'

The sisters find themselves in a queue of girls, lining up to give their details to the white-shirted clerks sitting at desks in the middle of the chaos of the base.

'Are we safe, is the war over?' Cibi asks.

The clerk looks up, a warm smile on his face. 'You are safe, and yes, the war is over. The Nazis have been defeated.'

'Are you sure?' Magda asks.

'I am.' The clerk's grin grows wider as he says, 'Hitler is dead.'

'Dead?' whispers Livi. 'Actually *dead*?'

The girls stare at the clerk, desperate to believe him. He's still smiling.

'What do we do now?' asks Cibi, finally. 'Where do we go?'

'We'll feed you,' a clerk tells Cibi. 'And give you and your sisters a place to sleep.'

They are allocated a place to sleep inside a concrete block.

Livi starts to tremble as she enters the room lined with bunks.

'Livi, it's OK, my love, we're free now. This is just a room,' soothes Cibi.

'And those are just beds,' adds Magda.

In between meals they walk around the base, looking for familiar faces from Auschwitz, but find none. Cibi is restless, keen to be on the move again. For the first time in many weeks, she is not in control of their daily routine.

'We won't be here much longer,' Magda says, as they patrol the lines of tents, still hoping to catch sight of a friend. 'Tomorrow we'll find out when we're going home.'

The next morning, a female Russian officer appears in the block. She sits at a desk at the front of the room and beckons forth the girls for questioning.

Cibi is tired of answering these questions. She can't help fearing that one of her responses might elicit some sort of punishment. She reels off the details again: we're from Slovakia, we escaped from Auschwitz. *My family is dead.*

'Three weeks!' Livi explodes. 'We have to stay here, in this camp, for another three weeks?' Despite her temper, Livi is looking well. Her cheeks have filled out and the khaki trousers and white shirt they were issued on their arrival suit her, but her eyes still blaze with the same defiant fire. An officer has just informed them that in three weeks they will be taken by bus to Prague.

'The time will fly by,' says Cibi, trying to sound hopeful. 'It always does.'

'But I've had enough, Cibi!'

'We've all had enough,' says Magda, an edge to her voice that she cannot hide. 'What good does moaning do? Where did complaining ever get us?'

'Our house will be there when we get back, whether it's in three weeks or a month or a year,' Cibi adds.

'But Mumma won't be there.' The defiance is gone from Livi's tone. She heads for their bunk, climbs in and pulls a blanket over her head. Magda takes a step towards her, but Cibi catches her sleeve.

'Leave her, Magda. She needs to feel her pain. We can't pretend that Mumma will be there.'

The weeks do fly by – Cibi was right – and now the girls will be boarding a bus in three days' time. Their names are once again checked off a list. When the clerk has confirmed their identities he looks at Eva, whose name is not on his list.

'And who are you?' he asks.

'Her name is Eva, she's with us,' Livi pipes up.

'Where are you from, Eva?'

'She's from Yugoslavia, but she is with us,' Livi says, firmly.

'I'm sorry, Eva, you have to come with me. You will go back to Belgrade.'

'But she can't,' says Magda. 'Her family is dead.'

'You don't know that, miss. There may be someone in Belgrade who will take her in. A cousin perhaps, an aunt. Our instructions are clear – only citizens of Czechoslovakia are to return to Prague.'

'When will she leave?' Cibi asks.

'You need to say goodbye now. I will take her to the Belgrade block.' He nods up and down, urging the farewell to begin.

Eva starts to cry and Livi throws her arms around the little girl. Cibi and Magda join the hug and the girls hang on to one another for a long time.

'I am sorry, girls, but I need to take Eva now. Please, let her go.'

Slowly, the sisters release the child in their midst. The clerk takes Eva by the hand and walks away. Eva doesn't resist, but she turns round, holding out an arm as if to catch hold of their hands.

'How many more people can they take away from us?' sobs Livi.

'They will never take *us* away from one another again,' Magda says, fervently.

In silence, the girls return to their block and wait for the final three days to pass.

It is a warm, late summer morning when the sisters join one of the five buses heading for Czechoslovakia. Livi gazes out of the window without speaking, lost in her thoughts of home and what awaits them. When the absence of her mother becomes too awful to contemplate, her mind darts back to Auschwitz, to Birkenau. Is that it? she thinks. They went through all that horror, and now they're just being sent home, on a bus, as if nothing had happened? Rage spikes her body. Who is going to say *sorry*? Who is going to atone for their suffering, the senseless deaths?

But six hours is a long time to keep hate alive in your heart, and on the third go around, Livi joins her sisters and the rest of the bus in a loud rendition of the national anthem of Czechoslovakia, and a recital of prayers. Livi notices that while Cibi sings the songs, she clamps her mouth shut for the prayer.

The sisters stare at the countryside as it sweeps past. The chatter around them falls silent as they move through the ruins of Berlin and Dresden. They watch men, women and children picking through the rubble. They all look up as the buses sweep by, holding out their hands for food. These are the people who enslaved, starved, tortured and murdered us, thinks Cibi, bitterly. And now they dare to beg for our compassion.

The mood on the bus becomes more alert as they cross the Charles Bridge into Prague.

Some of the passengers are *home*.

The bridge is lined with hundreds of people, waving hands, flags and flowers, *welcoming* them. As they drive onto the bridge, Cibi thinks of the hypocrisy of these citizens. They had once thought nothing of turning their backs on the Jews of their city, willingly handing them over to Hitler.

She turns to Magda, her eyes flashing. 'I never thought I'd see this,' she breathes. 'They abandoned us and now they're welcoming us home?'

The convoy of five buses has to pull over after they have crossed the bridge, as the crowds are impassable. Then the doors are opening and the exuberant hordes are boarding the buses. The sisters are offered cake, chocolate, water, fruit – a man presses money into Magda's hands. Livi starts to cry, overcome by the genuine outpouring of affection, by the cheering and clapping that engulfs them.

An elderly gentleman takes Cibi's hand and raises it to his lips. Just moments ago she was angry, furious that their welcome was nothing short of hypocrisy, an act displaying not joy at their return, but guilt for doing nothing to save them. She is not so sure now, as she struggles to make sense of what is happening around them.

The bus driver takes the wheel, blasting his horn again and again to clear a path through the masses gathered outside. Soon the convoy arrives in Wenceslas Square, where the mayor is waiting to welcome the return of Czechoslovakian citizens. The sisters step off the bus, hand in hand, wary of becoming separated amongst the roaring crowds.

'Prominte! Prominte!' they shout. 'We're sorry!'

The mayor joins in the chant before calling for quiet. He tells them he is so happy they have returned home, that from now on they will be cared for. That what happened to them will never happen again.

Loaded with flowers, chocolate and cake the sisters join the other passengers and reboard their bus. Exhausted, exhilarated, they are taken to nearby army barracks where they will spend the night, in bunks they don't have to share. They sleep well.

Their journey home only really starts when they take the train to Bratislava the next day.

Stepping onto the platform, each of the girls is struck with fierce, painful memories. On the tracks is a normal enough looking train; at least, it's not made up of coal or cattle wagons.

But it's a symbol of their captivity all the same.

'Cibi,' says Livi, her face crumbling. 'I don't think I can . . .'

Cibi is already weeping and Magda is shaking.

'We can,' sobs Cibi. 'We've come too far, kitten. And this is the way home. Do you remember?'

The sisters hold on to each other as they cross the platform, hold on tight as they climb the steps, whisper words of strength and courage as they walk down the aisle and find a seat.

Three sit on a seat made for two. They cannot be apart, not now.

They had been given new clothes at the army barracks, as well as a little money, and Cibi notes how they don't look much different to everyone else on board, save for the sunken eyes, hollow cheeks and gaunt frames identifying them as the victims of a terrible war.

The ticket collector hangs his head as he approaches. He won't take their money. '*Prominte*,' he whispers and shuffles away.

Their arrival in Bratislava is a far cry from the welcome in Prague. Other returning survivors slink away from the train station, still fearful of lurking enemies. Cibi asks at the office when the next train to Vranov Nad Topl'ou will be leaving.

'Not for two days,' she is told with a sneer.

'Can we stay here in the station until then?' she asks. The clerk shrugs his shoulders and turns away.

274

For the next couple of days, the sisters sleep on the benches, use the toilets and wait patiently for their train to arrive.

Other trains pour into the station, from all corners of Europe, returning Slovakian survivors to their homes.

Livi becomes transfixed by the appearance of these survivors. 'Do we look like them?' she asks her sisters, over and over. Cibi and Magda wonder the same thing. These were happy, healthy young people who have been ravaged by inhumane torture and degradation. How did it happen? Who let it happen? Everything that made them human had been wiped out. They were skeletal figures now, hunched over by the burden of their experience.

When it's time to pay for their tickets, Cibi approaches the window, half expecting her money to be refused. But the man holds out his hand, a glint of steel in his eyes, and takes it.

They are finally on their way.

The sisters step onto the platform where it all started. The sun is shining, at least. Cibi holds Livi's hand and Magda slides her arm through Cibi's. They begin to walk, each of the sisters trying hard not to think about what awaits them at the end of this final leg of their journey.

They walk slowly, taking their time to immerse themselves in the familiar streets. At the corner of their road, they stare up at the Catholic church whose bells have sung to them the whole of their lives. They peer through the iron gates to the priest's house next door, and marvel at the linden tree in full bloom. No neighbour steps out of their house to greet them, but Cibi notices the curtains pulled aside at their approach and then hastily drawn as they pass.

They stand outside their home looking for signs of life.

'We don't have the key,' Livi says. 'Do we break in?'

'I think we knock,' says Magda. 'Mumma was pretty sure someone would move in.'

'Into our house?' Livi is indignant. 'Who?'

'Whoever got there first,' Magda replies.

Cibi takes the initiative and strides up to the front door and knocks loudly. They can hear movement inside, footsteps, and then the door is flung open by a man in a stained string vest and grey underpants.

'What do you want?' he asks, gruffly.

'We want our house back,' says Cibi, evenly.

'And who the hell are you? This is my house. Now get out of here before I throw you onto the street.'

'This is our home!' yells Livi, taking a step towards him. 'It's you who doesn't belong here.'

'Bloody Jews,' he curses. He doesn't move and the sisters lock eyes with him until Magda nudges Livi aside.

'I'm coming in,' she says. 'There is something of mine in there and I'm going to fetch it.'

The man shoves Magda away and tries to shut the door. But the sight of this ugly figure attempting to close their own door in their faces flicks a switch in Cibi's head. She kicks him hard in one leg and then she kicks him in the other.

Livi manoeuvres behind him and shoves him onto the path. Magda sidesteps the man and runs through the door into the living room, where she finds herself face to face with a woman and two small children. They stare at her and she stares at them. No one says a word. The children cling to their mother's skirts. Magda can hear Cibi and Livi screaming at the man outside.

276

Grabbing a chair from the kitchen she takes it into the hallway and places it beneath the trapdoor. She's through the door in seconds, wriggling to the far end of the cavity. She grabs the pillowcase, feeling the edges of the candlesticks and the smooth, flat surface of the photos inside.

They're safe. Their memories are safe.

The woman has pulled her chair away and Magda crashes to the floor on her exit. But she's on her feet in seconds, running for the front door just as the unkempt man is coming back inside. She pushes past him and is on the street again, waving the pillowcase triumphantly in the air.

'I got it! I got it!' she yells and the three of them run down the road. They do not stop running until they are two streets away. Only then does Magda realise she is limping. She has twisted her ankle in her fall.

'Are you all right?' Cibi asks.

'Yes, I just hurt my ankle when I fell out of the ceiling,' Magda says.

'You fell . . . what?' says Livi.

'Never mind.' Magda smiles. 'I have what I wanted.'

'But what do we do now?' Livi persists. 'Someone is in our house.'

'Well, we can't stay here. I think we should go back to Bratislava. At least we'll be amongst all the other survivors,' Magda suggests.

'Well, whatever you've got in that pillowcase, Magda, it had better be a miracle, because that's what we need right now.' Cibi is grinning, trying to infuse in her sisters the courage she is yet to feel herself.

Part III
The Promised Land

CHAPTER 26

Bratislava
July 1945

Again, the three girls squeeze into a seat made for two
on the train to Bratislava. They take no notice of the
countryside as it streams away. There is nothing here for
them any longer.

Instead, they pore over the photos in the pillowcase.

'I wish we knew what happened to Uncle Ivan and the
cousins,' says Livi, staring at a photo of their uncle and
mother as teenagers.

Magda sighs, and touches her sister's shoulder. 'We will
find out sooner or later. They might even be in Bratislava,'
she says.

Magda watches her sisters as they re-acquaint themselves
with the family snapshots. They had been apart for over two

years and the siblings she found in Auschwitz in no way resembled those she knew in Vranov. Magda feels guilty – she can't help it. While they suffered, she slept in their bed, ate the food they should have been sharing, enjoyed the company of the mother they so desperately miss. How will she ever find her way back to them, separated as they are by their experiences? She reaches over to stroke Livi's hair, now thick and strong with the telltale reddish hues she and Cibi envy. She pulls a strand away from Livi's face, tucking it behind her ear.

'Bratislava is huge, Magda!' Livi throws a photo onto the pile. 'How would we find them? What are we going to do? Walk the streets hoping we'll bump into them like they're our neighbours?'

'If you've got a better idea, then please tell us,' Magda fires back. She is exhausted too.

But Livi is furious. Not with Magda, but with those who decided putting them on another train and abandoning them to their fates is some kind of recompense. Someone is living in their house. Their *mumma*'s house.

Magda gathers up the pictures and thrusts them back into the pillowcase, which she clutches to her chest.

Hours later, the sisters are crossing the main street of Bratislava. Several shops are open and there is an air of business as usual in the bustling city. It is late afternoon and their feet ache from pounding the pavement, hoping to spot at least one friend from Auschwitz or Vranov.

Livi's eye lingers on the two, very thin, young men approaching.

'They look Jewish,' Livi says, nodding at the men.

'*They look Jewish*,' mimics Magda, with a grin. 'How is that helpful?'

'Well, they *do*!' Livi pouts. 'Aren't we looking for Jews?'

'That's enough!' snaps Cibi, and her sisters fall silent.

Cibi steps up to the young men. 'I was wondering if you could help us,' she says.

The men glance at each other and then at Cibi.

'Happy to, if we can,' says one.

'We've just arrived in Bratislava,' Cibi begins.

'Which camp?' the other asks.

'Auschwitz-Birkenau.'

The men exchange another glance.

'I'm Frodo, and this is my friend, Imrich. We were in Auschwitz, too. Where do you live?'

'Vranov. But someone has taken our house,' Cibi feels like crying, right there in the street. This is too hard. Every word spilling from her mouth paints a picture of their never-ending despair, but Frodo is smiling, nodding his head.

'Don't worry,' he says. 'We can help. There's space in an apartment in our block where you can stay for a bit. The girls who live there are survivors too.'

Cibi notes her sisters' wary faces and makes the decision for them. 'Thank you. We've got a little money.'

'Keep your money,' Imrich says.

Cibi nods and holds out a hand. 'I'm Cibi, and this is Magda and Livi. We're sisters.'

As they walk, Cibi and Livi tell the men about their time in Auschwitz, about the death march and then their escape, the full horror of their ordeal spilling easily from their mouths as the boys nod and listen. Cibi feels better afterwards, and decides she will talk to whoever is ready to listen, but Magda has added very little during this exchange. Learning once more of the horrors her sisters endured in her absence only compounds her guilt.

They navigate their way across a bombed-out estate of houses, until they reach Frodo and Imrich's apartment block.

'Who owns the building and how come you can stay here?' asks Cibi, as they begin to climb the flights of stairs.

'No idea, we're squatting. But there's running water. No electricity, though, so it's a little romantic dining by candlelight.' Frodo laughs.

'We're *all* survivors here,' says Imrich. 'Some of us have already found work. We share what we make. It's a bit like a commune.'

On the second floor, Imrich leads them to Apartment 8. He knocks and a female voice calls out, 'Come in.'

The door opens onto a small lounge. Two girls around Cibi's age, who had been lounging on a mattress in the middle of the room, jump to their feet. They hug the men, and Cibi instinctively feels they can trust these young people.

'This is Klara and Branka,' says Imrich to Cibi. 'The girls need a home,' he tells his friends.

'Of course,' says Klara, the taller of the two women. 'There's plenty of room for you – a whole room, in fact, which you could share.' She turns to Branka. 'We just need more bedding, don't we?'

'Klara and I sleep here.' Branka points at the mattress. 'And Kamila and Erena share the other bedroom. We're a cosy family.'

Cibi's eyes well up. She feels for her sisters' hands. 'How do we thank you?' she says.

'Don't be silly.' Klara laughs, throwing her arms around Cibi. 'You've just forgotten what it feels like to have friends. We all have.'

Magda and Livi watch in silence as Cibi weeps in Klara's arms; their brave older sister, undone by this simple gesture of kindness.

Frodo and Imrich make their excuses and leave and the sisters are shown to their new bedroom.

'It's perfect, isn't it, Cibi?' Magda asks.

Cibi is rubbing her eyes, but she's smiling and nodding.

'Help us with dinner,' Klara calls, and once the girls have opened a window to air out the room, they join their new landlords in the tiny kitchen.

Cibi and Livi find the cutlery and an odd assortment of plates and lay the table. The sun is setting and the room dims.

'I've got some candles in a drawer, I'll get them,' says Branka. 'Magda, can you find something to put them in? We don't want them falling over and burning down what's left of the building.'

As Branka pulls two candles from a drawer, Magda gasps. 'I've got just the thing,' she says, leaping from the table. Moments later she returns, holding the silver candlesticks, now liberated from the pillowcase. 'Will these do?' she asks.

'They're perfect! Where did you get them?' Branka asks, delightedly.

'They're all we have left of our mother,' says Magda, in a whisper.

'Mumma would love the thought of them at our first meal with new friends,' Cibi says, her voice dropping to a whisper too.

'I'll light them,' pipes up Livi, taking the candlesticks from Magda. 'Cibi's right. Tonight we eat by the light of Mumma's watchful eyes.'

Later that evening, after a meal prepared with the apartment's final two residents, Kamila and Erena, the women retreat to the large flat on the top floor which has access to the rooftop. Survivors from other apartments gather to share their stories of life in the camps, and life after.

The sisters learn that every day, the men and women go out looking for work. Some are lucky, and those who aren't are tasked with making their living conditions more comfortable, by scouting the other flats for food, furniture and toiletries.

'Tomorrow, you must visit the Red Cross offices,' Branka tells the sisters. 'They'll register your return and help you find family and friends.'

'Someone will help us? Actually *help* us find our uncle?' Livi's voice is shrill and the rooftop falls silent.

Branka reaches for her hand. 'I hope so, little Livi,' she says, softly. 'I really hope so.'

The evening draws to a close and people begin to shuffle to their feet and head for their beds. Cibi is aware that several young men and women linger to finish their conversations, their heads bent close as they talk. Normal life might be possible after all, ponders Cibi. She remembers Yosi, the cheeky boy from the *Hachshara*, who so loved to throw his bread at her head. Maybe, one day, she too might find someone to love.

The sisters' lives fall into a pleasant rhythm, each of them happy to lose themselves in a new, independent routine. Cibi is the luckiest, finding short spells of office work where she uses her typing skills. Livi and Magda find themselves office work too, filing paperwork and helping tally the accounts of small businesses, or cleaning. When they're not working, they fix up the apartment.

Cibi and Livi had spent enough time watching the Russians construct Birkenau, so it's no surprise that they prove to be dab hands at mixing cement and fixing broken bricks back into the walls of their flat, to afford them some protection over the winter months.

'You girls sure know your way around construction,' Frodo says, watching in awe as Cibi and Livi slap the bricks with mortar.

As the weeks pass, the sisters feel like they're waking up from a bad dream. Each night, before they go to bed, the girls look through the photos, their hearts aching as they relive their happy childhoods, before it all went so wrong. But it's no longer unbearable to face these memories. Livi cries herself to sleep every night, the pain of losing their home in Vranov still so fresh in her mind. Her dreams are confused things: the thug at their house shoving them into the street, into the arms of an SS officer who orders them onto a cattle wagon which is laden with actual cows. But each morning she wakes up and decides life must go on and, slowly, she begins to feel stronger.

Cibi visits the Red Cross at least once a week, scanning the lists for her uncle and aunt's names, but so far she has had no luck.

One afternoon, two months into their residence in Bratislava, she returns home to find a man lurking outside the door of their apartment. Friend or foe, she wonders, instinctively, but Cibi reminds herself she is safe here, that a single cry for help would bring people from every apartment running to her aid.

'Can I help you?'

The man turns round slowly. He is clutching his hat in his hands, twisting it round and round with thin fingers. 'I'm looking for . . .' he begins.

Cibi gasps, reaches for the wall for support. 'Uncle Ivan?' she whispers.

'Cibi!' he cries. In seconds they are hugging, each of them sobbing onto the shoulder of the other.

Cibi recognises him by the glint in his eyes, the shape of his nose – but everything else about her uncle is different. His once proud posture is stooped, his black hair is now white and straggly. Lines etch his features, but his smile is as wide and warm as it had ever been. 'Magda? Livi?' he says, hesitantly.

'They're fine. We're all fine. And Aunt Helena? The children?' It's Cibi's turn to sound hesitant. Ivan looks at his misshapen hat. 'The children have been through a lot; it will take some time for them to adjust.'

'Aunt Helena?'

Ivan hangs his head as the tears begin to spill down his cheeks. 'We lost her, Cibi. She's gone,' he croaks. 'She fell on the death march . . .'

He doesn't need to say anymore and Cibi doesn't press him. Once more they're crying in each other's arms.

'I want to see Magda and Livi,' Ivan says, finally.

Cibi nods, takes his hand and leads him into the apartment.

The next day the family gathers at their uncle's apartment block, mere minutes from their own. The sisters listen as their cousins recount the moment their mother fell and was then shot by an SS officer. It is painful to hear, but Cibi knows now that talking about it will help them, however distressing the memories.

'There is an empty apartment above,' Ivan tells the sisters. 'It would make me very happy if you girls moved in. We could be a family again.'

The sisters don't even need to discuss it. That same afternoon, they say goodbye to Branka and all their friends, with promises to stay in touch, and move their meagre possessions to Ivan's block.

They celebrate the first night of their reunion with their uncle, drawing up chairs and crates to sit round a small table and eat. When the table is set and the food steaming in mismatching bowls, Magda reaches for her bag and pulls out the candlesticks, replete with the long tapers given to her by Branka.

Livi strikes a match and the room glows in the yellow flickering light.

'Are these . . .?' Ivan begins, but can't continue, because he has started to cry.

The children circle their father, patting his back, wiping away his tears. 'It's OK, Daddy,' they say over and over.

Slowly Ivan sits up, arms around his children 'Where . . .? How did you get them?' he says.

'I hid them in the ceiling of our house, Uncle,' says Magda. 'Before we left. And then I went back for them.'

'There are photos,' Cibi says. 'Magda hid those, too.'

While the rest of them eat, Ivan doesn't put a single morsel into his mouth; he is lost in the memories stirred up by the black-and-white photographs. Gradually, the solemn mood shifts into something lighter as the children become enamoured of these images of their father as a young man.

'Daddy, you were a *boy* once!'

'Aunty Chaya is so pretty.'

By candlelight, they all begin to recall episodes from the lives of the brother and sister, their spouses, and Grandfather.

Ivan rubs away the melted wax from the silver surface of the candlesticks. 'I feel Chaya is with us,' he says. 'Looking at these photos in this special light, we have remembered the past without grief. And if we can do that, we can also look ahead without fear.'

*　*　*

Cibi recognises the move to their uncle's block as a new chapter in their lives. While work is still irregular and poorly paid, and the daily and not so subtle anti-Jewish sentiment that seems to be imbedded in Bratislavan society is increasingly grating, the sisters are thankful to be with family once more. Slowly they begin to build a life together in Bratislava.

Nor was Cibi misguided in her musings about romance that day on the rooftop. Mischka, a friend from the old apartment, is very keen to remain in touch and Cibi finds herself looking forward to his visits, despite the fact that Magda and Livi waste no opportunity in making fun of their big sister.

'Oh, Mischka, I love you!' Livi teases, in a high squeaky voice.

'You are so handsome, Mischka. So strong!' Magda moans. 'Cibi, marry him quickly or one of us will.'

'Yuk,' laughed Livi. 'That would be like marrying your brother!'

But the teasing stops when, one evening, Cibi breaks the news.

Uncle Ivan, her cousins and sisters are gathered together in her uncle's apartment, playing a game of charades. Cibi stands up, sits down, stands up and begins to pace.

'What is wrong with you?' asks Livi. 'You're ruining the game.'

'I have something to tell you,' says Cibi, sitting down once more.

'Well, tell us then,' says Magda, when Cibi says nothing.

'OK, OK. Give me a second.' Cibi is flushed, happy, grinning stupidly. 'Mischka has asked me to marry him!'

The sisters stare at Cibi in silence, waiting for more. Ivan leaves his chair to sit beside his niece.

'And?' he asks.

'I've said *yes*.'

The room erupts. Both Livi and Magda burst into tears. Ivan is holding Cibi tight, telling her Chaya would be so proud, that Mischka is exactly who she would have chosen for her eldest daughter. When the noise abates, Ivan is still holding Cibi's hands.

'I have an announcement too,' he says, blushing.

'Uncle!' yells Livi. 'You're getting married too?'

'I am. Her name is Irinka. She is also a survivor.'

A few weeks later, in April 1946, Cibi marries Mischka. She couldn't have cared less it is on Hitler's birthday; Cibi was glad, in fact. She wished every Jew could find something to celebrate on this day, to show this man and his army of murderers that hope flourishes in the darkest of places. The couple move into another apartment in their uncle's block, ready to begin their lives together.

Not long after the wedding, Cibi and her sisters are having coffee and cake in their favourite café, a routine that hasn't ceased despite her newly married status. The groaning hunger that defined so much of their experience in the camps is now part of their DNA; they will never forget their desperation to put something, anything, in their stomachs. These days they savour every mouthful, but, more than that, they cherish the freedom to move around the city as they choose, no longer under the watchful and penetrating gaze of a *kapo* or worse, an SS officer.

'The other day,' Livi tells her sisters, biting into flaky pastry and moaning with pleasure. 'I stood in front Madam Cleo's boutique. You know the one?' The girls nod. 'Just because I *could*. 'No one was going to tell me to go and clean the toilets or dig holes or sort the mail of dead people; I was just *free* to stand there and dream myself into those dresses.'

'I know what you mean,' says Magda, about to launch into her own stories of the incredulous wonder of being in control of her own body, but she doesn't, because she has noticed that Cibi has gone very red in the face.

'Are you OK?' she asks Cibi. 'You've gone all . . .'

'I'm having a baby!' Cibi blurts.

The sisters slam down their coffee cups and burst into howls of excitement.

'If Grandmother were here she'd deliver the baby,' says Livi finally, turning back to her pastry.

'She'd put ruby earrings into her ears,' says Magda, gulping down her now cold coffee.

'Would she still do that if it was a boy?' Livi asks.

The girls dissolve into laughter.

Every day and for the next seven months, Magda and Livi visit Cibi; they feel the baby kick and they marvel at the expansion of Cibi's belly. They quiz her midwife, letting it be known they will be present at the birth. Mischka, however, won't, and it's not expected of him.

Magda and Livi turn up unexpectedly at Cibi's apartment one day, demanding she accompanies them on a secret mission.

'I don't want to go anywhere! Look at me, I'm an elephant,' she wails.

'Even elephants go shopping.' Livi giggles. 'Come on, Jumbo. Get up.'

'Where are we going? You wouldn't do this to me if you knew what it was like to have a giant football in your tummy.'

'We don't know, you're right. And that's because you, as the eldest, have taken it upon yourself to do everything first,' Magda says.

'But I look so bloated and puffy.'

'You've looked worse, trust me,' Livi says, grinning.

'That's not fair! You looked just as bad as me,' Cibi throws back at her.

'I never looked as bad as you two did, did I?' Magda says, suddenly serious.

'But you would have, if you'd been there as long as we had,' Livi says, and immediately wants to bite back the words. 'I'm sorry, Magda, that came out wrong. I'm an idiot.' Livi hangs her head.

'I know it did. It's OK. Just help me get the elephant up off the sofa, into her shoes and out of the door.'

Cibi lets herself be dragged out of the apartment and onto the busy high street. Livi lingers by every clothes shop they pass and each time Magda urges her on.

'This trip is for Cibi,' she says, impatiently, 'not you. Come on, we're nearly there.'

Magda and Livi stop in front of a large shop, its windows full of prams and cots and tiny mannequins sporting colourful children's clothes.

'We're here!' Magda announces, finally.

'I can't afford anything in there,' Cibi says, deflated.

'But we can, Cibi.' Livi takes her arm to lead her into the shop, but Cibi resists.

'It's OK,' Livi soothes. 'We've saved a little money from our wages these past few months and now we have enough to buy a pram for that soccer ball.'

'All you have to do is choose the one you want,' Magda says.

'We weren't going to have a pram; we can't afford one.'

'You are going to have a pram, Cibi Meller!' Livi insists. 'Mumma would have wanted you to have one, and we want you have one.'

'Will you please come inside and choose one?' Magda takes Cibi's arm and, finally, Cibi allows herself to be dragged inside the shop.

An hour later, Cibi is pushing a brand-new pram all the way home. The sisters are quiet, aware of the those who can't be here as they prepare to welcome a new generation of Mellers, but it's Cibi who looks the saddest.

'Are you OK?' Livi asks, taking her hand. 'Is it the pram?'

Cibi seems to come back from far away. 'No, Livi. Of course not, I love the pram. It's everything I could have wished for.'

'Is it Mumma, then? Are you thinking about her?'

'I'm always thinking about her. But that's not it, either.' Cibi pushes the pram to the side of the pavement and the sisters follow.

'What is it then?' asks Magda, puzzled.

'It's Mischka,' says Cibi. She meets her sisters' eyes and looks away. 'This isn't his first child,' she says.

Livi and Magda stare at Cibi, waiting for more.

'I don't understand,' says Magda, finally. 'He has another child?'

Cibi nods. 'Mischka has been married before and he has also been a father before.'

The truth behind Cibi's words hits Magda and Livi at the same time. They each place an arm around her shoulders and draw her close. Poor Mischka, thinks Magda. Just like us, he has lost so much.

'Thank you for telling us,' Magda whispers, her voice breaking, her heart breaking for the brother-in-law they have come to love.

'Is he happy that you are having a baby?' Livi asks, tentatively.

'Oh, Livi, yes, he is. Very happy. He calls it his second chance.'

'Then it will be a very special baby,' Magda says. 'Has he told you much about his first family?'

'Before we were married he told me everything. And we haven't spoken about it since.'

'His child, was it a son or daughter?'

'A daughter. Her name was Judith.' Cibi falters, clears her throat. 'She was three years old when she was taken away with her mother.'

Livi stamps her foot, turns away, looks up at the sky. The sisters are sniffing, wiping their eyes, each of them recalling the terrifying images of very young children being lowered into the arms of their mothers and fathers from the cattle wagons. They had been too young to know what was going to happen to them, but old enough to realise they had arrived in hell.

Cibi notes the flame in Livi's eyes, the flare of her nostrils. 'It's all right, Livi, honestly, he'll be fine. Mischka will hold this little baby in his arms, and he'll remember Judith and the first time he held her. And then he will love and protect his second-born child with his life. I know he will.'

'His new son will fill the hole in Mischka's heart, Cibi,' says Magda. 'Just as you have done.'

'Oh, Magda, when did you become so wise, and how do you know I'm having a boy?' Cibi is smiling now, happy to have shared her husband's story with her sisters.

'I have always been wise, the two of you just never saw it. And I do believe you will give Mischka his first son.'

* * *

That night, Magda crawls into bed with Livi, who is sobbing into her pillow.

'Do you want me to give you a cuddle?' she asks Livi. 'I can tell you've been thinking about Mumma all day.'

'I have, and Mischka too. His little girl.'

'I know,' says Magda. 'Me, too. But you cry every night, Livi – are you dreaming about Mumma?'

'No, I wish I did,' says Livi, wiping her nose on the sleeve of her nightdress.

'What do you dream about, then?'

'I think about Mumma and our little house before I fall asleep, and then, for the rest of the night, I'm back in Birkenau.'

Magda wraps her arms around her sister. What can she say to this? She pulls Livi close and sings her a child's lullaby until she falls asleep.

When Cibi goes into labour, her sisters are by her side, taking turns to hold her hands, bathe her with wet flannels and encourage her with advice neither is qualified to give. A whole day and night passes like this and still the baby hasn't arrived. When the sun begins to set on the second day, everyone is exhausted and subdued. And then, suddenly, Cibi breaks the monotony of their patience with a piercing scream.

'It's coming!' Cibi yells. 'Now!'

Magda and Livi snap to attention: Livi wipes Cibi's face clean of sweat and tears; Magda, at the foot of the bed with the midwife, yells, 'Push! One more time, Cibi. Push!'

The sound of a newborn fills the room. Magda and Livi promptly burst into tears.

'Mumma should be here,' sobs Livi.

'I can feel her here,' says Cibi, tiredly, touching her chest. 'I really can. But I can *see* my sisters.'

'Don't you want to know what you've got?' asks Magda, nestling a small bundle of blankets in her arms.

Cibi stares at the new baby and nods.

'A boy,' says Magda.

'I have a boy?' says Cibi softly, taking the bundle. She looks into the wrinkled face of the newborn. 'Magda, Livi, we have a baby boy.'

'Would you like me to send the father in to see his son?' asks the midwife.

'In a moment,' says Cibi, gazing into the blue eyes of her son. 'Just give us a few minutes. He'll understand.'

Livi reaches over, gently stroking the face of her nephew. Cibi places the squirming bundle into her sister's arms and Livi looks into his puffy, little red face as she begins to sing.

My Little Angel	*Hajej můj andílku*
Lie my little angel, lie and sleep,	*Hajej můj andílku hajej a spi,*
Mum is rocking her baby.	*matička kolíbá děťátko svý.*
Lie, sleep sweet, little one,	*Hajej dadej, nynej, malej,*
Mum is rocking her baby.	*Matička kolíbá děťátko svý.*
Lie my little angel, lie and sleep,	*Hajej můj andílku hajej a spi,*
Mum is rocking her baby.	*matička kolíbá děťátko svý.*
Lie, sleep sweet, little one,	*Hajej dadej, nynej, malej,*
Mum is rocking her baby.	*Matička kolíbá děťátko svý.*

When Mischka steps into the room, the tears flowing freely down his face, Livi takes Magda's arm and the sisters leave husband and wife alone to welcome this precious child into their family.

As the months pass, Magda and Livi watch Karol grow from a tiny baby into a big baby, but Livi also watches her big sister ease into being part of a new family. Their uncle now has Irinka, who is adored by his children. What does Livi have? She is beginning to feel restless, but Magda has no desire to shake up their lives again.

It is an everyday act of racism, one of the many that have come to define the boundaries of their existence in Bratislava, which makes up Livi's mind.

'Chocolate! Can you believe it?' Livi has just stormed into their apartment, rage painting her features. 'I've just been abused for having the gall to buy some chocolate.'

'What are you talking about, Livi?' Magda asks.

'Two anti-Semitic imbeciles came into the shop as I was handing over my money, and do you know what they said?' Livi is pacing the floor.

'I have no idea, Livi, what did they say?'

'One of them looked down his nose at me, and it was a big nose, and in his stupid loud voice, so everyone in the shop could hear, he said, "Bloody Jew. Who do they think they are to eat good chocolate?"'

'What did you do?' Magda is calm; she doesn't want to inflame Livi any further.

'I put the chocolate down and left.' Livi rounds on her sister. 'I don't want to live like this anymore. I want to be somewhere where I'm not abused because I'm a Jew, somewhere I can buy chocolate and not feel threatened.'

'What are you saying?' Magda asks, worry creeping into her voice.

'Something needs to change, and I don't think it will in Slovakia.'

Over the next few weeks, Livi talks to fellow survivors about leaving Slovakia. Now under communist rule, they receive little news about the situation in Palestine and the efforts to create a new state of Israel.

When Livi shares her frustrations with her friends, a few of the boys speak up and tell her they are leaving for Israel soon, when they have done their training with the *Hachshara*. She imagines living a life where her hard work will be fairly rewarded, where she won't always be the last one chosen for office work because she's a Jew, where she can believe that those around her want the same things for themselves as she does. In the end, she is surprised at how easy it was to make up her mind.

'I want to join them,' Livi tells her sisters one evening. She and Magda are in Mischka and Cibi's apartment. Livi is bouncing Karol on her knee. 'I want to join the *Hachshara* movement and then go to Israel. I want us all to go to Israel.'

'That's crazy talk,' Magda explodes. 'First of all, no one is allowed to leave this country – we're all communists now, in case you didn't know. Also, haven't you heard what the British are doing to Jews who try to make it to Israel? They're turning migrants right round and taking them straight back to refugee camps.' The three sisters flinch at the word 'camp'. 'They've even boarded the boats bound for Israel.'

This is true. Britain, fearing the loss of their position as the dominant power in the Middle East has no desire to aid the creation of a Jewish nation, which might provoke the Palestinians and thus jeopardise the British power base there.

'I've done my research, Magda, thank you,' says Livi, her mouth set in a straight line. 'That's what the training is for. Don't you think our freedom is worth fighting for? We didn't leave one prison only to find ourselves in another.'

Magda is silent.

'Haven't you had enough of Slovakia?' Livi asks her sisters. 'When was the last time you got a job lasting longer than a week, Magda? And you, Cibi, do you want to bring up your baby in a country which still seems to hate its Jews?'

Magda opens her mouth, but Cibi lays a hand on her sister's arm. Magda turns to her. Cibi is smiling. 'She's not wrong, Magda, and I was in the *Hachshara*, remember? They will look after her.'

'We are not allowed to leave this country!' Magda repeats. 'No one is. What will they do to her if they capture her?' Magda shivers.

'No one will capture me,' says Livi. 'And I won't be allowed to leave until I'm ready.'

'Livi is a woman now, Magda. She's twenty-one years old. Let's just hear her out.'

Magda rounds on Cibi. 'Why are you keen suddenly to get rid of our sister? I thought we had a pact. I thought we were supposed to stick together, to look after each other. We promised father, we . . .'

'Magda, listen to me,' says Cibi. 'You must go with Livi. Do the training and get to Israel.' Cibi's voice is calm, reassuring, as if Livi's choice is the obvious one to make. 'And then Mischka, Karol and I will follow you.'

Magda's mouth falls open.

'We won't be joining the *Hachshara* because of the baby, but we'll find another way.'

'See, Magda?' Livi is on her feet, punching the air. 'Cibi is going too, it's decided.'

'Nothing is decided, little sister.' Magda is quiet, imagining life in Bratislava on her own. It's an impossible picture. 'I need to think.'

'But you're open to the idea?' Livi says, hopefully. Magda doesn't say yes or no, but gives a single nod instead.

'God will watch over you,' Mischka says. He has been silent during this exchange, but now he comes to stand by Cibi's shoulder. 'It is the right thing for us, for the whole family.'

Livi grins and says, 'See?' to Magda, who ignores her because she is busy, thinking.

CHAPTER 27

Bratislava
October 1948

Magda and Livi watch Cibi and Mischka, baby Karol in his mother's arms, walk back to their car and drive away. Minutes before, Magda had reluctantly handed Cibi the pillowcase with the candlesticks and photos, and extracted a promise that she would soon follow them to Israel and 'give them back to me'.

Now, two sisters wait by the side of the road for the other young Jewish men and women to arrive. Jewish men and women who, like them, have decided to join the *Hachshara*. They will be part of a cadre willing to risk everything to make a new life for themselves in Israel.

It had been hard to say goodbye to Cibi, of course it had. Magda views her older sister as an extension of her own body; to Livi she is a mother and her saviour. But there was also an air of celebration to the farewell. It is October 1948 and Cibi's twenty-sixth birthday. Vows had been renewed: they are an invincible unit, and while two of the three sisters might soon be 3,000 kilometres away, this distance will not so much as scratch the exterior of their promise. But it is time for them to move on again, to make new lives for themselves and thankfully, Magda had finally agreed she was ready.

'Strength and hope,' she told Cibi the night before their departure. 'That should be enough to build a new world, shouldn't it? But we need your help to do it, so don't waste any time.'

The men and women arrive in their hundreds and begin to board the trucks idling by the side of the road. Livi isn't sure if she's excited or terrified as they begin to pull away. What if this is a terrible mistake and she has dragged Magda right back into danger? The canvas flaps are drawn against the prying eyes of the Bratislavans as they move out of the city, and Livi wonders if there will ever come a time when they can freely, openly go wherever they want.

They bounce along the gravelled road, bumping over small rocks, swerving round craters while Magda's mind drifts back to her time in captivity, when a similar truck had delivered her to a prison. She wonders what happened to Mr Klein. But the excitement in the vehicle is infectious and soon Magda finds herself relaxing into the company of cheerful and hopeful young men and women.

It is cold, with winter just round the corner, but the sisters are snug in thick scarves, hats, warm coats and sturdy footwear. They are strong and healthy again, and now three hours and 150 kilometres later, the truck stops in a plot of mud and forest vegetation. This will be their home for the next three months.

'Breathe in the air, Magda! How wonderful it feels! It reminds me of the forest back in Vranov,' Livi squeals.

Magda has to agree: the smell and taste of forest air is like no other. She thinks of home, of Grandfather.

They are told that they have crossed into the Czech side of Czechoslovakia; they are in the woodlands of Moravian Karst, near Blansko. But this information means nothing to Livi and Magda: their feet are cold and they are desperate to get inside.

Their accommodation consists of small huts: girls on one side, boys on the other, arranged around a large central building where they will gather for meals and lessons to prepare them for what lies ahead.

After they unpack, Magda and Livi follow everyone else into the main hall.

They are informed that their training will be intense and require courage; they will soon embark on a journey across a hostile European landscape, through countries now under communist rule, closed to the outside world.

'You will learn to travel light, move unseen and fight when you have to,' their instructor tells them. 'We are not communists, we are Jews, and we have paid dearly for the freedom to choose where we want to settle and live our lives.'

While they feel daunted by the idea of 'training', both Magda and Livi are eager to begin the journey, desperate to believe the memories which haunt them will magically disappear once they set foot in Israel.

That first night, they fall asleep filled with a sense of purpose, of hope that they will acquire the tools to carve out a future for themselves, and eventually for Cibi, Mischka and baby Karol. They triumphed when the world was against them, and have come so far. Magda is determined that the hope which kept them alive in the camps will drive their ambition to finally determine their own fate.

They train in the Moravian forests and what many lack in fitness, they make up for with enthusiasm. Magda and Livi find themselves in caves and canyons, in dense woodland and deep snow, challenging the elements as they are tasked with surviving the night in the wild, with few provisions.

The girls' stamina grows and they discover their appetite for the challenge is huge, and soon they are sailing through their exercises.

'We faced much worse at Auschwitz,' is Livi's cheerful and constant refrain.

It is when the sisters are handed revolvers that they face their first real hurdle. Neither want any part in learning how to fire a gun. And they are not alone.

'The Communists will not let us leave Europe,' their instructor tells them. 'And the British do not want us to travel to Israel. We are still being rounded up, whether on land or at sea. Who here wants to be sent to a detention camp, have their freedom ripped away? Haven't we suffered enough?'

His message is clear: to move to the next level of training, they will have to learn how to use a weapon.

At the shooting range the next morning, the sisters accept the guns offered to them and Livi proves to be a skilled marksmen, to Magda's astonishment.

'How?' asks Magda, staring at the scattered tin cans on the ground.

'If you imagine they're Nazis,' says Livi, cheerfully, 'it's really very easy.' For Livi, each tin can is the face of Isaac, with his greasy black hair and yellow teeth. Every time she hits her target.

Magda raises the weapon to the cans lined up on a tree stump in the distance, and while her aim is not as accurate as Livi's, she hits more cans than she misses.

'You're right.' Magda turns to her sister, grinning. 'They're all dead!'

Livi's restlessness eases as the days became weeks, and she blossoms in the company of the other men and women in the camp. There are dances, indoor sports, games and meal times. For the first time in her life Livi feels truly independent, amongst these friends who all share the same goal.

She is surprised to learn that some of the group are Christians, joining the *Hachshara* to show solidarity and support for the Jewish dream of establishing a home in the promised land.

Romance also blossoms in the woods, and Livi is flattered when Zdenko begins to ask her for every dance.

The date of their departure draws ever closer. Soon they will begin their trek into Romania, and from there to the port of Constanta. Part of their journey will involve travelling through Ukraine or Hungary, both of which have closed and heavily patrolled borders.

Magda and Livi listen intently as the dangers of such an expedition are explained to them. Livi wonders if everyone feels the same as her, that this part of the journey is almost an extension of their captivity, and simultaneously the last hurdle in their bid for freedom. They walked away from the death march, didn't they, and that took so much more courage; Livi feels ready to walk away again, but she can't pretend she isn't scared.

Travelling in small groups will provide some protection, but they will have to be very careful. If they make it to the port of Constanta in Romania, they will find a ship waiting to take them to Haifa. It will be leaving with or without them.

On the day of departure, Magda and Livi's group of around one hundred trainees travel by truck back to Bratislava. With money in their pockets, they will take trains where they can, otherwise hitch rides or walk. Each of them has a gun and a supply of bullets. Livi and Magda put the bullets in their bags; the guns they shove deep into their coat pockets.

'Are you upset that Zdenko isn't in our group?' Magda asks.

'A bit, but not really.'

'Do you like him, Livi?'

'Of course I like him.'

'No *romantic* feelings?'

'No. He's a friend, that's all.'

'Friendship is a good basis for something else,' Magda teases.

'Well, Magda, when you have found *the one*, you can tell me what it feels like, then I will know what to look for. Until then, sister, mind your own business.'

'Are you scared, Livi?' asks Magda, suddenly solemn.

Livi looks at her big sister and sees her own fear reflected in Magda's eyes. 'It can't be worse than a death march, can it? Or a selection?' she replies.

'I guess that's one way of looking at it,' Magda says.

'It's the only way.'

The trainees take trains to a range of different towns, from where they will position themselves to cross into Romania. Vranov was one of the options, which Magda and Livi rejected; they choose instead to travel to Košice, and make their way through Hungary. From there, they hope the locals will direct them to Constanta.

They have been given maps and a guide: Vlad. With three other boys, the sisters listen while Vlad tells them they will have to cover another 500 kilometres once they are in Romania.

'Do you think we will have time to visit Father's grave in Košice?' Livi whispers.

'I don't think so, Livi. We need to keep moving. We'll come back one day,' Magda says.

Livi leans back and shuts her eyes and lets the motion of the train lull her to sleep.

Arriving in Košice, the group of six are aware of their friends also disembarking the train, but they ignore one another, as they have been instructed to do. The group is now on their own.

'Only thirteen days to go and you'll be on the boat,' Vlad tells them, as they walk the city streets of Košice. 'Let's find somewhere warm to spend the night.'

'A hotel?' asks Livi, hopefully.

'A barn,' he replies.

'No soft blankets and feather mattresses for you, Livi,' one of the boys teases. 'Will you be OK or should we shoot some ducks and pluck them for your pillow?'

'That would be lovely, thank you,' Livi fires back.

It's getting dark when they reach the outer limits of the city. They are on a deserted road, woodland to the left and right of them, but no sign of any barns. The boys want to camp in the woods, so does Vlad, but Livi wants to hold out for shelter.

All six heads turn round at the sound of the clip-clopping of a horse. Vlad's hand goes inside his jacket. Livi tenses: this is where it falls apart, where they will be taken captive once again, punished for wanting more than a life lived in the shadows. Magda takes a deep breath, trying to control the trembling in her hands. She'll never shoot anyone, she knows that now, because how can she, when, at the first sign of danger, she falls apart?

'Where are you off to?' A farmer whose cart is being drawn by a fine black mare has pulled up.

Vlad withdraws his hand and waves. Both Livi and Magda exhale.

'To Trebisov,' he replies.

'You're Jews?'

'We are.'

Livi glances at Vlad, but his eyes are fixed on the farmer. If he's not worried, then neither is she.

'Hop on the back and I'll take you as far as I can.'

They climb aboard. The cart reeks of animal dung, but they're comfortable enough in the straw.

'Sorry,' calls the farmer. 'I had pigs in the back.'

They trot along in silence for about an hour. Vlad holds himself erect the entire journey. He might as well be on a train or in a car, thinks Livi, adjusting her own posture. The farmer eventually pulls up at a fork in the road. 'Trebisov is about ten kilometres down the road. You can walk there now, or you can sleep in my barn tonight – it's up to you.'

'It is getting late,' Livi says, hopefully.

'Thank you,' says Vlad to the farmer. 'We would be grateful. I promise we'll be gone before you wake up in the morning.'

'I doubt that.' The farmer grins. 'You ever run a farm?' He winks.

With a flick of the reins, the horse continues down a narrow track to a small farmhouse, beside which looms a large barn.

'Make yourselves at home in there,' he tells them. 'There are still a few pigs inside, but they shouldn't bother you. And my wife will bring you some food in a bit.' He offers a wave and strides off to the farmhouse.

'Thank you,' they chorus.

While they are making beds from the abundant piles of straw, the farmer's wife enters the barn. 'Will someone give me a hand?' she calls.

Vlad and Magda help her with the mugs of tea and a huge plate of steaming potatoes and roast pork. There are six forks.

'This is so generous of you,' Vlad says.

'Leave the dishes by the door when you're finished, I'll collect them later.' The farmer's wife pauses in the doorway before she leaves. 'We've helped other groups, you know, just like you, and we'll do what we can for those that come after you.' With that, she is gone.

Still unused to the random kindness of others, Livi feels a lump in her throat.

'Livi, don't look so surprised,' Vlad tells her. 'Not everyone hates Jews!' The boys and Magda burst out laughing. 'Let's eat.'

They gather around the plate of food. 'Maybe she doesn't know that Jews don't eat pork,' says one of the boys.

'He did warn us he had pigs,' sighs Magda. 'But, Livi, do you remember the house with the Russians?'

Livi nods. 'When we have no other food, we eat pork.'

The boys are still laughing when they all pick up their forks and dive in.

The next morning, the farmer wakes them with tea and fresh bread. He offers to take them to Trebisov.

'Day two of fourteen,' Vlad announces.

In Trebisov they buy food and head for the border. They are in Hungary. That night, they sleep in the woods. Livi would rather sleep in the open now, as far away from people as possible. While she has the skills to survive in the wilds of the countryside, her nerve for any confrontation with an enemy will fail her, she is sure. She wishes Cibi were with them – the promise that they will always be together weighs heavy in her mind. Are they tempting fate by leaving her behind?

Over the next ten days they hitchhike, walk, and travel by train until they arrive in Constanta, two days ahead of schedule. They have met little resistance and both Livi and Magda are wildly grateful. They have been lucky, they acknowledge this to one another, and pray this 'luck' holds out for the voyage.

At the port the ship is already docked, awaiting its cargo of excited migrants. The evidence of a war recently fought surrounds them: many buildings sit in heaps of rubble still waiting to be cleared, but in town the ancient buildings still stand tall and proud, untouched by the chaos that rained down on the port.

A day later, the one hundred trainees from the Moravian Karst forest camp, the first to arrive, are joined by hundreds more from other camps across Europe.

Magda and Livi feel a thrill of exhilaration as they mill around the port, caught up in the anticipation and excitement for the journey ahead.

'Everybody on board and be quick about it!' Vlad is rounding up the young men and women, urging them towards the ship.

Magda takes Livi's hand at the foot of the gangplank. 'This is it, little sister,' she says. Her eyes are shining. Livi knows Magda's tears are for Mumma, for their grandfather, but they are also for herself and Livi too. They are not only about to embark on a voyage across the ocean, but they are crossing over from one life into another.

'I'm ready,' says Livi. 'Let's walk up together.'

Livi thinks of the three sisters on the platform of the train station in Bratislava, on their way back to Vranov. They had been so scared they had clung to each other the whole way. She doesn't feel like that now, she isn't scared, and she is glad Magda is beside her, but then Livi feels a familiar tingle up her spine, a note of dread. Again, she wishes Cibi were with them, the constant protector who kept her alive in Auschwitz through sheer will and determination. Not now, she tells herself, but how do you embrace the future with an open heart when that same heart has been broken over and over again, the shards of it hammered into dust? Maybe that's what this is all about, Livi thinks, as the ship pulls away, putting our hearts back together. Cibi is safe with Mischka and Karol and soon they will honour the promise and follow them to the promised land.

Hundreds of young men and women line the decks, hanging over the sides to watch the waves roll away. Livi puts a hand in her pocket and feels the gun. Her fingers move past the weapon to find the tiny knife, her talisman. It is as much a part of their struggle to survive as their mother's spiritual presence.

'Magda,' she says, quietly. 'I'm going to chuck my gun into the sea.' It doesn't belong with the knife. While they could both kill, the knife has only ever come to her aid.

'What? Don't be so stupid, Livi. Someone will see.'

'They're not looking at me.'

'You can't know that for sure. Please, leave it alone.'

And before Livi can take the gun out of her pocket to launch it into the waves, they are joined by a couple of the girls they had trained with. 'Did you hear?' says one, breathlessly.

Magda, instantly on the alert, stares into the vast expanse of empty sea, the port in the distance growing smaller and smaller, and then into the clear skies. No Communists or British ships in sight. So far, so safe.

'There's not enough bunks below for all the passengers so they're looking for girls to sleep on deck with the boys.' Magda can tell from the glow in their eyes, the pink of their cheeks, that they're excited, thrilled by their daring. 'We're going to say yes. Do you want to join us?'

Magda allows herself to feel the same thrill. 'Sure,' she says. 'Why not? Livi?'

'I signed up for adventure,' says Livi, taking her hand out of her pocket. 'Of course I'll sleep on deck.'

'We'll be in Israel in less than a week,' says Magda, staring at the unending sea ahead of them. 'I think five nights under the stars is a great way to prepare ourselves.'

'Let's go and find the perfect spot,' urges Livi.

'Well, that will be wherever the boys are, right?' says the breathless girl.

'I was thinking as far away from the engine as possible, if we're to get any sleep,' says Magda, sensibly.

'Who wants to sleep?' asks the girl. 'I don't think I will ever sleep again.'

Livi takes Magda's hand as the girls lead the way to their new sleeping quarters. 'Please tell me you're excited, Magda,' says Livi.

'I am, I really am. But I'm scared too, Livi. I really hope we make it without any trouble. But, I guess' – Magda pats her pocket – 'we have these *guns*.'

The girls duck under a rope and Magda follows, unaware that Livi is hanging back. When she realises her sister is no longer by her side, she turns round to see Livi facing a man with greasy black hair. He's older than the sisters, and there is something wrong with the expression on his face. He's sneering not smiling. Livi and the man don't move. They look like statues.

'Livi!' shouts Magda. 'Come on. What are you waiting for?' Magda starts forward, ducking back under the rope until she's standing beside her sister.

'Well, well,' says the man to Livi. 'Who do we have here?'

'Stay away from me.' Livi's voice is trembling.

'Livi. What's going on? Who is this man?' Magda takes her sister's arm to pull her away, but Livi doesn't move.

'Going to the promised land, are you?' he hisses. Magda shivers as she sees his mouth open in a leer to reveal chipped yellow teeth. He takes a step towards the sisters.

Magda's hand goes to her pocket.

The man catches the movement and steps back. 'I never thought you'd make it,' Isaac says.

'Same,' snaps Livi, emboldened a little by Magda's presence. 'You should have been shot along with the Nazis for what you did.'

Magda, her hand still in her pocket, positions herself in front of Livi, blocking her view of the man. 'Livi. Who is he?' she says over her shoulder.

But Livi leans past her and spits into the man's face.

'You going to be a problem for me?' he asks, dragging a sleeve across his cheek.

'I might be. And what will you do about it without any of your Nazi friends to save you?'

'I'm entitled to a fresh start. Just like you.'

'I'm *nothing* like you.' Livi grabs Magda's hand and drags her away.

'It's a big ship,' he calls, as they walk away. 'Who would notice if a little mouse fell overboard?'

Magda turns round, drawing the butt of the gun out of her pocket. 'And who would care if a big oaf like you got a bullet in the back of his head?' she snarls.

The sisters walk away.

When they are at a safe distance, Magda rounds on her sister. 'Livi, tell me who he is. What was all that about?' Magda is scared by the look in her sister's eyes.

'It's nothing, Magda. He's someone from the past,' says Livi, trying to smile but failing.

'But *who* is he?'

'You can guess, can't you? A dirty *kapo* from the camps. A Jew, if you can believe it, but I don't want to talk about it. I want to forget he ever existed.' Livi walks off to join the girls on deck, leaving Magda to trail behind her.

Livi feels lightheaded as the scenes of Isaac's cruelty come back to her. Once more she is standing by the gates of Birkenau watching an SS officer hand his baton to the greasy-haired *kapo*, who proceeds to batter the bodies of prisoners returning to camp.

'I'll remember you, girlie. Isaac never forgets a face,' he had told her, and she knows now that she will never forget his. But what really appals her, what has utterly stumped Livi, is the fact that he could have killed her just now, while she was too immobilised to move or to call for help. Is this her reality now? Must she carry this crippling fear into her new life? She may no longer be a prisoner, but will she ever be truly free?

The sisters walk past a gaggle of girls, giggling and pointing at a group of boys who are preening at their attention. Seeing it, Livi feels like she's stepped back out of the camp and into daylight. *This* is normal life, she reminds herself. People flirt and gossip and do whatever the hell they feel like without being plagued by the dark shadows of Auschwitz every minute of the day. Isn't it enough that she has to dream about Birkenau every night? During the day, she promises herself, I will look to the light.

'Look at those boys,' mutters Magda. 'Peacocks.'

Livi looks at the boys. They are smartly dressed, wearing better than most in their refugee castoffs. The boys are eyeing the girls, grinning and waving, except for one man, who stands apart, leaning against the railings lining the deck. He's looking straight at Livi. She averts her eyes, suddenly self-conscious, and when she glances back, he's still watching.

'Who are they?' Magda asks one of the giggling girls.

'The fly boys,' she tells Magda.

'The what?'

'Pilots, technicians. Great husband material.' The girl is still laughing at her last remark as the sisters walk away.

For the next couple of days Livi forces herself to join in with the others' merriment, but Magda senses her growing discomfort.

'I'm just feeling seasick,' she says, or, 'Magda, you're smothering me. I'm not the "kitten" anymore.'

Livi takes to sitting alone in the evenings, at the front of the ship, staring into the horizon for the first signs of Israel. She hasn't seen Isaac again and hopes that she never will. But, if she does, this time she vows she will call to the others. She will tell them what he has done and they will throw him overboard. Strangely, the thought of his body disappearing beneath the waves doesn't make her feel better.

They pass through the Dardanelles channel and into the Aegean; Livi's senses are overwhelmed by the colour of the sea, and overwhelmed again when they hit the Mediterranean, skirting the coastline of Turkey. Next stop, Haifa, she thinks and it will all be behind her: Auschwitz, Isaac, the death march, all of it.

As the sun dips below the horizon on the fourth day, Magda joins Livi at the bow. 'I can see why you like to sit here,' she muses. 'It's so peaceful. Maybe tomorrow you'll be the first to spot land.'

'I feel safe here, like nothing can harm me,' Livi says. 'Does that sound strange?'

'A little. But you are safe now. We both are. Whoever that man was, Livi, you have to put him out of your mind. Once we land, you'll never see him again. Now, let's go and eat before it's all gone.' Magda stands up and holds out a hand to her sister, who takes it.

As they turn to head towards the dining room, they hear them before they see them: the Peacock Boys, as Magda has taken to calling them. They're talking loudly amongst themselves, but it's for the benefit of the girls who have gathered to watch this display.

'Not this lot again,' says Magda, loud enough to be heard by the boys and the girls. Livi's laughter dies in her throat when she sees him again: the lone 'fly boy', standing to one side, looking at her. Blushing, she grabs Magda's arm and they run to dinner.

In the late afternoon of the following day, the port of Haifa looms into view. The ship is instantly filled with cries of excitement and cheer. Feet pound the deck in a restless enthusiasm to set foot on dry land.

And then the world tilts. Livi's screams pierce the air as a gun explodes. She is immediately on all fours, hunkering to the ground as the joyful cacophony continues around her. She runs her hands over her body. Has she been shot? Did he get her?

'Livi! Livi! What's wrong?' Magda is kneeling beside her. 'It's just some idiot firing his gun into the air to celebrate. Come on.'

As Livi stumbles to her feet the captain steps onto deck, and instantly the cheering stops. His face is red, and there is fury in his eyes as he raises a bullhorn to his mouth. 'Who just fired a gun on my ship?' he roars.

No one speaks, although the hands of all the men and women go to their pockets, feeling for their own guns.

'I will not ask again,' bellows the captain. 'I will turn this damned ship round and take everyone back if you don't come forward right now.'

A hesitant hand is raised in the crowd. 'I'm sorry, Captain.' The culprit, a young man, continues: 'I just got carried away. I won't do it again.'

'Come here,' the captain orders, holding out his hand. 'The gun, please.'

The man steps forward and places the weapon in the captain's hand. The captain pockets the gun and slaps the man hard across the head. He takes his punishment without a word.

The crowd is more subdued after that and Magda and Livi head for the bow of the ship, from where the port of Haifa is steadily growing in size.

They are home.

CHAPTER 28

Haifa, Israel
February 1949

The sun is shining as the gangplank is lowered to cheers of excitement and whispered prayers of thanks. It's cool, but not cold. The port of Haifa swells with the new arrivals and quayside spectators.

Magda views the milling crowds with a sense of wonder. So many Jews and no one is about to round them up and put them on a train for their beliefs. They will finally be able to proclaim their names, and bare their arms without fear of reprisal or the taunts of anti-Semites.

'Magda,' whispers Livi. 'Are you ready?' She is gripping her sister's arm; if she lets go, she might float away, up into the sky. But then the weight in her pocket slams her back down to earth. 'Do you think we'll be searched before we get off the boat?'

'No idea,' says Magda. 'But if we are, then we're all going overboard and will have to swim to port.' Livi starts to laugh, and begins to tell Magda that would be a pity when the words dry in her throat.

'Smart girl. You kept your mouth shut,' jeers Isaac, standing before them.

Livi instantly feels the familiar dread, the pressure on her bladder, the fear, exhaustion and misery of the camp. Her hand is in her pocket, but instead of the gun, her fingers close around the small knife. She withdraws it slowly and holds it by her side.

Isaac doesn't move. He eyes flick to the knife, to the other passengers crowding the deck.

'If I scream now,' Livi tells him in a low voice, 'who do you think my brothers and sisters will believe? You or me?'

'Don't be a fool,' he hisses.

'Let's try it, shall we?' Magda says, lifting her chin.

Isaac's eyes are suddenly wide and wild. He holds up his hands and backs away.

'Where are you going?' says Livi, raising her voice. But the *kapo* has turned round and is running for the gangplank.

'You know, Livi,' says Magda. 'I almost wish you'd done it.'

'What? Stabbed him or called for help?'

'Both.'

Now Magda places her hands on her sister's shoulders. 'That is the last we'll ever see that guy, Livi. We are not bringing him to Israel with us. Take a final look as he runs away and then we'll forget him.'

Livi is breathing hard – the memories are threatening to rear up again – but she nods, wishing that Isaac was the only thing she had to let go of.

From the top of the gangplank they look down at the dock, wanting to fix this picture in their minds for ever. Before they can take a step, a young man pushes past them.

Livi tenses, but it's just a boy in a hurry to get ashore. 'Sorry,' he mutters.

Livi is surprised to see it's the lone 'peacock'. 'It's OK,' she says, grinning. The boy winks at her and then he's swallowed up by the crowds of men and women spilling off the ship onto the dock.

'Ready?' asks Magda.

With a case each, their arms linked, Magda and Livi step in time down the ramp, pausing at the bottom.

'Now!' says Livi.

As the sisters step onto dry land for the first time in a week, tears spilling down their cheeks, their faces are turned not to the sun, but to the ground beneath their feet.

Standing in the crowd on the quay are two men dressed in military-style uniform, their berets bearing the insignia of wings around a Star of David. They wave to the Peacock Boys, who follow them to a truck adorned with the same insignia.

'Must be the air force,' Magda says.

'Israel has an air force, already?' Livi asks.

But they don't have time to ponder this or the Peacock Boys any further, as the new Israelis are called to line up for registration and the allocation of a new home.

Magda and Livi are aboard an open truck with other men and women, driving through the streets of Haifa. The people on the pavements wave and cheer their arrival and everyone aboard the truck waves and cheers right back. On the outskirts of the town, the sisters marvel at the huge groves of orange trees; the air is heavy with their sharp, sweet aroma.

They are a little way out of Haifa when the truck turns off the road and onto a rough track, which they bounce along for a good half-hour.

They pull up inside a small compound of huts and barns, a clearing within an abundant orange grove. A man emerges from one of the huts and watches the men and women clamber out of the vehicle.

'*Shalom aleichem!*' He is smiling, spreading his arms wide to welcome the travellers.

'*Aleichem shalom,*' they call back.

'Welcome to Israel. Welcome to Hadera. Welcome to your kibbutz. Thank you for making the dangerous journey to be here, to be part of the founders of your new home.' The men and women gather around him.

Magda holds Livi's hand and Livi shakes her off. 'Too tight,' she says, and Magda takes her arm instead.

'My name is Menachem, I am the supervisor and your friend,' the man continues. 'As you can see, you are standing in an orange grove. Right now, there are no oranges to pick but there is plenty of work to do as we prepare for picking season. I want you to spend your time here getting to know one another. You are the future of this land – respect her, and she will look after you.' He points to the huts. 'This is where you'll live.' Menachem gives them a wry smile: 'Boys on one side, girls on the other. But should you meet in the middle, well, so be it. Over there are the kitchens and dining area where some of you will work, because I'm not going to cook and clean for you. Now, go and find yourself a place to call home and I'll see you at dinner.'

'When will we know it's dinner time?' a voice pipes up.

'Ah, someone who thinks about his stomach. Good, you can only work and play if you are well fed. To answer your question, there is a large cowbell outside the kitchen which you'll all hear when it's time to eat. Now, go.'

'He has Father's name,' says Magda.

'It's a good sign, isn't it?' Livi is staring at the supervisor. The girls and boys are all heading towards the huts but the sisters haven't moved.

Menachem too has not moved. '*Shalom*, ladies, is everything all right?'

'Everything is wonderful, it's j-just . . .' Livi stammers.

'Go on.'

'You have our father's name,' she says, shyly.

'I am honoured to have the same name as your father. And what are your names?'

'I'm Livi and this is my sister Magda.'

Menachem glances at the girls' arms.

'Show me?' he asks.

Magda holds out her arm and they both inspect the tattoo.

'Livi, Magda, you are both safe here and I am honoured to meet you. If there is anything you need, please come and find me. Promise me you will?'

'We will,' Magda says.

As the sisters walk away, Livi is still solemn.

'Are you OK, kitten?' Magda asks her. 'Was that upsetting?'

'I wish we could remove them, Magda,' says Livi. 'I wish I could cut my arm off.'

Magda lays an arm around Livi's shoulders. 'And give the Nazis our limbs too? They've taken enough.'

'Are you happy, Magda? That we're here?'

'I just want to feel safe again, Livi, and isn't that just what Menachem promised?'

'Magda, wake up. Wake up.' One of their four roommates is hovering over Magda's bed. It is still dark outside, but the moon is out, throwing pale white light over the figures asleep beneath their blankets. The camp is quiet.

'What is it?' Magda asks disoriented, drowsy.

'It's your sister. She's crying and calling out – I think she needs you.'

Now Magda hears the muttering, the sobbing from her sister's bed. She's out of bed in moments, crossing the room.

'Cibi? Cibi, where are you?' Livi is repeating over and over as she twists and turns under her covers.

'Livi, it's all right, I'm here.' Magda sits down on Livi's bed and takes her shoulders. 'You're OK, Livi.'

'I need Cibi. I need Cibi,' moans Livi.

'It's Cibi, Livi. Right here.'

The other girls in the room are all awake now, sitting up in their beds, watching the exchange between the sisters.

Magda wraps Livi in her arms.

Livi seems to hear Magda's words, as her body relaxes and she falls back to sleep and Magda climbs into bed with her.

The next morning, Livi is perplexed to find her sister asleep beside her. She shakes her awake. 'Why are you in my bed?'

Magda, once again, wakes up disoriented. For a moment, she too has no idea why she's there, and then she remembers. 'You had a bad dream, that's all,' she tells Livi. 'And I thought a cuddle would help.'

Livi gets out of bed and heads for bathrooms in the hut next door to theirs.

'I had a sister who used to sleep-talk, and cry out.' The roommate who had woken Magda is moving around the room, picking up the clothes she dropped the night before. 'My mother said it was best if we never told her about it.'

'Maybe you're right,' sighs Magda.

'Who's Cibi?'

'She's our older sister. She and her family will be here soon.'

'And Livi is close to her?'

'Very. They were in Auschwitz together for nearly three years.'

'What about you? I've seen the number on your arm.'

'I came later, much later. I didn't go through half what they did.'

The girl lays her dirty clothes on her bed and crosses the room to give Magda a hug. 'Livi will be fine, we're all one family now.'

'And you? Do you have anyone here?'

'I don't.' The girl frowns and turns away to look out of the windows at the glorious sunshine. 'They're all dead and I don't know how or even why I survived, but I did.' The frown is gone as quickly as it had appeared and now she's smiling. 'We owe it to those who died to live our best lives, become our best selves, and here we can.'

Livi bursts into the hut, her arms flung around the shoulders of two girls. 'Magda! Look who I found!' she squeals.

Magda looks at the girls, who are holding on to Livi as if they will never let her go. 'Who have you found, Livi?'

'It's Shari and Neli! They're sisters too. We were in Auschwitz together, they worked in the *Kanada*.'

Shari and Neli extend their hands to Magda.

'We heard so much about you,' Shari says. 'Livi and Cibi talked about their family all the time. I am so happy they found you.'

'And Cibi will be here soon,' Magda tells them. 'Any day now.'

The four girls head for the kitchen, for their first breakfast, on their first day in their new land.

Magda and Livi settle into the routine of life on a kibbutz and begin to learn Hebrew, the language of their new country. They attend talks given by officials from Tel Aviv and Jerusalem, where they learn of the plans to turn Israel into a home for Jews across the world. They will fill the country with businesses and babies, they will remember the dead and celebrate the living. They will never forget, but they must also live their best lives. Much of this feels inspiring to the sisters, but often, at the end of one of these talks, Livi feels very small, too small to be charged with the monumental task of creating a new homeland on behalf of all those who were murdered. But Magda is more hopeful.

'You're just missing Cibi,' she reassures her. 'She's coming, Livi, and when she gets here, we can stop worrying about her.'

The task they are most devoted to is their Sunday evening ritual when they sit down to write to Cibi. Livi's letters beseech Cibi to come soon, that there is so much there for her to love, but she must hurry, while Magda's are more practical, containing lists of things that would be useful in this new climate.

Cibi writes back to tell them she, Mischka and Karol will be arriving in May.

With Cibi's arrival date on the horizon, Livi's mood is better. She begins to feel the past receding, just a little, with each day she spends in the orange groves, amongst the trees, watching the fruit grow, their hues shifting from green to pale yellow, to brilliant orange. The first fruit she picks makes her face pucker as she tastes its bitter juice, but she drinks it down just the same.

'Too soon,' Menachem tells her, with a grin. 'Another month, young Livi.'

Eventually, the large trucks arrive. It is time to pick the oranges. Everyone is shown how to secure the wicker baskets to their bodies, and they march into the fields, line up in front of the rows of trees and begin to pick oranges. It's not supposed to be a race, but Livi can't help herself: she is the first in the kibbutz to haul an overflowing basket to the sorting shed.

The sisters collapse into bed straight after dinner during picking season; the long days have robbed them of any desire to socialise, and it is the same for everyone. But, four weeks later, when the last orange is plucked from the final tree, they are allowed a week off. They can go to Haifa or stay and recuperate on the farm.

The sisters stay where they are, enjoying the silence of the empty fruit groves, a silence which is soon shattered by cries of delirious excitement when Cibi's letter arrives, informing them of her departure date.

'We'll be together again, Magda,' says Livi, waving the letter in the air. 'The Meller sisters in one place, just as they should be. She says they're sailing from Italy – didn't you once want to go to Italy?'

'Did I?' Magda can't recall wanting anything for years other than her sisters' safety.

'You did, but never mind. Hopefully Cibi won't decide to stay there.'

'I wish we knew more about their trip.'

'You know they can't put too much in their letters.' Livi opens her eyes comically wide. 'There are eyes everywhere!' she booms.

Magda laughs and mimics her expression. 'Spies every-where!' But then she seems to deflate, the joke over. 'This place, though? Can they really come here? There aren't even any children on the kibbutz.'

'Can we worry about that later?' Livi folds the letter and puts in her pocket. 'Don't spoil it just yet!'

* * *

'Just how much have you packed, Cibi?' Mischka sighs, looking at the three open suitcases on their bed, brimming with clothes, books, toys and – sticking out of the sleeve of a winter coat – Chaya's precious candlesticks.

'What would you have me leave behind? Kari's toys? Your clothes?' Cibi says, with a pout.

'We can buy Kari more toys in Israel. I can *make* him more toys – but at least let's leave behind his enormous yellow truck?'

'Can we take his train at least? You made it, and he would be heartbroken to leave it here.'

'The train can stay, but not the truck. And only two books – the others we can give to your uncle's children.'

Reluctantly Cibi removes the wooden yellow truck and several books from one of the suitcases. 'I will only take one extra pair of shoes,' Cibi says, examining the two pairs she has packed, deciding which to discard. 'And food? For the journey?' She doesn't intend to stuff tins of sardines in between her son's toys, but the inclination to is strong.

'Again, not too much. We're not abandoning civilisation, you know. We can buy what we need as we go,' says Mischka.

'Uncle Ivan will be here in the morning to help us, so he can take anything we don't want.'

'Will Irinka be with him?'

'No, he's coming alone. He said he'd be much more useful if he was on his own. And anyway, their baby is so small still.' Cibi looks wistful for a moment. 'Hopefully he will join us very soon and then the whole family will be together.'

Only the whole family will never be together again, thinks Cibi. Packing these suitcases has returned her to an earlier time, one she would rather forget, where she and her mother had carefully gathered clothes for two small suitcases that she and Livi were never to lay eyes on again once they had entered Auschwitz.

'What do you want to do today? We should mark it – our last day in the country of our birth,' Mischka says.

Cibi pushes aside the discarded books, sits on the bed, and sighs deeply. 'You don't think we'll ever come back?'

'I don't know. Maybe for a visit.' Mischka sits beside his wife and puts his arm around her.

She leans into him. 'When Kari wakes up, let's put him in his pram and go for a walk. I think that's how I'd like to say goodbye, with one last stroll around town.'

Slowly, the small family makes its way through the streets of Bratislava. Cibi sees the chocolate shop where Livi had once been humiliated for having the audacity to buy a treat. It was the incident which broke the camel's back, thinks Cibi. It broke all our backs. She's ready to say goodbye.

'Let's go home, shall we?' she says to Mischka, who turns the pram round.

Uncle Ivan struggles with the pram, all too aware of the bus driver huffing and sighing as he waits to load it into the back of the bus with the rest of their luggage. Mischka, Kari in his arms, is trying to stifle his giggles as he and Cibi watch Ivan fumbling and cursing.

'Give him a hand, Cibi, please. Put him out of his misery,' Mischka says, eventually.

Ivan holds up his hands in surrender and Cibi takes the pram and hands it to the bus driver in a single swift manoeuvre.

Ivan shakes hands with Mischka, pats Kari on the head and opens his arms for his niece. 'Irinka, the children and I will be with you before you know it,' he says.

'We won't rest until we're together again,' whispers Cibi. 'And safe.'

'This bus is leaving with or without you,' the bus driver grumbles.

Cibi, Mischka and even Kari wave at Ivan until he is out of sight.

On Cibi's lap, Kari is glued to the window, transfixed by the buildings, the cars and the people outside. Say goodbye, little baby, thinks Cibi. We're going on an adventure. A big adventure too: they have borders to cross, documents to be examined and questions answered before they reach – and cross – Italy, where a ship awaits them in Genoa for their passage to Haifa. It's the questions to be answered that gnaw at Cibi: she has had her fill of army officials in spotless uniforms standing between her and her freedom.

'How long before we get to the border?' Cibi asks in a small voice. They are the only ones with so much luggage; it's obvious to everyone on the bus that they're trying to leave the country. With a defiant tilt of the head, Cibi meets the glares of some of the other passengers aboard, who muttered 'Jew' under their breaths as she and Mischka moved down the bus.

'Which border?' Mischka asks.

'Austria, our first test.'

'Not long, half an hour. Depends how many stops we make. We'll be fine because we have all the right documents. Will you stop worrying?'

Cibi squeezes the handles of her handbag, their future contained therein: government documents granting them permission to migrate to Israel. 'Good riddance,' the town hall official had said when he handed them over. But Cibi hadn't cared: she'd felt the same about him.

Two stops later, the bus is pulling in behind a line of cars and trucks at the border between Czechoslovakia and Austria. Cibi's pulse quickens when she spots the armed soldiers walking up and down the rows of vehicles. Their brown uniforms, whilst simple and unadorned with medals, nevertheless send a shiver down her spine. Instinctively, she clutches Kari to her chest. He lets out a cry and Cibi releases him.

Beyond the barrier she sees the Austrian soldiers wandering along the rows of vehicles waiting to enter Czechoslovakia.

The barrier is raised and lowered, raised and lowered, and very slowly the vehicles begin to inch forwards. Cibi watches as most of the cars are waved through the border, but notes, with a growing sense of dread, that some are being turned back.

Finally, the doors of the bus slide open and two soldiers step aboard, one heading for the back of the bus and the other starting at the front. Knowing what to expect, all the passengers have their documents ready and hand them to the officials when requested.

Cibi passes their papers to Mischka who offers them to the approaching soldier. Kari squeals with happiness while they are being examined. The soldier offers the baby a smile before saying, '*Jude?*' to Mischka.

'Yes. We are moving to Israel,' Mischka tells him.

'Why? Don't you want to live in the country of your birth?' The man has a steady gaze and Cibi wants to slap it off his face. *Would* you *want to stay here after what we've been through?* she wants to scream.

'The only family we have left are in Israel and we want to be with them,' Mischka tells him, with an equally steady gaze.

'Good luck.' The soldier hands the documents back and they have passed the first test.

Cibi closes her eyes, exhales, unaware she had been holding her breath. Mischka settles back in his seat and offers Cibi a small, triumphant smile.

Across the border, the Austrian soldiers insist on checking the paperwork for their transit from Genoa to Haifa, and then warn them to proceed with haste through Austria: they have no visa permitting them to stay in the country for even a single day.

Cibi scrambles to produce the train tickets for Vienna to Spielfeld later that day.

'And from there?'

Cibi hands over further train tickets: from Spielfeld, through Yugoslavia, to Trieste in Italy, but, she notes, her heart sinking, this journey is not until tomorrow.

'Where do you plan to spend tonight?' asks the soldier.

'We'll sleep at the station so we can be on the first train out of Austria tomorrow morning,' Mischka told him.

'Well, you had better not miss it.'

An hour later, the bus stops at the Hauptzollamt train station close to the city centre. Cibi and Mischka collect their luggage and strap Kari into his pram. They have a little time before their train and Cibi insists Mischka finds a place to deposit their cases while they look around.

'It's a food hall!' gasps Cibi. They are standing in front of a vast building filled with stall upon stall of tempting foods. Cibi has never seen so much food: cheeses, breads, meat and poultry. She wants to buy it all, and proceeds to devour every sample offered by every trader as they make their way up and down the rows of laden tables. In the end, Cibi buys a selection of her favourite things, enough to last them the few days until they reach the Italian port from where they will sail away from Europe, perhaps for ever.

Back in the railway station, Cibi settles Kari into his pram to sleep and stretches out on the bench, her head in Mischka's lap, to doze before the next leg of their journey. Mischka watches over them.

The next morning, their train arrives on time and the second test looms: Cibi, Mischka and Kari wait on the

334

platform for officials to arrive and process their entry into Yugoslavia.

Cibi feels the tension flood her body, but takes long, calming breaths.

'We'll be fine, Cibi.' Mischka tries to reassure her. 'Look, they're barely even looking at the papers.' Mischka is right: the officials are offering only cursory glances at the documents of the boarding passengers.

Finally, it is their turn, and Cibi hands over their papers and train tickets for their journey to a uniformed official.

'What is this?' the official says, waving their papers at them after attempting to read a language he obviously can't speak. While Cibi has no knowledge of Yugoslavian, Mischka knows enough to recognise there is a problem.

'Do you speak German?' Mischka asks.

'*Ja.*'

Mischka tells him where they have come from and where they were going, while Kari begins to fuss, insisting he be allowed out of his pram.

'The little one is in a hurry to get going,' says the guard, patting the baby on the head.

'Yes, we all are,' says Cibi.

'Then you had all better get on board. The train is about to leave.'

'Thank God for Kari,' says Cibi, collapsing into her seat. 'No one likes a crying baby.'

Four hours later, they arrive at a small station on the outskirts of Trieste. Two soldiers wearing the pale blue berets and uniform of the United Nations climb onto the train and begin to check the passengers' papers. Once again, Cibi is reassured that the papers are handed back to the other travellers without question – until their own are inspected.

The men pass the papers back and forth between them.

'Speak German?' Mischka asks, for the second time that day.

'*Ja*, but you are not German.'

As Mischka outlines their travel itinerary, Cibi can tell his answers are not what they want to hear. The men step aside to speak in low voices.

'You cannot continue on to Trieste,' they are told. 'You must collect your luggage and leave with us now.'

But Cibi doesn't move. 'We have permission to migrate,' she insists, pointing at the documents. She is suddenly very hot. 'It is legal and we're leaving.'

'Miss, please calm yourself. All migrants to Israel are being held while we assess the rightful territory of Trieste. Currently, it's a disputed area.' The soldier smiles, but Cibi is not reassured. 'The United Nations is not your enemy, but we need further clearance before you can proceed.'

Cibi is uncomfortably aware of the other passengers' impatience as she and Mischka unload their luggage, and this only further intensifies her ire: what's a small delay to these people when the future of her family hangs in the balance?

After a short ride in the soldiers' white jeep, they arrive in Trieste, pulling up outside the United Nations headquarters and are shown inside to a large, airy office while their documents are removed for inspection.

'May we offer you some food or coffee? Milk for the little one?' But Cibi waves away their hospitality. She is thinking only of her sisters now. They are waiting for her, and these people are standing in her way.

'We don't have tickets from Trieste to Genoa, Mischka,' Cibi whispers, when they are alone in the room. 'We should have tried harder to buy them.'

The couple had assumed it would be easy enough to buy bus or train tickets for the last leg of their landbound journey, but this oversight is now their downfall.

An official comes back into the room. 'How did you imagine you would cross from Yugoslavia into Italy without a visa or right of passage?' he asks them, to which they have no reply.

We've been fools, thinks Cibi. And all the while we thought we were so clever.

They have been escorted to the dining room, but Cibi can't eat or drink a thing. Her stomach is in knots. Magda and Livi are waiting for them; her thoughts are spiralling, she knows, but there is little she can do about it.

'Cibi, the last thing we need right now is for you to fall apart,' insists Mischka, handing her a cup of coffee. She takes it and gulps, scalding her tongue.

One of the blue berets is approaching their table and Cibi sits up straight, desperate to hear the news that they may proceed with their journey.

'I can't find an Italian senior officer to consult with,' he tells them. 'They will need to grant you entry.'

'And if they don't?' asks Cibi, feeling the last ounces of her energy drain away.

The blue beret looks at his feet. 'Then you will have to go home.'

'Home?' explodes Cibi. She shrugs off her coat, her cardigan and pulls up the sleeve of her jumper, thrusting her tattooed arm under his nose. 'This is what happened to me at home!' she tells him.

The officer's face falls as he studies her arm. 'I am so sorry,' he says.

Mischka pulls down Cibi's sleeve and puts an arm around her shoulders, drawing her close. 'We have been through too much already,' he tells the officer. 'Please help us.'

'Madam, sir, we will not resolve this today.' The officer has regained his composure, but he addresses them with more kindness now. 'Tonight you will be our guests.'

But there is no sleeping to be done. Their bedroom, on the upper floor of the headquarters, is stuffy, and Kari isn't happy, despite the fuss that is made of him in the dining room at supper.

'We just need to get through the night,' Mischka tells Cibi, but Cibi can't so much as blink. Everything hangs in the balance, in the hands of anonymous officials who have no idea what they have endured to come this far.

'I need to be with my sisters, and I will use Auschwitz and Birkenau and the death of my mother to get to Israel,' says Cibi.

The next morning, back in the dining room for breakfast, the senior officer has arrived and now he takes a seat at their table.

'Here are your tickets,' he says, handing Cibi an envelope containing tokens for the fourteen-hour bus ride from Trieste to Genoa, where they will have to wait until their ship is ready to sail. To cover this, there is also a voucher for two nights' accommodation. 'The hotel is very close to the port. This little one must be eager to get home,' he says, offering Kari a warm smile.

Cibi's eyes fill with grateful tears and Mischka takes her hand. The kindness of others, she thinks. When did she

338

forget such gestures were still possible? She looks around the room, catching the smiles and nods of good luck from everyone present.

'We are all keen to get home,' Mischka says.

And soon they are speeding through the Italian countryside, the first blooms of summer wishing them well as they speed by. They pass through small towns, and tiny villages, through the cities of Venice and Verona, and then on to the coast.

At last, Cibi sets eyes on the dazzling blue of the Mediterranean and the ships docked in the port. Which is ours? she wonders. The *Independence*? A good name for a ship, because that's how she feels in this moment: independent and free to proceed to the promised land.

On the day of their departure, hundreds of other passengers materialise from the edges of the town to join them; Cibi and Mischka hold hands as they walk up the gangplank to their future, Kari in Cibi's arms.

On the deck of the *Independence* the couple watch the waves roll away. Cibi is as calm as the waters that carry them. Mischka's arm is around her waist while Kari sits on his shoulders.

'I'm coming, dear sisters, I'm coming,' whispers Cibi to the setting sun.

* * *

After the week's break, the sisters' work in the orange groves is easier. They make sure the trees are healthy, ready for another abundant crop the following year. With summer edging ever closer, the weather is warmer and the sisters revel in the heat. Lying on their backs, day after day, they gaze at the beauty of Mount Carmel, its slopes featuring a lush oasis of vegetation. Livi wonders if they will ever walk its limestone ridge. Maybe one day.

They are lying in the shade on the day Menachem appears by their side with news, a broad grin on his face. 'We've just had word that the next ship will be here in two days. That's your sister's ship, isn't it?'

They girls sit up.

'The *Independence*?' Livi is now on her feet.

'That's right.'

'What's the date? I've lost track of time!' Magda is still dazed from the heat, but now she too stands up.

'The 15th of May. The ship is docking on the 17th.'

'Then we need to go to Haifa! We need to be there when they arrive!' Livi gasps.

'Slow down, Livi. He said two days. Haifa is an hour away.'

'But how will we get there?'

'You will be there to meet the ship, I will organise it,' Menachem assures them. 'But you should know that all migrants are now taken to a camp in Sha'ar Ha'aliya – it's not far from here, don't worry. They'll have health checks and registration. It's just a precaution, and I'm told most people are only there for two or three days.'

The sisters are instantly despondent; they had wanted to pick Cibi up from the port and bring her to the orange groves. Livi has been dreaming about taking Karol up and down the rows of trees in the early evening, beneath a brilliant red sky . . . now she will have to wait even longer.

The dock looks different, Magda observes. Barricades have been erected to separate the new arrivals from the locals.

Magda and Livi position themselves by a barrier close to the point where the gangplank will drop. As they watch the *Independence* sail into the port, Livi and Magda scan the faces of all those on the decks.

The docking is painfully slow, but, finally, the new migrants to Israel are streaming onto the quay.

'They won't be first, Livi,' warns Magda, as Livi attempts to climb the barricade. She yanks her back down. 'Have some patience or you'll get us in trouble. They have a baby, remember. They're not going to risk having him hurt in the crush.'

Buses are lined up on the docks to take the new migrants to Sha'ar Ha'aliya. Men, women and children climb aboard, eager and excited to get on with this first stage of their new lives in the promised land.

'They're taking for ever,' Livi moans.

'No, they're not,' says Magda, her voice breaking. 'They're here!'

Cibi has spotted them on her way down the ramp and now she hands Karol to Mischka and sprints through the crowd towards her sisters. Cibi falls into their arms, heedless of the thin wire of the barrier between them.

None of the women speak for a long time. Mischka watches in silence, too overwhelmed by the sight of his wife's reunion with her sisters, to say a word. It is Karol's grizzling in the end that wrenches the sisters apart. Livi wipes away Mischka's tears, while Magda strokes the cheeks of her baby nephew.

'Thank God you're here,' Magda says.

'He had nothing to do with it, Magda,' Cibi replies.

Magda and Mischka exchange a glance; Mischka smiles. Nothing has changed where Cibi and God are concerned.

'We have to have health checks,' Cibi says, sighing.

'But it's not for long, Cibi. Just a day or two and we'll be there when you get out.'

'Move along, come on. You can't stay here,' a voice calls, but it is the kind voice of an official who has just watched this tender encounter.

'The candlesticks, have you got the candlesticks and the photos?' Magda calls out as Cibi is lead away.

'Yes, Magda, I have the candlesticks and photos, they are in my bag. I promise I will give them to you as soon as I can.'

'We'll see you in a couple of days,' Livi tells her sister.

'Better make it three,' the official says.

'Two,' insists Livi, said with a grin.

'Two it is, then.'

Magda and Livi watch until the bus carrying their sister is out of sight.

After dinner, Magda and Livi corner Menachem and ask him to take a walk with them outside. Boys and girls wander through the trees hand in hand. Excited chatter from the dining hall reaches every corner of the kibbutz; it is like this most evenings, and the sisters will miss it.

'We're thinking of leaving,' Livi tells him. She wants to feel sad about it, but she can't. More than anything she needs to be with *both* of her sisters.

'It's lovely here, and if it wasn't for Cibi we'd stay.' Magda picks up a leaf from the ground. She breaks it in half and holds the citrus smell to her nose. The evening is warm, almost too warm, but it's still cooler than being inside. 'This is a wonderful place, but it's not for families.'

'I understand,' says Menachem. 'I'll be sad to see you go. Do you know where?'

'Not really,' says Magda. 'We were hoping you could help us with that too.'

Menachem laughs, and thinks for a moment. 'There is an area, about a hundred kilometres from here, called Kfar Ahim. It's where a lot of migrants are choosing to settle and start farming. You could be part of something special there.'

Two days later, Magda and Livi are standing outside the quarantine facility with the car and driver provided by Menachem. Their father's namesake has come through for them.

The sisters talk incessantly on the way to Kfar Ahim, but Karol won't stop crying, unable to settle in the heat. Mischka is the only one who is quiet, taking in the noise and the scenery with a big smile on his face.

The government has assured all new migrants they will be housed, and now the family stand before a row of identical prefabricated dwellings, each with two small bedrooms, a kitchen and bathroom. Inside their allotted accommodation, Cibi and Mischka take their cases into one room and Magda and Livi take theirs to the other. Instead of half the world, the only thing that stands between the siblings now is a thin wall.

They are together again.

Kfar Ahim, with a population of 200, is an emerging farming town, its fertile land perfect for growing and processing oranges. The sisters are soon back on familiar territory, working amongst the orange groves. Mischka finds work too and soon he and Cibi and Karol move into a small one-bedroom home, only a few streets away from the sisters, with enough land to start their own farm.

The sisters watch the town grow and, as migrants continue to arrive, the need for accommodation grows. When Livi hears the local authority is asking for volunteers to help build new homes, she and Magda immediately put themselves forward.

'I'm going to help too,' says Cibi, when she hears the news. 'I want to give something back to Israel for taking us in.'

'But you've got Karol,' Livi reminds her.

'I will find someone to watch him.'

For three days a week Cibi joins her sisters at the building site. They aren't the only women, they are pleased to discover. Dressed in trousers and shirts the sisters get to work. More than once Livi and Cibi exchange a glance, and even a tear, as they recall their 'jobs' at Auschwitz and Birkenau. The bricks, the mortar, the rubble – it is complicated, but over time, and in the company of so many new faces and new stories, the sharp edges of their brutal recollections dull a little.

Long lines of women form to pass the bricks all the way to the construction site. The first brick is picked up by the first woman in line and passed on to the next, who receives it with the words, '*Koszonom*, Hungary.'

'*Dyakuyu*, Ukraine,' says the next.

And on it goes, each woman saying 'thank you' in her mother tongue and then her country of origin.

'*Blagodaryat ti*, Bulgaria.'

'*Danke je*, Netherlands.'

'*Hvalati*, Bosnia.'

'*Dakujem*, Slovakia,' says Cibi.

'*Efcharisto*, Greece.'

'*Dekuki*, Czech.'

'*Spasibo*, Russia.'

When they take their break, the women gather around to admire the work of the bricklayers as the first foundations go up. Cibi tells the story of another construction site, this time in Poland, where she and Livi had helped to build Birkenau.

Sitting on an empty crate, Livi is shivering as Cibi speaks, feeling a sudden chill despite the soaring temperature. She looks into the faces of the women as they listen to her sister, their eyes downcast. She shifts her focus to the beautiful hills beyond, the land that will become her home. So much space, so much colour, hope and promise; so why does she feel the walls of a concrete building closing in on her?

'Are you OK, Livi?' Magda has joined her on the crate.

'I'm fine, I think,' whispers Livi. 'It's just that sometimes it's like I'm still back there, you know?'

Magda nods. 'I know. We've moved continents, put seas between then and now, and yet . . .' her voice drifts, but Livi understands. They are still under the same sky and their memories are woven into their flesh. It will take more than the soil of a new earth under their fingernails to feel safe again.

As the summer's heat intensifies, so do Magda's feelings for a young man working on a nearby site.

Walking home one evening, Magda is unusually quiet.

'Is something wrong, Magda?' Cibi asks.

'No.'

'You've been quiet for a few days now. Are you ill?' Cibi persists.

'If you must know, I've been talking to a boy,' Magda says, bright red.

Cibi and Livi stop walking.

'When?' Livi demands to know.

'A while now.'

'And? Are you in love?' Livi is equal parts shocked and delighted.

'You know, I think I am,' replies Magda, beaming. 'His name is Yitzchak, just like Grandfather's.'

'When can we meet him?' Livi asks, thrilled.

'Cibi, you even know his sister; she lives across the road from you,' Magda teases.

'That is so funny!' Cibi bursts out laughing. 'Yeti told me she had a handsome brother who she wanted to introduce to my sisters, but now we don't need to set you up because you've done it all by yourself.' Cibi is thrilled: her responsible middle sister is in love!

'So, when can we meet him?' Livi repeats.

'Slow down, we haven't known each other that long,' Magda says, in no hurry to pander to their intrigue.

'OK, we'll slow down, but you're not getting any younger, Magda.' Cibi's eyes twinkle mischievously.

'We're going for a walk later. He says he needs to talk to me.'

'*He*'s not slowing down, is he? He's going to ask you to marry him, I just know it!' Livi is beside herself.

From the living-room window, Cibi and Livi watch their sister walk towards a tall man with dark, wavy hair. He has a green blanket tucked under one arm, and he's smiling.

That smile tells the sisters all they need to know: it's the look of a man in love. Livi and Cibi sigh in unison as the couple head off on their walk, hand in hand.

*   *   *

Yitzchak leads Magda to a small park not far from Cibi's house. They stand beneath an orange tree, its ripe fruit threatening to drop any second. The sunset mimics the deep tones of the oranges poised above their heads. Yitzchak kicks away the fruit on the ground, creating a space for them to sit before he shakes out the blanket and lays it on the grass. Magda sits down and takes up an orange from the ground. Sliding a nail over the dimpled flesh, she lifts it to her nose, its sharp, sweet scent returning her instantly to the kibbutz.

'You said you wanted to talk to me,' Magda prompts. She feels suddenly shy with this man, and can barely meet his eyes.

'I do, Magda,' he says. 'There is something I need to tell you before I ask you a question.' Yitzchak takes the orange from her and Magda looks him in the eyes. 'My sister has told me all about you and Cibi and Livi and your time in Auschwitz.'

'They were in the camps much longer than me,' says Magda. 'I was there for less than a year.'

'And you all survived the death march,' he continues, and Magda nods. Yitzchak is the one to look away now. 'I am so sorry that you and your sisters were in that evil place.'

'Well, we're here now and that evil place is behind us.'

Yitzchak rolls up the sleeve of his shirt to reveal a tattoo of numbers. Magda's mouth drops open. 'You were there too? In Auschwitz?'

'I was there, with my brother, Myer.'

'And you survived too,' says Magda, with a grin. But Yitzchak is not smiling; he looks worried. She waits for him to say something, but he has fallen silent, staring at the numbers on his arm. 'What is it, Yitzchak? Is there more?'

'It's difficult to explain. I heard your story from Yeti; it was awful, the worst story I have ever heard. I can barely understand how you are all so sane, given what you had to endure.'

'We had each other,' says Magda, simply.

'It wasn't like that for me.' Yitzchak looks away into the distant edges of the parkland.

'You weren't in a holiday camp, you were in Auschwitz,' exclaims Magda. 'No one had an easy time of it. You mustn't compare our experiences. Please, Yitzchak, it will drive you mad.'

'How can I not, Magda? My brother and I survived because we were cooks. We prepared meals for the SS and what they didn't eat, we did. I don't remember ever being hungry.'

'You feel guilty? For not suffering as much as my sisters did?'

'I do,' says Yitzchak, fervently. 'Very much so.'

Magda reaches for his hand. She understands this feeling. 'I know how you feel; I was living at home with Mumma and my grandfather for two years while my sisters suffered. Can you imagine how I reacted when I saw them again? I was healthy and they looked like they were dying.'

'But still . . .'

'But nothing! My sisters won't let me feel guilty; there is nothing I can do to change what happened in the way it happened. I'm learning to live with it, but this is what I truly believe – you and I survived and that's all that matters. We all *survived*. How we did it means absolutely nothing. We're here now, in our promised land.'

'Are you saying your sisters would forgive me?'

'For what? Having a full belly? Do you think we wouldn't have swapped places with you in a heartbeat, Yitzchak? There is no honour in suffering, that's what I'm trying to tell you.' Magda's eyes flash as she speaks and she knows her words are for herself as much as this tall, kind man. 'Thank you for telling me your story; it makes no difference to how I feel about you.'

Yitzchak squeezes Magda's hand. 'There's more,' he says.

'Go on,' Magda says, warily.

'I was married before the war,' he tells her, looking up into the orange tree.

'A lot of people were married before the war. Mischka was too.'

'Cibi's husband? I didn't know that. Not only was I married, Magda, but I had two little girls.' His voice breaks and his face crumbles.

'Oh, no, I am so sorry,' Magda whispers.

'I lost them in Auschwitz.'

Magda draws closer to Yitzchak and gently wipes the tears from his cheeks. His eyes meet hers, and there is pain in them, but there is something else too – something she recognises: hope. No more words are needed as Magda understands the ways in which they can share their pain and grief.

Yitzchak leans across the space between them to tuck the wayward strands of Magda's hair behind her ears, a smile slowly forming on his mouth. Right here, right now, thinks Magda, is where we found each other.

'I said to you there was something I needed to tell you and a question I had to ask you.'

'So, the question,' grins Magda.

'Magda Meller, will you marry me?'

Magda looks over his shoulder as the last rays of sunlight disappear. A full moon is already in the sky, shining its pale light on them.

CHAPTER 29

.

Kfar Ahim
1950

M agda and Yitzchak are married in Cibi's front garden,
amongst the flowers, and the friends they have made
since arriving in Israel. When the glass, wrapped in a fine
linen cloth, breaks beneath the couple's feet, the crowd erupts
with cries of, '*Mazel tov!*'

In the early hours of the following morning, Magda waves
goodbye to her sisters and takes her leave with her new
husband. Cibi and Livi linger in the garden until everyone
has left.

'She looked so happy, didn't she?' Livi says.

'She is happy. She's in love.' Cibi is absentmindedly folding
napkins.

'Do you think I'll find someone?' asks Livi, wistfully.

Cibi drops the napkins and takes both her sister's hands in her own.

'Of course you will, kitten. You may have already met him, you never know.'

'I'm not in a hurry, Cibi.' Cibi raises her eyes to the dawn sky.

'Who's ever in a hurry these days? Life brings what it brings. Do you remember what Grandfather used to say about 'time'?'

Now Livi fiddles with the napkins. Her eyes narrow as she casts her mind back to their childhood in Vranov. 'Something about life being long if you savour every moment?'

'Exactly. That we shouldn't look at each day as a series of tasks we have to get through, but to see each twenty-four hours as a gift from God and cherish individual moments.' Cibi gulps. The words 'gift from God' stuck in her throat.

'You're still not praying?' Livi asks, folding napkins. She hates putting Cibi on the spot, but sometimes it happens.

Cibi shakes her head.

'That's OK. You will again.'

'I'm not sure I will, Livi. God used to live in here.' Cibi touches her chest. 'But now my sisters fill that space.'

'If your heart is full, then maybe it's the same thing.'

'I have always had my sisters, Livi. There has never been a time when one or other of you wasn't there for me, but we needed *God* in those camps, and where was he?' Cibi says, firmly.

Livi has no response for this. Her sister's heart was broken, just as hers was, and Magda's. Like Cibi, she has no idea if, when or how they will begin to heal.

352

Cibi stands and takes Livi's hand. 'The sun is coming up and we have all the time in the world to discuss your love life and my faith, or lack of it. Right now we need some sleep before Karol wakes up.'

A week later, Magda and Yitzchak and Livi return to Cibi's house for dinner. Cibi thinks Magda looks pale. While memories of the wedding party are recalled and savoured, Magda stays ominously silent. Maybe her sister has an announcement, Cibi wonders mischievously, but when Cibi tries to catch her eye, Magda looks away.

'I've got some good news,' says Cibi, wondering if this is just what Magda needs to cheer up. 'Uncle Ivan wrote to me. He, Irinka and the children have been given permission to come to Israel. Isn't that wonderful?'

'It's wonderful!' says Livi, clapping. 'We'll be a family again, all of us together.'

'Do you think it's wonderful, Magda?' asks Cibi cautiously, when her sister fails to show the same enthusiasm as Livi.

'Of course I do!' says Magda. 'Irinka's pregnant, isn't she?'

'Yes, they want their new baby to be born in Israel. Isn't that romantic?'

Magda nods.

'Magda, come on!' says Cibi, while their husbands are taking the plates through to the kitchen. 'Tell me what's going on with you. You've barely said a word all evening.'

'Don't forget she's a newlywed, Cibi,' says Livi, cheekily. 'Maybe she's just too happy to talk.' Livi winks at Magda.

Magda raises her eyes, and both Livi and Cibi startle: Magda looks scared.

'You're worrying me now. Please,' says Cibi.

'Yitzchak,' calls Magda. 'Can you come in?'

The sisters are still sitting, side by side at the table when Yitzchak and Mischka come back into the room.

'You're right, Cibi.' Magda swallows. 'I have something to tell you and you're not going to like it.'

'What is it?' asks Livi, her hand at her throat. 'And why don't I know? I live with you, for God's sake.'

'We wanted to tell you both at the same time. As you all know, I have loved living here.' She looks at her husband. 'It's where I met Yitzchak after all. But' – Magda takes a deep breath – 'we want to move.'

Cibi looks confused, Livi startled.

'What are you saying? You want to leave Israel?' Cibi whispers.

'Of course not!' exclaims Magda. 'How could you think *that*, of all things? We want to move to Rehovot. It's a bigger town and it's growing. It's better for us, for our futures.'

Cibi rounds on Yitzchak. 'Is this your doing?' she demands.

'Of course not!' says Yitzchak, showing her his palms. 'It's not what you think, Cibi. This isn't about abandoning the family.'

'Cibi, please don't be silly. Look at me,' says Magda. 'This is a farming town and I'm not a farmer. Neither of us is. I want to do something different with my life, that's all.'

Cibi doesn't know what to say. She stares at her hands, rough, a little calloused – but she doesn't mind. She has found she loves the land.

'Let's just hear them out,' Livi says, letting out a long breath. She nods to Magda to continue.

'It wasn't an easy decision, but when have any of our decisions been easy? Anyway, there are more work opportunities there, and we want to start a family.' Magda's faltering voice seems to reach Cibi from a long way away.

'And you think this is OK, do you?' Cibi says finally, turning to Livi.

'I didn't know, Cibi, so please don't think I'm in on it. But they're a couple now and couples have to make their own decisions, don't they?'

Cibi is hurt. 'I thought you'd be on my side.'

'It's not about sides. I want Magda to be happy and if that means she has to leave, then I think she should,' Livi says.

'And our promise to Father?' persists Cibi. 'What about always staying together? Does that mean nothing to either of you?'

Magda reaches for Cibi's hand, but Cibi snatches it away. 'Cibi!' says Magda, firmly. 'If I thought for one moment my moving away would mean the end of our promise I wouldn't do it, how can you not know that? How can you not know I would do anything for you and for Livi?'

'Really?' snaps Cibi. 'Why don't you tell me what else I should know?'

'You should know I love you. That moving a few kilometres up the road has nothing to do with our promise to Father and Mumma.'

Magda's eyes flash as she talks, but Cibi's soften. She lets Magda take her hand. 'You're right. Of course you're right,' says Cibi. 'And you are both pretty useless on the farm, anyway.'

Magda draws her into a hug. 'Scrabble around in the dirt if you must, I'll love you just the same,' says Magda. 'I'll be half an hour away, and haven't we been apart before? Haven't we always found our way back to each other?'

'Let them go, Cibi,' says Mischka to his wife. 'Let's all give them a chance at making a life in Rehovot. If it doesn't work, we'll always be here for them.'

Cibi sighs. 'When will you go?' She reaches for the bottle of red wine and fills up her glass.

'Yitzchak has friends in town who we'll stay with until we find our own place.'

'My sisters . . .' Yitzchak says now, 'I will always look after Magda, but we would love your blessing.'

'I don't like it, I can't pretend that I do, but Livi is right, even if it means moving away, then of course you have my blessing.' Cibi raises her glass to her lips.

The sisters share a hug that is about so much more than physical comfort. It is a bond which crosses time and space, which hurdles their pain and dulls their suffering. They each implicitly understand that mere distance will not break their bond.

Cibi thinks about the space in her heart where God used to live and wonders, for a second, if the peace she feels in her sisters' arms is a sign that maybe He never really left.

When they draw apart, Livi turns to Magda and then to Cibi. 'Cibi, you know I love you.'

'Livi!' warns Cibi.

'Let me go with them.'

Three weeks later Magda, Yitzchak and Livi travel to Rehovot.

Yitzchak finds a job in a butcher's shop and dreams of opening his own shop one day. Magda and Livi fall back into the casual work they enjoyed in Bratislava, managing the accounts of small offices, and even some volunteering work, helping new migrants to Israel settle.

The Jewish Agency has opened an office in Rehovot, to assist with work opportunities and accommodation. Magda and Livi register with it.

A month later, Yitzchak asks a friend to drive them to Kfar Ahim and the sisters are reunited.

'We're expanding!' Cibi tells Yitzchak and Magda. 'We have enough land for chickens and cows.'

'Chickens and cows!' marvels Magda. 'Well, I have got some news too.'

'Oh, dear,' says Cibi, frowning. She imagines Magda is about to announce a move to Tel Aviv.

'Not again,' pouts Livi. 'How do I not know?'

'It's good. Don't look so worried, Cibi,' says Yitzchak. 'You'll be happy to hear it.'

'I've been offered a job.' Magda is bright red, brimming with excitement to share her triumph with her sisters. 'I'm going to be working in the home of President Weizmann.'

'Are you joking?' Livi says.

'No,' say Magda, with a grin.

'The president? The president of Israel? Tell us everything immediately!' Cibi is just relieved to hear her sisters are staying put.

'The Jewish Agency told me there was a vacancy at the president's house for a maid and asked if I would be interested.'

'And what did you say?' Livi asks.

'Obviously, I said yes. I met Mrs Weizmann and she gave me the job. I start next week.'

'You met Mrs Weizmann?' Cibi is as excited as Magda now. 'What was she like?'

'She has the kindest eyes and she spoke to me like a friend. She asked me about you, as well.'

'About me?' says Cibi.

'About both of you – she wanted to know about my family. I showed her my arm and she wanted to know if you had numbers too.'

'What did you say?'

'I said you didn't. I told her the Nazis only blessed the special ones with a number.'

'Magda!'

'I'm joking! She asked me about Auschwitz and listened for ages while I told her our story. I probably said too much, but she let me talk.'

'This calls for a toast!' Mischka says.

Raising their glasses of iced tea, they chant, 'To Magda and President and Mrs Weizmann.'

Magda knows she was right to move to Rehovot when she starts her new job. As she makes her way to the Weizmann household, her heart expands to meet the day. In the president's beautiful home, where the staff are kind and her work is easy enough, she feels, maybe for the first time, she is making a valuable contribution to this new homeland. Magda knows herself well enough to recognise her demons are merely lurking for the moment, but she'll take the respite where she can. Losing herself in her work, she forgets, sometimes for whole hours at a time, that for two whole years she was oblivious to her sisters' suffering.

Livi has found work picking fruit on a local farm, and soon she is tasked with registering and overseeing the fruit pickers as well. She takes pride in the fact that her oranges are now among the thousands being exported to the rest of the world. But there is little continuity in casual labour; no sooner has she made friends they move on, to another community, or another part of the country, each one hoping to find a place they might finally call home.

Livi works alongside the new arrivals, but also with the Palestinians who regularly return to harvest the fruit. She enjoys the way her tongue folds around the Arabic words she is so keen to learn. *Sabah alkhyr kayf halik alyawm* was the first phrase Livi mastered, taught to her by a shy girl, Amara. She used it to greet her Arab friends every day: *Good morning, how are you today?*

Lina'a bikhayr kayf halik, comes the reply. *I am well, how are you?* to which Livi would respond: *Ana bikhayr shukraan lak. I am well, thank you.*

One morning, Amara arrives with a small bag of dates.

'They look ugly,' she tells Livi in simple Hebrew, 'but when they crunch between your teeth . . . ah, heaven!'

Livi takes the fruit and bites, her teeth landing hard on the stone. She winces.

'Oh, sorry!' says Amara. 'There's a stone.'

'I know that now,' grins Livi, chewing the sticky fruit. 'This is *delicious*,' she exclaims. 'Even better than oranges.'

Exchanges with new arrivals always begin with the same questions: 'Where are you from?' and 'Who do you know in Israel?' Livi is proficient in a number of languages; her time in Auschwitz taught her that languages can be a means of survival. And now she uses her new Hebrew, plus German and Russian, to welcome the fruit pickers to the farm.

It is during one of these exchanges that that she makes friends with a girl her own age. Soon they are heading into the groves together, picking oranges side by side in companionable silence.

'Do you have a boyfriend, Livi?' Rachel asks her one day. Nosy, thinks Livi. But all the talk amongst the young people on the farm is about who is dating who.

Livi lobs oranges into the huge basket. When it is full, they will heave it to the sorting sheds. 'No,' she says. 'I work here all day and then I go home to bed, and I don't fancy any of these boys.' Livi waves a hand at the pickers.

'I know someone you might like. He's my cousin. And he's not a fruit picker.'

Despite Livi's protestations, and with Magda's firm encouragement, Ziggy Ravek is invited to lunch the following Saturday.

Livi spends the rest of the week trying to concentrate on her work and failing. She can't decide if she is looking forward to meeting this stranger, or terrified. It is probably a little of both, she decides.

But Saturday rolls around anyway, despite her misgivings, and Livi is getting ready.

'You look nice.' Magda appraises her little sister with a critical eye. 'But your hair needs some work.'

Magda sits Livi at the dressing table in her bedroom and pins up her curls. She adds a little blusher to Livi's cheeks and swipes a pale lipstick across her mouth.

'Much better,' says Magda, standing back to appreciate her work. But Livi isn't so sure.

'I look like a painted doll,' she complains, just as the doorbell rings.

'I'm nervous, Magda,' says Livi, grabbing Magda's shoulder as she turns to leave the room.

'Nervous about meeting a *boy*?' jokes Magda. 'After everything we've been through?'

Livi can't help laughing. 'Why are you comparing meeting a boy to being starved in Birkenau?'

'I wasn't. You just did that all by yourself, little sister.'

Livi follows her big sister into the living room, to where a tall man with thick black hair is holding out his hand to her.

'Have we met before?' says Ziggy.

'I don't think so,' says Livi, enjoying the warm handshake.

'You look familiar.'

'I have one of those faces,' Livi says. 'I look like everyone else.'

Ziggy bursts out laughing. 'You have a sense of humour,' he says. 'I like that.'

Later, as they eat their lunch, Livi catches Magda's nod of approval when Ziggy tells them he is an aircraft technician working for the Israeli airline, El Al. She wishes her sister wasn't always right, but Livi's nerves dissolved the moment she shook Ziggy's hand.

After lunch Ziggy asks Livi if he may see her again.

'You may,' she says, coyly.

'A film perhaps?' Ziggy suggests.

'That depends,' says Livi.

'On what?'

'On who's paying,' says Livi, with a smirk.

'Livi, you can't say that!' Magda gasps.

Ziggy laughs. 'Yes, she can, and I would like to take you to see a movie, my treat.'

'Then thank you very much, I would like that too.'

Livi meets Ziggy twice a week, enjoying his easy company and fierce intelligence. There *is* something familiar about Ziggy, but she can't put her finger on it. Maybe they are kindred spirits, she ponders.

'Thank you for sharing your story with me,' he tells her after their fourth date. They are on a park bench by the

children's playground. It's an unusual spot to divulge a horri-
fying tale of torture and death, while kids' joyful screams fill
the air. And Livi was reluctant at first to talk about the
sisters' lives in the camps with Ziggy; she doesn't know him
well enough yet, and the memories are painful, but afterwards, she feels better. He knows everything about me now,
just as kindred spirits should, she tells herself.

'Will you talk about what happened to you?' Livi asks.

'Maybe one day,' Ziggy says, sighing. 'But today the sun
is shining. Don't you think one concentration camp story is
enough for now?'

Livi laughs, marvelling that she is laughing at all. He
listened to her and even held her when she had cried. That
anyone, aside from her sisters, should make her feel so safe
is a surprise to her.

Safe, that word again. Like an itch that no amount of
scratching seems to ease for very long.

*   *   *

'I'm pregnant!' announces Magda to Livi, who stands on the
doorstep, her key poised. Livi has dirt under her fingernails
and is tanned from her long days in the sun; she feels exhausted
and happy, keen to tell Magda about her recent date with
Ziggy, but he is instantly forgotten when she hears the news.

'Another Meller baby!' cries Livi. 'I'm to be an aunt *again*.'

'You are. And thank the Lord you'll be around to help me.'

Livi is finally allowed into her house and now the girls
sip from tall glasses of orange juice while Magda tells Livi
how she feels.

'I'm hungry all the time, mainly for olives. And there are
loads of olives at the Weizmanns'.'

362

Livi's mind instantly goes back to the story Cibi told her of the first time she tasted olives, when she had believed they were plums – only to sink her teeth into the hard bitter flesh. All food was precious in the camp, so maybe they should have just choked them down, but the Greek girl's delight when Cibi gave them to her had been a bright spot in her day.

'How long will you keep on working?' Livi asks. What might be the residual effects of near starvation on Magda's body? she wonders. But Cibi had a good pregnancy, didn't she?

'Ah, I'm glad you mentioned that. I've got some good news for you, little sister.' Magda points to Livi's hands. 'Maybe you can say goodbye to all that mud under your nails.' She is beaming.

'My nails?' Livi looks at her hands, confused.

'Forget about your nails. Mrs Weizmann would like to meet you and, if she likes you – and how could she not – you could have my job when I leave.'

'Your job?'

'I'm pregnant, Livi, catch up! Are you interested?'

Livi takes a gulp of juice. A job in the president's house? She can't begin to imagine it. The orange groves are all she knows these days. The town is growing, but not fast enough for Livi to find a permanent office job. This could be perfect.

'Of course I'm interested,' she says.

'Good. Because I've arranged an interview for you. Not for a few months, but Mrs Weizmann said that if you're half as good as I am, you're good enough for her.'

'Half as good as you? The cheek!'

'OK, maybe she didn't say that.'

'So, when are you leaving?' Livi's eyes are shining. She's already imagining meeting the president.

'Now who's being cheeky?'

That night in bed, Livi thinks about working in a place where she isn't a nameless face among many, doing the same job as everyone else. She feels a thrill of hope for a different kind of future. Maybe tonight she won't cry herself to sleep as she has done every night since the sisters were thrown out of their home in Vranov. She never means to cry, but as her eyes close her mother's face appears. Mumma had loved that house; she had worked so hard to make it into a beautiful home. And now a brute and his family were eating off their crockery, sitting in their chairs, lying down in their beds. When her head hits the pillow, Livi is always transported back to that day: once more, she is kicking that brute in the leg, shoving him away from Magda.

She draws a long breath and feels her throat constrict. Despite all Livi's optimism for a new job, that night is no different, but, as she drifts off, she whispers a promise to her mother, between sobs.

I will make you proud of me, Mumma.

Three months later, on the day of the interview, dressed, brushed and polished, Livi heads off to the president's house, Magda on her heels, begging her to slow down for the pregnant lady.

Now she is finally inside the house, her excitement is whittled down to a nub of dread. Nervous and dry-mouthed, Livi enters the living room where Mrs Weizmann sits on a small white sofa, her hand outstretched. Livi takes it.

'Do sit down, my dear.' Mrs Weizmann points to a chair. 'I find it easier to speak in German, do you mind? Or in Hebrew, if you're more fluent than your sister, that is. But my Slovakian, I'm afraid, is non-existent.'

'German is fine,' replies Livi.

'Tell me about yourself.'

'There's not much to tell,' says Livi, thinking that there isn't enough time in the world to talk about herself, about everything she has lived through.

'Oh, I don't believe you, Livi. Magda has already told me quite a lot but I would like to hear it from you.'

An hour later Livi stops talking. She has given Mrs Weizmann the condensed story of her life, and is offered the job on the spot.

For the rest of the week Livi is on a high. She has met a man who makes her laugh, and now she works in the household of the president of Israel; her sisters are happily married, one with a child, the other pregnant.

But am I truly *happy*? she wonders.

It is at moments like this, when she is poised on the cusp of great change, that what starts as a tingle along Livi's spine begins to pulse. She felt it just before they stepped onto the gangplank at Haifa, and then again when she, Magda and Yitzchak drove to Rehovot to make a different life for themselves, and once more on her first day at the Weizmann house. Usually, Livi takes it at face value: she's just excited to be on an adventure, why wouldn't she feel a tingle of anticipation? But, at other times, like tonight, the feeling along the length of her spine takes her back to Birkenau, to the hospital, where she was being treated for typhus.

There is one specific memory from her time in Birkenau that makes her feel like she does not deserve her good fortune.

She and Matilda had lain in identical hospital beds, each of them feverish, each of them suffering, but a strange twist of fate had meant that Livi had survived the night and Matilda hadn't.

While Livi was being 'saved' – forced to lie on a latrine floor, her nightdress soaked in excrement – Matilda had been taken from her bed, straight to the gas chamber. The girl had been denied a new life in Israel, denied a job at the Weizmann household, and the love of two sisters. It's crazy, she knows that, but it's how she feels right then – as if she is walking in a dead girl's shoes.

Livi doesn't understand why this particular memory comes to her at times like these: she doesn't blame herself for Matilda's death, but she suspects she will always wonder whether, if she had lived, she might not be there, tingling with excitement for a new adventure?

Cibi and Magda offer words of comfort, share their own stories of certain events which take centre stage above all others, but neither of them can explain why Livi relives this girl's death over and over again. Maybe it's because this simple story has come to symbolise the microcosm of her entire time in Birkenau, a night in which she lived and another girl died.

A night in which Mala, with a few words spoken into a wisely chosen ear, had saved her life.

There's an awful symmetry to these memories, Livi thinks, as she sees herself wheeling the body of the dead translator to the crematorium.

CHAPTER 30

Rehovot
1951

The heat of the midday sun is relentless and Livi and Ziggy escape into a café for a few minutes' respite. Livi is both nervous and scared: nervous of broaching a subject that will hurtle Ziggy headlong into a past he would rather forget – that much is obvious to her now, as they have been together for two months and Ziggy hasn't once opened up about his life in captivity; and scared, because if he can't share this part of himself, they probably have no future.

'You look so worried, Livi,' Ziggy tells her as they take their seats. 'You've hardly said a word all the way here.'

'I'm not worried,' says Livi quickly. And then adds, 'Maybe a little.'

'Will you tell me?' When Ziggy focuses his whole attention on Livi, as he is doing now, she becomes flustered, tongue-tied.

'Shall we order some drinks?' Livi picks up the menu.

'And then you'll tell me?'

Part of Livi wishes she hadn't decided to confront Ziggy today. Or any day.

They sip their iced coffee and share a pastry in silence. Ziggy is a patient man, thinks Livi. He'd probably just sit here for an hour waiting for me to say something.

'Ziggy, you've told me so much about your life since you arrived in Israel,' says Livi, finally. 'But I don't know what happened to you.'

'Is that what's on your mind?' he asks, setting his glass on the table. Ziggy suddenly looks very tired, and Livi wants to take back her words. 'I've told you. It's all in the past, Livi. What does it matter?'

'It matters to *me*. You know everything about me. Won't you tell me a little about your family, and where you were born at least?' she persists. She firmly believes her story is a part of what makes Livi *Livi,* however painful it is to remember the past.

Ziggy sighs, running his hands over his face, drawing his fingers through his thick hair. 'I come from a town called Český Těšín, in Moravia,' he begins. 'Well, it was Moravia when I lived there. It's now part of Czechoslovakia.'

'And your family, are they still alive?' Now Ziggy has begun, Livi is impatient to hear it all at once

'OK, Livi, I'm getting there. I was one of four boys, the youngest brother. My father was a tailor in town and my mother . . .' Ziggy stops talking, hangs his head and sniffs.

She feels his pain, of course she does; it is her agony too, and the agony of every survivor, but Livi also realises she has to let him tell her in his own time.

'My mother . . . oh, Livi, she baked the best cakes in town; every day we'd come home from school to a house that smelled like heaven. Bread, cakes, biscuits . . .' Ziggy drifts off, no longer sniffing, but smiling at the memory. 'When things started turning bad for us and we weren't allowed to go to school, or to work, my oldest brother went to fight with the Russians and was killed. My father was worried about me being so young so he sent my mother and me to an uncle in Krakow. We were there for months, and finally Mother wanted to go home, to my father, my brothers, and of course, her kitchen.' Ziggy sighs again. He pushes his plate away and signals to the waitress for more coffee. 'On the way back we were stopped by the Nazis.' Ziggy is now clutching the front of his shirt, twisting the fabric, and a button pops.

Livi reaches out and places a calming hand on top of both of his. He smiles and lets go of his shirt.

'They beat her, Livi. In front of my eyes they beat her, and didn't lay a finger on me.'

Livi squeezes his hand hard, hoping the gesture will make him feel less alone in his memories.

'When they finally let us go, I helped Mother back to our uncle's place in Krakow. Maybe a few weeks passed, not long, and we heard they had started to round up all the Jews in the area for transportation. Mother and I hid in a cupboard, but they found us and then . . . then we were all taken into the town square and there they separated us. That was the last time I saw her.'

Livi doesn't say a word because she knows Ziggy is gathering his strength to tell her the worst part of his story, just as she had stumbled over hers.

'She was taken to Auschwitz and she never left.'

'Oh, Ziggy, I am so, so sorry.' Tears are flowing down Livi's face.

'Anyway, I was moved between camps in Freiburg and Waldenburg where they set me to work making optics for German submarines, then to Gross-Rosen and finally Reichenbach.'

'You did get around,' Livi says, with a small smile.

'That's one way of looking at it. I was liberated at Reichenbach and taken back to Prague, but eventually I headed home to Moravia.' Ziggy takes a drink from the long glass of cold coffee which the waitress has just placed in front of him. 'Home, ha!' Ziggy snorts. 'There were Germans living in our house, so I kicked them out and—'

'Wait,' Livi interrupts. 'You kicked them out?'

'Of course. They had taken our lives, Livi, they weren't having my house too.' Ziggy's eyes flash and Livi has no trouble imagining this strong, handsome man chasing those Germans out of his home and down the street.

'Go on,' says Livi, sipping her coffee, wishing Ziggy had been around to dispatch her own intruders in Vranov.

'Well, I moved back in and then, one day, a knock on the door and it's my father standing there. Can you believe it? He and my two brothers had been taken to Łódź in Poland and when the Russians came through, they ran away and joined the Czech Legion. My brothers were still in Prague, but eventually we were reunited.'

'Ziggy, thank you for telling me your story.'

Ziggy sighs, closes his eyes and shakes his head slowly. 'I had a relatively easy time during the war, Livi – weren't you listening? I didn't suffer like you or your sisters. I don't even have a number on my arm.'

'A number on your—? Ziggy, what are you talking about? It isn't a competition. It's a terrible story, all our stories are equally awful.'

'I'm just saying, your suffering was worse, much worse than mine. I can still see it in your eyes, Livi . . . whenever you think no one is watching, you disappear.'

'And so do you!' Livi snaps. 'We all do. Now please, Ziggy, you have your father still, your brothers. I have my sisters. Let's just take our good luck and appreciate it. Do you think it matters whether you had more soup than me? Or that you had two blankets instead of one? We were prisoners, they took us from our homes for no reason and killed our families.'

Ziggy sets down his cup and takes Livi's hand. 'I live with my father in Rishon, Livi. I would very much like you to meet him.'

Livi is surprised. She has been with Ziggy for months, but he never once mentioned his father. But at the same time she also knows there is nothing sinister about Ziggy; that this part of his life is so closely entwined with the tragedy of his past, to talk about one he would have had to discuss the other, and, until today, he just wasn't ready.

'I would like to meet him,' says Livi, trying to control the tension in her voice. She too is ready is move on from their stories for the moment.

'Good, because he is dying to put a face to the beautiful girl I have been telling him about.' Ziggy opens his mouth to say more, but closes it, peering at Livi intently.

'Have I got something on my chin?' she asks.

'It's just that odd feeling that I've seen you somewhere before, Livi. It's driving me crazy.'

'Well, I guess we might have been on the same ship, and we might have just caught each other's eye at some point.' Livi is grinning, relieved that Ziggy is not dwelling on the past, that they can now move on and . . . something snags at the back of her mind and now she is staring at Ziggy just as intently.

A group of show-offs surrounded by adoring girls.

'You're a Peacock Boy!' she whispers, delighted.

'I'm a what?' Ziggy looks appalled.

Livi remembers the young man, standing alone while his 'fly boy' peers basked in the golden attention of pretty girls.

'That's what Magda called you. Not just you – the group you were with on the boat. The pilots, technicians. Fly boys.'

Ziggy is quiet, and then his face breaks into a huge grin. 'Of course! You're the girl who always looked so serious. You didn't give any of us a second glance.'

'That's not true, Ziggy. I gave you two, at least.' Livi is blushing.

This coincidence thrills Livi. She hadn't met Ziggy on the whim of a fruit picker she met on a farm; Ziggy *was* her kindred spirit, and maybe even more than that: her destiny.

They drink more coffee and share another pastry. Livi is unsettled, though: Ziggy has moved on – now he recounts funny stories of his workmates, tells her of his engineering ambitions and mulls over the best cafés for iced coffee, as though he has entirely forgotten that moments ago he was crying for his dead mother.

*　*　*

Mrs Weizmann greets Livi with a big smile.

'My husband returned home last night and as he hasn't had a chance to meet you, I wondered if you'd like to come along to his office and say hello.'

'Say hello to President Weizmann?' Livi asks, with a tiny tremble in her voice.

But Mrs Weizmann is striding ahead. She knocks on the president's door and opens it without waiting for an invitation. 'Chaim, this is Livi, the new maid who is keeping us all on our toes.'

'Hello, Livi.' The president rises from behind his desk. He has a goatee beard and round glasses; he looks like a university professor. 'I've heard a lot about you.'

His eyes are friendly and Livi finds herself warming to this man. He holds out his hand and Livi takes it. As is her instinct, she slides her left arm behind her back, a gesture the president is quick to catch. He reaches for her arm and, very gently, he pushes up her sleeve. Tenderly, he traces his fingers over the tattooed numbers.

'There is quite a journey in these numbers, isn't there?' he says, softly.

Livi nods.

'Will you tell me about it?'

'When he held my hand, I thanked God for a man like Chaim Weizmann, a man who has such vision. I really felt, probably for the first time, that I was making a contribution to the promise of Israel.' Livi is having dinner with Magda and Yitzchak, regaling them with every nuance of her meeting with the president. 'He didn't say one word as he listened to my story. Not one, he just let me talk.'

'Poor man,' says Magda, laughing. 'That's the second time he's heard our story then.'

'Mine is different to yours,' says Livi, regretting her words the moment they leave her mouth. 'I didn't mean it like that, Magda. I'm sorry. I'm sorry.'

Magda smiles. 'Don't worry, Livi. I know you didn't.'

But Magda once again feels the dual twinges of guilt and despair whenever any reference is made to the fact that her sisters spent two long years in the camps while she was at home with Mumma, oblivious to their suffering. 'Well,' she says, now. 'All I know is that he's earned the right to be called Father of Israel, and I think Mrs Weizmann should be called Mother of Israel by now.'

When Magda retreats to her bedroom to lie down after dinner, Livi joins her. Magda can tell her sister is still feeling contrite.

'Livi, it's fine. I didn't for a second think you were trying to hurt me.'

Livi's eyes are full of tears. 'I'm glad you weren't there, Magda, I really am. Do you know that's what kept me and Cibi going? Believing that you were back in Vranov, taking care of Mother and Grandfather.'

This doesn't make Magda feel any better. 'What hurts the most,' she says, heaving herself up into a sitting position, 'is remembering our last days in Vranov. Night after night we'd sit down for dinner – we never had much, but certainly more than you – and we'd sit down, say a prayer for you both, and eat. I took the food for granted, took Mumma and even Grandfather for granted sometimes. They were always telling me to hide, to stay out of the way, to be a ghost. And I used to lose my temper, screaming at them to let me come and find you.' Magda wipes a tear away.

'I'm sorry, Magda,' says Livi.

'My safety meant as much to them as it did to you, but I didn't want to *be* safe – I wanted to be with you and Cibi. And then I got my wish, which wasn't your wish or Mumma's, but it was mine. And then no one was happy, least of all me.' Magda is crying now, fat tears falling onto the bump of her stomach.

Livi gets onto the bed, and the sisters lie down in each other's arms.

'Magda. Do you think we didn't know how painful it must have been for you wondering what had happened to us? It must have driven you crazy. If I had been you, I know I would have done something stupid.'

'Like giving yourself up to Visik?' Magda smiles through her tears.

'That guy, I hope he's dead,' says Livi, bitterly. 'But yes, I wouldn't have cared what Mumma or anyone said, and I would probably have got myself killed.'

'Well, I guess I should be glad I was the one who got left behind then.'

'But then you arrived fat and strong, Magda,' teases Livi, and then she's serious again – 'and thank God. For how else would we have survived the marches if you weren't?'

Magda and Livi receive word from Cibi that she is pregnant again, and Yitzchak asks a friend to drive him and the sisters to the farm. Soon there will be three Meller children, Livi thinks. These new babies will be born against the backdrop of the national ambition to make this country into a prosperous and cultured Jewish homeland, in which they will play a part.

'Hurry up and marry, Livi,' Cibi tells her. 'We want to fill our houses with babies.'

'I'm not marrying someone just to give your children another cousin,' Livi says, indignant.

'I'm not suggesting that's the only reason, kitten,' says Cibi. 'But you love Ziggy, don't you?'

'I don't know!' snaps Livi.

Cibi looks at Magda. 'Is she OK?'

'I'm right here, Cibi, you can ask me yourself.'

'Oh my God, what's wrong with you?' Magda says. 'Is it Ziggy? Is something wrong?'

Suddenly, Livi is crying. 'I'm sorry,' she sobs. 'I'm not unhappy, just . . . just confused.' Livi sits on the sofa, a sister either side of her, each with a hand on her back.

Cibi is back on familiar territory now: she knows how to comfort Livi; hasn't she done it before, and in worse places than her own house in the promised land?

'Confused?' says Magda. 'Will you tell us what's happened?'

'Nothing has happened,' says Livi. 'But it *is* about Ziggy. More than once now, whenever we talk about the camps, he says he shouldn't even be complaining when we suffered so much.'

'It's not a competition,' says Cibi, frowning.

'That's what I said.'

'Livi, listen to me,' says Cibi, suddenly serious. 'From what you've told us about Ziggy's story, it's obvious he was on his own – he didn't have his brothers around to help make sense of what was going on.'

'That's right,' says Magda. 'You two had each other and then I joined you; one way or another, we went through it together.'

'Maybe he feels guilty,' says Cibi.

'Guilty?' wonders Livi.

'Well, if he feels his experience wasn't as bad as ours, then maybe somewhere, deep down, he believes it should

376

have been – God knows there are some terrible stories out there. He probably thinks he got away with something he shouldn't have.'

That night, long after her sisters have left and while Mischka is putting Karol to bed, Cibi gets into bed herself and closes her eyes. The exchange with her sisters about Ziggy's possible guilt has triggered a powerful memory in Cibi, one that she wishes wouldn't visit her so often.

However hard she tries to put their faces out of her mind, they come unbidden to her.

Warm in her bed now, Cibi thinks back to that night in Birkenau when – shivering in their bunk, the night she and Livi had decided to kill themselves before the cold took them, the night they were saved by a girl they didn't know and who they never met again – the girl had pulled the blankets off a couple in another bunk to give to them.

The next morning the girls had been dead, their bodies curled around one another in a bid to eke out the warmth that never came.

Maybe the girls had already been dead when their blankets were snatched away, but Cibi will never know. Cibi didn't steal those blankets, but she accepted them.

Does this make her complicit?

Cibi turns over, restlessly, in her bed now. A week ago, at the baker's in town, shopping for *challah* and buns, she caught sight of two teenage girls in the kitchen at the back of the shop: the baker's daughters, helping their mother after school. They had just pulled a tray of tins from the oven and were delighted with the golden loaves and pale sponges. They had fallen into a hug, and there was something about their embrace that had sent Cibi straight back to that chill morning. Arms looped around each other's backs, chins nestled into shoulders, eyes wide open, they had adopted the self-same posture as the dead girls. Cibi had shivered, turning away without buying a loaf and hurrying home. That afternoon, she had retrieved her mother's candlesticks and filled them with new wax tapers which she lit in memory of the dead girls, all the while knowing the gesture was about assuaging her guilt.

How many stories like these do survivors have to endure? she wonders.

*   *   *

Magda has had a good pregnancy: having Cibi to talk to about her various twinges and cravings has helped, but she has never missed Mumma more than she does now. When she goes into labour, she's grateful for Livi's presence, and to hold her hand, and how she encourages her to push when it's time, but it's her mother she wants, and her grandmother, who had been a midwife to so many in Vranov.

There is no question in her mind as to the naming of her baby daughter: her mother's name means 'life' and that's what baby Chaya means to Magda right now. A new life, together with this chance in Israel – she hopes she can begin to let go, a little, of the remaining threads of guilt she feels whenever Cibi and Livi discuss their time in the camps.

Her guilt had really started in Bratislava, at their apartment, with their friends on the rooftop of their building. When the survivors began to share their stories, Magda's advantage was given the spotlight: she hadn't been starved to death or suffered from typhus or even had her head shaved. The number on her arm had been given to her by a kind man at Cibi's request, not a Nazi's. Appalled when she finally came face to face with her sisters, barely recognising them as her kin, her first feeling had been one of anger at her mother: why hadn't she just let her go? This was the guilt that lingered: that she hadn't been there for Cibi and Livi.

'I'm glad you weren't there,' Livi had told her on that rooftop, as she has so often since. 'We would never had survived the death marches without you.'

'Don't you remember, Magda, the stories you told us?' Cibi had said, incredulous that Magda couldn't see it. 'Those memories helped us all to keep putting one foot in front of the other. The chocolate snow!' Cibi had crowed, suddenly, and Magda's heart had broken at those words.

She had looked at her sisters, still far more ravaged by their experiences than her, and swept them into her arms, so grateful to them for trying to making her feel better.

'And your day in the woods with Grandfather,' added Livi. 'Magda, I'm serious, we wouldn't have made it without you. Thank God you were in hospital when they came for us.'

God, thinks Magda. Now, where had God been? Unlike Cibi, Magda continues to pray, but her faith is shaken, badly shaken. It was only when they stepped onto land in Haifa that she gave thanks for the first time in years, and now, looking down into the face of baby Chaya, Magda gives thanks once more, and begins to let go of her guilt.

Soon after, Chaya has a new cousin, when Cibi gives birth to Joseph just three weeks later.

Holding her nephew in her arms, Livi becomes aware, very quickly, that Karol is less than enamoured of his new sibling. He loses his temper whenever Cibi picks up the baby, throws a tantrum when Cibi disappears to put Joseph to bed and generally suffers from the withdrawal of the attention that has, until this point, been his exclusive domain.

Livi's presence allows Cibi to spend more time with Karol and, gradually, the little boy, once more the apple of his mother's eye, comes to love his baby brother.

Back in Rehovot, Livi is regaling Magda with tales of Karol's transformation from fearsome monster to devoted big brother, when her sister punctures these happy memories with a dose of unwelcome reality.

'You must invite Ziggy to celebrate Hanukkah with us,' Magda suggests. 'We haven't seen him in a while.'

Livi is instantly morose. 'I haven't seen him either,' she says, sullenly. 'Maybe he's found someone else.'

'Will you tell me what happened?'

'Nothing's happened, it's just that . . . well, it's what I told you about. And Cibi was right, Ziggy *does* feel guilty. Whenever I talk about the camps, he goes quiet and then I feel strange, as though I shouldn't be talking about it, but I'll go mad if I can't, Magda!' Livi sighs. 'Don't you see? I just can't do it.'

'It was the same for Yitzchak, don't you remember, Livi? The man lost his wife and children and yet he still thinks he didn't suffer enough. Guilt is a powerful emotion, Livi,' Magda tells her sister, feeling her own flare in her chest. 'We all have it, don't we?'

Livi nods. 'But we *talk* about it, we talk about everything. Ziggy doesn't.'

'Then you have to decide if he's worth fighting for, Livi. Is he?'

'I don't know.' Livi is pacing the small living room, her hands on her hips.

'Do you care, Livi?' prods Magda.

'Of course I care, but what can I do?'

'You have to tell him how you feel.' Magda is all business now, rummaging through a desk drawer, extracting a sheet of paper and a pen, thrusting them into Livi's hands. 'Invite him to Hanukkah – if he comes then it's not over between you, you have more to say to one another. If he doesn't, well, that's your answer.'

Livi has no desire to do this, but she realises she does need to know, one way or another, where they stand.

Under Magda's watchful gaze, Livi scribbles out a brief note.

'Take it now, while the ink is wet,' Magda urges, fetching Livi's coat.

All the way to Ziggy's house, Livi debates whether to just throw the note away and go home, but then she's on the doorstep, ringing the bell to his apartment. When there's no answer, she takes the note from her pocket, meaning to tear it into tiny pieces. But how would she face Magda? She has never lied to her sister, and Livi is not a coward. She slips the note under the door and hopes that someone will take it up to Ziggy's apartment.

'He wasn't there,' she tells Magda when she returns home. 'So, either he'll turn up or he won't. We'll find out in three days, in any case.'

'He'll come,' says Magda. 'Whatever is going on between the two of you isn't over yet. Remember, I'm your big sister and I'm always right.'

* * *

Livi has filled the Weizmann house with flowers. The beautiful blossoms overflow from tall vases, abundant and irresistible. From the very first time she placed a glass vase of roses in the Weizmann's bedroom, she was given the role of flower arranger for the whole household. Even the president has been caught admiring the large displays in the foyer or on the dining table before a formal dinner.

'Take a break,' the cook advises, as Livi washes and dries empty vases in the kitchen.

'Thanks. The roses are so wonderful right now, I might just go and sit in the garden for a bit.'

Finding a bench in the shade of the Jerusalem pine, Livi tilts her face to the sun and inhales the scent of flowers. She closes her eyes and thinks about Ziggy. Will he come to dinner later, and if so, what will she say to him? What will he say to her?

'Ah, I see someone else enjoys sitting under my magnificent tree.'

Livi's eyes snap open and she jumps to her feet. 'Mr Weizmann,' she says, blushing. 'I didn't see you coming.'

'Sit down, Livi. I'm just an old man, out for a walk.' He gives her a wide smile and Livi settles back down on her seat. 'Is everything all right, my dear? You seem preoccupied.' He points to her bench. 'Would you mind if I sat with you a while?'

'Of course not. Please.'

'Then we can sit and talk or sit and say nothing, and just enjoy the garden. I know you love it as much as I do, and I've watched you gather the flowers for the house. You never take too much – that's what I like.'

'It's so peaceful here,' says Livi. 'And you have both worked so hard to make it beautiful.'

'We have,' the president agrees. 'Can I tell you something?' He doesn't wait for Livi to reply. 'I would much prefer to be out here than in any other room in the house. Oh, don't get me wrong, I love the house, but this' – he waves a hand across the gardens – 'this is where I feel at peace, and it's where I can hide from prying eyes.' The president laughs and Livi imagines him sneaking out of the house and making his way across the lawn to disappear amongst the bushes.

'That's not entirely true, is it?' Livi says, with a grin.

'What are you saying, young Livi?'

'I've seen you and Prime Minister Ben-Gurion sitting out here many times, and for long periods. You always let him find you.'

President Weizmann laughs out loud. 'You are so right, Livi. Can I tell you another thing? It is Prime Minister Ben-Gurion who asks to come out here, so there is another who also finds peace in my garden.'

'I should get back to work now. There was something on my mind, you were right, but after talking to you . . . I don't know, but I feel so much better.'

'Boyfriend problems?' probes the president.

Livi laughs. 'Yes! How did you guess?'

'Like I said, I'm an old man, and there's not much I don't know. But you must tell this young man of yours he is lucky to even know your name, let alone have you in his life.'

Livi ducks her head. 'I will. Thank you.'

The Hannukah meal on the table, Livi, Magda and Yitzchak exchange a glance.

Livi shakes her head slowly. 'It's OK,' she says, suddenly despondent. 'Let's eat. It's Hannukah, we're supposed to be celebrating.'

They're about to sit down when three sharp knocks at the door echo into the house.

'I'll get it,' says Yitzchak. 'You sit down.' He looks at the food on the table and sighs, longingly.

'Welcome, Ziggy.' The sisters hear Yitzchak's greeting in the hallway.

Magda grins and puts a finger to her lips. 'Be nice,' she warns Livi.

'Come in, come in.' Yitzchak ushers Ziggy into the room.

Livi notices he is smartly dressed. Maybe his new girlfriend chose those clothes for him, she thinks.

Ziggy nods at Livi and hands Magda a plain box, which she opens to reveal chocolate coins wrapped in gold foil. 'And this is for you, Livi,' he says, holding out a scroll of parchment.

Livi unfolds the sheet of paper and reads.

'*Baruch atah Adonai Eloheinu Melech ha-olam, she-asah nisim la-avoteinu v-imoteinu ba- yamim ha-heim ba-z'man ha-zeh.*'

Blessed are you, Our God, Ruler of the Universe, who performed miracles to our fathers and mothers in their day at this season.

Livi feels a lump in her throat, and the room feels suddenly too hot. She mutters a 'thank you' to Ziggy, without meeting his eyes, and leaves the room.

'But we're about to eat,' Yitzchak calls after her.

'Just give her minute,' Magda tells him. 'Why don't you offer Ziggy a drink?'

Magda finds Livi in her bedroom, sitting on the edge of the bed, staring at the scroll. 'Are you all right?'

'I'm fine,' says Livi, holding up the parchment. 'It's just this prayer . . . no boy has ever written me a letter or even a note before, and when one does, it's the beautiful Hanukkah blessing.' Livi's eyes fill with tears. 'I'm confused, Magda, and I didn't want to cry in front of him.'

'Ah, Livi,' says Magda, sitting down beside her sister, taking her into her arms. 'There are worse things . . .'

'Don't say it, Magda!' giggles Livi. 'I *know* there are worse things than crying in front of a boy. I just wish you wouldn't drag Birkenau into everything.'

Magda chuckles. 'Look at us,' she says, 'laughing about a concentration camp. Come on, Yitzchak is starving – haven't you noticed?'

Livi races Magda back to the dining room.

At the end of the evening, on the doorstep of the small house in Rehovot, Ziggy asks Livi if she will take a walk with him in the morning.

'To talk?' Livi asks.

'To talk,' he confirms.

It is a cool day, but at least it's not raining. Livi takes her coat off the peg and steps outside.

They walk in silence for a while, waving at neighbours, bestowing blessings. Ziggy steers Livi to the park, where they take a seat once more beside the children's playground.

She has to confess she is happy to see Ziggy again, and the prayer he gave her is a promising sign.

'Ziggy, please, just tell me what's going on with you. I want to hear whatever you have to tell me.' She's about to say she's handled much worse but thinks twice.

'Something is going on, Livi, you're right.' Ziggy takes a deep breath. 'I want to marry you. I want you to be my wife.'

Livi is lost for words. *Marriage.* She didn't see this coming.

'Marry me? How can we marry, Ziggy, when you never tell me what you're thinking?'

Livi knows she sounds angry and maybe she is, but when Ziggy hangs his head and stares at his hands, her heart melts. His gesture is enormous, overwhelming, and she wants to say yes.

'Ziggy, I'm sorry,' says Livi. 'That came out wrong.'

'Don't be sorry, Livi!' Ziggy's hand snaps up. 'Please, don't ever say sorry to me. You're . . . you're an angel. I don't deserve to sit on the same bench as you.' Ziggy reaches for her hand.

'Please, if you start that again, we have to say goodbye to each other right now.' Livi looks hard at Ziggy. 'You feel guilty, I know that. I even understand, but *I* feel like I'm being punished when you withdraw.'

Ziggy sighs, deeply. 'Livi, I don't know if two survivors can be happy together.' He looks at the sky. 'All that pain – sometimes it's just too much. But I have heard you and if you're willing to take me on, then I will try. I promise you.' Ziggy's eyes are beseeching her to say 'yes', and she can see he's struggling, but still she holds back.

Will just *trying* be enough?

Ziggy pulls up the sleeve of his jacket to reveal bare skin. 'As you can see, Livi, I don't have a number on my arm.' Ziggy hangs his head.

'As you know, Ziggy, I don't *care*. I don't care if you lied, cheated and stole to stay alive – no one can judge us for what we went through. I just want us to be close enough to share our stories, whenever we want. And I'm not a saint *or* an angel – we all survived by doing whatever we had to do.'

Now is the moment, Livi sees, that she has to tell him what she wants, and either he will agree or she will never see him again.

'I'll marry you on one condition, Ziggy Ravek,' Livi tells him. 'That we talk about what happened to us whenever the mood takes us, that we tell our children and grandchildren what happened, that we never stop talking about it. We can't hide this stuff or pretend it's in the past and try to forget about it.' She pauses. 'Tell me, have you even forgotten one thing about the camps?'

Ziggy shakes his head. 'I remember every second of every day,' he says.

'That's a lot of memory, isn't it? Unless we want to spend the rest of our lives trying to shut the door on something that nearly destroyed us, we'd better get used to the fact that the camps are as much a part of our lives as each other.'

'You said you'll marry me.' Ziggy is grinning, reaching into his pocket for a small box. He flips it open and takes out a ring which he slips onto Livi's finger.

She holds up her hand to admire the tiny green stone. 'It's the same colour as the woods in spring in Vranov,' she exclaims.

CHAPTER 31

Rehovot
1952

L ivi wanders through the rose gardens of the Weizmann household, her arms full of blooms with which to make new flower arrangements. She places them on a garden bench and continues her journey amongst the bushes, alert for the tiny buds which will return an abundant crop of roses the following year. The gardeners have turned the soil earlier that morning and the rich earth is dark and so inviting that Livi bends to pick up handfuls of it, which she lets sift through her fingers.

'You are *my* land now,' she whispers to the earth. 'My home. Thank you for taking us in.' Livi does not hear the president approach with Prime Minister David Ben-Gurion; when she turns back round, the men are sitting on the bench where she placed the roses, watching her intently.

'Ah hem,' President Weizmann says.

Livi is startled, the soil still falling from her hands. 'I'm sorry, I'm so sorry, I—'

'Livi, what ever are you sorry about?' says the president, laughing. 'You are right, this *is* your land.' He turns to the prime minister. 'David, maybe you would agree it's more Livi's land than ours.'

Ben-Gurion nods, with a sad smile.

'You have lost so much, Livi, suffered more than any of us can imagine; if anyone has earned the right to be here it is you and your sisters,' continues the president.

Livi rubs her hands on her apron, stepping off the soil onto manicured lawn. Briskly, she walks over to the bench and gathers the flowers.

'The president's right you know, Livi. This is your home now, and it is our honour to watch you claim it.' Ben-Gurion stands and gives Livi a short bow.

'Thank you, Mr Prime Minister. I will leave you both as I'm sure you have important matters to discuss.' Livi is blushing, keen to be on her way.

'Have we, David? Do you have anything important for us to discuss?' President Weizmann asks, playfully.

'Oh, I'm sure we can think of something,' Ben-Gurion replies, as Livi hurries away.

* * *

Livi no longer skips to work and she hasn't for a while: the president is very sick and Livi's worst fears are realised when, in November, she arrives in the kitchens to be told that he died in the night.

For the rest of the day, Livi watches hundreds of men, women and children gather outside the gates to weep for the man who had dedicated his life to giving them their promised land.

Livi thinks about promises as her own tears fall. Vows and pacts and bonds and pledges, they all amount to the same thing, really: a declaration to fulfil a dream. Israel has already given her more than she dared to hope for. Her sisters have looked after her, as they promised their father they would, and she knows she has looked after them. Her fingers close around the small knife; it's always on her person, whether it's in her bag or in a pocket. She remembers how Cibi used it to feed her slices of onion – such a small thing, but as much a part of their pact as Mumma's candlesticks. Hell had escaped its moorings and risen to earth in the shape of Auschwitz and Birkenau and all the other camps, and yet, and yet, she had found the knife, and the sisters had found Magda, and Magda had kept them alive on a march to their deaths. Even in hell, they found enough hope to help them fulfil a promise.

As Livi watches Chaim Weizmann's coffin being carried through the house and outside to await the thousands gathered at the gates to pay their respects, she bows her head and whispers a prayer of thanks for the man who had given the sisters a safe place to heal, and to create a new family of their own. His coffin is laid on the heavy framework of a catafalque in the rear garden within a canopy of heavy white drapes, beside his beloved rose garden. From the foyer of the Weizmann household, Livi watches as his wife, Vera, on the arm of Prime Minister Ben-Gurion, is escorted outside to sit with her husband one final time.

Livi is still in the foyer with the other staff when the first lady returns. They haven't exchanged a single word from the moment the coffin was taken into the garden.

'Why don't you go now and pay your respects to Chaim before the public is allowed in?' Mrs Weizmann suggests. 'I know you all loved him and I hope you know he loved you.'

'I did love him,' says Livi, fervently. She realises she must have been scratching her tattoo when Vera takes her hand and presses it to her heart.

'It meant so much to him to have you here, young Livi,' she says. 'You have no idea.'

When Mrs Weizmann leaves, the prime minister steps forward. 'And it means so much to me,' says David Ben-Gurion, with a short bow to Livi. 'Please, all of you, go and say goodbye to your president.'

Soldiers stand to attention at each corner of the catafalque in the dazzling sunshine. Livi's knees almost buckle as she approaches the president's coffin, but fortunately the gardener is there to catch her as she stumbles.

'I don't know what to say,' Livi croaks.

'You don't have to say anything, Livi,' the gardener says. 'All you need to do is stand here and feel the love Chaim Weizmann had for this land.'

Livi tries to recall the many conversations, the small talk, the funny jokes she had shared with the great man. What she remembers, instead, is the last time she saw her mother and grandfather in Vranov in their little cottage; they come to her with such clarity now that she may as well have only said goodbye to them that morning. Livi closes her eyes, feels the intense love Chaim Weizmann had for Israel and its people, and asks that Mumma looks after her friend in heaven.

'We're about to open the front gates,' a soldier informs the staff. Livi looks towards the crowds waiting to come

391

inside and bid a final farewell before she slowly makes her way back to the house, which will never feel the same again.

*   *   *

Livi and Ziggy collapse onto Magda's sofa; they're exhausted after a weekend of walking the streets in their hunt for a place to live. They have spent every weekend for months looking for an apartment. The problem is money: Ziggy, a specialist technician for El Al, a growing – but still small – airline, isn't earning very much, and Livi's hours have been cut in the Weizmann house since the president's death.

'We can't afford any of them,' Livi tells Magda, exasperated. 'And don't get me wrong, it's not like they're expensive.'

'And there are so many people in Israel now; it's like everyone wants to live in Rehovot,' Ziggy complains.

'You have time, you'll find something,' comforts Magda.

'I want to find the perfect place for your sister,' Ziggy tells her.

Livi leans in, turning her face to receive his kisses. 'I don't care where we live, as long as we're together,' she says.

'You might eat those words if we don't find something soon.'

'Wherever it is,' Livi says, wisely, 'you can bet your life we've all lived in worse places.' Magda and Livi laugh, but Ziggy remains solemn.

'You're the only person I know, Livi Meller, who jokes about living in a concentration camp.'

'She's not joking, Ziggy,' says Magda, and he cracks a small smile.

'Anyway, as a last resort, I have a friend, Saadiya Masoud, who has a small farm with a few dwellings on his property, just outside town.' Ziggy sighs. 'I could ask him if he has an empty hut we can have.'

'An empty hut would have been a dream come true at Birkenau,' says Livi, a twinkle in her eye.

A week before the wedding, Livi and Ziggy are shown into the only vacant building on Saadiya's farm. 'I used to keep my goats in here on cold nights,' he says, with a grin.

Livi doesn't care that he's an Arab. She came to Israel with hope in her heart, and this man has given them a home. To Livi, he is a friend.

Now, she peers inside. The hut has no windows and there is still a hole in one wall for the goats to enter and exit.

'We can clean it out and I've got a small gas cooker you can have. There's a tap nearby for water and you're welcome to use the bathroom facilities in our house. Up to you, but it's yours if you want it.'

'What do you think?' asks Ziggy. He wrinkles his nose. Livi can hear the hesitation in his voice – this place is worse than he imagined.

Livi sighs, but she's smiling too. 'Like I said, I've lived in less pleasant places. We can clean it up and there's plenty of room inside for a bed. We can eat outside in good weather.'

'Are you sure?' Ziggy is surprised.

'I won't be living here alone, you know,' she tells him. 'If I suffer, you suffer. So we'll both have to just make the best of it for a while.'

The morning of Livi and Ziggy's wedding finds the house in chaos. Cibi and Mischka arrive early with Karol and Joseph in tow. With their cousin, Chaya, the children run amok, trailing their mothers behind them to feed them, fix plasters to grazed knees and change the babies and then change them again. Throughout the mayhem, Livi remains calm, enjoying the noise and excitement small children bring to any occasion.

Cibi is once again trying to fathom from Livi why the wedding is being held on the rooftop of an apartment building.

'Because, and as I've already told you, Ziggy's uncle has a flat in that block with access to the rooftop.' She takes her sister's arm. 'I know you're worried the children will jump over the side.' Cibi's look of horror makes Livi laugh. 'Come on, Cibi, don't you remember those nights in Bratislava with our friends, talking all night in the open air?' Livi looks wistful. 'That's when I first felt like a grown-up. And what could be more grown up than getting married?'

After changing baby Chaya's outfit for the third time, Livi is finally happy. Her niece looks adorable.

'Now it's time to get you into your wedding dress,' Magda tells their youngest sister.

'If you must,' replies Livi, with a grin.

Finally ready, Livi and her sisters, urged on by the well-wishes of their neighbours, walk the three blocks from Magda's house to the rooftop wedding. And Livi's spine begins to tingle. Not now, she thinks. But she doesn't resist the memory and lets her mind drift back to the hospital, to Matilda. The girl is with her on her wedding day and Livi realises she will be with her when she has her babies, her grandchildren, when she is old; that she is as much a part of her story as this happy day. Livi lifts her chin and starts to climb the stairs to the rooftop.

The balcony is perfect. The sisters gasp in unison as they take in the garlands, the floral arrangements sitting in the middle of colourful tablecloths, and the canopy above their heads, draped in a heavy fabric featuring wreathes of olive branches. The rich aroma of hot food permeates the air, spicy and sweet.

Mischka and Yitzchak take charge of the children and Cibi and Magda escort Livi up the aisle towards Ziggy, who awaits his bride with an enormous smile. Livi hurries to his side, not wanting to delay the moment of their union any longer.

The third glass is smashed and the third sister is married. Shouts of, 'Mazel tov', and cheering, fill the air. The melee begins with feasting and ends with dancing.

Livi has never been happier, but then, of course she has. She remembers the sisters breaking away from the death march, tired, almost dead, certainly too wrung-out to feel much of anything, but that had to count as a defining moment, the beginning of their journey back to life.

Mrs Weizmann, now a widow, takes Livi and Ziggy aside before she leaves. 'I want to wish you a long and happy life together. If you have a marriage even half as loving as my own, you will have succeeded,' she tells them.

Livi hugs Mrs Weizmann and, for a second, she lets herself believe this is her mumma, here on the rooftop to witness her marriage, to share the love and good wishes of their friends, to celebrate her youngest daughter's happiness.

When she draws away, Mrs Weizmann wipes a tear from Livi's cheek. 'I am sorry your mother isn't here,' she tells the young woman, as if she has just read Livi's mind. 'But you have wonderful sisters, and now a wonderful husband.'

After the last dance, Livi breaks away from Ziggy to find her sisters. They link arms and whisper a prayer for Mumma and Father and Grandfather, and in doing so, they renew their promise.

'Can you feel their presence, Livi?' whispers Cibi. 'Because I can. I can see Mumma in her best dress and Grandfather in his suit. He's holding a bunch of gladioli, and . . .' Her voice breaks.

'And Mumma is smiling, Livi,' says Magda, squeezing Cibi's shoulder. 'It's that smile she used to give us before saying goodnight.'

'Usually it's only their absence I feel,' says Livi, her eyes shining. 'But tonight, that space is filled with my happiness. I think that's what you mean, Cibi, by their presence?'

Cibi nods, then looks at her youngest sister. 'I was four years old when you were born, Livi, and I remember it clearly.'

'I remember it too,' says Magda. 'Even though I was only two.'

'You don't!' says Cibi. 'How could you possibly?'

'Well, I do. Father took us both in to see the new baby.' Magda looks at Livi. 'You were so tiny, like a newborn kitten.'

'Don't start all that again, it's my wedding day,' says Livi, laughing.

'Well, Father let me hold you,' continues Cibi. 'I had to sit down in his big chair and he carefully laid you in my arms.' All around them the wedding is winding down: guests are leaving and dirty plates are being stacked. 'He told me that having a new sister is a bit like keeping a special secret.'

'I don't remember that,' says Magda.

'See?' says Cibi. 'You were too young. Anyway, with special secrets, you have to keep them forever, that's what he told me. They have to live inside you.' Cibi touches her heart. 'There is nothing that anyone can do to make you give up your secret. And that's how Magda and I were to keep you safe.'

'You have kept me safe,' Livi says, taking her sisters' hands. 'But you mustn't give up now, OK?'

'Maybe just a little,' jokes Magda. 'I mean, Ziggy might have something to say about it.'

'Don't even joke,' chides Cibi, serious. 'Husbands don't stand a chance with us around.'

As she drifts off to sleep that night, Cibi recalls the day of Livi's birth in even greater detail. Livi's blanket was soft and yellow. Their mother, exhausted, offered her only a weak smile when she was allowed in to see her. Cibi worried she was dying, until Father reminded her that Mumma had delivered a whole baby, and she was allowed to be tired. She had sat on her mother's bed, holding her hand, and Mumma had told her to give thanks to God in her prayers that night for the 'kitten'. And Cibi had.

Just as she's falling asleep, she recalls one more detail: while she was praying, her father had come into the bedroom she shared with Magda, and told her it was time to go to sleep, that God would be around tomorrow too, to hear her thanks. *God would be around tomorrow too.*

Cibi's eyes flick open. She reaches for Mischka's hand. God is here today.

The next morning, Livi and Ziggy are woken by the calling of the rooster, loudly proclaiming the dawning of a new day.

'I can't believe we live in a goat shed,' Livi announces, looking around the windowless room.

'I promised you it wouldn't be for ever. You deserve a palace, fit for a queen, and that's what I'm working towards,' Ziggy tells her, pulling her close. He kisses each of her cheeks and then her mouth.

'I would just like some windows,' manages Livi, before she kisses him back.

397

Once dressed, they open their front door to find two large crates of oranges sitting on the ground. A third crate is covered by a white linen cloth, which Livi removes to reveal a platter of food and a small note: *Your wedding breakfast! Blessings on your marriage, from Saadiya, Leah and family*, it reads.

The couple take their breakfast to a couple of tree stumps in the clearing around their hut and eat in joyful silence, savouring every mouthful of the warm bread, cheese, hot coffee and slices of orange.

'So this is married life,' says Livi, wiping her mouth. 'I think I like it.'

'I like it too. And in the spirit of sharing our stories,' says Ziggy, pouring more coffee, 'there's something I need to know.'

'Ask me anything,' says Livi. Ziggy sets down his cup and takes her hands in his and, for a moment, Livi feels unnerved by his sudden focus as he meets her eyes. 'What is it?'

'Livi, I am on your side now. I find this stuff hard to talk about, and you don't, so please be honest with me. Last night you cried yourself to sleep. I don't want to think it's because ... well ... because of anything I did ... we did. I just ...' Ziggy is blushing.

'Ziggy, no!' Livi is alarmed that he might blame himself for her nightly grief. She takes his face in her hands. 'I don't want to cry every night, but the tears are for Mumma, for her house in Vranov. I can't seem to get past that day when that pig threw us out of our home.'

Ziggy looks confused, but also a little relieved. 'You're upset about a house?'

'I know it sounds crazy, after everything else. But when I close my eyes at night, I see Mumma cooking in the kitchen, making the beds, sitting in her chair.'

'Livi, it's OK. I just needed to understand.'

Livi wants this marriage to be perfect. Was Ziggy right to worry? Is it stupid to think that two survivors might be happy together? She shakes this thought away. They *are* making a life for themselves. Didn't they just get married?

'I hope I don't cry for ever,' says Livi, in a small voice. 'I'm sorry, Ziggy.'

'I told you once before to never apologise to me, Livi. Cry all you want, but one day I hope I'll make you happy enough to forget about the house in Vranov, or at least for the memory to be less painful.' He stands up and holds out a hand to Livi. 'Now, let's go and see your sisters before Cibi goes home,' he says.

Livi is immediately excited. 'Do you really want to?'

'I want to.'

Arriving home after her first day back at work, Livi is delighted to find her husband sitting outside the hut with a meal on the rickety table donated to them by Saadiya.

'I have news,' he announces, as Livi sits down. 'My boss called me in today to tell me I've got the job I applied for at El Al, and I've been promoted.'

'Promoted?' Livi asks, spearing a green bean. 'To what?'

'You are looking at the technical manager of a new fleet of Constellation aircraft.'

Livi swallows. 'Ziggy, that's . . . that's amazing.'

'And more money, Livi. Soon I will be able to give you windows.'

A month later, Magda and Yitzchak help Livi and Ziggy move into their new apartment just a few blocks from their own. It is the home Livi never allowed herself to dream of.

'I saw a lovely sofa on sale in a shop in Tel Aviv,' Ziggy tells her. Livi is pushing a wayward spring back into the ageing sofa given to them by a neighbour.

'Do we need a new sofa?' Livi is grinning. She doesn't care about the furniture. She is delighted by everything, whether it's second hand – and most of it is – or new.

'You never complain, Livi. We have so little, and yet you never complain.'

'I have everything that matters,' Livi tells him.

'That's what I love about you.'

'Is that all that you love about me?'

'I love everything about you.'

CHAPTER 32

Rehovot
1954

Two years later, on the day that Livi's first child is born, she and Ziggy make a vow to tell baby Oded their stories, and more importantly, how they survived to share this part of themselves with him.

'It's so sad, though,' Livi muses. 'But to know us, he must know what happened to us.'

'Livi,' says Ziggy. 'Our baby was born just yesterday and last night was the first time you haven't cried yourself to sleep. Do you know why?'

Livi is quiet, thoughtful. Oded nurses at her breast, even though she's not sure her milk has come in yet. 'I do, Ziggy. I think it's because I'm a mother now. I will always miss

Mumma, but last night I felt her beginning a new journey, that she was guiding me to become the mother she was. Our house is gone, but Mumma isn't. She's bigger than the house in Vranov. This baby is bigger.'

When Oded is a month old, the sisters meet in Livi's apartment. Their husbands are at work and the children are happy enough, racing through the flat as they play hide and seek.

Magda is heavily pregnant with her second child.

'I hope it's a girl,' she says. 'I like the idea of two girls.'

'I hear you,' laughs Cibi. 'My boys are driving me crazy.' Karol and Joseph are screaming at Chaya to come out from her hiding place.

'You're quiet, Livi. Still exhausted?' Magda asks her sister.

'I'm OK, I'm just thinking about someone.'

'From the camp?' asks Cibi.

'From the camp, yes. The girl I was with in the hospital.'

'Matilda.' Magda and Cibi say together; they know the details of their sister's ordeal.

Magda shivers. 'I think we all have one memory that stands out above all the others.'

'Well, you both know mine.' Cibi sighs.

'The blanket girls,' say Livi and Magda.

Cibi nods, also shivering.

'I don't know yours, Magda,' says Livi. 'Do we, Cibi?'

'Well, I have a few jostling for the top spot.' Magda smiles sadly. 'But there's one I come back to more than the others. Do you remember that day Volkenrath brought me to Auschwitz?'

'When she didn't tell you where you were going?' says Cibi.

Magda nods. 'She didn't say one word the entire journey, but it was before she ordered me into the car. I was in the sorting room, miserably opening those parcels for the dead, when she came in and called my name.' Magda swallows. 'Well, I'd made a friend there, a girl my age, she was Czech and she had a sister at Auschwitz. She asked me to pass a message to her, to tell her that she was fine and trying to find a way to get back to Auschwitz herself.'

'Did you?' Livi asks, wondering why she has never heard this story.

'I found out her sister was dead. I could have sent word to her with one of the prisoners who was still going to Birkenau to work, but I didn't.' Magda hangs her head.

'Will you tell us why?' asks Livi.

'I think I know why,' says Cibi.

'I imagined myself as that girl receiving the news that you or Livi was dead.' Magda draws a deep breath. 'I couldn't stand the thought of it, so I just forgot about her.'

'Only you didn't,' says Cibi.

'In that inhuman place we still managed to feel guilty.' Livi shakes her head in wonder. 'Can you believe it?'

The children are all crying now; even Oded has woken from his dreams and is grizzling for food. Livi puts him on her breast while Magda and Cibi rustle up some food in Livi's tiny kitchen.

'Eat,' says Magda, passing Livi a plate piled high with *latkas*. 'They're good for your milk.'

Livi pops one into her mouth and chews. The children are bouncing on Livi's bed and no one tells them to stop.

'I think I would like to live in this moment for ever,' Livi says, taking a smaller bite of another *latka*. 'I'm with my sisters and our children and . . .'

'And we have *latkas* and, if I'm not mistaken, some of Ziggy's excellent wine for later,' says Cibi. 'You know, one day we'll be grandparents, maybe even great-grandparents.'

'You won't live that long, Cibi. As the eldest, you'll go long before great-grandchildren,' says Livi, giggling.

'I might be around, you never know. Well, I'm just wondering if we'll still feel the same about each other.'

'Of course we will,' says Livi. Oded has fallen asleep again and she takes him through to his bassinet in her bedroom. The cousins are fast asleep on her bed, exhausted by their bouncing.

'Let's have a glass of Ziggy's excellent wine, shall we? Just a small one?'

Magda shakes her head and points to her belly. 'I'd like some orange juice, though.'

The sisters raise their glasses and, as one, they say: 'To Mumma.'

Magda thinks of the last time she saw their mother, in that classroom. She and her grandfather were insisting they accompany Magda to wherever the Hlinka were taking her, but she had reassured them she would be back soon, even though she knew it was probably a lie.

Magda watches her sisters as they sip their wine and munch on *latkas*. She was deferring her mother's pain, she realises, it wasn't much more than that. A small act of kindness and that's what binds these sisters now: small acts of kindness, of consideration. They no longer need to renew their vow to look after each other, as their promise is as much a part of them as their children. But, all the same, she raises her glass once more.

'To the promise.'

The sisters clink and the children, all at once, wake up.

Four years after the birth of her son, Livi and Ziggy are blessed with a little girl. They name her Dorit. Odie relishes his role as big brother, protector of his sister and, in his mind, his Ema.

EPILOGUE

Rehovot
December 2013

'They're here! Oded, take the lift and bring back your aunt! I can't wait to see Cibi,' yells Livi.

Livi is hanging over the balcony of her first-floor apartment, looking down onto Moshe Smilansky Street below. The street she has lived on for twenty-five years.

Her daughter, Dorit, and Oded's wife, Pam, join her on the balcony to wave at the people below. Three generations of the descendants of the Meller family are making their way up the street, in a cacophony of hugs, laughter and the cries of children. Each adult is carrying either a large basket, or a tray of food.

'*Shalom, shalom!*' they call to the women above.

'Odie is bringing the lift down,' Dorit shouts.

At last, Livi sees her sisters. Magda is holding a walking stick in one hand, the other the hand of her eldest daughter, Chaya. Cibi is behind her, in the wheelchair she increasingly relies on since the day she fell and broke her hip. Her son, Yossi, pushes his mother along the pavement. Magda and Cibi both look up and spy Livi. Magda waves her stick, Cibi blows a kiss.

'Go and help them with the food,' Livi urges her daughter and daughter-in-law.

Livi knows she will have less than two minutes before her home swells with the people she loves most in this world: her family. She spends one of these minutes looking at the building across the road, to its rooftop where, seventy years ago, she stood with her sisters, friends and a rabbi, and married the man she loves.

Ziggy is in the bedroom, preparing for the onslaught that is part and parcel of marrying a Meller sister.

'Ema, Ema!' the cries of her grandchildren snap Livi's attention to the present and away from the memories of her wedding day.

She remains on the balcony as the sisters' extended families stream inside to receive her special kisses and hugs.

'What about me?' Ziggy calls out as he enters the living room. 'Don't I get a hug?'

The younger ones rush at him, and he leans back against the wall to welcome their onslaught.

Livi hears the lift door ping open. Who will it be first? Cibi exerting her oldest sister rights, or Magda, who will have pleaded the right to sit down because, unlike Cibi who is already sitting down in a wheelchair, her need is the greater?

Cibi is wheeled in by Yossi.

'I thought you would let Magda come up first,' Livi says, as she bends to plant kisses on her sister's cheeks.

'She's younger than me. She can afford to wait,' Cibi says, with a flick of her wrist.

'Come in. Come in! You want to stay in that thing or sit in a proper chair?' Livi asks.

'I'm fine where I am. And, this way, when I have had enough of you, I can wheel myself out of here.'

'If only I didn't love you so much, I would push you down the stairs for that.'

'You keep on like that and I'll push myself down the stairs.'

They both hear the lift door ping open once more.

'There she is! How long is she going to keep reminding us she is the eldest?' Magda says, joining Livi and Cibi.

'All the days of our lives,' Livi answers.

'All the days of her life, and then it's my turn.' Magda kisses Livi.

'What? Your big sister doesn't get a kiss?' Cibi says, indignant.

'I gave you a kiss in the street, or have you forgotten already?' Magda snaps back. 'Livi, where's Ziggy's chair? I need to sit down, and his is the most comfortable you have.'

'Did I hear someone say my name?' Ziggy asks, as he takes his sisters-in-law in his arms.

'Magda wants to sit in your chair,' Cibi says. 'Tell her she can't.'

'Do *you* want my chair, Cibi?' Ziggy asks.

'No, I'm happy in my own chair – one I can run away in.'

'Come on, Magda, come and sit down,' Ziggy says, taking her arm and escorting her into the living room.

'I have to go back to the car to get some drinks. Are you OK now, Mumma?' Yossi asks Cibi.

'I've got her, Yossi. I've always got her,' Livi says, taking the handles of Cibi's wheelchair and pushing her into the living room, dodging children and coffee tables as she goes.

'Put me in a corner somewhere,' Cibi says.

'No, I will not. This is a party and you're to enjoy yourself. Come and say hello to Odie and Pam. They arrived all the way from Canada only two days ago.'

'Aunty Cibi, how are you?' Oded kneels to hug and kiss his aunt.

'You look older,' Cibi tells him.

'I *am* older, Aunty. It's just that you don't see me enough. I wish we could afford to fly over more often.'

'Just stop getting older. You're making me feel really ancient. Now, where is your wife?'

'I'm here, Aunty Cibi.' A beaming Pam kneels beside her husband and holds both of Cibi's hands in her own.

'She doesn't look any older,' Cibi says to Odie. 'But she is even more beautiful.'

'Aunty,' says Pam. 'Odie and I have something very special to show you, all of you, later.'

'You can't show me now?'

'No, you'll have to be patient, but I can get you something to eat,' Pam offers.

'A glass of red wine would be nice.'

Livi looks around her home. Every inch of the large dining table is covered with plates of food. Glasses are being filled, small hands sneak into bowls of fruit, crisps, small cakes, and snatch the food away.

Cibi's great-granddaughter is crying. 'Will you take her?' her granddaughter asks, thrusting a squealing baby into Cibi's arms.

The baby reaches a fat hand for Cibi's glass of wine.

'You're too young for that, but in a few years come and see me,' Cibi says to the one-year-old.

'You won't be around when she is old enough to drink.' Livi laughs.

Livi weaves her way through her family, ducking as Yossi throws his eight-year-old granddaughter in the air. The young adults, the third generation of the family, have escaped onto the balcony.

'Mind if an old girl joins you?' Livi asks her grandson, stepping outside.

'Ema, I will be old before you are,' he says, taking his petite grandmother in his arms and lifting her off her feet.

'Have you seen all the food in there?' Livi says.

'It's about normal,' her granddaughter says. 'You know we'll eat it all, don't you?'

'Hey, I'm hoping we don't eat it all so I can take some away. I rely on these family gatherings to feed me for a week,' her cousin insists.

'I will leave you to talk about whatever it is young people talk about these days,' Livi says, as she turns to go back inside.

'We talk about what you and your sisters talked about at our age.'

'That's what worries me, and that's why I am leaving.'

Ziggy grabs her as she comes back inside, placing a loving arm around her waist. 'Come and get something to eat. God knows there's enough food,' he says.

'So much noise, Ziggy. I don't know if I love it or hate it,' Livi says, leaning into him.

'You love it – always have, always will.'

'I will put some food on a plate and go and talk to Magda. Everyone is standing up and she is the only one sitting down,' Livi says.

'Cibi's sitting.'

'Cibi's in a wheelchair.'

Livi drags a chair next to Magda. Without an invitation, Magda begins to pick from the plate. 'Cibi doesn't look good,' she says.

'If only she would get out of that wheelchair and use her legs, she would get better much faster,' Livi replies.

'Ema, Aunty Amara and Uncle Udom are here!' Dorit yells from the other side of the apartment.

Livi looks round to see her daughter wrap her arms around Amara, her friend from the orange groves, the shy girl who introduced her to dates. Her husband, Udom, is holding a huge plate of falafels and a small wicker basket of dates.

'Take the plate, Dorit,' Livi yells back, rising from her chair and making her way across the room. 'Now the whole family is here.' Livi beams as she hugs her old friend.

'I think Odie wants your attention,' says Amara.

Odie is clinking a knife against his glass, asking for quiet. The chatter in the room rises in volume as each person tells the one next to them to be silent.

The young adults step inside the room, and the younger children immediately seize their opportunity to claim the balcony for themselves.

'Ema, Aunty Magda, would you please come and sit next to Aunty Cibi?' Odie says.

The three sisters sit side by side at the front of the room.

Odie reaches for Pam's hand. 'Pam and I are so happy to be here with you all and we thank you so much for coming. I want to take this moment to show you something very special.'

'What is it?' Cibi says, in a loud whisper to Livi.

'Let's just all wait and see,' Livi tells her.

'Pam and I have been working on a glass sculpture for a long time now. It is currently on display in an exhibition called "WAR Light Within/After the Darkness" at a gallery in Toronto. We called it *The Miracle of Three Sisters*.'

'Have you got it here?' Magda asks.

'No, Aunty, it's too big to bring all the way over to Israel, and anyway, it's still in the exhibition. But we do have a photo of it here, in the gallery catalogue.'

Odie hands the catalogue to Livi. Cibi and Magda lean in to look at the photo.

They gasp as one when they see etched into the base of the towering glass structure the numbers 4559.

'That's your number,' Cibi says.

Livi cannot speak. Ziggy makes his way over and places both his hands on her shoulders. Cibi takes a sip of wine, her breathing slow and heavy. Magda wipes her eyes and turns to her daughters, who are leaning in for a hug.

Pam is trying to speak, but her tears are making it difficult to get the words out. 'Do . . . do you like it?' she manages, finally.

Livi hands the catalogue to Magda and embraces her son and daughter-in-law. Odie cries on her shoulder. 'I didn't know how else to honour the three of you and what you did to survive and give us our lives,' he sobs.

'You honour me by being my son,' Livi tells him, setting Pam off once more.

Karol is on his knees, hugging his mother. Eventually, he gets to his feet and picks up his glass, clinking it with the ring on his finger. Once more there is silence in the room. 'As the eldest of the sisters' children, I would like to say a few words,' he announces.

'Like mother, like son,' Magda says.

A moment of stunned silence is followed by raucous laughter.

'OK, OK, so I learnt from the best – thank you, Mother,' Karol says to Cibi. 'No, seriously, just for a moment, before we return to our merrymaking . . .'

'And more drinking,' Cibi adds.

'And more drinking,' Kari agrees, then continues: 'We have always known we have a very special family and everyone who has joined us continues to make it special. Odie and Pam, we miss you in Canada and don't see enough of you, and now you present us with this amazing tribute to the sisters. We want to thank you for what you have created in their memory.' Raising his glass, he yells, 'To the Three Sisters.' A chorus of 'To the Three Sisters,' rings out.

'My glass is empty,' Cibi says.

'Someone please give my mother another glass of wine,' Yossi calls out.

Within the rush to fill glasses, help themselves to more food, and resume conversations, Livi, in the middle, stretches an arm around each of her sisters.

'Where's Ziggy? He should be with us,' Magda says.

'I'm right here, Magda,' Ziggy says behind her, leaning between Livi and Magda. 'If I had a glass in my hand, I would raise it and say, "Cheers to Mischka and to Yitzchak,"' he says.

'To Mischka and Yitzchak,' the sisters say, looking around the room. The six of them made each and every one of the people present today.

Cibi starts to say something and stops.

'What is it, Cibi?' Ziggy asks.

Cibi closes her eyes. A thousand memories race through her mind. 'We kept our promise, didn't we? To Father, to Mumma and Grandfather.'

Livi takes her sister's hand. 'Do you remember the onion, Cibi?' she says. Cibi nods. 'To this day, whenever I chop an onion, I think of how you saved my life.'

'The bunk,' whispers Magda. 'Remember the bunk we shared? Every night, however terrible that day had been, I knew that if I could cuddle up close to you both in the dark, I would never be alone.'

'We saved each other's lives,' says Cibi. She raises the sleeve of her left arm and her sisters do the same. Their skin is wrinkled now, but the numbers are as clear as the day they were stabbed into their arms. 'When they put these numbers into our skin, they sealed our promise. Somehow, they gave us the strength to fight for our lives.'

The sisters are silent as the party mills around their hunched frames. The dead are never far from their thoughts, and now each of them pictures the countless empty rooms around the world that should be filled with laughter, with husbands, sons and daughters, with grandchildren, nieces, nephews and cousins.

'We might not be much to look at now,' says Livi, grinning. 'But once we were the Meller girls.'

AUTHOR'S NOTE

Menachem Emil (Mendel) Meller, the sisters' father, died on 27 October 1929. He is buried in the Jewish Cemetery in Košice, Slovakia.

Civia 'Cibi' Meller was born on 13 October 1922 in Vranov nad Topl'ou, Slovakia. She died on 25 November 2015, in Rehovot, Israel.

Magda Meller was born on 1 January 1924 in Vranov nad Topl'ou, Slovakia. She lives in Holon, Israel.

(Ester) Gizella 'Livia/Livi' Meller was born 16 November 1925 in Vranov nad Topl'ou, Slovakia. She lives in Rehovot, Israel.

A fourth daughter, Emilia, was born three months after her father Menachem Meller's death and died of tuberculosis before her third birthday.

The sisters' paternal grandparents, Anyka and Emile Meller, lived and died in Vranov nad Topl'ou, Slovakia.

The sisters' maternal grandmother, Rosalie Strauss, died in 1934 in Vranov nad Topl'ou, Slovakia. She was a midwife, and delivered all of the Meller girls.

The sisters' maternal grandfather, Yitzchak Strauss, was murdered in Auschwitz-Birkenau on 24 October 1944.

The sisters' mother, Chaya Sara (née Strauss) Meller, was murdered in Auschwitz-Birkenau on 24 October 1944.

Cibi's husband Mischka was born Mordechai Maximilian Lang on 2 April 1908. He died on 30 March 2000 in Kfar Ahim, Israel.

Magda's husband Yitzko was born Yitzchak Guttman on 1 November 1911. He died on 5 May 1982 in Holon, Israel.

Livi's husband, Shmuel, known in the family as Ziggy, was born Viteslav Zigfried Shmuel Ravek on 8 April 1925 in Moravia. He died on 14 December 2015 in Rehovot, Israel.

Cibi married Mischka in Bratislava, Slovakia, on 20 April 1947. Their son Karol (Kari) was born on 16 March 1948 in Bratislava. Their second son Joseph (Yossi) was born on 12 August 1951, in Israel.

Magda married Yitzko in 1950 in Israel. Their daughter Chaya was born on 28 May 1951, in Israel. A second daughter, Judith (Ditti), was born on 22 September 1955, in Israel.

Livi married Ziggy on 2 May 1953 in Israel. Their son Oded (Odie) was born on 1 August 1955, in Israel. Their daughter Dorit was born on 12 July 1959, in Israel.

The sisters' uncle Ivan (Strauss), his wife Helena and children Lily, Gita and David, arrived in Auschwitz-Birkenau on 25 October 1944. There was no selection for the gas chambers that day, or any subsequent day. The war was nearly over. Taken on a death march, Helena, weak and sick, fell and died. Ivan and his children made their way back to Bratislava where they were reunited with the sisters. There he met his second wife Irinka and moved to Israel in 1949. They had three further children.

Dr Kisely was the Christian doctor who saved Magda from deportation by admitting her to hospital. Magda remembers his name clearly.

Before they were taken to Auschwitz, Cibi had been passionate about travelling to Palestine, to be part of the creation of a Jewish homeland. A wealthy local Jewish man who had converted to Christianity acquired a property 30km from Vranov. There he provided *Hachshara* training for young men and women, teaching them about farming, large-scale cooking and other survival skills that would be essential in a new land, with a climate and terrain very different to Slovakia.

Visik was the same age as Cibi. He had been a friend for many years and was part of a social group of young, idealistic women and men, predominantly Jewish, who met regularly, often in the Meller home, to dream, plot and scheme for a better life. He joined the Hlinka Guards and tried to intimidate and harass Cibi while they walked from the synagogue to the train station in Vranov as they were deported for Auschwitz.

Cibi and Livi are listed on the transport leaving Poprad, Slovakia, for 'Poland' on 3 April 1942.

Mrs Marilka Trac lived opposite the Mellers and frequently hid Magda in her ceiling during the winter months of 1942 and 1943.

Ilava Prison in Slovakia, where Magda was taken after being captured, was the same prison in which the tattooist of Auschwitz, Lale Sokolov, was imprisoned in 1948.

The Theresienstadt family camp was emptied, and all occupants murdered in the gas chambers, on 8 and 9 March 1944.

Maria Mandel (10 January 1912–24 January 1948, also known as Maria Mandl), was tried, sentenced and executed for war crimes. https://en.wikipedia.org/wiki/Maria_Mandl

Elisabeth Volkenrath (5 September 1919–13 December 1945) was tried, sentenced and executed for war crimes. https://en.wikipedia.org/wiki/Elisabeth_Volkenrath

Heinz Volkenrath (28 December 1920–13 December 1945) was tried, sentenced and executed for war crimes on the same day as his wife.

Mala Zimetbaum (prison number 19880) (26 January 1918–15 September 1944) was the first woman to escape from Auschwitz-Birkenau. She fell in love with a Polish prisoner, Edward (Edek) Galinski. They escaped together on 24 June 1944. Galinski turned himself in to the SS when he saw Mala being arrested. Interrogated and tortured, they were to be executed at the same time in the men's and women's camps, respectively. Galinski attempted to jump into the noose before the verdict was read, shouting the words 'Long live Poland!' The prisoners, forced to watch, took their caps off as a mark of respect to Galinski, incurring the fury of the guards. The reports of Mala's death vary in the official records. Livi confirms the report that she bled to death on the cart as she was taken to the crematoria. A musical (*Mala, the Music of the Wind*) and a film (*The Last Stage*) have been made about Mala. https://en.wikipedia.org/wiki/Mala_Zimetbaum

During World War II, Banská Bystrica became the centre of anti-Nazi opposition in Slovakia when the Slovak National Uprising, one of the largest anti-Nazi resistance events in Europe, was launched from the city on 29 August 1944. The insurgents were defeated on 27 October 1944.

24 October 1944 was the last day the gas chambers and crematoria were operational in Auschwitz-Birkenau. Livi saw her mother and grandfather at the train line inside Birkenau. Not knowing what to do, she ran to find Cibi and tell her. The scene described is as it happened: Cibi confronting Kramer, then managing a brief exchange of words with her mother and grandfather as they entered the gas chamber.

Eva, the young Yugoslav girl the sisters cared for during the death marches and at the end of the war, told them that her father had been the personal physician to President Tito. This position did not save his Jewish wife and daughter from being taken to Auschwitz. Eva had been with her mother when she died on the death march. It is not known what happened to Eva after her return to Yugoslavia.

The candlesticks and photos Magda hid in the ceiling of their home in Vranov nad Topl'ou remain in her possession.

The Three Sisters glass sculpture featured in the epilogue was created by Pam and Oded Ravek. It is both a tribute and a memorial. It is a memorial to the 6,000,000 Jews murdered by the Nazis (expressed by fragmented scattered roses with thorns on the base) and to the memory of the 1,500,000 children under the age of thirteen (twelve nascent roses on the second tier without thorns). The intentionally rough-cast numbers on three facing sides are the actual numbers that were burned into the arms of the three sisters. The side with no number serves to illustrate that a number may be filled in by the viewer in his/her mind, and also honours those who perished in the Holocaust who were not inked.

Magda worked for President and First Lady Weizmann from 1950 until the birth of Chaya in May 1951.

Livi worked for President and First Lady Weizmann from March 1951 until June 1955.

President Chaim Weizmann and First Lady Vera Weizmann are buried in the grounds of their home in Rehovot, now a public garden. Livi visits them, taking her children and grandchildren, giving them a special tour that transcends time and brings the gardens and historic figures to life.

AFTERWORD FROM LIVIA RAVEK

From the moment that Heather walked into my home, I instantly liked her. I was drawn to her beautiful smile, cheerfulness and her lovely accent. To me, it was miraculous that Heather would come to see me. I was astonished that she would make a change to her busy touring schedule and come to Israel to meet with me, from South Africa, before returning to her home and family in Australia.

We do have something in common. Heather wrote her first novel, *The Tattooist of Auschwitz,* about Lale and Gita, and I knew them from a young age – 'before' – back home in Slovakia. Heather has Lale and Gita in her heart, and great love and empathy for people.

The rest is history. It was unbelievable that Heather would write about the lives of my sisters and me. She has a gift of being able to quietly listen and understand. *Three Sisters* has been two years in the making. I have grown to know Heather, consider her a sister and part of my family, and I love her deeply. I am so proud and honoured to know her.

My family and I look forward to seeing Heather in Israel again soon.

AFTERWORD FROM ODED RAVEK

Sometimes the stars align and, by a zillion-to-one chance, you discover that dreams, every now and then, do come true.

Ever since I can remember, I've longed for the life story of my mother, Livia, and her two older sisters, Cibi, *z"l*, and Magda, to be told. In the spring of 2019, my wife, Pam, and I were about to embark on a trip to visit our adult children and family in Israel, and to celebrate the wedding of our niece. While doing some last-minute shopping, the novel *The Tattooist of Auschwitz* caught my eye, and we purchased it to read on our trip. Little did I know that the purchase of *The Tattooist* would lay the foundation towards the fulfilment of my long-held dream.

We joyfully reunited with our children and my mother, my *Ema*, in Israel; at the same time Heather Morris was preparing for her South African book tour to promote her bestselling, powerful novel about Lale Sokolov, *The Tattooist of Auschwitz*. Giving Ema the book to read, she was delighted to realise that she knew Lale and, without reading ahead, knew that his beloved wife was Gita, her former schoolmate.

An email from Pam to Heather set the wheels in motion. Heather changed her plans to return to Australia from South Africa, and arrived in Israel a few days after our family celebration, to meet with Ema and our family. In Heather's skilful hands, a compelling, inspirational story of the life of the three sisters began to form. My long-held wish was beginning to come true.

The story of my mother, Cibi and Magda is testament to the power of love and devotion. Against all the odds, the three sisters survived the most heinous, systematic genocide that the world has ever known. And yet they went on to live and work in a new country, the country of my birth, learning a new language and culture. They lived lives full of laughter, fulfilment and joy, always surrounded by love, with each successive generation of sons, daughters, grandchildren and great-grandchildren growing and thriving in freedom.

This book brings together all of the stories that I'd heard from a young age. Heather captures the beautiful, peaceful lives that Ema and her family enjoyed in Vranov, and the helplessness, chaos and horrible tragedies that these strong, incredible sisters endured and witnessed.

As a child, I saw the sadness in my *Ema*'s eyes. I felt her sorrow, but didn't understand. I would save my small birthday and holiday gifts of money, and purchase presents for her so that I could see her beautiful smile light up her eyes. My sister, Dorit, and I had the best childhoods ever, filled with love and laughter, security and liberty. We were blessed that my father, my *Aba*, and my *Ema* were open with us, and didn't keep their lives before we knew them a mystery.

As the years went by, I began to understand that they had survived the unimaginable.

Engraved in my mind is a pivotal moment when I stood with Ema next to the fence at the death camp, Auschwitz-Birkenau. Ema described to me the depravity that went on in that place and about life beyond the dividing electrical fence. She told me: 'It is the same blue sky and sun that is over the death camp and the fields and forests beyond, on the other side of the fence.' She could see families together, children playing, and people working in the fields. They totally ignored what was going on in the death camp, continuing to live and go about their business as though it were an ordinary day, as though those on the other side of the fence were invisible. Here, where Ema stood, on one side of the fence, was the stench of death, murder and misery, yet on the other side there was life and freedom. And it was all under the same blue sky. How could it be?'

Later, at a newly opened boutique hotel at a ski village not far from Auschwitz-Birkenau, Pam and I returned to the car. We told Ema and Aba, Dorit, and our niece, Ruth, what we'd just learned. This converted mansion had an infamous history. It had been a retreat for SS officers who worked at the death and extermination camps. 'Shall we look for other accommodation?'

Ema's response, as always, was insightful and succinct: 'We are here. They are not.'

AFTERWORD FROM AYALA RAVEK

I remember.
   I remember, as a child, tracing my fingers on her arms, over the faded numbers.

I remember coming home one afternoon to see my *Safta* speaking to a stranger, with tears in her voice, immortalising her story into a camera; and being scared and curious, and not knowing what to do or say.

I remember the small knife she always carried in her purse, next to the mints she would share with me during car rides; the knife that she would occasionally take out and cradle in her hand, working her thumb over the worn handle.

I remember the first time she told me where she found the knife – in the camp – after asking her where the knife was from, and I said, 'Cool.' We were in the middle of a mall, sitting on a bench. I was a child but, still, I remember the feeling of instant regret, knowing I had said the wrong thing and not really understanding why; but I understood the sadness in her eyes.

I remember, years later, that the knife was lost in a taxi, and that I cried to myself that night, feeling a loss I could not explain.

I remember the sleepovers in my grandparents' room, and sitting outside in the sunshine eating ice cream, after having walked by the water in the summer sun.

I remember the laughter around the table as bellies ached and tears rolled down cheeks, our laughter so hard we couldn't catch our breath; as the pain that was always there below the surface found its release.

But what I remember most of all are the hugs when Safta would whisper: 'You are my victory. My family is my victory.'

AFTERWORD FROM YOSSI LAHAV (LANG)

I would like to thank Heather Morris, who dived head first into this project and brought the remarkable tale of the three sisters into existence. Their path will for ever be documented in this book.

In addition, a big thank you to my cousin, Oded Ravek, and his wife, Pam, who initiated the collaboration with Heather Morris.

I was born and raised in Kfar Ahim, a community of Holocaust survivors.

At the time of my birth, my mother suffered from tuberculosis and couldn't take care of my older brother and a new baby – we were assigned to children's homes. The first two years of my life I spent in Jerusalem, while my brother was in Tiv'on.

As I was growing up, my parents, Cibi and Mischka, were busy building a new life in a new country, after surviving

World War II. They were never outspoken about what happened to them 'before', and us kids never really asked or were concerned about my mother's arm tattoo. Maybe it was because my parents were never particularly interested in sharing, or because nobody else in my immediate surroundings ever voluntarily shared their past, I didn't feel like something was amiss.

Not until I met my future wife, Ronit (Sophie), and discovered she had known her great-grandparents, was I struck by how much I had missed – I had missed a generation I never met or even imagined could be present in my life.

It was only when my daughters, Noa and Anat, grew up enough to start asking questions, that I was confronted with the scope of what had happened to my mother. This was the first time I realised her heroism: the way my mother and her two sisters survived those horrible times.

The story of these three sisters, Cibi, Magda and Livia, is an amazing tale of wits and courage. Their incredible survival, their arrival to and settlement in Israel, and their thriving 'tribe', are all evidence of their victory.

A my sa zas tholíme a ideme dolej. Prechádzame okolo lágru. Je to taký zvláštny pocit, ale sme ešte dosial nemohly. Dnes mešením nás pustili za dráty! Ploten hrady sú zrušené – mohlo tam nie je, lebo by na nás strielali, keby sme chceli vyjsť.

Kirov.

Skoro nepoznávame Kirov, je to malé mestečko, chodily sme sem častr pre mliečko o máte pre lágru. Tu je viac miestr Kirova, len zbombardované domy, horiace skladoly, vypálené obchody – holé do neba trčiace, dymiace hosky. Je to strašný pohlad, na dvoroch zhorený dobytok – jak strašne to smrdí!! Ideme dalej, velmi pomaly nám to ide, lebo je už poludnie a tiež má dost tihne začíne zohrievat. – Konečne zas dedinka, kde sa dobre umyjeme, najíme, vyspíme a zajtra ráno zas s novou silou sa dáme do cesty. Našly sme si tichú izbičku, velmi dobre si tu odpočnieme. Kirov je velmi malinké dedinka,

The document on the opposite page is an extract from Magda's diary. Magda found a notebook and a pen at Retzow (part of Ravensbrück Concentration Camp) after the sisters were moved there from Auschwitz-Birkenau, and kept it with her on the death marches and after they broke free. Here, Magda reflects on the news that the war is over. The sisters were by then in a small village in southern Germany, Mirow, which had been abandoned by its residents. Russian soldiers passing through the village told them the war had ended.

8th May 1945

We have packed up and are on the move once again. We passed our camp at Retzow. It feels strange not to be behind that fence and being pushed around. There's no one to shout at us if we choose to run away.

Mirow

Mirow is such a small town. We used to come here to get milk and meat for the camp (when we were at Retzow). We don't recognise it now though. Houses have been bombed, barns and shops are still burning. It's an awful sight – even the livestock have been burnt – the smell is terrible! The sun is high and strong. We continue walking. Soon, we are in another small village where we can wash and get our strength back for the next bit of the journey. We find a nice, clean room where we can stay. The name of this tiny village is Zirtow. It has been abandoned – there are no civilians here anymore. We are almost alone. There are Russian soldiers around, but they are quite kind and don't bother us. This is a pleasant surprise.

Midnight, 8th May 1945 – The End of War

We cannot imagine what other people are doing outside this village. This is not an easy thing to write: It is the End of War. This is not only the end of the war, it is the end of tears, the end of death, the end of the sound of gunfire, the end of air raids; and finally the capitulation of Germany.

It is the end of this massive sadistic German Empire. The Empire which believed it could not ever be defeated, by anyone. The end of an Empire which has enslaved thousands of good and honest people and many nations.

That Great Third Reich is now in ruins and her powerful leaders, The Bandits of Europe, now will be punished.

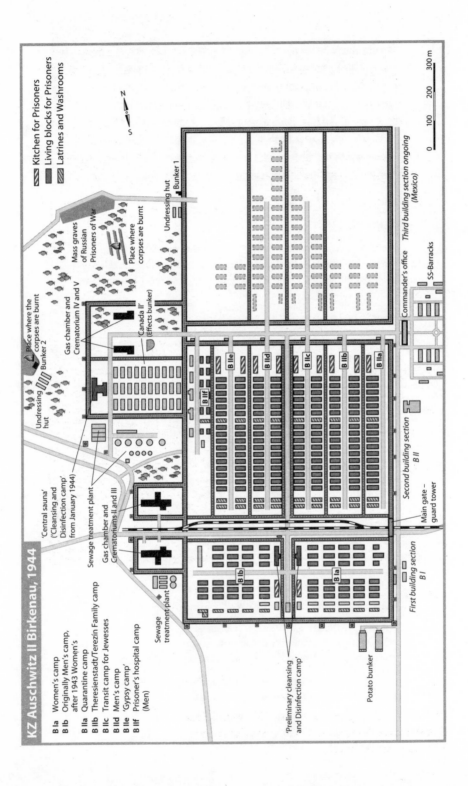

KZ Auschwitz II Birkenau, 1944

B Ia   Women's camp
B Ib   Originally Men's camp, after 1943 Women's
B IIa   Quarantine camp
B IIb   Theresienstadt/Terezin Family camp
B IIc   Transit camp for Jewesses
B IId   Men's camp
B IIe   'Gypsy camp'
B IIf   Prisoner's hospital camp (Men)

Kitchen for Prisoners
Living blocks for Prisoners
Latrines and Washrooms

'Central sauna' ('Cleansing and Disinfection camp' from January 1944)

Sewage treatment plant

Gas chamber and Crematoriums II and III

Sewage treatment plant

Potato bunker

First building section B I

B Ib

B Ia

'Preliminary cleansing and Disinfection camp'

Main gate – guard tower

Second building section B II

Commander's office

SS-Barracks

Third building section ongoing (Mexico)

B IIf

B IIe

B IId

B IIc

B IIb

B IIa

'Canada II' (Effects bunker)

Gas chamber and Crematorium IV and V

Mass graves of Russian Prisoners of War

Place where corpses are burnt

Undressing hut

Bunker 1

Place where the corpses are burnt

Bunker 2

Undressing hut

N
S

0   100   200   300 m

			Birkenau	- 20 -
MAYER	Erna		49 ys	Mikulov Prag
MAYER	Ernst			
MAYER	Gustaf		2.5.10	
MAYER Dr.	Paul		58 ys	Mikulov-Prag
MAYER	Pavala			
MEIJAR	E.			
MEINBACH	B.			
MEINBACH	E.			
MENIST	Simon		1.16.14	
MEISEL Dr.	Baruch	H.9.		
MEISEL	Sara			
MEYEROVICS	Ruzena		1918	
MELEROVA	XXX	Bl.21.		
MELLER	Alexander	7ᵃ.		Zilina
MELLEROVA	Cibia Cilla	Bl.21.		Poprad
MELLER	Livia		1925	
MENDELSHON	Bertha			
MENIST	Leopold		6.16.04	
MENDLOVIC	Manes	H.4ᵃ.	1916	
MENZER	Lazar			
MENDELSTEINOVA	Piroska		1926	Poprad
MENDELSTEINOVA	Ruzena	Bl.21.	1922	"
MESSINGER	Irene	H.8.	1911	
MEYER	Lustig Margot		7.18.21	
MEYER	Margot		1921	
MEYER	Theodor		11.07.20	
MIADOVNIK	Bernat		1919	
MICHEELS	Ina			
MICHELS	Louis		6.06.17	
MICHELS ?	Louis		6.06.19	
MIKULINSKI	Lea			
MILCH	Margarethe	Stabsgebeude	1911	
MILCH	Margit			
MILDER	Ruzena		1921	
MILGRAM	Samuel		10.88.12	
MILIET	Sali	5ᵃ.		
MITTELMANN	Andrej	H.21.	1915	
MITTELMAN	Emanuel	H.7.	1925	
MITTELMANN Dr.	Mayer	H.16.	1916	
MITTELMANN	Hermann	H.7ᵃ.	1907	
MITTELMANN	Lad.	Bl.21		
MITTELMANN	Lea	Bl.14.	1920	
MOFFIE	David		3.11.15	
MOK	Benjamin		7.01.11	
MONAS			9.09.17	
MORDKOVIC	Haju	Bl.14.		
MORDKOVIC	Helene	H.14	1925	
MORGENSTERN-GRUENBERG	Lucie		.1.04.10	
MOSER	Christina			
MOSKOVIC	Jolana		1928	
MOSKOVIC	Magda	H.15	1916	
MOSKOVIO	Sara			
MOSKOVIC	Serena	Stabsgebeude	1920	
MOSKOVICOVA	Gizella		1924	Poprad
MORDKOVICOVA	Haja			
MOSKOVICOVA	Lilli			Poprad
MOSKOVITS	Eva		12.14.22	Zilina
MUEHLRADOVA	Lisi	Stabsgebeude	1924	

Various lists concerning Auschwitz-Birkenau prisoners
(postwar collection), 1.1.2.1/517828_0_1, ITS Digital Archive at USHMM

List from Birkenau, at some time after June 1942, when Cibi and Livia were moved there from Auschwitz, showing the sisters as prisoners housed in Block 21

```
x č.611   Adler Isak, Haus 18 a
x   612   A dlerová Pipi p.A.Hellinger Magda Bl.14
x   613   Amster  Ruth p.A.Schwarz Piri,Block 14
    614   Baum Sura p.A.Weinfeld Ida, bl.27/4692
    615   Becherová Manci p.A.Weinfeldova Ida bl.27/4692
x   616   Beer Elza p.A.Trenkova Elze Bl.21/3807
x   617   Billig Růžena
    618   Brand Jakob
    619   Braun Bora p.A.Teichnerova Baba,St.
x   620   Braun Ladislav .
    621   Braunova Lulu p.A.Teichnerova Baba St.
    622   Braun Manci p.A.Teichnerova Baba,St.
x   623   Citron Helene
x   624   Citron Hinda p.A.Weinfeldova Ida,bl.27.4692
    625   Cinnova Piri,Block 21
    626   Cuprova Hilda p.A.Schlesingerova Zela,4125/bl.21
x   627   Delikat Fiera
x   628   Deutsch Bozena p.A.Hellingerova Magda,Block 14
x   629   Einhorn Gisela p.A.Zoltanova Lenk,Block 25
x   630   Einhorn Magda,Block 21
x   631   Engelmannova Edit p.A.Weinfeld Ida bl.27/4692
    632   Farkasova Paula
    633   Farkasova Růžena p.A-Treuhaft Helene bl.27:13268
x   634   Feldmannova Erika p.A  Gross Johna,Block 9
x   635   Fischer Lily
x   636   Fischer Olga p.A.Gross Jola,Block 9
x   637   Friedova Magda p.A.Schwa rz Piri,Block 14
    638   Friedbergova Lili p.A.Silbermann Margit 4093
x   639   Friedmannova Hedy p.A.Trenkova Elza bl.21/3807
x   640   Friedmannova Martha Block 1
x   641   Friedrichova Ida p.A-Weinfeld Ida bl.27/4692
x   642   Furhmannova  Gita p.A.Heller Cibia,Block 21
    643   Gartnerova Malci p.A.Treuhaft Helene,bl.27/13268
    644   Gelbova Cili p.A.Rothova Grete  St.
x   645   Gelb Fritz Haus 12a
    646   Goldblum Sara,Block 11,
    647   Grünbergerova Kata p.A.Steinerova Anna, 4049/bl.21
x   648   Guzik-Weinstein Sara p.A-Schearz Piri,Block 14
x   649   Hammerova  Etel
    650   Hammerschlag Rudolf p.A.Hammerschlag Stella bl.20/4531
    651   Hammerschlag Stella,bl.20/4530
x   652   Hausner Lili p.A.Weinfeld Ida, bl.27/4692
x   653   Heitlinger Aranka Stbg
x   654   Hellerova Růžena
x   655   Hellingerova Magda Bl.14
    656   Hoenigova  Jolanka p.A.Rothova Herta
    657   Kacerova Krete p.A.Szivessy  Maria St.
x   658   Kaempfner Alice
x   659   Katzova Ilonka
x   660   Kollermannova Erika
x   661   Kleinova E
x   662   Kleinova Růžena .
x   663   Kohnova Magda Block 9
x   664   Kornova Libuša
    665   Kornhauserova Mira p.A.Hammerschlag Stella bl.20/4530
    666   La ndauova Eta, 6037
    667   Laxova Erica
    668    Laxova Paula
    669   Lissauerova Elza p.A.Trenkova Elza,bl.21/3807
x   670   Lissauerova Luize o.A.Trenkova Elza bl.21/3807
x   671   Loewenbergova  Eleonore
    672   Loewy Livia 4752,Block 3
x   673   Lustigova Aliska p.A.Sternova  Ema,3993/bl.13.1919
    674   Lustigova Kata p.A.Sternova Ema,3993/bl.13.1919
    675   Lustigova Klara p.A. Sternova Ema 3993/bl.13.1919
    676   Magyarova Baba p.A.Rothova Grete St-
x   677   Markovits Helene p-A.Weissova Berta,Block 2
    678   Melerova  p.A .Trenk Elza bl.21/3807
    679   Hellerova Cibia,Block 21
```

List from Birkenau, at some time after June 1942, when Cibi and Livia
were moved there from Auschwitz. At line 642, the names of Cibi and
Gita Furhmannova, future wife of Lale, the Tattooist of Auschwitz, are
shown side by side, housed in Block 21, a remarkable coincidence

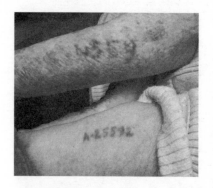

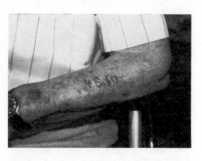

Magda's (bottom) and Livia's (top) numbers
— A–25592 and 4559

Cibi's number — 4560

Livia, Cibi and Magda (left to right) as children.
Vranov nad Topl'ou, circa. 1930

Livia, Cibi and Magda (left to right).
Bratislava, circa. 1947

The girls' parents, Chaya Sara (née Strauss) Meller and Menachem Emil (Mendel) Meller. Vranov nad Topl'ou, circa 1920–22

Livia and Magda on Magda's wedding day, 1950

Cibi and Mischka on their wedding day. Bratislava, 1947

Ziggy and Livia on their wedding day with Vera Weizmann, the first First Lady of Israel, 1953

Cibi and Mischka with their children Yossi (left) and Kari (right), circa. 1957

Magda and Yitzko with their children Judith (Ditti) in Magda's arms and Chaya, Israel circa. 1956

Livia holding the knife

Livia and Ziggy with their children Oded (left) and Dorit (right) at their home in London, England, circa.1962

Magda, Livia, and Cibi (left to right), the last time all of the families were together, Purim 2014, as re-imagined in Heather's epilogue. The sisters discuss the glass art sculpture THE THREE SISTERS

Photograph courtesy of Pamela Ravek

Livia and Magda (left to right) holding the candlesticks in Magda's apartment in Holon, Israel, 2020

Heather's second visit to Israel, with Livia (left) and Magda (centre), January 2020

Expressed in luminous glass art, capturing the essence of the sisters' unwavering bond, devotion, and love for one another, THE THREE SISTERS sculpture, created by artists Oded and Pamela Ravek, is dedicated to Oded's mother Livia and aunts Cibi z"l and Magda

ACKNOWLEDGEMENTS

Livia and Magda, thank you for inviting me into your homes, sharing your meals, showing me the candlesticks and photos, trusting me to tell your story. You have my undying love and devotion, my respect and admiration for your courage, resilience, commitment to each other and Cibi, and your families.

Kari and Yossi, my heartfelt thanks to you for your support and encouragement to tell the story of your amazing, much loved, mother – Cibi. Her strength continues to give me strength, her love for her family will inspire others to emulate her values in caring and loving unconditionally, no matter the risks.

Chaya and Ditti, thank you so much for your support and encouragement in obtaining memories from your mother, Magda, and sharing them with me. Without this, I could not have told the story of *Three Sisters*. Her courage, love and compassion are a beacon lighting the way for others who may at times feel lost and alone.

Odie and Dorit, no words can express the love and gratitude I feel towards you for inviting me into your world, into your mother Livia's home and life. You have been my guide in obtaining the memories – painful and joyful – from Livia, which have brought this story to life, to the page. The many hours I have spent with you, in person or via video, have been joyous, sad, hilarious.

Kari, Yossi, Chaya, Ditti, Odie and Dorit, I wish to acknowledge my gratitude for the sometimes very painful journey you have all experienced as you have relived the evil period of history your amazing mothers endured and survived. I am eternally indebted to you for the emotional rollercoaster you undertook to ensure I could tell the true story of *Three Sisters*.

Pam, you started this wondrous, life-changing adventure for me. Thank you so much for writing that first email which I opened in the small hours of the morning in South Africa, telling me about your mother-in-law, Livia, who had seen a copy of *The Tattooist of Auschwitz*, recognised who the story was about, and her connection to Gita. You set in motion a sequence of events which has led to this publication. Thank you.

To my daughter Azure-Dea who sent me multiple text messages while I was in South Africa, telling me, 'Mum, you have to read this email: Mum, open this email, you have to read it now.' Who immediately saw in a small email the story which needed to be told; and that I should do all I could to tell it. Thank you, honey.

My dedication in this novel included the grandchildren of Cibi, Magda and Livia, most of whom I have had the pleasure of meeting, and whose support I am most grateful for. I can only imagine how proud you must be of the grandparents whose survival and bravery placed you on this earth.

Kate Parkin, managing director of adult trade publishing, Bonnier Books UK. In *Cilka's Journey* I called you my friend; I now call you my dear, dear friend. From the moment I sent you Pam's email and said I wanted, no, needed to follow this story, you have supported and encouraged me to write it and tell the world about three amazing sisters. You are without measure, and I remain honoured and blessed to be in your life.

Margaret Stead (Mav/Maverick), publisher, Bonnier Books UK. This is as much your novel as mine. Your brilliant writing and editing, capacity to see the stories behind the story, the depth and meaning behind the experiences of Cibi, Magda and Livia is what makes this story brilliant, even if I say so myself. It would not exist without you. You have travelled with me, been both friend and companion, as we met family and planned the best way to tell this story. I am a better person and writer for having you in my life. *Ko taku tino aroha me taku whakaute I nga wa katoa. Mauruuru.* (My deepest love and respect always. Thank you.)

Benny Agius, general manager, Echo Publishing Australia. What can I say to express my love and thanks to you for being my friend, my manager, my driver, my advisor: so much wisdom. You make me laugh; you make me cry. You are, simply, the best. I cannot wait for our next adventure.

Ruth Logan, rights director, Bonnier Books UK: what a gal! Your openness and friendship have come to mean as much to me as your brilliance in getting my stories into many,

many territories and translations. You do not do this alone: Ilaria Tarasconi, Stella Giatrakou and Amy Smith – you are learning from the master. Thank you for all your efforts.

Claire Johnson-Creek – I apologise for my tardiness in providing you with copy in need of so many corrections. Your skill is what the reader ultimately sees; I am most grateful, and I thank you.

Francesca Russell, publicity director at Zaffre and Clare Kelly, publicity manager, Zaffre – my companions, my Mary Poppinses. I love my time with you in person, over Zoom or email. Your talents in putting me on the stage and on the page are so appreciated. You know I love to perform, and you make it possible. Thank you.

Blake Brooks, brand manager at Zaffre, you have laughed and cried as you became involved in telling this story. Thank you so much for connecting with the families in Israel and Canada, making the amazing videos we now have. Your efforts have been immense, and I appreciate your passion and commitment. Thank you.

There is a team at Zaffre who contributed to *Three Sisters* now being in your hands. Their brilliance lies in the art department, marketing and sales. Nick Stearn, Stephen Dumughn, Elise Burns and her team, and Paul Baxter. Love being part of your teams.

Celli Lichman, you have been part of telling this story throughout its development. Without your expert translation of the testimonies of Cibi, Ziggy and Livia the story would not have been told. Thank you so much for your dedication to honestly and passionately translating the words I only had access to through recorded testimonies, and for your sensitive and perceptive read of the final manuscript.

My love and sincere thanks to Lenka Pustay, from Krompachy, Slovakia, without whom so much valuable information and documents identifying names, dates of birth etc., would not have been found. You are a wonder.

Sally Richardson, Jennifer Enderlin at St Martin's Press in the US, you embraced this story hearing only the vaguest outline. You welcomed me with open arms with *Cilka's Journey* and now again in celebrating Cibi, Magda and Livia. Along with Kate, Margaret and Benny we form a band of women celebrating and honouring strong, courageous women. I am so grateful for your warmth, keeping in touch with me, and making me welcome when I visit – thank you.

The rest of the team at St Martin's Press US, please accept my sincere thanks – I will acknowledge individually in the US edition.

I have spoken of Benny from Echo Publishing Australia and the significant role she plays in my Aussie publishing life; however, she does not work alone. He has left Echo, but I need to say thank you and acknowledge James Elms for his technical expertise getting me zooming around the globe, but mostly for his dedication and wonderful attitude to helping me at all times of the day and night. Miss you, James. My publicist, Emily Banyard, your bubbly, always smiling approach I hugely appreciate. Tegan Morrison and Rosie Outred, I so enjoy having you on my Aussie team.

To the team at Allen and Unwin Australia, my books wouldn't get read if you did not make it happen, distributing them in Australia and New Zealand. My sincere thanks to you all for being this important cog in my 'home' territory wheel.

To the management and staff at Saffire Freycinet in Tasmania, thank you for your pampering, catering and interest in writing this story, and in providing me with an oasis to hide away in and concentrate on writing when I fell behind. Isolation during a pandemic did not provide me with the environment to be creative; your amazing corner of the world did.

Peter Bartlett and Patrick Considine, so grateful for your continued advice and support.

Kevin Mottau and Adriano Donato, one and one would not make two if it wasn't for you. Ta.

Lastly, the people who make my waking up each day, a good day: my family. Steve, Ahren and Bronwyn, Jared and Rebecca, Azure-Dea and Evan, my love and thanks once again for putting up with me as I waxed and waned in your lives: there one day, not the next. And to the five little people who continue to bring me such joy and laughter: Henry, Nathan, Jack, Rachel and Ashton – you light up my life. Love you beyond measure.

HEATHER MORRIS

If you would like to hear more from me, why not join the
Heather Morris Readers' Club?

I'll keep you up to date on all upcoming
projects, with early exclusives like extracts, videos and
behind-the-book details; as well as more on all my published
titles including real-life research, deleted scenes and
giveaways.

You can join anytime at
www.heathermorrisauthor.com/heathers-readers-club

Dear Reader,

Thank you very much for picking up *Three Sisters*, a story I feel honoured to have had the opportunity to tell. Throughout my career as a writer I've been lucky enough to meet and talk to some amazing people. It's because of your help and support as readers that I have been able to share the stories of Lale and Gita, of Cilka, and now of Cibi, Magda and Livia.

The story of these three incredible sisters came to me through a most extraordinary set of circumstances. I was in South Africa on a book tour, when my daughter contacted me to say she'd had an email from a man who had been visiting his mother Livia in Israel and had brought a copy of *The Tattooist of Auschwitz* for her, as she and her sisters are Holocaust survivors. 'That must be Lale and Gita's story,' Livia said when she saw the book. 'I was in Birkenau with them – and Gita and I were at school together.' This man, Oded Ravek, who I now think of as a brother, asked if I would come to Israel to meet Livia and her sister Magda. Their older sister, Cibi, is sadly no longer alive.

What could I do? I got straight on a plane to Tel Aviv, where I met Livia and Magda, and heard the incredible story they had to share and which you have just read. The sisters were from Vranov nad Topl'ou, Slovakia. At just fifteen, Livia was ordered to Auschwitz by the Nazis. Cibi, only nineteen herself, followed Livia, determined to protect her sister, or die with her. Magda, aged seventeen, escaped capture for a time but was transported to the death camp. Reunited, the three sisters made a promise to each other: to live. Their fight for survival took them from the hell of Auschwitz-Birkenau, to a death march across war-torn Europe and eventually home to Slovakia, now under Communist rule. Determined to begin again, they embarked on a voyage of renewal, to Israel. Magda and Livia are in Israel today, surrounded by family and friends. Livia and

Magda and their children and grandchildren have become family to me. And I was truly honoured when they entrusted me with their story, and asked that I reimagine it in *Three Sisters*. It is my pleasure to share *Three Sisters* with my readers. It is a heartbreaking, inspirational and uplifting story that I am honoured to tell the world. I hope you enjoyed it.

If you would like more information about what I'm working on now or about my books, *Three Sisters, The Tattooist of Auschwitz, Cilka's Journey and Stories of Hope*, you can visit http://eepurl.com/dIuF-P where you can join My Readers' Club. It only takes a few moments to sign up, there are no catches or costs and new members will automatically receive an exclusive message from me. My publisher, Bonnier Books UK, will keep your data private and confidential, and it will never be passed on to a third party. We won't spam you with loads of emails, just get in touch now and again with news about my books, and you can unsubscribe any time you want. And if you would like to get involved in a wider conversation about my books, please do review *Three Sisters* on Amazon, on GoodReads, on any other e-store, on your own blog and social media accounts, or talk about it with friends, family or reader groups. Sharing your thoughts helps other readers, and I always enjoy hearing about what people experience from my writing.

Many thanks again for reading *Three Sisters*. I hope, if you haven't done so already, you might like to read Lale and Gita's story in *The Tattooist of Auschwitz*, Cilka's story in *Cilka's Journey* and find out about the inspiration behind the books through a series of tales of the remarkable people I have met, the incredible stories they have shared with me, and the lessons they hold for us all in *Stories of Hope*.

With my very best wishes,

Heather ♡

READING GROUP QUESTIONS

- What do you think it was about these three sisters that meant they survived the Holocaust when so many others didn't? Was it luck or something else?
- Why do you think the girls were so often treated better than other prisoners, by the block kapos and other guards, another fact which meant that they survived?
- How important were relationships in the camps – between family, friends and those in charge?
- There is a sense that Magda felt guilt at not having been in the camp for as long as her sisters. Is this justified?
- How do you think being in the camps shaped the people these three sisters became?
- How does *Three Sisters* change your perceptions about the Holocaust in particular, and war in general? What implications does this book hold for our own time?

- Why do you think the sisters chose to leave their home in Slovakia after the war and embark on a journey to Israel? Do you think they would have done this had it not been for their experiences in the Holocaust?
- How do you think the sisters' experiences affected the relationships they formed after the Holocaust?
- The scene where the group of girls who have just survived the death march find an abandoned house and decide to take the dining table outside to eat is incredibly powerful. Why do you think they did this after everything they'd been through, rather than eating inside, and would you have done the same?
- What was your overwhelming feeling when you finished the novel? Was it one of hope?
- The sisters were barely older than children when they were taken to Auschwitz – Livia just fifteen. Do you think their youth gave them an advantage, or was the opposite the case?
- Each of the sisters married a Holocaust survivor, with his own story of survival. Why do you think this might be?
- Do you see the sisters as heroines, or ordinary women?

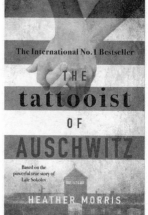

Your Stories of Hope

'Just as I was able to honour Lale Sokolov, I would like to extend this opportunity to others to share their family stories and join a global conversation of hope.'

The Tattooist of Auschwitz has triggered an extraordinary response in its readers – many people have wanted to share their own experiences of reading the book and the stories from their own lives that resonate.

Just as Heather was able to honour Lale Sokolov – she would like to extend this opportunity to others to share their stories of hope and join a global conversation.

If you have a story that you would love to share, maybe even one that has remained untold for decades and generations, Heather would love to hear from you.

Find out more at
www.yourstoriesofhope.com